"SOON I'LL BREAK YOU, AND I'LL LOVE DOING IT."

Ben's promise was uttered breathlessly. Hungrily, he pulled Natalie to him, lowering his mouth to hers and then trailing hot moist kisses along her sensitive neck.

"I'm not going to play by your rules," he went on. "I won't settle for knowing just part of you." His dark eyes seemed to drink her in as the rhythmic motion of his hands caressed the sensuous contours of her body.

Reeling and raging like a tropical storm within, Natalie fought to resist him. But inside his powerful embrace, she drifted on a current of liquid fire; her flesh flamed under his touch; her fears dissolved to ash.

"Soon we'll make love—soon I'll know all of you," he murmured huskily.

Though her head vowed never, her heart cried out a resounding yes....

AND NOW...

SUPERROMANCES

Worldwide Library is proud to present a
sensational new series of modern love stories —
SUPERROMANCES

Written by masters of the genre, these longer,
sensuous and dramatic novels are truly in keeping
with today's changing life-styles. Full of intriguing
conflicts, the heartaches and delights of true love,
SUPERROMANCES are absorbing stories —
satisfying and sophisticated reading that lovers
of romance fiction have long been waiting for.

SUPERROMANCES
Contemporary love stories for the woman of today!

CHRISTINA CROCKET

TO TOUCH
A DREAM

A SUPERROMANCE FROM
WORLDWIDE
TORONTO · NEW YORK · LOS ANGELES · LONDON

Published March 1983

First printing January 1983

ISBN 0-373-70055-5

Printed in Canada

CHAPTER ONE

NATALIE BISHOP brushed aside a wisp of sun-bleached hair that had strayed across her lightly freckled nose and reached upward to tug closed the sunroof of her little red Mustang. The familiar gusty winds sweeping across the highway bolstered her courage as she eased up on the accelerator and glanced out at the unsightly rows of hamburger shops, gas stations and motels lining the first stretch of the Overseas Highway. She had traveled this narrow highway hundreds of times before; it stretched out in alternating bridges and roadway strips linking the string of Florida Keys to the mainland.

Traffic moved at an erratic pace along the more populated Upper Keys, but gradually the commercial sites became fewer and the bridges more frequent as Natalie passed Plantation Key and continued southwest toward the Lower Keys. Palm trees waved their umbrella-spoked fronds in the brisk April breeze, swaying with the irregular burst of wind from the east. Natalie smiled at the row of fat-bellied pelicans perched atop the bridge pilings. Obviously the fish were running well as the waters of the Atlantic and the Gulf became warmer, and the pelicans, full and satisfied, were enjoying their sunny siesta.

"I know just how you feel, boys," Natalie declared. She had often stretched out her long-legged body to bask in the sunshine on the Keys after stuffing herself with Aunt Evie's conch chowder and fritters. Natalie's smile faded as her guilty conscience and earlier misgivings nudged aside the pleasant memory. Aunt Evie wouldn't approve of Natalie's current venture. For that matter, the entire Bishop family would be dismayed if they knew where Natalie was at this very moment. However, what she had set out to do had to succeed or fail without the assistance or the support of the family she loved.

"This is *my* show," Natalie murmured aloud. Her dad and two brothers were across the Gulf of Mexico on their twin trawlers, harvesting the pink-tailed shrimp from the rich shrimping grounds in the Bay of Campeche off the Yucatan Peninsula. They would be gone for at least five weeks. By mid-May the Bishop fleet would be back at Key West only long enough to unload their catch, and head out to the Dry Tortugas to trawl its coral mud bottom for shrimp, or try their luck in the northern Gulf of Mexico off the coast of Alabama and Texas. Natalie should be able to make it well into the summer without her father or brothers' being any the wiser. By then, she would know for herself precisely what she could do on her own.

With a bit of luck, Natalie reflected, *my plan should work perfectly.* Janie Hitchcock, her college roommate, would forward all Nat's mail to her from the sorority house in Atlanta, and Nat's letters back to the Bishop clan would be relayed through Janie so they would bear the Atlanta postmark that her family expected to see. No one would be apprehensive. No one would use his or her influence to help her. Natalie's calm life at college would appear to continue without any interruption.

I simply have to do it, Natalie thought as she watched the two-lane ribbon of a bridge stretching before her. Something within her craved a challenge. Something inside made her yearn for a less conventional, less predictable life than her father had planned for her. Whatever that *something* was, she was finally giving it full rein.

Thick clumps of dark-needled pink trees spread to the left of the road on the next small key she reached. Natalie slowed her sporty Mustang to a cautious speed and eased past a cluster of picnickers laden with baskets of food, blankets and surf-casting rods. Nat's eyes lingered momentarily on the fishing gear as she instinctively assessed the equipment. The line looked a bit heavy, and one of the group was carrying some live shrimp. "Not much of a contest," Nat shrugged. The odds were all in favor of the fishermen; the fish wouldn't have a sporting chance. Her dad had taught her to even out the competition by using lightweight line so a feisty fish could put up a fight and snap it if she wasn't skillful, and to try lures and jigs instead of shrimp for bait.

Suddenly Natalie was anxious to reach her new lodgings and get out her own fishing gear. Something about the contest—a fair match between fisherman and fish—excited her. Succulent young pompano should be plentiful now right off shore. All it would take was a light touch and the right technique.

Nat's brow furrowed as she reached the busy commercial strip of Marathon. Shops here were strung out casually for six miles, unlike the slick air-conditioned shopping complexes in Atlanta where shops were neatly stacked on top of one another. She had been homesick even for those.

Finally, the highway leaped out over the clear blue waters of Knight Key Channel, and Seven Mile Bridge reached far ahead toward the Lower Keys. The sight of beautiful little Pigeon Key, which had rich underwater banks to the southeast, prompted her to smile wryly. At one time, Natalie had begged to study at the Marine Laboratory of the University of Miami. The university leased Pigeon Key and offered courses in marine biology, which brought students there to dive beneath the clear water and probe the offshore reefs.

Almost four years earlier, however, when Natalie had thought that was what she wanted, Bill Bishop had opposed her. "Just because you have saltwater in your veins and sand in your shoes," he teased, "doesn't mean you have to make a career out of being a beachcomber or a skin diver. You have a natural talent as an artist. Your mother saw it, and she would want you to develop it. So I want you to get off a bit, study, develop your talent," he counseled his only daughter.

Mr. Bishop's sunbaked face and steady, steel-gray gaze had not wavered when Natalie had tried to persuade him to let her attend a college near the Keys. She even tried convincing him that she could combine both fields—marine biology and art. "Give yourself a chance to see what you can do," he countered. "Don't hold on to what you feel safe with—all this water and sea life you've grown up near. Let's give you some time with your brushes and canvases," he advised. "Time *away* from here so you can get a different perspective on what life has to offer you." Bill Bishop had watched Natalie from childhood as she turned to paints and crayons for both amusement and solace. Now he wanted her to give that talent a chance to blossom.

"First, you go to a college with a good art department," he insisted. "Your fine fingers will be trained to capture whatever your eyes see and your spirit feels," he declared poetically. Then his innate practicality surfaced. "You pick up a teaching certificate, just in case. You can get a job in a nice school, make a decent living and do what you want on your own time—even bake in the sun and let the saltwater wrinkle your skin," he grinned.

The idea of being able to study with excellent instructors and experiment with a variety of styles and artistic media appealed to Natalie. Leaving home—leaving Key West—did not.

"It would be nice to have a college graduate in the family," Mr. Bishop cajoled. "You might end up as an elegant, refined lady, Natalie—not just another weathered old Conch." All the longtime residents of the Keys claimed the nickname "Conch" after the tough-shelled mollusk from the waters off Key West. Natalie wasn't sure whether she considered the name a compliment or a criticism.

The Bishop family traced its lineage back to the old Bahamian settlers who colonized the Florida Keys, so the name Conch was particularly appropriate for them. These human conchs, the early colonists, took a lesson from the hardy mollusks and built their own protective coverings—hardwood, gabled houses, with metal-shingled roofs to withstand the winds, rains and termites of the tropics. The subsequent generations of Conchs were a unique and tough lot whose stubborn nature and single-mindedness often made them seem callous or insensitive. But, unlike the sea creature that gave them its name, Key West Conchs concealed within their hardened exteriors the softest of hearts.

Bill Bishop's head had told him that he had to send Natalie off to college. A squarely built seaman, not quite six feet tall, Bishop could look almost level into the gold-flecked eyes of his daughter. Tall, with waist-length brown hair streaked with blonde from the sun, Natalie, eighteen at the time she'd left, had still been his baby. His heart wanted her to stay. But opportunity lay elsewhere.

"The boys and I are rugged," Bill Bishop said quietly with a firmness that Natalie recognized. "We're built for this sea life. Shrimping is part of our character. It's all we know. But you're like your mama—" he softened momentarily "—slender and gentle. It's time we put aside this tomboy business and stopped using you as an extra hand on board. You have a life and talent of your own. So like it or not, young lady," he informed her, "you're getting away for a few years to find out what else you can do. I won't let you get bogged down here and spend your whole life wondering what you missed." The gray eyes misted over for a few seconds. "I waited too long to pamper your mama," he whispered sadly. At forty-three, Anna Bishop had suffered a stroke and had died quietly in her sleep only a few months before Natalie was to graduate from high school.

"Now that your mama is gone," Mr. Bishop continued, "I only have you to pamper. So you pick a college that is *not* near water and send them your application. We're going to do this college business with style."

After three and a half years of college in Atlanta, Natalie had all the so-called pampering she could endure. Her talents with watercolors and acrylics had indeed blossomed, and her practice teaching had proved that she had an affinity with children, but something inside still resisted like a moored boat tugging against its anchor. She wanted to be out on the open water. She ached to be back in the Keys permanently. It was only on holidays—Thanksgiving, Christmas, spring break and summer—that she'd been home in Key West, swimming in clear water and breathing the salty air that sustained her. While her father and brothers went off shrimping, Nat had hung around her Uncle Buzz's marina, sometimes sketching, sometimes watching him repair motors and propellers and often actually helping him with the labor. Working with Uncle Buzz had given her an education of a totally different kind.

Now, at twenty-one, Natalie was not so timid or yielding as she had been at eighteen. She had tried to make his dream for her come true. She had worked diligently in all her classes and had managed to complete her course work a quarter early. However, before the graduation ceremony in June—and before she accepted a teaching job at any school—she was determined to try a different dream of her own.

Nat's dream depended on proving that she could make a living for herself in the Keys—on her own.

This time it was not her skill as an artist that would pay her way. It was her Conch blood and her instincts developed in the Keys over the years that would help her earn enough to support herself and her art. This time it was Uncle Buzz's kind of training that had to show a profit.

"Oh, boy," Natalie whistled at the approach of Big Pine Key. Beneath its dense buttonwood and evergreen trees, tiny key deer found refuge, protected by government managers. Nat had a friend there on the Refuge, but first she had to settle something a little farther on. With only a sidelong glance at the dense green Refuge compound, she crossed the bridge over Big Pine Channel onto the next key.

The large, weather-worn sign pointing to the left caused her to brake suddenly and follow the cutoff down Little Torch Key. Dense mangrove trees, squat scrub pine and bedraggled paper bark trees clung together along the channel coast, lacing their roots together like gnarled old fingers in a desperate attempt to survive the constant ebb and flow of the tides. Less than a mile farther on, Natalie reached her destination—the Gold Coast Fishing Lodge.

Nat took a deep breath and turned her little car onto the white crushed-shell drive. It curved through the thick pine trees toward a grassy clearing, then it spread wide again before a horseshoe-shaped inlet rimmed by well-trimmed coconut palms.

Sprawling along one side of the parking area, the lodge itself was a modest, low one-story building with a long shaded porch jutting out toward the inlet—Newfound Harbor Channel. The farthest end of the lodge, standing out above the water on barnacle-encrusted pilings, housed a small restaurant. Through the ceiling-to-floor windows of the immaculate white building, Nat could see several empty tables from which a diner would have a fine view of the marina and the channel beyond.

Directly in front of her, a network of moorings and wooden walkways lined the water's edge. Only a small runabout and a sixteen-foot skiff were tied to the dock. To the right, a sparkling white building similar to the lodge was spread along the other side of the marina. The first entrance led clearly to a bait-and-tackle shop; the second was marked Charters and Guide Bookings.

Natalie slid her large-lensed sunglasses into her shirt pocket, tucked back an unruly strand of hair and shook her head so her thick tawny braid hung squarely between her shoulders. Calmly she slid her hands over her hips to smooth out the wrinkles in her slim-fitting ivory slacks. With a soft, "Here goes," she headed for the door marked Charters, pushed it open and stepped inside.

"Be with you in a moment," a man's raspy voice greeted her from somewhere behind a long storage locker. As she looked around, Natalie was rather startled by the peculiar architecture of the building. She stared past a series of coiled water hoses to the covered moorings that took up most of the building's space. The entire rear wall of the Charter building had been removed to allow docking space for four good-sized boats. All the slots were currently unoccupied except for the last one. There an old model forty-three-foot cabin cruiser, suspended above the water by giant hoists, was undergoing considerable repairs. The paint had been stripped from her underside, and the name and numbers had been sanded off.

"That was a magnificent cruiser in her day," Natalie commented to the unseen person still rummaging around in the storage locker.

"You're right about that," the voice replied. "She'll be a sight to behold when she's finished."

"Would you mind if I take a closer look at her?" Natalie asked impetuously as her eyes scanned the vessel.

"I wouldn't mind a look-see myself." A head popped out abruptly. A short, stocky fellow of fifty with close-cropped gray hair grinned up at her appreciatively. "Name's Mac Butler," he announced. "I'll let you gawk at her—if I can gawk at you. I've been staring at nothing but ugly old fishermen all day, and you're a welcome change."

In her ivory loosely woven knit top and ivory slacks, Natalie was a pleasant sight indeed. The slender gold serpentine chain around her neck echoed the gold flecks in her eyes and the sun-streaked strands in her hair. Stretching out her hand gracefully toward the man's extended hand, Natalie chuckled aloud at his unrestrained admiration. "Hi—I'm Natalie Bishop, and you've got yourself a deal." She found herself grinning back at the fellow as he escorted her to the dry dock and gave her a running commentary on the old cruiser.

"Come on board and take a peek," he insisted, hoisting his leg over the side and reaching down for her hand. "Beautiful she was in her heyday," he went on eagerly. "Teak...." He touched the dark wood panels along the side of the cabin. "This is pure mahogany." He ran his thick, rough hands over the pilot's chair. "A real prize," Mac Butler breathed with obvious reverence. "All brass fittings," he said, pointing behind her at the bridge from which inset dials, now long outdated, had been removed.

"She even smells good," Natalie declared as she gazed at the handcrafted details that testified to the skilled workmanship employed in the craft's construction. "She smells like something natural and alive. . . not like those factory-made fiberglass jobs."

The gray-haired fellow shot her a surprised look and grinned more broadly. "You've been around boats before, I see," he remarked. "Would you like to take a look below?" He watched with pleasure as Natalie's eyes flashed eagerly to the cabin door.

"I'd love to," she answered quickly.

Mac was just beginning the tour of the stateroom when the steady hum of a diesel inboard echoed through the marina. "One of the charters is getting in," he said uneasily. "I'd better go topside and give 'em a hand. You stay here and look around, Natalie," he insisted. "It isn't often someone gives the old girl the respect she deserves. You take your time." He ducked through the doorway and disappeared.

The glorious old cruiser had apparently slept at least six people, Natalie observed as she continued her tour: four bunks, and a stateroom with a berth big enough for two. Natalie scrutinized the interior as she slid her fingers lovingly over the burnished wood furnishings that someone had been fastidiously polishing and restoring.

Natalie must have spent fifteen minutes below deck, touching, examining, exploring and inhaling the scents of the rich old wood and the chemicals that would revive the original luster. "You're absolutely lovely," Natalie whispered as she trailed her hand along the smooth wooden bulkhead.

"Just what are you doing aboard my boat?" a deep voice snapped from the shadows. Natalie had been so preoccupied with her self-guided tour, she had not heard anyone approaching. Now she drew in a sharp breath and turned to face the man.

"I was just looking at her." Natalie tried to smile at the dark-haired figure blocking the doorway. His furrowed brow cast a dark line across his eyes, making his expression inscrutable. Her smile did not soften his features.

"She's a beautiful boat." Natalie reached out and touched the sanded wood once more with her fingertips. "You're doing a remarkable job with her...."

The man did not respond. He just stood blocking the doorway, his eyes still obscured in the shadows. Natalie couldn't tell where his gaze was directed, but she suddenly felt a creeping uneasiness from the silent stranger's appraisal of her. The ease of his stance suggested to her that he may have been there some time before he spoke, watching as she moved below deck, listening to her murmured comments intended only for the old boat.

"She's not open to the public." The man finally altered his position and emerged into the light. He was tanned a deep golden brown and had slight lines on his handsome face that spoke of years on open water cruising in the salty air. "I suggest you leave."

He issued the order in a low growl. He stepped back into the gangway to clear the exit route for her.

"I am sorry if I trespassed," Natalie said softly, as she started to move past him in the narrow gangway. His arm shot across in front of her, momentarily blocking her way.

"That's precisely what you did—you trespassed," he replied solemnly. "This is private property. I don't intend to be liable if anyone prowls around a boat that is being worked on," he stated. The scent of sea air clung to his pale gold V-necked skirt that accented his deep tan. The shirt clung to his powerful, muscular shoulders and arms. "This area is restricted to crew members only. No one else."

"Then if you'd move your arm," Natalie said with an angry edge to her voice, "I will gladly get off your boat." She didn't dare look up at him; she didn't want to make a big production out of an already unpleasant situation. She just wanted out. For an instant, she considered telling him that she had actually been invited aboard. Instead, she decided to keep that piece of information to herself and spare Mac Butler a similar reprimand from this stern, solemn man. Natalie stood rigid until he dropped his arm and let her proceed. With considerable relief, she reached the main deck and saw Mac and a young fellow unloading gear from the charter cruiser. The tall man followed her, stepping up onto the deck behind her.

"Mr. Butler," Nat called out clearly, now that she was free from the penetrating stare of the angry boat owner. "Could you tell me where I could find Captain Andress?" she said with authority. "I have business with him." Natalie hoped the mention of the owner of this charter and guide service would decisively end this unreasonable man's treatment of her.

Mac's seemingly permanent grin drooped in bewilderment for a second, then it returned, wider than ever. "He's the one you've just passed below deck. Can't imagine how you two missed each other. Ben, this is Natalie." Butler jerked his thumb toward the man standing astride the cabin hatch. "Natalie, Ben Andress."

Natalie hid her dismay and turned with a sheepish smile to acknowledge the introduction. Andress tipped his head slightly and ran his long fingers through his tousled black hair. There was a trace of an amused smile on his lips when he looked up. "Now what business could you possibly have with me?" His face became serious again as he leaned back against the boat. His deep brown eyes scanned her from her open-toed sandals to her streaked, braided hair. Natalie knew that she looked out of place at the moment, among the hard-muscled, weathered men in the vast charter building. Ben, Mac and the young man were all damp with perspiration and salt air, and she was the obvious outsider... or so the look in Andress's eyes seemed to suggest.

"I'm a few days early, but I'm supposed to report to you," Natalie managed to say, with only a single break in her voice. She glanced toward the dock for the reassuring, friendly face of Mac Butler, but he was concentrating on some tackle. When she again met Andress's brown eyes, his expression was wary.

"Report?" he drawled. "I don't have the remotest

idea what you're talking about." Suddenly he seemed very impatient. He was not a man for idle conversation. "If you want to see about a charter or a fishing guide," he dismissed her politely, "you can make those arrangements with Mac." Andress abruptly turned and in one smooth leap vaulted onto the dock.

"The letter said to see *you*." Natalie raised her voice. "You are Captain Ben Andress—" she fumbled in her pocket for the letter "—and I am Nat Bishop." She snapped open the letter and thrust it down for him to see.

"Oh, brother...." Mac Butler chortled from the dockside, as he stood with his arms crossed, grinning at her. He had finally caught the drift of the exchange between the two.

Ben Andress looked from Natalie to Mac, then to the letter that fluttered in the afternoon breeze. His face was expressionless as he glared at the paper, then at the young woman who held it toward him. He didn't need to read it.

"*You* are Nat Bishop?" he finally said. "*You* are a rated charter captain?" he asked with a half-smile. Natalie folded the letter and held his gaze.

"Yes, sir," she said evenly.

"Well, Miss Bishop," Andress replied tersely, "Buzz Cochran recommended you highly. He just omitted a few significant details." He placed his hands on his hips and stared at her glumly. "Buzz said you had your captain's license and were qualified to take out fishing parties."

"That's quite true," Natalie answered. "I took my Coast Guard pilot's training in Key West. If you recall, I sent you a copy of my license."

Ben stroked his day's growth of beard thoughtfully as his dark eyes studied the ivory-clad visitor with the long, lightly tanned arms and graceful hands. "You've actually fished these waters?" he queried.

"I grew up in the Keys," Natalie replied honestly. "I've fished both coasts from Key Largo to the Dry Tortugas." She stopped herself before she added, "with my father and brothers." From the corner of her eye, Natalie could see Mac had totally abandoned his chores and was sitting, pipe in mouth, on a wooden crate listening intently to the conversation.

Suddenly Ben stepped forward and reached his right hand up toward Natalie. Apprehensively she took a step backward, beyond his grasp. Ben's thick eyebrows arched in surprise.

"I wasn't trying to grab you," he snapped. "I just want to give you a hand down. We'll discuss this misunderstanding in greater detail—in my office," he added, as he shot a dark look toward Mac. The older fellow merely shrugged and grinned as Natalie, without Ben's assistance, climbed from the boat and followed Ben toward the glass-enclosed room in the far corner of the boathouse.

"You realize, of course, that the job offer was intended for a man." Ben turned on her after he closed the door behind them. "Buzz Cochran has done me a lot of favors over the past year, and he's never asked for anything in return—except for giving me your name and suggesting you replace Charlie until summer as captain of the *Calusa*. I hired *N.C. Bishop* on his recommendation." He spoke calmly as he slid behind the broad desk and waved Natalie toward a nearby chair.

His long, tanned fingers rested atop a flat brass paperweight, shaped like a starfish, holding a stack of papers in a neat pile on one corner of the desk. "I'm sure you'll understand if I rescind my offer now that I've seen you." He raised one finger to silence her as Natalie opened her mouth to protest.

"Look, Miss Bishop," he said, leaning forward earnestly. "I'm finally getting things operating smoothly. Everyone who works here permanently has a piece of the profits. We all pull our share of the work and divide up the rewards." He once more scanned Natalie from head to toe. "I just don't think you'd fit in."

"Aren't you making that judgment a bit prematurely? You haven't seen me work yet," Natalie replied evenly. Her serene countenance concealed the bitter disappointment she felt. She had anticipated some sort of resistance, however, and she had come prepared. "You could at least give me a chance to prove myself."

"Prove what?" he almost sneered. "Let me assure you, Miss Bishop, piloting a charter boat is one heckuva lot tougher than it looks from the deck chairs. Oh, I forgot," he added unconvincingly, "you've been to Coast Guard school."

Natalie felt like throwing the brass paperweight at the smug face that confronted her. He knew well that to get her license Natalie had done more than just casually attend some classes and take a few deep-sea fishing trips. She had demonstrated her competence in everything from interpreting nautical charts and fixing positions by taking bearings on fixed objects to effectively sending and receiving radio signals.

Natalie remained calm. She had too much at stake to be goaded into a show of emotion. Instead, she slowly turned her head to gaze at the framed operator's license in the name of B.R. Andress that hung over a small counter to her right. Ben's dark eyes followed hers. "I'm a hard worker and I'm qualified," Nat said evenly.

"It's not just the heavy work," he replied. "There are other risks—engine trouble, storms, sharks." He recited the perils at sea. "And there's always the threat of hijackings. Any contraband runner looking for a cruiser to take over would not consider a female captain much of a deterrent. Once the word is out, they'd come looking for you. Dope runners know easy pickings when they see them. I'm sure you'd bring out the pirate in them...or in any man." He lowered his eyes and stared at the deep V of her knit sweater.

When he looked up, Natalie met his gaze steadily. She was not going to be scared off—or stared off—the job by Ben Andress.

"Look, Miss Bishop," he said, rolling back in his chair. "I've had a look at that snazzy car you parked outside. You obviously don't need this job. Work is erratic. Some days we're booked up and some we're not. The pay isn't that good."

Natalie stared at him stonily.

"You wouldn't pull in enough to make your car payments, let alone anything else," he added.

"I'm here for the experience, not the money," Nat shot back.

"Well, I'm not in the business of providing experience," Ben answered. "I don't have the time or the patience to fool with you. I need a strong worker who can handle the gear, the passengers, a .357 Magnum and the helm of a cruiser—without my having to keep an eye out all the time to see that everything is going well. You're very attractive," he noted without enthusiasm, "but my passengers want *fish* in their photos, not a pretty face." He gave her a patronizing smile. "So I'm still stuck. I need a temporary captain. I thought I was set. Buzz Cochran must be out of his mind to set me up with you," he concluded in exasperation.

This time he rocked his chair forward and glanced above Natalie's head toward the door. The gesture was clearly a formal dismissal. Nat didn't move. She had hoped to be able to reason with the stern, handsome man who had hired her at Buzz Cochran's request.

"You can't have the job, but I will reimburse you for your travel expenses—" Ben started to reach for the drawer to his right.

"I'll take you to court," Natalie cut him off coolly. "I have a letter signed by you acknowledging my qualifications and promising me the job—and suitable accommodations—until your other captain returns." Her cheeks were crimson as she proceeded efficiently. She had come this far, and she wasn't about to give up. "My Uncle Buzz would not have recommended me unless he knew I could handle the job. You may refuse a favor to him," she said haughtily, "but this has gone beyond merely returning favors. You have a legal commitment to me, and you cannot dismiss that so readily. I'll sue you."

Ben's dark eyebrows arched, with increased attentiveness, at her defiance. Then his expression became inscrutable.

"I'm sure the newspapers will pick up on any discrimination suit," Natalie stressed. "They could have quite a time spreading this around the country while we wait for a court date. I wasn't intending to stay here forever, Mr. Andress. We could handle this all quietly and discreetly—and inexpensively," she noted, "or we could make a real mess of things. You offered me a job for which I am qualified, and I accepted," she stated flatly. "You honor your commitment and I'll honor mine."

"Why did you have to pick on my outfit for this? We're just a small deal. Pick on one of the bigger marinas," he argued. "They can afford to take a chance. We can't."

"I didn't pick your outfit," Natalie stressed. "You just happened to have a temporary vacancy, and I wanted a job. Maybe it will be fairer if you take less of a chance. Try me for a month. Give me a chance to prove that I can handle all the responsibilities. If you can find a legitimate reason for firing me, I won't challenge your decision. Otherwise, I leave here now, contact my attorney and take you to court." Her gold-flecked eyes were riveted on his.

He held her gaze as he began slowly drumming his fingertips on the scarred old desk. "Your *Uncle* Buzz, huh?" he mused aloud. "And *your* attorney...." He stopped drumming, leaned back and rubbed his index finger over his upper lip thoughtfully. His eyes lingered on the gold chain around her neck as he regarded her intently. Natalie couldn't imagine what he was thinking. His behavior only minutes ago aboard his precious old cruiser showed that his mood could be as cloudy as an October morning off Key Largo.

"Would you please step outside for a moment," Ben said icily. Nat lifted her chin slightly, then nodded in agreement. Without a word, she walked out of the glass-walled office, pulling closed the door behind her. He already had the telephone receiver to his ear as he dialed a number.

Natalie waited by the door while he spoke to someone, hung up, then dialed another number. Studiously, she turned her attention to the thirty-six-foot sports-fishing boat being hosed down at the far end of the building. Mac was lugging tackle out onto the wooden dock, occasionally glancing over at her and at Ben behind the glass partition, still engrossed in his telephone conversation.

"You can come back in." Ben startled Natalie once more by jerking open the door and speaking abruptly, summoning her into his office. He waved her toward a chair, then settled in his own swivel chair behind his desk. For a moment, he simply glared at her, his dark eyes remote and cautious.

"It seems that you've got me...." He clipped the words as he spoke. "You and Buzz Cochran set this up quite effectively," he stated grimly. "At least that's what *my* attorney tells me."

Nat regarded him closely. He was obviously displeased about the situation, but he knew his legal limitations. Natalie could stay.

"Actually, you've got me." Nat tried to lessen the tension between them. He was going to be her boss; the least she could do was to help make the relationship more bearable. "You've got me for a month, perhaps more." She wasn't going to take more than she deserved—a fair chance to prove to herself that she could handle the work. In the process, she would prove to Ben Andress that she was qualified for the job. "I'll stand by my earlier proposal," Nat insisted. "If I complete one month to your satisfaction, then I get to stay on. If not, I'll leave quietly."

"It's very generous of you to make concessions," he noted dryly. "Particularly since I have no other legal options at this moment."

"I am trying to be fair about this," Nat declared.

"*Now* you can be fair." He eyed her skeptically. Slowly a slight smile spread across his tanned face, but the eyes remained cold. "I suppose if you should choose to quit during that month, I would not be liable for any legal action?"

"If I quit, your obligations are at an end, captain," Nat conceded, wondering what this man could possibly be planning. "However, I'm not a quitter," she asserted. "I intend to stay here and do the job very well," she concluded with determination.

"In any case—" Ben picked up a pen "—let's make sure there's no further misunderstanding each other." He rapidly wrote out the terms of the agreement: one month trial, no further claims if she quit. "I don't intend to be sued," he attested, "so if you will simply sign this and date it, Miss Bishop...." He turned the paper so it faced Natalie.

"This isn't necessary." She inspected the document then accepted his pen to sign her name.

"I'm not so sure," he responded quietly. Once Natalie had completed her name and the date, he added his own to the agreement. "I'll have a copy made for you," he said as he examined the paper.

Natalie slid out of her chair and walked toward the door. She turned, with one hand clasping the door handles. "I came a few days early so I could look around and become familiar with the routine here," she informed him. "If you don't mind, I'd like to move into the 'suitable accommodations' you referred to in your letter. . . if the place is available."

Ben merely looked at her.

"If it isn't convenient," Nat said with forced dignity, "perhaps someone else can direct me."

He stood and walked toward her, cupping his hand over hers on the door handle. "I will show it to you personally," he said softly, resting his other hand on her shoulder. Natalie slowly dropped her eyes from the amused glint in Ben's. Abruptly he snatched open the door and proceeded out ahead of her.

During their conversation, two thirty-three-foot cruisers had maneuvered up to the dock. The crewmen all turned to stare at the tall young woman in ivory who stepped rapidly across the wooden floor in the wake of their stern-faced boss. Only Mac made any move. Grinning and giving her the thumbs-up sign, he bobbed his head up and down in obvious delight. When Nat flashed him a grateful smile, all eyes shifted curiously from the girl to Mac. Natalie guessed that a flurry of questions would erupt in the boathouse as soon as she stepped out onto the crushed-shell parking lot and heard the door slam behind her.

Moving hastily along a narrow walkway that meandered past the boathouse and out amid the mangroves and palms, Natalie followed the rapidly disappearing form of Ben Andress. Somewhere ahead, obscured by the trees, was her new room.

A one-month trial, she reminded herself. *Anyone can stick it out for that long.* When she caught a glimpse of Ben standing impatiently ahead of her, she wasn't so sure. She'd promised him a month trial period—and this man looked like someone determined to make those thirty days extremely difficult.

"Your room's in this one." He pointed to the first of four beach houses raised on barnacle-encrusted pilings. "A bit primitive for your tastes, perhaps," he remarked, watching Natalie raise one hand to shield her eyes from the late-afternoon sun as she peered up at her proposed abode. "The fellows bunk here most of the time—except for their occasional all-nighters when they go out partying and then find a warm body to snuggle up to."

Natalie ignored his comment and climbed up the rear stairway onto the low porch that encircled each beach house. She opened the rear door and stepped into the modest dwelling. Swiftly she scanned the rectangular kitchen-living room that ran the length of the beach house. A room-size air conditioner built into the rear wall was turned off. From the ceiling, a large fan was suspended. Ben reached out and flipped on the switch. The fan blades slowly rotated, sending a current of cool air across the room to welcome her.

"It's really quite pleasant." Natalie turned to face her employer. He had followed her across the room and stood much closer than she had anticipated.

Again she found herself stepping back to avoid contact with him.

"The bathroom is through there." He pointed to the closed door next to the kitchen end of the cottage. "You can sleep in here," Ben said, as he reached past her and opened the door farther down on the left side of the main room. A simple wooden army cot was backed against the far wall of the bedroom. A bureau with several drawers, a low table, and a yellow canvas deck chair were the only other furnishings. "Not quite the Hilton, Miss Bishop—" he smiled coldly "—but it is provided free of charge," he added in a matter-of-fact tone. "If you prefer something fancier, then you'll have to locate it yourself." He leaned against the doorjamb, studying her expression.

"This will do nicely," Natalie said, nodding slowly. "I'll bring in my things." She started for the doorway, but he didn't budge.

"You're sure?" He regarded her cautiously.

"Positive," Natalie asserted cheerfully, though inside she was somewhat apprehensive about his reference to the "fellows" bunking in the adjacent cabins.

A trace of a smile tilted the corner of Ben's mouth. "Then pull your car over here, and I'll get Hector to help you unload. Just drive right along the path." He preceded her down the rear stairway and walked two strides ahead of her to the parking area.

"Hector!" He waved at the dark-haired crewman who stood with several other men on the porch of the Gold Coast Lodge. With a can of beer clasped in his hand, the swarthy-skinned young man muttered something to his comrades, then bounded over the rail and loped toward his boss and the lady in ivory.

"Give Miss Bishop a hand with her things, will you?" Ben said amiably to the young man, whose bright black eyes gazed evenly into Natalie's.

"Thank you, I can manage by myself," Natalie said softly. "I don't have that much."

Ben pivoted to glare down at her. "You'd better let Hector help you get settled. You'll need to straighten out between you who puts what where."

Natalie's eyes widened uncertainly. "I don't understand," she murmured.

"Hector Ortiz, meet Natalie Bishop. She's temporarily replacing Charlie as skipper of the *Calusa*—and she'll be bunking with you in Beachside One." Without another word, Ben slapped Hector on the shoulder and strode across the parking area to the cluster of crewmen gawking from the porch of the lodge.

Natalie managed to close her mouth and turn toward her red Mustang before the soft laughter from the porch brought a deep red glow to her cheeks. There had been another door on the far side of the main room of the beach house. Nat had assumed it was an unoccupied bedroom. Apparently she was wrong. Recovering her equilibrium, Nat grabbed her car keys and slid in under the wheel.

"Hop in, Hector," she said solemnly as she reached across and flipped up the passenger side door lock. The young man dropped into the seat next to her and pulled the door closed. He sipped his beer in silence as Nat maneuvered the car along the shell path to the beach houses. Over and over she thought to herself, *if papa and the boys find out....* "But a deal is a deal," she stubbornly reminded herself.

"Pardon?" Hector's eyes darted anxiously over toward the tawny-haired young woman at the wheel.

"Just mumbling, Hector," Natalie apologized. "Bad habit of mine," she added.

"I have a few bad habits myself." Hector smiled back at her and crushed the empty beer can against his knee.

And I'll probably get to know about them all, Natalie silently shrugged. After all, bunking in the same beach house would be a pretty chummy situation. *Natalie,* she lamented, *have you bitten off more than you can chew?*

Forcing a brave smile, she pulled to a stop at the foot of the stairway of Beachside One. Fleetingly she recalled a line she'd learned in her sophomore literature class—a line by Alexander Pope—about fools rushing in where angels fear to tread. Yet she was determined. *I won't quit,* she inwardly affirmed. *I'll show that smug-faced Ben Andress.*

Resolutely she began passing boxes and suitcases toward the outstretched hands of Hector Ortiz. When she reached alongside the driver's seat and eased her spin-casting rod from its secure nest, the young Cuban's quick gaze shifted, and he whistled a low salute.

"Nice gear," he noted. The wide fiberglass tackle box brought another startled glance. "You really do fish...." He sounded surprised.

"I really do," Nat replied. "I may be a little out of practice, though."

Hector looked away, cleared his throat and scratched at the day's growth of beard on his cheek. "You...want to do a little casting?" Hector asked eagerly. "Say in an hour—once you get settled, I mean?" he added in a weak attempt to veil his curiosity about his new housemate.

"I guess there are some pompano...maybe gray snapper." Natalie avoided his eyes as she smiled and proceeded up the steps ahead of him. "Maybe we could try a few casts before dark. Just give me some time to hang up my things and get out of these clothes."

From below her on the stairs, Hector chuckled. "You bet!" Then came a long pause and a hasty, "Yeah, pompano—we'll get some action for sure."

The low sun sent an orange flame shimmering across the surface of the inlet and flooded the beach house with a warm glow.

Almost there, Natalie thought as she stood in her room hugging herself as she gazed to the southwest out over Little Torch Key. In the distance sprawled Ramrod Key, low and dark in the fading light. Beyond that, the Overseas Highway led to Key West— and home.

CHAPTER TWO

THE LOW SUN was at their backs as Natalie and Hector stood thigh-deep in Newfound Harbor inlet cross-casting with spinning rods. Initially Hector had watched Natalie intently as she'd selected a yellow bucktail jig—a single hook fringed in nylon and weighted with a lead head. When she tied it skillfully to the monofilament line, Hector turned his attention to his own efforts.

He dug his toes into the wet beach sand after a receding wave and prodded aside shells until he spotted a burrowing sand flea. He slipped it onto his own hook that he'd weighted with a sinker, then cast first one way then again in the opposite direction, making the trail form an X. He dropped the next cast in the center of the X and waited for a pompano to follow the scent of the sinker trails toward the bait.

Nat made no comment on Hector's technique. Her father had always taught her that any method was all right—just as long as it worked. She calmly cast her jig well out into the water, slowly jerking and retrieving it as it shimmered and spun beneath the breaking waves.

Hector's line was hit first. He pulled the line to set the hook in the fish, then he frowned and muttered something in Spanish as the line abruptly went slack.

The unseen fish had got away—taking the bait with it.

Nat reeled in slowly, cast again, then retrieved. On her third try, the line was hit—and this one stayed on. Efficiently she drew the pompano closer to shore, then hoisted it with pride before the admiring eyes of her companion.

"About a three-pounder," Nat guessed. Hector simply glared at it and frowned. "Too big for one person to eat alone," Nat grinned. "How about it, Hector? Shall we dine together tonight?"

His disappointment at losing his fish was replaced with a flash of anticipation. "You cookin'?"

"You bet," Nat said as she waded in to shore. "You washin' the dishes?" she shot back over her shoulder.

"I don't wash no dishes," Hector responded grumpily. Nat shrugged and continued on toward the beach house. Hector remained behind, making holes in the sand with his toes, then at last, followed her.

Nat cut off the gills and all but the top of the head of her fish, then she scaled and cleaned it. She located a metal grill pan in the small kitchen, sprinkled the cavity of the fish with salt and pepper, then basted it with butter. Other than three cans of beer, the forlorn single stick of butter had been the only item in the refrigerator.

"Obviously you don't eat in much," Nat noted as she slid the fish under the hot broiler. The oven was spotless.

"I don't cook," Hector muttered. "I eat with the guys—sometimes at the lodge, sometimes out."

"And who pays for the meals?" She eyed him curiously.

"Breakfast comes with the job," Hector explained. "On Saturday night we get a big fish dinner, too. Anything else comes out of our pay. It don't cost much."

"Nothing is as cheap as this...." Nat peered at the sizzling fish. She reached for the butter and basted it once more. "Cheaper than *free*?" she smiled.

"Sure—" Hector shook his head slowly "—but I don't know much about cookin'."

"Then let's discuss a deal," Nat proposed as she sat cross-legged on the floor next to the oven. "You do the dishes, we'll split the cost of some groceries, and I'll cook for both of us. I don't like to eat alone, but I will if I have to. If you want to share, we'll both save some money."

Hector glared down at the young woman. "You got a nice car," he said evenly. "You got nice fishin' gear—expensive stuff. That chain around your neck ain't cheap. You tellin' me you wanna save money?" His lips twisted sardonically.

Natalie sighed. "Yes, I want to save money," she replied flatly. Momentarily she considered taking the brown-eyed young man into her confidence. Having him on her side would be a big advantage. However, Hector was Ben Andress's mate. His loyalties lay elsewhere, and she was determined not to give anyone more information than she had to. Hector would have to draw his own conclusions.

"I'm here to work, Hector. I'm on my own. I intend to live on the money I make with the charter outfit—and to save as much as I can.'' She stared at the firm, defensive set of Hector's jaw. Just a little while before, when they were casting in the surf, she had seen the gleam of admiration in Hector's eyes—a veiled look of approval at the skilled manner in which she'd handled the spinning rod and brought in the now golden pompano. Now his eyes held only cold distrust.

"Take it or leave it, Hector," she declared. "Do we make a deal and eat—or don't we?" She uncrossed her legs and stood to confront him.

Hector stared at her uncertainly. In her cutoff jeans, with her hands braced on her hips, Natalie looked as independent as she claimed to be. The aroma of the broiled fish filled the room, and its tantalizing scent made his mouth water. Gradually the coldness faded from his dark eyes.

"We eat," he conceded.

Natalie waited. "And. . . ." She prodded him.

"And I do the dishes," he conceded. "Only you don't tell the guys."

"It's a deal," Natalie agreed, reaching out her hand to shake on it. Hector was almost crimson when she turned to snap off the broiler.

Later, over their modest meal of pompano and grapes—which were all that had remained in Nat's ice chest after her drive—she and Hector hesitantly discussed the Gold Coast Lodge and the charter business. Hector hadn't attended the Coast Guard school, nor had he taken the test for his operator's license, but he knew a great deal about the charter routes, offshore wrecks and reefs and the kinds of fish that were running. She had considered asking him in detail about Ben Andress and the other men who worked the charters, but Hector was still somewhat uncertain about the gold-eyed girl with the long braid, who looked like a lady but fished like a true Conch. At least for the first month, until she had secured the job, Natalie would steer clear of anything personal and try to take this housemate business one day at a time.

"YOU COMIN', NAT-A-LEE?" Hector dragged out the name with obvious pleasure. Natalie rolled over on the small cot, fumbled for her watch on the dresser top, then finally focused her eyes on the dial: 5:00 A.M. She swung her legs sideways, planting her feet firmly on the floor as she peered toward the window. The pale gray early-morning sky was slowly yielding to a brighter blue that promised good weather. Natalie padded over to the closed door. All she had on was the oversize Atlanta Braves T-shirt that she slept in. She cracked open the door and peeked out as she spoke to the dark-eyed young man.

"Good morning, Hector." Her voice was still thick from sleep. "Am I supposed to be somewhere?" she asked.

Hector shrugged. "I don't know if you're workin' today or not. I just figured you'd get up with the rest of us. We eat at the lodge between five and five-fifteen on the days we got a charter." He shifted feet uncomfortably as he caught a glimpse of the long slim legs beneath the shirt. "I got a charter today. On the *Southwind* . . . with Ben. . . ." He broke off awkwardly.

"Captain Andress didn't say I was to start until

next week." Nat tried to ease the fellow's discomfort. "But thanks for getting me up. I'll get dressed
and go eat with you. I'd better get acquainted with
the routine around here. Give me a couple of minutes
and I'll be ready." She managed to elicit a weak
smile from the young man.

"You bet," Hector breathed in relief, as Nat
pushed closed the door and reached for her clothes.

There were still a few problems of logistics to work
out between them. The only way to the bathroom
was through the living room, and that was where
Hector was pacing. Natalie pulled on her clothes,
then hurried past him into the bathroom to splash
warm water on her face and brush her teeth. Hastily
she rebraided her hair and ran her lipstick over her
lips, then she was ready to face the world.

At precisely 5:12 A.M., Natalie crunched along
beside Hector on the path leading toward the Gold
Coast Lodge. In her bright yellow rolled-sleeved shirt
and khaki jeans, she looked considerably more like a
beach native than she had when she arrived the day
before.

"The guys are gonna wonder about you and me,"
Hector said without looking at her. "Bein' in the
same house...." Shoulder-to-shoulder, they continued walking briskly along.

"There isn't much to tell them," Nat replied in her
matter-of-fact manner. "Let them wonder."

"Sure," he muttered sullenly. Nat suppressed a
small smile. She'd seen the same symptoms in her
older brothers when the boys had hung around the
back porch, each one trying to seem more successful
with the ladies than the next one. Hector didn't have

a thing to brag about...at least not as far as the fellows were concerned. After dinner the night before, he had helped Nat unpack her stereo tape player and set it up in the living room. Then he'd sifted through her tapes and played a couple of them while they sat out on the rear balcony sharing a cold beer and listening to the music. When Nat finally said good-night, they had each gone their separate ways, quietly closing their doors behind them.

"I guess they'll expect to hear that you made some move," Nat observed. "Lots of clutching and grabbing and heavy breathing." She watched his firm lips soften.

"Something like that," he confessed.

"Tell them I'm not your type," she suggested. "Or tell them you haven't made up your mind yet...." She lowered her voice. "Or tell them it's none of their business." She had to skip a couple of steps to keep up with him.

"Maybe they won't ask," Hector said unconvincingly.

"At least not while I'm there," Nat added. But sooner or later, she knew they would get Hector aside, and when they did, Nat had no idea what her soft-spoken housemate would say.

The lodge foyer was abandoned when they entered.

"There are three rooms for guests that way," Hector explained, pointing to the left. "The back end is where Mac lives. We go this way to eat." He guided her toward the window-rimmed room overlooking the inlet. As they stepped into the room, five pairs of eyes turned to stare at them. Five cups of coffee paused in midair as the twosome approached. Hector had a half smile on his face and Nat felt a flush of embarrassment creep up her neck as she noticed five pairs of eyes watching her and her housemate. She refused to imagine what naughty thoughts they might be considering.

At the end of a long table sat Mac Butler. He was grinning like the cat who'd just dined on the canary. He stood to greet them.

"Natalie. . . Hector." He nodded. "Boys, this is Charlie's replacement—Nat Bishop." He pulled back a chair for the young woman. "Natalie, this is Fuzzy, skipper of the *Suds Buggy*," he stated, pointing to a wiry bald fellow who simply blinked at her. "And Herb, mate on the *Suds Buggy*." Herb was about thirty—a few years younger than Ben Andress. Herb's pale blue eyes and almost white hair made his deep tan seem almost black in contrast. Herb glared at her and grunted an acknowledgment. "And Greg—" Mac pointed at the bearded young man at the far side of the table "—will be your mate on the *Calusa*. And, of course you know Ben," Mac chuckled as Nat's gold-flecked eyes shifted to the blank countenance of Captain Andress.

"Glad you could join us," Ben said politely as Natalie settled into her chair. "I hadn't planned on working you till after the weekend. The job officially starts then," he remarked pointedly. "But as long as you're up and about, you can follow Mac around today and get your bearings. Tomorrow I'll take you out on the *Calusa* to see how you handle her." His even voice seemed unexpectedly reassuring. Natalie felt the color rise in her cheeks as he regarded her intently. "Is that acceptable, Miss Bishop?" He maintained a businesslike tone.

Before Nat formed an answer, a portly woman of forty came bustling out of the kitchen followed by a young dark-haired girl whom she guessed was of Cuban descent like her housemate, Hector. Each of them carried a tray laden with platters of eggs and sausage and baskets of freshly baked rolls.

"So you're the one Mac's been tellin' me about." The older woman burst into a grin and stretched a moist hand toward Natalie. "He's been moanin' about fallin' in love with some long-haired amazon," she chuckled. "I expected a woman wrestler," she joked. "Mac said you were tall, but he didn't tell me you were so pretty."

Natalie's face was now a full, deep crimson.

"I'm Maggie Butler, Mac's wife. He may be in love with you for now—but he's taken," she cackled. Mac reached out and slid an arm around her broad waist and gave her an affectionate hug. "Don't blame ya for tryin'." Maggie nudged him as she continued to study Nat's freckled cheeks and thickly-lashed eyes.

"Maggie runs the lodge," Ben explained calmly, amid the guffaws and mumblings of the crewmen. "She's in charge of the rooms, the restaurant and just about anything else she takes a mind to run." His voice was openly affectionate. Nat jerked her eyes from Maggie to the face of Captain Andress, intrigued to see the warmth in his expression. It was not the guarded look he reserved for her.

"You make me sound like a bossy old woman," Maggie scolded.

"If the shoe fits. . . ." Ben smiled slowly.

"Watch it, buster," Maggie warned as she playfully rolled up her sizable fist. "You fellas stop gawking and get this food before it gets cold," she insisted, as her assistant, the silent young Cuban girl, laid down her tray of food and stepped back. There was a blur of motion as the serving platters were emptied of food.

Natalie stared in distress at the bare platters. Maggie simply shook her head and winked at Nat. "Until you get a little faster on the draw, you'd better come up front with me and fill your plate in the kitchen. It's the only way to guarantee you'll get breakfast today." With a loud laugh, Maggie strode off to the kitchen, with Natalie, clasping her empty plate, following behind.

At 5:45 A.M. every morsel had disappeared from all the plates, and the coffee cups were drained dry for a second or third time. "Let's go." Ben stood first and started out of the room while chairs squealed across the floor and the others went after him.

On the way out, the procession passed several eager fishermen rushing into the restaurant for a quick cup of coffee to brace themselves before setting out. "Ten minutes," one fellow called to Ben, who simply nodded and kept on walking.

Natalie walked along in the midst of the men, slightly behind Ben and Hector but in front of the other crewmen, who seemed to be in no hurry to reach the boathouse. She couldn't hear the conversation between Ben and Hector, but she noticed that Hector kept shrugging and nodding his head as if to indicate that things were all right so far. She skipped a step to get a little closer to the two men, staring at Ben's broad shoulders as they swayed slightly from side to side with each stride. When he stopped abruptly and turned to speak, Nat walked right into him.

"It's a little early for dancing, Miss Bishop." Ben caught her by the shoulders to steady her. Herb and Fuzzy broke into cackling laughter. "Maybe we could just talk." Ben moved her aside so the two men who had been amused by the collision could move past.

"Mac is taking out the *Calusa* today, and you might as well go along for the ride." Ben released her as he spoke. "Just remember that he's in charge, so keep your mouth closed and stay out of the way as much as possible. No more collisions," he said without any trace of his earlier joking manner. Without an audience, he didn't make jokes.

Natalie felt her face stiffen at his condescending tone.

"And," he went on in the same flat voice, "keep reminding yourself that this may be a *very* temporary situation if you mess up."

"Yes, sir." Nat raised her free arm in a snappy salute. "Whatever you say, sir," she added sarcastically, clicking her heels together.

For a moment Ben's dark eyes narrowed angrily, but instead of tightening his grip, he slowly let his hand slide from her arm. "This is really quite a lark for you, isn't it, Miss Bishop?" he said in a controlled voice. "You and Buzz have set me up—and you seem to be delighted with this little game."

Again his dark eyes glared at her. "Well, for me it's very serious business—" he emphasized each word "—and I don't take any of it lightly. I don't know why Buzz Cochran has it in for me—but I'm stuck with you. At least for the time being. And I don't like your attitude," he glowered at her.

"Mr. Andress," Nat said between her teeth, "I take this business more seriously than you realize. And I'm not particularly thrilled about your attitude either. One minute you're kidding, the next minute you're giving me a lecture. How about if you just treat me like one of the boys—and not like a child," she added angrily.

"Fine!" Ben blasted back, causing Fuzzy and Mac to look up from their schedules and stare at the two of them. Lowering his voice suddenly, Ben stepped closer. "Then, as one of the boys, you can damn well start loading the gear."

"I was hired as a captain. Loading gear is a mate's job," Natalie replied icily. "However—" she reconsidered as Ben tensed visibly "—just to show you that I'm a good sport, I don't mind helping out the mates now and then," she sniffed.

"How about *now*," Ben breathed ominously.

"I'd be delighted." Nat assumed an aloof expression, turned on her heels and headed for the *Calusa*. As she stepped aboard with a cooler full of crushed ice, she caught a glimpse of Captain Andress ducking into his glass-walled office. Maybe it was a trick of the low early-morning sun, but Natalie thought she saw on the stone face of Ben Andress the beginnings of a smile.

Nat sat up front with Mac on the trip out to deep

water. Leaning forward eagerly, watching the bright surface of the water, Nat couldn't help smiling as the steady wind in her face seemed to blow away her misgivings. Mac glanced from the water ahead to the intent, radiant face to his left, and found himself grinning, too.

"You're gonna love this little boat." Mac tilted his head toward the stern of the craft. "She's light, quick...skims along like a bird. She doesn't have as much engine as the other boats, but she gets the job done."

Nat leaned back against the canopy support over the cockpit and looked at her companion. "You sound like you take her out a lot," she noted. "I don't see what Captain Andress needed another charter operator for...."

"I'm just the backup man," Mac said with a trace of regret. "Most of the time I get the dull end of the work...signing up charters, managing the supplies, seeing to the repair work. When I do get out, I take it easy...but I love it," he chuckled aloud. "This boat needs a full-time captain...and it looks like you're it."

"It looks like it," Nat agreed with a satisfied sigh. Here out in the Atlantic she felt unrestricted. For the first time in months, she felt as if she was breathing real air. "Boy, I've missed it down here," she confessed.

"If it's in your blood, there's nothing like it." Mac seemed to understand. "I came down here on a fishing trip, years ago, when I was still in the army. Once I got the sand in my shoes, I just kept comin' back for more."

"Is Captain Andress from this area?" Nat ventured to ask.

"Ben?" Mac shook his head. "He was an army brat," Mac smiled. "I don't think he really is *from* anywhere. When I got to know him, he was flying helicopters. He had no family left. We just struck up a friendship." He slowed the boat down to trolling speed as he spoke.

"How about it, Mac?" one of the passengers called up to him. "Are we ready to get down to some serious fishing?"

"You bet," Mac replied. Without needing any further direction, one passenger settled into the single fighting chair, while the other settled comfortably on the built-in bench on the side of the craft. Greg Owens, the mate on the *Calusa*, shifted into motion, setting out the lures and bait. For the next several hours, the routine would be the same.

"Who named this boat the *Calusa*?" Nat asked curiously. "I remember hearing tales about them when I was a kid."

"Ben named her." Mac kept his eyes on the clear, deep blue water as he chatted with her. "Some kind of Indian tribe, wasn't it? He comes up with the strangest things sometimes. What do you know about them?"

"My dad says they were here before anyone else," Nat replied. "They were the earliest inhabitants of the Keys and most of the west coast of Florida. He said they were great fishermen and excellent seamen." She fell silent a moment as the memory of what else her father had said came back to her.

Mac gave her a sidelong glance as if he was waiting for more. "And?" he prompted her.

"And...depending on your point of view...they were fearless scavengers...or pirates and cut-throats," she continued. "They weren't too hospitable to ships and passengers caught on the reefs. They usually pillaged the ships and left the crews to the sharks."

"They sound charming," Mac muttered. "I can't see what the other point of view could be. A pirate is a pirate."

"They considered wrecks as gifts from the sea," Nat countered, defending the long-extinct tribe. "All the gold and food and supplies were rewards for some deed they had done. I guess they considered the crew simply delivery boys. Once the Calusa men took what they could carry in their canoes, they let the people perish. Maybe they thought the gods of the sea would take the people and use them again."

"Maybe they didn't care one way or the other," Mac said. "I sure wonder if Ben knew all that stuff about them when he came up with the name? I wouldn't put it past him."

"It's a nice name," Natalie stressed. She didn't want Mac to mistake her curiosity for disapproval. "I like *Calusa*."

"You'll like her even more when you get behind the wheel." Mac winked at her. "You want to try your hand at it?" He stepped back and invited her to take the pilot's seat.

"I sure do." Nat almost leaped across the boat. "You don't think Captain Andress would mind?" She hesitated.

"If this is going to be your boat, he'd better get used to seeing you behind the wheel," Mac said firmly. "And if you're going to stick around, you'd better not be too concerned about what Ben thinks. You'll never know what he's thinking until he's darn good and ready to tell you."

"So. . .I'll drive." Nat beamed. The thirty-three-foot stark white *Calusa* eased ahead beneath her touch. Gleaming like a white gull on the water, she would pause from time to time as Greg netted one of the fish that the passengers had pulled alongside. *It's going to work,* Nat kept reassuring herself as the smooth motion of the boat put her increasingly at ease. *I'm going to do it. . .and it's really going to work.*

THE NEXT MORNING, Andress was ready to see for himself what Captain Natalie Bishop could do. The *Calusa* was booked for a five-hour run out through Hawk Channel into the Atlantic to a place just beyond the massive reef that paralleled the Keys. The two passengers aboard sat on padded blue seats, peering expectantly out over the clear blue water along the edge of the Gulf Stream. The springtime sky was lightly overcast—comfortable for fishing—and the glassy water shimmered as Nat perched in the pilot's seat, scanning the bits of driftwood and gulfweed that sheltered fish.

Expressionless but efficient, bearded Greg Owens served as mate, checking the tackle, handling the gear and occasionally pausing to stare at the young female captain who seemed to know precisely where to find fish. Ben had come along only as an observer. He sat on a high swivel stool in the pilot's area with his battered once-white cap pulled low over his eyes. He rarely spoke; he just observed. Natalie was conscious of every movement he made as he evaluated her performance from his vantage point only an arm's length from her. She had told him that she took the job seriously, and she was determined to prove just how skillful she could be.

The two fishermen had wanted bonito—the feisty little tuna that reached a top weight of about twenty-five pounds. They were not out for trophy fish; these two were sports fishermen out mainly for the contest and the excitement. While Greg armed the men with light spinning gear and bucktail jigs, Nat trolled along at a good clip, scanning for any surface disruption that would mark the location of the little tuna.

April was a good month for bonito, Nat remembered as the cruiser knifed through mats of gulfweed. Springtime meant the water was getting progressively warmer. Fishing would pick up considerably and get better as the hot weather approached and the fish became more plentiful. It took her fifteen minutes to spot her first school, but when she did it was an active one. The tuna slammed into the lines, running with the hooks, giving her passengers the thrills they had come for.

The tuna made fierce sustained runs then cut and swerved with ferocious bursts of power that had made these bonito famous as rough and tough adversaries. Nat let the boat drift with the current as the men reveled in their pump-and-wait game of tug-of-war with the spunky fish. The men were hooting with delight one minute and cursing with equal enthusiasm the next, as the shiny bomb-shaped fish tested their spirit and tortured their wrists. Nat was caught up in their excitement, shouting encouragement, laughing and making suggestions and always keeping her attention on the location of the lines and the motion of the boat. Ben's dark eyes were constantly locked on her, observing, evaluating and reminding her that this was more than a simple fishing trip.

After nearly two hours of fighting the bonito, the two fishermen had had their fun and selected only one specimen each as a "keeper." The battle, not the quantity of prizes, was what interested them. Ben finally abandoned his post up beside Nat and climbed down to spend the latter part of the trip talking quietly with the two passengers or helping Greg. All the other fish caught on the trip were released along the way by Greg or Ben. They would lean over the side, dragging the limp creatures openmouthed in the clear salty water. After a few seconds, the fish would be sufficiently revived to plunge again into the depths of the Gulf Stream, eventually to fight again another day with another fisherman.

All the way back to the lodge marina, Natalie gripped the wheel of the *Calusa* tightly, resisting the urge to look down over her shoulder at the expression on Ben's face. She was eager to hear *something* from him—some comment about how she had handled the charter, but she didn't want to press him before he was ready to discuss it with her.

Nat steered the boat into Newfound Harbor, maneuvered it expertly up to the dock, unloaded passengers and fish, then waited impatiently while Ben stepped out without a word to her and began talking with the satisfied passengers.

"Take the boat around into the boathouse and wash her down," Ben finally said. "Nice trip, Miss Bishop," he added politely, then turned his attention back to the two men.

Nat bit her lip to stop herself from saying anything in front of the customers. She backed the *Calusa* away from the dock and pulled it around into the covered boathouse where long hoses and the storage sheds reminded her that she still had a good hour of work to do. Silently, she pitched Greg the tie lines and began the task of cleaning the gear and spraying down the *Calusa*. Her arms ached from the tension of clutching the wheel and operating the boat under Ben's watchful eyes, but Nat wouldn't slack up. She worked alongside Greg, scrubbing, hosing down and storing gear just like any other crewman.

"I'd like to see you when you finish." Ben paused on the end of the unloading dock on his way toward his favorite project. Nat nodded and watched him stroll off and climb aboard the hulking, grand old cruiser he was restoring. He disappeared below deck to the place where Nat had first looked into his dark, hard eyes.

"Yes, sir," Natalie whispered in dismay. She'd been expecting some kind of evaluation, certainly more of a critique than "Nice trip, Miss Bishop." Apparently she was going to have to trespass on his beloved old boat if she was going to hear what else he had to say.

When the swabbing down was completed, Greg grunted a brief farewell and walked out of the boathouse, leaving Nat on dockside alone. She walked around to the side of the cruiser in dry dock and called from the dock into its dim interior. "I think everything is cleaned up satisfactorily," she began. "You wanted to see me?" For a moment there was no reply.

"Captain Andress?" she said loudly.

"I can't hear you. Come on down here," he called from below deck. Hesitantly Nat pulled herself aboard the cruiser. At least this time, it was at Ben's invitation. Nat took a deep breath before going below, hoping that this confrontation would be nothing like the last one they had had on this boat.

Ben had stripped off his loose navy shirt and was on his knees in tight, well-worn jeans. He was diligently scraping paint from the floorboard of the cruiser. In the still, moist air within the narrow corridor, he labored methodically. His dark hair, wet with perspiration, lay pressed against his forehead in slender spirals and the hair on his chest and on his bronzed arms glistened as he moved. Natalie watched him silently, entranced by the power and the beauty of his tanned body.

Finally Nat cleared her throat to let him know she was standing there. "You wanted to see me?" She forced out the words.

"Oh...I've seen you...." He picked up a cloth and brushed aside a few flakes of paint. Then he stood and stared at her. "I watched you most of the morning," he reminded her.

"I'm well aware of that." Nat was not amused. "You said you wanted to see me *now*, so here I am."

"Are you worn out from the trip?" Ben looked at

her closely. "Any sore muscles?" He reached out and clasped her upper arm as if to check. Natalie flinched at the contact, unable to conceal the discomfort in her strained arms.

"I figured you might be tired," he said, beginning to massage her arm gently. Natalie started to resist, but the warm rhythmical pressure of his hands on her arms was too deliciously comforting. Yielding beneath his touch, she let him turn her around so his strong hands could relax the muscles in her shoulders. She had come to him expecting an analysis of her labors; she had not anticipated the gentle, firm stroking of his hands. Ben Andress continued to surprise Natalie. There was no way to anticipate what he would do or what he was thinking.

"You impressed me," Ben said quietly as he rubbed her shoulders. "I didn't think you could handle the boat as well as you did." He seemed reluctant to say any more.

"I tried to do a good job," Natalie answered softly. She knew that she had a lot in her favor that day—the weather was perfect and the fish plentiful. Not all charters would go that smoothly.

"Maybe you should try to get some rest." He kept up the mesmerizing motion of his hands on her arms. "You're really tight in there. I think you overdid it a bit...." His concern once again veered toward a reprimand.

"If I'm through for the day, I've got some other things I have to do." Natalie left her specific plans vague.

"You're going off somewhere?" The movement on her arms halted as he waited for her reply. Natalie turned and looked up into black, questioning eyes.

"I have a few arrangements to make. . . if I'm taking over the *Calusa* full time," Nat explained. "I *am* taking her over, aren't I?" She finally summoned the courage to ask directly.

"Oh, you're taking over all right," Ben conceded. "I was just curious about what else you're up to. Do you have family nearby—besides Buzz Cochran, I mean?"

Natalie found herself withdrawing again, retreating from the closeness with him that the contact with his hands had established. When he'd touched her, she'd felt warm and protected, but when he started questioning her, looking at her with his dark cautious eyes, it became clear again that he didn't trust her any more than she felt she could trust him. They were still adversaries. He had been tricked into hiring her, and only her threat to prosecute had forced him to keep her—even temporarily.

"Buzz is the only family nearby," Natalie replied. It wasn't quite a lie. The Bishop men were off across the Gulf on their trawlers. Natalie didn't know what Ben was after, but she didn't want him to know any more than necessary. All he had to see was that she could handle the job, regardless of family or anything else.

"Is there anyone I should contact in case of an emergency?" Ben tried again. "Friends? Anyone close to you?"

"Just Uncle Buzz," Natalie insisted. "He's been my guardian angel," she added honestly.

"Is that who you're going to visit?"

Natalie shook her head in distress. "Remember

how you don't like people trespassing?'' She frowned. "Well, I feel like you're prying into my personal life...and I don't like it. I owe you a good day's work," Natalie stressed. "But what I do away from here is my own business.''

"Maybe...maybe not." Ben glared at her. "That depends on what you're doing.''

"You don't act this way with the men!" Nat protested.

"The men don't have freckles and golden skin... and a voice like soft bells in the wind...." He reached out and clasped her shoulders. Instantly the hostility was gone. There remained only his dark, liquid eyes and the warmth of his hands drawing her near. He pulled her against his bare chest, sliding his hands down her back, lifting her to him as he pressed his mouth against hers.

Natalie responded instinctively, letting her slender hands trail over the bare expanse of his back. His skin was soft and velvety to her touch, its tanned surface surprisingly smooth over the powerful corded muscles beneath. The moist, pliant pressure of his mouth and the luxurious feel of his body next to hers seemed vaguely familiar, as if Natalie had played this scene before, somewhere in a dream, and now was experiencing it again in the real world.

Ben once more began the stroking motion that had eased her aching arm muscles, but now the rhythmical pattern extended down over her hips, tracing the slender contours of her body, pressing her against him so the increasing hardness of his response pressed against her lithe form. Almost breathless, Ben pulled back and stared down at her. Seeing no protest, only the eagerness in her eyes, he lowered his mouth once more, trailing hot, moist kisses down the sun-bronzed column of her neck.

Never before had Natalie felt the overwhelming heat that Ben set raging within her. The salty, manly scent of his body mingled with the rich aromas of the old cruiser, filling her with an intoxicating sensation of sea and timelessness and passion. It was as if some natural force had been pent up within her, and only the contact with this bronzed, unpredictable man had set it loose. Reeling and raging like a tropical storm, it surged within her as she clung to Ben, returning touch for touch as she marveled at the unsuspected yearnings that he seemed to elicit.

Ben broke away abruptly, holding her away as they both stood gasping for air. There was no gleam of passion in his eyes—only a dark, unsettled look that sent a wave of uneasiness through Natalie. "Do you have any idea what you're doing to me?" Ben finally said. "You just catch fire when I touch you...." He sounded disconcerted. "I didn't think it would be like this...."

Natalie looked at the bewildered expression on Ben's face. Even with the flush of passion still glowing on his bronzed skin, there was an enigmatic remoteness that chilled her. *What did he think it would be like,* she wondered. What had he been planning or expecting when he kissed her?

"You weren't going to stop me, were you?" he challenged. Natalie regarded him uneasily. Was that what he wanted? Had he planned to pressure her sexually until she fought him off? Did he want to see how far he could go before she broke away? Suddenly the small corridor below deck became horribly oppressive. Had he called her down here just for this? Here, where no one could see them, was he going to break her reserve and shatter her control?

"There were *two* of us involved in this," Natalie retorted. "I hadn't made any plans about what I was going to do." She bit off the words. "I don't *plan* what I feel."

"What you *feel* is pretty dangerous, Natalie—unless you can control it or accept the consequences." Ben dropped his hands from her shoulders once more, breaking the contact between them.

"I think you have a share in those consequences," Natalie stressed. "I wasn't doing anything alone... and I didn't start this either," she reminded him.

"No, you didn't," he conceded. "And you didn't try to end it...and I'm not sure what would have happened if *I* hadn't come up for air." Natalie merely looked at him. She had no answer for that. She had been seized by a wave of emotions more powerful than any she had felt before. She had no idea what would have happened if they had continued touching, kissing, feeling the eagerness of each other.

"Maybe you'd better leave and take a little time to think about this...." He thrust a hand through his thick hair.

"Maybe you'd better think about it, too," Nat returned pointedly. "It seems as if you're the one with all the plans and all the self-control," she observed.

"My self-control may not be enough for both of us," Ben asserted. "There's something going on between us—underneath every conversation and every look, there's another form of communication going on...and I think it just told us that we may both be in deep water if we aren't careful.''

"It only happens when we touch...." Natalie couldn't stop the words from slipping out.

"Then you'd be safer if you didn't touch me, Natalie...." Ben crossed his arms over his chest. "And I'll try like hell to keep from touching you." There was a distinct tone of resignation in his voice. "After all," he noted solemnly, "you're just passing through. Whatever it is you're trying to prove has nothing to do with me. You've made it clear that your life beyond the lodge and the marina is none of my business."

"That's right," Natalie agreed. Somehow there was no victory in hearing him acknowledge the limits of their relationship.

"Then go and have a pleasant afternoon, Miss Bishop." Ben again assumed his formal mode of address. Without further comment, he bent down and resumed the slow, deliberate scraping of old, chipped paint from the floorboard of the cruiser.

Natalie almost ran along the shell pathway that took her from the boathouse to Beachside One. She wanted to put some distance between Ben Andress and herself so she could recover from the contrary emotions churning inside her. Hastily she grasped her art portfolio from her bedroom, pitched it into the rear seat of her car and drove out through the lodge roadway beyond Gold Coast Lodge to the Overseas Highway and toward her destination.

Within minutes, she was on Big Pine Key, turning down the gravel drive beneath the sign National Key

Deer Refuge. An open Jeep parked by the cottage ahead bore the insignia of the U.S. Fish and Wildlife Service. Retrieving the portfolio from the back of the car, Nat clasped it under one arm, then walked with long strides to the cottage. Here she could be someone else. Here she could begin a second test of her skill under perhaps easier circumstances.

"You made it at last...." The blond-haired man came to the doorway to greet her before she had a chance to knock. "Come in and make yourself at home." His eyes shifted to the portfolio at her side. "Let's see what you've done since I last saw you." His angular hands reached out to receive her carrying case full of artwork.

"Pardon my manners...." He turned apologetically and glanced over his shoulder at the uniformed young man standing on the far side of the room. "Jack, this is Natalie. Natalie, meet Jack Wilson, one of the Refuge managers here. Natalie is the student I've been expecting."

"So you're going to be around here working with Roger." The young man stepped toward her, reaching out to shake her hand in greeting. "That's great." His youthful face brightened as he inspected her from head to toe. "I guess we'll get to see each other a lot." His obvious interest in her made Nat smile. Wilson was close to her age. His blond hair and blue eyes reminded her of her brothers.

"I'll only be here part of the time," Nat replied. "Roger has agreed to let me follow him around and study his technique whenever I'm free. I have a job farther down the Keys. That will take up the rest of the time I have." She saw a glimmer of disappointment in Wilson's eyes. Obviously he was already hoping for an opportunity to get to know her.

"You sound pretty busy," Jack remarked.

"She's been busy all right," Roger Embry interrupted. "Look at some of this stuff...." He grinned, raising a pen-and-ink sketch she had made of an old ramshackle cabin. "Natalie came to a show in the Memorial Art Center in Atlanta last November," Roger commented as he passed one sketch after the other to Jack. "We discovered we share a common interest in the birds and the bees," Roger joked. "I put her on to the possibility of a career as a wildlife illustrator and agreed to give her a little help getting started. Looks like she's off and running," he murmured as he studied the last of her recent sketches.

"Very nice work," Jack acknowledged. "You'll give Roger a little competition," he chuckled.

"That's all she'll give me," Roger assured him. "When I got this commission and told my wife I would be spending the late spring with another woman, Sue was not thrilled. Then I showed her some of Natalie's work, and she knew I was serious—about a student-teacher relationship. As long as Sue is bogged down in her shop in Atlanta," Roger asserted, "she figures I won't get too lonely with Natalie for company. Nothing like another artist to keep me on my toes. We'll get twice as much done trying to show off for each other."

"You're from Atlanta, then?" Jack tried to sound casual as he passed the drawings back to Roger.

"I was in school there," Nat answered. "I've been finishing art classes, and I was planning to go into teaching, until I met Roger.'' She watched with pleasure as he gave each of her sketches another close look. "I like drawing outdoors," she explained. "Teaching all day doesn't give me a lot of time to work outside while the light is good. But jobs like Roger's are not easy to come by," she conceded. "So I'm hoping that a crash course with him and a little exposure to some of his contacts may get me some commissions of my own."

"And a fat portfolio full of samples wouldn't hurt either," Roger interjected. "Remember that business about a picture being worth a thousand words?"

"You really prefer working down here to being in the big city?" Jack regarded her with curiosity.

"I run a little low on inspiration in the city," Natalie replied.

"Some people call it homesickness," Roger teased.

"You mean you come from here. . .?" Jack's look brightened. "What's your last name? Maybe I know your folks. . . ."

"Ahh. . . ." Roger saw where this line of conversation was leading. "We need to keep Natalie's whereabouts a bit confidential," he stressed. "You see, Jack," Roger added with a wriggle of his eyebrows, "the lady is playing hooky. That and the fact that she'll be pressed for time would make it really nice if she was just free to work on her own—without her family's becoming concerned."

"Once I see how this works out," Natalie said, "I'll let my family know that I'm around. I simply need some time to myself." Jack looked a little bewildered by the explanation, but he smiled amiably.

"So I call you Miss X?" he kidded.

"You call me Natalie—Nat Bishop," she smiled. "Just don't call it out too loudly."

"Whatever you say," Jack agreed. "If you intend to be coming in and out of here, I'll even get you a Refuge sticker for your car. You can park on the compound anytime—no questions asked." He was getting into the spirit of this good-natured conspiracy.

"Then get the sticker. . . ." Roger shooed him out the door. "Natalie and I have to set up some kind of schedule—and get down to work."

"I've got to get back to work, too." Jack fumbled with his hat, pausing for a final friendly nod in Nat's direction. "Hope to see you around here," he called before he climbed up into the Refuge Jeep.

"I'll bet he does." Roger grinned at Natalie. "Nice fella. Might provide a little diversion during your stay here," he teased.

"I have no time for diversions." Natalie rolled her eyes playfully. Jack Wilson was young, he had boyish good looks, and he was obviously attracted to her. But it was no contest between Jack and Ben Andress. Ben was no mere diversion; he was a complete detour. Enticing as he was, he was a formidable distraction that could consume her precious time and sap her powers of concentration.

"Tea?" Roger offered. "Then I'll take you back into my studio and show you my etchings." He struggled to keep a straight face.

"Easy there, or I'll tell your wife," Natalie teased.

"Then she'd have to get away from her antique shop and come down here to check out the rumors of hanky-panky,'' Roger declared. "And I'd get to see her...."

"That certainly isn't the best scheme I've ever heard." Nat laughed as she followed him into the kitchen. "I gather you have more than a trace of homesickness yourself."

"It's Sue, not Atlanta, that I miss," Roger declared. "Sue-sickness...." He chortled. "Six years and two kids...and I'm still lovesick."

"It's nice that it's incurable." Natalie leaned against the counter while Roger thrust the teakettle under the faucet.

"Incurable, yes...." He grinned. "Too bad it isn't contagious, as well." He tilted his head toward the direction in which Jack Wilson had gone. "Maybe you'd catch it and spice up your life a bit. Maybe someone tall and tanned—in a uniform?" he hinted.

"Tall and tanned...." The description set Natalie's thoughts racing back to Ben Andress. "I think I'd simply like some tea." She struggled to focus her attention on her work schedule with Roger. But the image of Ben—bare-chested and wearing faded jeans—kept easing all else aside. She found her memory of him bombarding her with a myriad of impressions: Ben's angular profile as he stared intently out over the surface of the ocean; his muscular, golden brown arms straining under the weight of the gear; his rough hands gently supporting a gleaming fish until it revived and could swim off on its own; the traces of humor and warmth when he spoke with Mac or Maggie.

Watching Ben had an almost hypnotic effect on Natalie. He fascinated her with his hard exterior that seemed to mask an elusive, even gentle, quality that he revealed only to those he trusted. *And he doesn't quite trust me,* Natalie mused. Not that she could blame him. She had come to him without an identity and forced him to keep her on the job. She couldn't take him into her confidence and tell him more about herself. She had promised herself that she would let her work speak for itself. Either she did the job well or she did not—regardless of any extenuating circumstances.

But in the shadows of the old cruiser, there had been no need to know facts about each other. Touching, kissing each other, they had responded simply as a man and a woman. The contact of his skin on hers had elicited a flood of emotions she could neither explain nor ignore. Ben possessed something akin to the natural forces that had drawn her back to the Keys. All appetite and instinct, she had exulted in his embrace. She had felt as free and unhampered here as she felt when she raced a boat across the open sea or caught the image of a creature with the strokes of her pencil.

"Remember me?" Roger nudged Nat out of her daydreaming.

"I remember," Nat replied in embarrassment. She had been staring off into space while Roger set out tea and thick slices of pumpkin bread.

"Tune in to this world long enough to tell me your plans for working with me," Roger joked. "I get up early, sleep in the heat of the day and go out again in the afternoon," he informed her. "Does any of that jibe with your routine?"

"I can make the afternoon shift." Nat picked up

the buttered bread and bit off one corner. "Maybe the occasional morning, depending on the weather."

"Then we're off to a good start," Roger asserted. "We'll begin with a tour of the compound." He pointed out the window toward his favorite sketching sites.

Outside, high above the water off Big Pine Key, a large brown pelican circled in the cloudy sky. Natalie narrowed her eyes and watched it until it disappeared behind a clump of low mangrove trees. Here at the Refuge she would have a tranquil haven, a place to draw and watch and learn from her talented friend. She could fill her mind and canvases with other images—ones that did not tempt her the way Ben Andress did.

CHAPTER THREE

FOR THE NEXT FOUR DAYS, Natalie buried herself in her work, deliberately arriving early for breakfast and then hurrying off to the boathouse when Ben entered the lodge. To everyone else, it simply appeared that Natalie was overly conscientious. Only the few times that their eyes met in passing did a brief flicker of comprehension pass between Natalie and Ben. The magnetic attraction was still there, charging the fleeting exchanges with a mysterious electricity.

Natalie ran three half-day charters. The fourth day, when the *Calusa* had no charter booked, she fished along the reef with Fuzzy and Hector, stocking up on fresh fish for Maggie's restaurant. Gradually Nat was making a place for herself in the easygoing routine at the lodge. She even managed each morning to load and store the on-board hijacking protection—a sleek .357 Magnum handgun—without conspicuously flinching.

Day five began with a glare of morning light breaking through a shroud of mist. Nat pulled her sunvisor cap low over her eyes as she strode toward the boathouse. The day would be a scorcher as soon as the sun burned off the moist haze, so she packed extra ice aboard for her passengers. They would all be needing cool refreshments as the day progressed.

Nat and Greg were still waiting at dockside after Ben and Fuzzy had each left on their charters. Finally at six forty-five her two passengers arrived—noticeably late—each carrying a squat zippered bag. The unmistakable odor of liquor on their breath was Nat's first indication of trouble. It seemed these men had brought refreshments of their own and had already started on them.

"Looks like a hot day ahead," Nat commented, greeting the men pleasantly. "Let's load up and see what's out there." The two men ambled slowly to the dock where Greg waited to help them board.

Art Thompson, the shorter of the two men who both appeared to be in their late fifties, looked up toward the pilot's seat where Natalie was stationed. With a bit of difficulty, he focused his gaze on Natalie. "Well, hello, sugar," he chuckled. "I'd like to start the day off with you anytime."

Nat sighed and shook her head in Greg's direction. Stoney-faced and inexpressive behind his beard, Greg merely shrugged and undid the tie lines.

"Nice buns," the second man remarked in a half-whisper as he settled down on one of the padded chairs. "Might as well enjoy the scenery," he joked to his companion. Nat considered stopping them right there, but she reminded herself that these fellows had paid well for the charter. They expected to be free to talk loud, spit, curse and do anything else they would normally do in front of a male captain. But they were obnoxious, Nat noted silently, and she was the one with the obligation to give them their money's worth. Ben expected her to do the job.

The *Calusa* hadn't cleared the marina before the

two fellows were unloading bottles of Scotch from their bags and sending Greg below for "big glasses of ice." For the time being, Nat's passengers had no intention of rushing into any activity that might interrupt their drinking or require them to exert any energy. They were out for a good time and they had paid well to insure that they would get it.

Nat muttered to herself as she negotiated a turn through the channel leading out into deep water.

"Just cruise up along the coast a while, honey," the squat Mr. Thompson said as he poured a second glass of Scotch.

Nat did as he directed and cruised along past nameless mangrove-shrouded islands that speckled the outer rim of the Florida Keys. About forty minutes later, Thompson was guffawing at some indistinguishable comment made by his buddy, Greg was below looking for more ice and Natalie was fuming over the incredible waste of gas, time and talent this ferrying around of drunks was generating. Resolutely, she turned the *Calusa* back south toward Little Torch Key and the lodge.

"Hey, honey, wassa matter?" the bleary-eyed Thompson finally asked.

"Nothing, sir," Nat replied tensely. "If you wish to drink yourself into a stupor, you can do it just as rapidly—and much more safely—back on shore. So that's where I'm taking you." She'd carefully considered her father's policy about not allowing big drinkers on his shrimp trawler. "Drunks get hurt. They fall overboard. They fall asleep. They get sick," he'd told her. "They don't belong on a boat— certainly not one of my boats," he always had insisted. So regardless of what Mac or Ben would say when they found out, Nat was going in.

"You can't do that," Thompson's buddy yelped. "We paid you. You drive this damn boat!"

Nat gave the red-eyed man a solemn look, then directed her attention to the view ahead. Mangroves, pines and low sandy beaches formed the irregular coastline. "Please stay in your seats," she said firmly. "You can discuss the finances and file your complaints with Mr. Butler once we reach shore."

"Butler, my foot!" Thompson blustered. "I'll have your job for this, sister. I don't need no hysterical woman tellin' me what to do!" Red-faced and screaming, Thompson gripped the sides of the fighting chair to stabilize himself. This time Nat didn't attempt to reply. Silently and efficiently, she steered the boat around the channel markers into Newfound Harbor and toward the dock. Mac came out of the boathouse and stood with hands on his hips, watching her.

"Something wrong, Natalie?" he called.

"You're damn right somethin's wrong!" Thompson shouted. "The broad's lost her mind. Screamin', bossin' us around!" he yelled. "I want my damn money back. She ain't givin' us our money's worth."

Mac shifted his gaze from the drunken men to the slightly pale face of the young woman at the wheel. "I see," he mumbled as he caught the bow line and secured the boat. "You go get yourself a cup of coffee," Mac told Nat and her mate as they stepped onto the dock. Greg nodded, dropped a coil of rope, and leaped from the boat to the dock and silently headed toward the lodge.

"I'll stay here," Nat began to protest.

"Coffee," Mac replied firmly without lifting his eyes from the two frowning passengers.

"Yes, sir." Nat surrendered, following the silent form of Greg Owens toward the lodge. It was only 8:00 A.M. but the bright day had become unexpectedly dismal for Nat.

Thirty minutes later, Mac stuck his head into the dining room. "Greg, give me a hand with the gear," he called. "Nat, nothing else scheduled for the *Calusa* today. You can knock off now."

She couldn't tell from his tone or expression whether he was angry with her, but at this point the offer of time off was a welcome reprieve. Hastily Nat dashed across the parking lot and along the shell path to Beachside One. Grabbing her sketch pad and pencils, she strode to her little car. Ten minutes later, she was driving down the shaded roadway of Big Pine Key toward Roger's cottage.

A whole day for sketching, she sighed in anticipation, *until I have to face Ben Andress,* she concluded weakly. She shook her head slowly to erase the mental image of his dark, angry face.

Later, she told herself, *whatever the consequences, I'll face them later.* But then she thought, *I was right. I did the right thing. I'll tell him... and he'll see I was right.* She took a deep breath to calm herself as she stepped out of her car. Her erect stance belied the uncertainty she felt. Resolutely she strode to the Refuge cottage.

"Hey, there, gorgeous." Roger yanked open the door and greeted her. "How long have you got?" he quizzed her.

"All day. Perhaps all summer," she added gravely. Roger arched his brows at the somber announcement.

"Nat, let me get my stuff and we'll go sit in the woods and see what comes along," he teased. "You can tell me why the world has come to such an abrupt end for you," he added sympathetically.

Things always seemed to fall into clearer perspective when Natalie was drawing. Little creatures with wide, anxious eyes peering through the woods—seen and captured on her sketch pad—smoothed away the harsh edges of the outside world. Delicate colors on the underside of a leaf could make the whole world seem magical again. So Natalie and Roger would draw. Perhaps later, somewhere among the trees, they would talk.

THE SUN WAS LOW IN THE WEST when Nat finally returned to Gold Coast Lodge. Without stopping at the main building, Nat swung her Mustang along the shell path and parked it at the foot of the stairs of Beachside One. A pot of water, boiling vigorously, sat on one burner of the small stove.

"Hector?" Nat called loudly. She reached over and turned off the burner.

"I got a problem." The familiar voice came from Hector's room.

"Join the group," Nat replied with dark humor.

"No, I mean I got a *real* problem," came the surly response.

"So what's the matter?" Nat addressed her question to Hector's closed door.

"I don't wanna talk about it," Hector grumbled.

"Come on, Hector—what's the trouble? Did you burn yourself trying to boil water?" she teased.

"Naww...." He drew out the word. "It's my pants."

"Your pants? What's the matter with your pants?" she asked from right outside his closed door.

"I don't wanna talk to *you* about my pants," he yelled.

Nat thought a second. "Is the zipper stuck?" she guessed.

There was no reply.

"Is it the zipper?"

"Yeah, yeah—so the zipper's stuck," he shot back.

"Hector, I've got brothers," she said, trying to reassure him. "You can trust me to take a look at the zipper to see if I can help."

"Your brothers ain't in my pants," Hector pouted.

"No, but *you* are," Nat snapped. "And unless you want to stay there, you'd better show me what's wrong. If we have to, we can cut the whole thing out and get a new zipper."

"Watch what you say about cuttin'!" Hector finally tugged the door open. "You sure you got brothers—big ones, I mean?" he demanded.

"Big ones," Nat laughed. Hector's olive skin became darker as he stepped into the living room, his apprehension lessening slowly. Natalie bent down to inspect the problem zipper.

"So—now you've seen it," he muttered. "What can you do to fix it?"

Nat reached forward and examined the opening. "If you hold it this way—" she directed him to grasp the top and bottom, stretching the zipper tight "—I'll wiggle the tab and try to ease it down over that little fold of fabric caught in the teeth."

Hector frowned but did as she directed. Still bending over, Nat took a firm hold on the little metal tab and tugged at it. Then she tried twisting it. Nothing. "Let me get some pliers from the car," she suggested. Suddenly she raced out the door. A moment later she was back, pliers in hand, pulling steadily at the slowly yielding zipper. Hector looked down at her, tilting his head this way and that, as if such movements might aid her in her task.

"I hope I'm not interrupting an intimate moment." Ben spoke from the open front door. As Nat stared up at him, a stray strand of hair drooped over her eye. Dark and imposing, Ben stood there regarding the two of them attentively. Suddenly the ludicrous nature of the scene struck her. Red-faced and flustered, Nat abruptly burst out laughing. Hector only moaned and shifted around with little shuffling steps until he had his back turned to Ben, while Natalie circled around with him, still clutching the pliers.

"It's my pants, Ben," Hector whined without daring to face his boss. "The zipper is caught." He paused, then looked over his shoulder in Ben's direction to add, "She says she's got brothers," he floundered. "She's just fixin' my pants."

"I'd rather hoped that's what it was." Ben broke into a grin. "You need any help, Miss Bishop?" he offered without moving from the doorway.

"We've almost got it," Nat said evenly, forcing her attention back on the job. With a couple more tugs, the teeth finally passed over the trapped cloth and slid free. "Were you putting them on or taking them off?" she called as Hector—with the pants' front clasped with his hand—leaped into his room.

"Off," he answered.

"Good," Nat called. "Before you try that pair again, let me tack the edges of the cloth back so it won't happen another time."

"How efficient," Ben commented dryly. "She cooks, she sews...and she drives a boat. Some wonder woman."

His peculiar tone prompted a cautious look from Nat. She'd been dreading a confrontation with him all day long, and now it sounded like it was going to be even more unpleasant than she had feared. "I guess you're here about the charter I brought back," she noted, her face as solemn as his.

"That's why I'm here," he agreed. Then he waited to hear what she had to say next.

Nat pulled herself up as tall as possible and looked at him steadily. "I brought them back because they were getting drunk," she said simply.

"And not because they were admiring your anatomy?" He matched her level gaze. "Greg repeated a few of their comments."

"The comments I can live with," Nat answered directly. "At least until I have a bit more job security," she added. "But drunks are a safety hazard. There are too many ways they could get hurt, so I brought them back." She kept her chin tilted at a confident angle. Ben seemed to be waiting for more.

"I'm sorry if you had to return their money," she conceded. Her voice was steady, but her hand trembled slightly. She could not read the expression on Ben's face. "I did what I thought was best," she concluded.

"What *you* thought was best?" He raised one eyebrow slightly. "With your entire week of experience as a captain—you did what *you* thought was best." His eyes narrowed slightly as he contemplated her somber face. "Your instincts are remarkable, Miss Bishop," he observed quietly. "You did the right thing. A few hundred dollars one way or the other doesn't come near what an accident liability suit would cost. I should have known you would pick up on the legal technicalities to be considered." He was obviously still bitter over her threat to fight him in court for the job. Nat stiffened in indignation. Ben merely smiled.

"About the racy comments—" he stepped forward and draped a comradely arm across her shoulders, lowering his voice in confidence "—you don't have to put up with them," he stressed. "Any rude personal remark—and you set them straight. You're the captain, Miss Bishop, not the on-board entertainment."

"I wasn't sure if you'd approve." Nat stood motionless and rigid beneath his touch. Surely he knew that he was breaking his own agreement—they were not to touch, they were not to get close again. She could breathe in the warm scent of his skin. All she could think about was how easy it would be to look up into his dark eyes and wrap her arms around him.

"I approve of a number of things about you." Ben tightened his grip on her shoulder slightly. "That's part of the trouble."

Hector's bedroom door lock clicked, then the door cracked open as he peeked out to see if Ben was still there. Ben abruptly dropped his arm and moved away a step. When Hector's door closed with a slight hand, Ben's face became stern and business-like.

"Passengers only pay for a fishing trip," he said clearly. "I expect a captain to behave in a professional manner. Letting the passengers get away with rude remarks is not very professional, Miss Bishop." He turned to leave. Then at the doorway he hesitated and added, "Besides, when Hector heard about it, I almost had to sit on him to keep him from tracking down the guys and punching them out. It seems you have acquired a housemate and a protector all in one," he observed. "I just wouldn't want Hector's personal feelings for you leading him into real trouble."

Nat clenched her fists and glared at Ben. He had managed to turn the conversation into a lecture again. "At least he has personal feelings...and he's not afraid to let them show," Nat blurted out. "If someone had been rude to Hector, I'd be angry too...and I'd let them know it."

"I hadn't realized you two were getting quite that close," Ben remarked as the remoteness in his eyes deepened.

"We're no closer in private than we are in public," Nat objected. "Hector doesn't check to see if he has an audience to decide how to treat me," she noted.

"He doesn't stop being my friend just because someone might overhear."

"Maybe Hector has less at stake...." Ben understood her implication that he treated Nat differently in front of others. "Good night, Miss Bishop...." He stepped out the door and closed it after him. Then, from halfway down the stairs, he added loudly, "Good night, Hector."

Alone in the kitchen, Nat stared at the closed door. "You don't have any more at stake than I do..." she said softly.

"You talkin' to me?" Hector emerged from the bedroom. He'd refused to come out while Ben was there, but now he ambled toward her wearing a different pair of jeans and sporting a sheepish grin.

"No, I wasn't talking to you, Hector," Nat sighed ruefully. "Just to myself again."

"Oh, okay." He looked a little puzzled. What he had heard through the bedroom door was unclear, but her expression indicated that her conversation with Captain Andress had not been particularly pleasant. "Hey, Nat-a-lee," he grinned at her, "you're doin' good. Even the guys think so, Nat-a-lee. Cheer up. Ben—he's kinda funny about the business. He takes it *real* serious. Havin' a woman on the boat...that's a little tricky." He bobbed around in front of her, trying to get her to smile.

"You did the right thing this morning. Don't let it get you down. Ben oughta be proud of you—he oughta tell you that."

Nat forced a small smile, just to show she appreciated his efforts. "He said I did the right thing," she assured Hector. "He just didn't say it as nicely as you did."

"Then does that mean we finally get to eat?" Hector beamed. Nat had forgotten all about dinner.

"Give me a few minutes and I'll see what I can come up with." She was glad to have something to occupy her mind. Ben kept her off balance—intriguing her, exciting her and infuriating her. When she was driving the boat, sketching or even cooking Nat felt that she had some control. But in Ben's presence, she never knew what to expect—from him or even from herself.

"How about an omelet?" Nat called out to Hector.

"Can I put hot sauce on it?" came the reply.

"It's your stomach," Nat chuckled. Hector put hot sauce on everything. At least, one man in her life was predictable.

ON SATURDAY, Nat docked the *Calusa* in the boathouse, pulling back on the throttle at precisely the right moment so the boat eased up to the tire-covered dockside with a gentle nudge. Mac stood at the bow line, grinning with approval, then hopped on board and brought his hand around from behind his back. Nat looked down to see a bottle of white wine with a pink ribbon around the neck.

"Congratulations," he smiled warmly. "You made it through your first week! When you make it a month, we'll have champagne," he promised.

Nat grinned in return and gladly accepted the reward. Her two passengers had been deposited on the main dock closer to the lodge and were making their way toward Maggie's restaurant.

"Good trip?" Mac eyed her warily. His eyes skimmed over the familiar clutter on deck, then hesitated momentarily on the compartment beside the pilot's chair where the .357 Magnum was concealed.

Nat nodded as she sipped the cool liquid from the plastic cup Mac had filled for her. "We got a couple of devilish barracuda," she answered as she stood and stretched her legs. "Real fighters. And we landed fifteen nice red snapper nearer to shore—out of that clump of mangrove trees just south of the inlet."

Mac smiled with satisfaction. "Good—but you look just a little weary, my dear," he observed. Nat's light blue shirt, knotted at the waist above her faded jeans, drooped limply from the damp sea air. Beneath her white visor, pale gold tendrils of hair clung to her forehead while others dangled down her neck where the perspiration had turned them into dark spirals. Already her skin was taking on a deep golden tan that had been usual when she was a kid.

"It was really hot out there." Nat shrugged and expelled a long loud breath. "I feel like a well-used dishrag," she smiled weakly. "I think I need a long, long shower." She wrinkled her freckled nose as she noted her disheveled appearance in the cabin window of her boat.

"Maggie's got a little treat for you at the lodge," Mac confided. "I was supposed to casually lure you over there. Can you come over for a few minutes—before your long, long shower?" He eyed her hopefully. "Just to celebrate your first week?"

Greg was bent over, several feet behind them, unloading the chilled fish caught by the passengers that day. Once that was done, he and Nat would hose down the boat so the *Calusa* would be ready for the next day. However, this was a special occasion. Perhaps the routine could wait.

"Greg, can you manage here alone for a little while?" Nat asked. "I'll come back to help scrub her down in a few minutes."

Greg looked up and nodded. Quiet and noncommittal, the bearded young man seemed unconcerned. But he had nodded, so Natalie trudged off with Mac to the air-conditioned lodge.

"If you can stand the way I look—" she draped one arm over Mac's shoulder "—I guess I can suppress my vanity and come along." Side by side, her head a good hand-span above his, they crossed the parking lot and climbed the steps of the lodge.

The dining room was sparsely populated. Nat's two passengers sipped cold beer, and another twosome from Ben's earlier charter aboard the *Southwind* sat nearby. They waved a brief hello to Mac as he guided Nat to a table by the window. Within seconds, Maggie's portly form emerged from the kitchen.

"Hurray for you!" Maggie Butler said gleefully as she held out a massive strawberry shortcake stacked high with heaps of whipped cream and plump scarlet berries. On the top, listing slightly to the left, a single lighted candle flickered merrily. "Hang in there, honey." Maggie hugged her as Nat puffed out the candle between chuckles. "I've got one for you, too," Maggie cackled at the look of envy on Mac's weathered face. In one more trip she returned carrying Mac's shortcake and three large mugs of coffee—one for each of them. A few minutes later, Hector ambled in, grinned in their direction and joined them.

"Is Ben working on his boat?" Maggie inquired.

"Nah," Hector groaned. "He's talkin' to that woman." His tone was flat and uncomplimentary.

"What woman?" Mac looked up from his empty plate with interest.

"Angela Sutton," Hector answered. "Her father is a rich old guy who owns a sporting goods business in Miami," he added for Nat's benefit. "Ben gets a lot of tournament work through Mr. Sutton."

"That's good," Nat remarked agreeably. Working as a captain for a tournament charter generally meant very good money.

"But Angela is another matter," Maggie frowned.

"Angela is sort of an old friend of Ben's," Mac tried to explain tactfully. "She used to be *Angie*—" he raised his bushy eyebrows and assumed an aloof air "—but since she joined the yacht-club set, she doesn't show up here very often. And when she does," he stressed, "she's *Angela*."

"So what's she doin' here?" Maggie grumbled.

"Her father has Ben booked next week for a tournament off Bimini." Mac stirred his coffee.

"Angela's probably booking Ben for the week, too," Hector sniffed. Maggie kicked him under the table. Hector reached for his shin and yelped as Ben and his dark-haired companion stepped into the dining room and glanced in their direction.

"Back to work," Maggie muttered, sliding out of her chair. Ben raised one hand to indicate that Maggie should stay seated, then he chose a table on the other side of the room and pulled out a chair for the young woman with him. As she was settling in, Ben crossed to the kitchen and called for Maria.

"A couple of iced teas, please, Maria," Ben requested of the yet unseen waitress, then rejoined the smiling Angela Sutton at the table.

Nat's friends all fell silent. Occasionally Maggie's eyes would cut across the room toward Ben and his companion. Mac kept his gaze focused on his coffee mug.

"All right, you guys," Nat chided them. "What happened to our celebration? How about a little conversation?"

"Want me to tell you about An-gee-la?" Hector leaned close to Nat's shoulder as he spoke. Both Maggie and Mac shot him threatening looks.

"Maybe later." Hector muttered. "Ain't very interesting anyhow," he grumbled.

Maggie sighed and leaned closer to Nat. "It's a long story, Nat," Maggie confided. "And I don't think we should spoil your celebration by cluttering it up with gossip about her." Again the uncharacteristic bitterness in Maggie's tone startled Natalie.

Natalie's view of Angela Sutton was cut off momentarily as the slender waitress, Maria, deposited two iced teas at Ben's table, then returned to the kitchen. Determined to shift the conversation away from Ben's visitor, Nat noticed the bright eyes of Hector still following the slender form of Maria. She had picked up on it before, during the morning breakfasts when Hector would watch Maria and occasionally give her a quick smile. Sometimes the olive-skinned young woman would smile back.

"Has Maria worked here a long time?" Natalie could feel Hector tense next to her.

"A couple of months," Maggie replied. "She's a good worker. She lives a couple of miles down the Key with an aunt and uncle and several cousins."

"She's very quiet," Nat commented. Even when just the three of them—Nat, Maggie and Maria—were in the kitchen area alone, Maria rarely spoke.

"She's a little shy." Maggie's eyes shifted from Natalie to Hector who kept gripping his coffee cup and pretending not to be interested. A slow smile crept across Maggie's face as she caught on to the motives behind Natalie's questions. "She doesn't have many friends her own age," Maggie offered. "She comes from an old family that's very protective. I suppose her family would have to give its approval before she could go out with friends."

"Ah...." Natalie nodded in acknowledgment. She knew many old Cuban families in Key West and often the traditions from their homeland lingered, particularly when it came to the courtship of a young lady.

"Speaking of friends...." Maggie smiled slyly as she turned the questioning to Natalie. "What about you, Natalie? Do you miss your chums back in Atlanta? Did you leave some fella waiting for you?"

"There's no one waiting for me." Natalie smiled. "All my old boyfriends have probably found someone else already...and my friends—" she grinned "—know where to write to me. I'm all right for now."

"No homesickness?" Maggie asked. Nat shook her head. She didn't want to explain that her homesickness ended when she came back to the Keys.

"And no fella?" Mac sounded surprised.

"She just hasn't met the right one," Maggie chuckled. "Give her time. She'll know a good one when she sees him."

Nat dropped her eyes to keep from glancing over at Ben. Nat had fallen in and out of love a number of times in college. She'd had a long romance with a young sculptor who had wanted her to move into his studio with him. But she had not felt that kind of commitment to him. She had always been able to cool a relationship and extricate herself when the situation became too involved. But she had never met anyone like Ben. Where he was concerned, she was no longer in control.

"I think we'd better get back to work," Mac broke in. "Enough of this sittin' around and gabbin'. Let's get the rest of the gear stowed and make sure Greg hasn't gone to sleep out there."

With Mac in the lead and Nat bringing up the rear, the three of them crossed the restaurant while Maggie picked up the few remaining dishes. From the table by the window, the pale blue eyes of Angela Sutton scanned the threesome, lingering slightly on Natalie, then gliding back to Ben's bronzed face.

"Sort of an old friend...." Nat recalled Mac's explanation of Angela's relationship with Ben. *An old lover, more likely,* Natalie concluded. It would take something more than a friendship to cause Maggie to be so harsh...and Hector's remark that Angela had booked Ben for the week indicated there was much more going on than just old friends meeting.

Catching a glimpse of her own reflection in the window of the lodge, Nat felt suddenly self-conscious. Hair disheveled, shirt stained with perspiration, jeans faded and oil-darkened above the front pockets, she looked like someone's kid brother as she loped across the parking area after Mac and Hector. She didn't mind that her appearance made it easy for Angela Sutton to disregard her. Ben hadn't looked her way at all. That bothered her.

I'm here to work.... Nat tried to stifle the realization that she resented Ben's looking at Angela, and not even noticing her. She wanted him to accept her as a competent captain, but she also wanted something more. She wanted to see the distrust in his eyes vanish. She wanted to see the gleam of desire in his eyes. She wanted a return of that closeness she had felt that afternoon on the old cruiser when he'd held her in his arms.

"Come on, hotshot," Mac called back to her. "Don't let a little success go to your head. You only finished the week. You're not home free yet."

Nat stretched her stride and caught up to Mac and Hector just as they reached the boathouse. Greg had already finished shifting the gear from the *Calusa* and was pulling the hose over to spray the decks. Nat kicked off her shoes, rolled up her pant legs and leaped aboard with scrub brush in hand.

"Fire away, Greg," she called, ready to swab the decks. Greg took a slow look at Mac, then did precisely what Nat had said: he fired away, shooting the spray all over Nat as well as the deck. Drenched to the skin, Nat pitched the brush at her bearded first mate and ducked behind the fighting chair. Hector had climbed aboard the *Southwind* at the next mooring and was hooting and clapping his hands.

"Not fair!" Nat yelled into the deluge. "Knock it off, Greg. I *mean* it!" She tried to sound serious, then gave up and stretched out, totally soaked, on the deck.

The fellows' laughter subsided suddenly. Nat lay there, laughing and gasping for air. Suddenly apprehensive that they might be planning another onslaught, she peeked cautiously over the stern. Stepping over the twisting coils, Ben crossed the wooden dock with the blue-eyed Angela Sutton behind him.

"Oh, brother," Nat groaned and ducked back down. Mac and Greg sheepishly wound up the hose while Hector disappeared into the cabin of the *Southwind*. Nat lay there, determined not to move until Ben escorted Angela toward his project—the still-unfinished old yacht.

"Have you named her yet, Ben?" Angela cooed as he hoisted her aboard the dry-docked boat. Nat couldn't distinguish his reply. Their voices became muffled as they proceeded into the cabin.

Nat peeked over the edge. Mac and Greg were at the far end of the boathouse busily hosing down the fishing gear. Nat made a lunge for the dock, hoping to avoid confronting Ben and Angela—especially in her current soggy state.

"Miss Bishop." Ben's voice stopped her as she reached the doorway.

"Yes, sir," Nat said without turning to face him.

Drips of water trickled down her legs, spreading into a dark puddle where she stood.

"Could you come over here for a minute?" he asked. "I'd like to introduce you to someone."

Nat's shoulders stiffened as she braced herself for the meeting. Determinedly, she held her head erect, smiled pleasantly and crossed toward the old yacht. "Yes, sir," she replied obediently. Ben stood with one foot propped on the side of his boat. The dark-haired woman was somewhere below deck.

"Miss Sutton's father is one of our regular customers," Ben explained smoothly as she approached. His eyes widened with surprise as she drew close enough for him to see that she was soaking wet. Ben glanced at the wet spots on the dock, then down to Mac and Greg at the hose. When his gaze returned to Nat, his dark eyes flashed with anger. "I thought you intended to take this job seriously," he said in a low voice. "Water fights are hardly appropriate," he hissed.

"We were just celebrating," Nat replied. "I made it one whole week," she started to explain, then felt her smile waver under his stern scrutiny. "Sorry, Ben," she apologized. Ben's frown softened slightly, but his eyes were still narrow and angry.

"So this is your temporary captain?" The dark-haired woman stepped up from below deck. She put considerable stress on *temporary*. "Daddy will be quite amused to hear you've hired a female." She addressed the comment to Ben, but her cool blue eyes studied Nat's wet clothing.

"Angela Sutton, this is Natalie Bishop," Ben said.

"You seem to have had an accident," Angela

noted. "Did you fall overboard, Captain Bishop?"

"Just a little horseplay with the guys," Nat answered. "I was the losing team," she added good-naturedly.

"I should say so," Angela mused as she draped one well-manicured hand possessively across Ben's shoulder. In pale yellow slacks and snug-fitting, low-necked T-shirt, Angela looked crisp, immaculate and elegant. Nat glanced down at her own damp, baggy clothes, then tugged at the shirtfront so the wet fabric no longer pressed revealingly against her skin.

"If you'll excuse me, I'd like to change." Nat kept her composure. "It was nice to meet you," she added politely.

"I'll be sure to tell my daddy's friends about you," Angela replied. "They're always looking for something new on the fishing scene. I'm glad I met you. Now I'll have something to spring on them."

Natalie forced back a protest. Twice Angela had referred to Nat as "something." Nat winced inwardly. Hopefully none of Mr. Sutton's buddies would make a special effort to seek her out—just because she was "something new." And hopefully no would-be pirates would get wind of the "something" and be tempted to take on the lady captain of Little Torch Key.

"So long." Nat forced a note of cheerfulness into her voice as she turned to leave. She could hear Angela say something to Ben, then laugh softly.

"Wonderful, just wonderful," Nat muttered angrily as she stalked off toward Beachside One. "I look like a drowned rat, he thinks I'm childish and she thinks I'm amusing," she huffed as she stamped up each step. But there was more than that involved, she brooded. She could stand Ben's reprimand, but something else gnawed at her... something about the way Angela draped herself on Ben's shoulder.

Nat struggled out of her wet clothes and flopped across the narrow bed. *One week and I'm turning into a nervous wreck.* She'd walked into a new job, a new field of art with Roger and met a man who haunted her thoughts night and day. Nat lay there several minutes, then flung her legs off the bed. "As long as I'm wet," she murmured aloud, then grabbed her two-piece swimsuit from the bottom drawer, "I might as well get *really* wet."

With her beach blanket draped over one shoulder and a sketch pad tucked under her arm, Natalie trudged barefoot along the seashell path toward the lodge, then cut through the parking lot toward the highway. Beyond the hot stretch of asphalt, a foot-path led through palmetto bushes and sea grass, over the sandy hills that separated the ocean from the highway. Nat glanced along the unoccupied beach and strolled to a secluded section where the sea grass formed an alcove in the sand. She spread out the big beach blanket, dropped the sketch pad, took off her loosely knitted white shirt, unbraided her tawny hair and raced toward the cool blue green water. She slipped below the surface, feeling the timeless motion of the waves coursing over her.

Breathless, Nat surfaced, then rolled onto her back, floating motionless in the salty water while her hair drifted like a golden fan. The gentle rise and fall of the waves gradually eased the tension she felt. Finally she rolled over and plunged again and again beneath the rippling surface, leaping up like a child, splashing the water in a great burst of exuberance.

Eventually Natalie waded in to shore slowly, eyes downcast, watching the small fish zip past as her footsteps disturbed the soft sand on the flat bottom. Only when she stepped out onto the beach did she see Ben stretched out on the sand beside her beach blanket, leaning back on one elbow, staring at her.

"You swim *alone*?" he asked critically. "Not very safe. What if you—"

"You sound like my father," Nat interrupted. "What if you get a cramp, what if you get hurt, what if you hit your head? I was being cautious," she asserted. "I could touch bottom. And as far as my swimming alone goes, I just felt like being by myself a little while. I wasn't being reckless." She stood before him, her long damp hair clinging to her shoulders.

"So now I'm the intruder." He gazed up at her solemnly. "You want me to leave?"

"No—" she held out a hand in protest "—I didn't mean it that way." She knelt on the blanket and looked over at him. "I just mean that it's been a very long week," she observed wearily. "I wish that at least *here*...away from the boathouse and the lodge...you could say something to me that doesn't sound like a reprimand. I'm tired of continually apologizing and defending myself."

Slowly a softening effect passed over Ben's handsome face. It was subtle, but recognizable—not a smile, but a slight difference in the set of the jaw and the look in his eyes.

"Nice day for a swim...isn't it?" Ben said

agreeably, as a smile made a brief appearance on his lips. Slowly Natalie looked over at him, surprised at the warmth in his expression. Then a second transformation took place, changing his scrutiny from polite to very personal. His glance drifted from her wide eyes down to the slender gold necklace, then lower over her slim tanned body in the white bikini.

"You look considerably different now than you did a few minutes ago back at the boathouse." Ben let his eyes linger on her curving waist. "And I had no intention of sounding like your father." Two dark eyes lifted to connect with hers.

Natalie felt her mouth go dry. This was the look she had longed to see. Ben's presence—when he was relaxed and off duty—was more compelling than she had anticipated. All week—aloof, businesslike and efficient—he had watched her from a distance. Except for the brief moments when he had interrupted the repair of Hector's trousers and spoken of the two drunks on the charter, everything she had heard from him had been delivered either as an instruction or as a criticism.

Now that he was alone with her on a secluded section of the beach, Ben seemed to find her enchanting. The intimacy of his gaze gave Nat a certain satisfaction and a flush of pleasure to know she had managed to dent his armor of indifference. He no longer viewed her as an employee—one he had accepted under duress—but he saw her once again as a woman...a desirable woman.

Natalie patted a towel over her lightly tanned body, then sprawled on her stomach on the thick beach blanket. Ben had followed her over here for a reason, and Nat was willing to take her time in finding out what it was.

"I didn't mean to spoil your celebration," he began in a low voice. "I came to apologize for snapping at you as I did. Once I realized what it was all about, I figured you deserved a little fun. You've worked hard." Nat turned her head to the side and peered up at him. He seemed sincere. Then she understood. They were alone again. There was no audience—not Hector or the men or Angela Sutton—to witness this side of Ben or to hear his apology.

Nat closed her eyes and pressed her forehead down on her arms. *Be cautious,* she warned herself. Ben's motives were never clear when it came to her. "I accept your apology," she said politely, then she lay very still in the hot sun.

Ben sat next to her without speaking, looking out over the clear water. Then he sat up, yanked off his shirt and dropped it onto the sand. Lying facedown, her cheek resting against her arm, Nat kept her long-lashed eyes half closed, trying to follow Ben's movements without being conspicuous. When he stepped out of his jeans, she kept her eyes riveted on his ankles. A moment later, she heard him splash into the water. Now it was her turn to sit and stare.

With slow, steady strokes, Ben swam out to the spot where the greenish ocean turned a darker blue green and dived beneath the surface, emerging again closer to shore. He swam back with equally rhythmic strokes, then stood, thigh-deep in the waves and walked toward her. His dark hair clung to his forehead and rivulets of salty water made silvery trails down his skin. His broad muscled chest glistened beneath the mat of crisp, dark hairs that diminished into a slender line at his midriff.

Ben moved with distinctive natural grace across the pale sand. Below his sleek navy swimsuit, the flow of dark hair continued down long, hard legs. Natalie couldn't pull her eyes away from him. He was a man who became a part of his surroundings—whatever they might be. He claimed the sand and the surf with every movement. He belonged. Nat found herself both admiring and resenting the elusive quality that Ben exuded.

"Can I share your blanket—" he paused by her feet to ask "—just long enough to dry off in the sun?" Wordlessly Natalie shifted her body to the left, allowing room for Ben on the far side of the bold-striped beach blanket. She lay on her back this time, letting the sun warm her skin. Ben sprawled on his stomach beside her, propping his head on one arm while he studied her profile.

"Natalie Bishop." He said her name softly. "Why on earth would someone like you want to work somewhere like this? We're in the middle of nowhere. I just don't get it." He spoke as if he didn't expect a reply. It was as if he was merely thinking aloud.

"You're a paradox, Natalie." The way he said her name quietly sent another surge of pleasure through her. "You show up here with no past—with only Buzz Cochran for family—yet you told Hector about big brothers, and you obviously have a protective father—somewhere. You're like one of those mangroves—" he tilted his head toward the sprawling roots of the trees along the water's edge "—you drift in, put down roots and start growing on everybody.

You send out shoots, touching the folks around you—and you hang on. The question is—'' he contemplated her still form ''—what happens if the wind changes? Do you simply drift off again... or slip away under the waves?''

Nat lay with her eyes closed, barely breathing, while his words, like soft waves, rippled over her. Already in her head she was visualizing something she would have to paint. Something massive and majestic. She would find a magnificent mangrove tree, one that had endured years of storms and tides, and she would paint it for Ben. Maybe that would give him the answer he sought.

''Where do you go in your little red car? Who do you run to see?'' There was no urgency in his voice— only a hint of amusement. Natalie could tell he had inched closer to her as he spoke. She could feel his breath fanning her cheek as he voiced his curiosity.

Natalie kept her eyes pressed closed and listened to his even breathing. She waited for him to make some move, but he remained at her side, not quite touching her. Apprehensively Nat lifted one hand to shade her eyes and cracked one eye open to look up at him.

''I'm still here.'' He smiled at her. ''I'm waiting for you to talk to me. I want to know what's going on inside that head of yours. I want to know where you've come from and where you're going.''

Nat dropped her arm and rolled onto her side, facing away from the dark, liquid eyes that watched her so intently.

''You can look the other way, Natalie.'' His breath whispered across her bare shoulder. ''You can hide behind that polite smile of yours. But you can't make me forget...and you can't stop me from wondering.''

Natalie wanted to get up and run away, far from the deep, calm voice that swept over her like a persistent wave, undermining the reserve that she tried to maintain. But a second powerful sensation, more overwhelming, like a riptide carrying her along, urged her to linger...to stay near the man who spoke to her so softly...and stirred such fire with his touch.

"Sometimes I catch glimpses of you when you're talking or laughing with someone...and I see the excitement in your eyes or the joy in your voice. I want that part of you. Then you get that determined set to your jaw, and your eyes become cautious and remote...and I don't know that part at all. That part is out to prove something to someone, not just to me." He drew in a slow breath. "But when I'm this close to you—" he lowered his head and brushed his lips over her bare shoulder, savoring the softness of her sun-warmed skin "—all I see is that you're the color of caramel, and the sweet taste of you chases all the questions away."

Ben slid his hand over her back, slowly rubbing his palm from side to side across the bare expanse of golden skin. "How many of you are in there, Natalie?" he mused aloud. "The tomboy on the dock, the zipper-fixer in the beach house, the charter captain, the velvet-skinned woman...." The rhythmic motion of his hand and the steady, pensive voice were unrelenting. The sensuous, gentle contact, the heat of the sun and the steady pounding of the surf all conspired to create the feeling they were suspended in time, she and Ben, in a golden world apart.

Then abruptly, his hand was gone. The magic cocoon of warmth disintegrated once the contact was broken. Natalie suppressed a sigh of disappointment as the enchantment passed. Ben cleared his throat and rolled to stretch out on his back.

"I'm going to Bimini next week," he announced softly, but with a growing detachment to his tone. "You'll be on your own. Just don't take any chances. Keep things on a business-only basis. Don't take nonsense from anybody."

Nat turned over so she could face him, intrigued by the abrupt separation he had placed between them. "You're sounding like my father again," she announced, grimacing at his list of instructions.

"I'm *not* being fatherly." Ben's voice rumbled low in his throat. "You have a genuine talent for turning every relationship you have into a safe one. Mac has taken to you like a father, and most of the crew feel like they're your big brothers. But it won't work with me, Natalie." He lay there with his eyes closed, blocking out the sun, with long black lashes against his tanned skin. "I'm not going to play by your rules. I won't settle for knowing just part of you." His eyes opened, then he rolled onto his side, facing her. "I've held you. I've felt you responding to me...touching me. I've tasted your lips and felt your breath against my skin. And I've seen you out there in the water, like a golden mermaid...." His voice had again turned low and thick. "You're not one of the boys, no matter how you try—and you'd better not mistake my reaction to you as brotherly or fatherly."

Suddenly his hand moved across and touched her

long, damp hair, sliding down it until his fingers cupped gently around her neck. In the beat of a heart, he moved toward her so his lips brushed hers, first gently, then more eagerly as she lingered within his grasp, neither retreating nor returning his embrace.

"Touch me, Natalie." He held his lips close to hers. "Let me feel your hands over my skin."

Natalie's breath faltered beneath the gentle pressure of his kiss. If she touched him, she knew she would not want to stop, and the impact of that passion would be irreversible. She could not speak. She could only shake her head slowly, not daring to reach out for him.

"Make love to me, Natalie," he whispered. "One of these days, you will," he added, more as a promise than a threat. "One day you'll stop dividing yourself into little compartments. When you finally let all the parts of you surface, I'm going to be there."

Gradually he eased her away a few inches so he could look into her wide hazel eyes. "You don't know if you can trust me, do you?" He grinned. Deep crevices made his dark tanned face even more handsome. "And I don't know if I can trust you. You do everything by your own rules—and no one but you knows what those rules are. I don't even know what the game is. I may not like it when I find out." He reached out and lightly brushed her cheek with his thumb. "You're a puzzle, Natalie Bishop. I want all the pieces. You're stubborn. But so am I. You can't walk into my life—into my business— without my knowing why. And I won't let you hide from me. I'll break you, Natalie Bishop. . . and I'll love every minute of it.''

He pulled her to him and kissed her once again, more forcefully than before, yet with a strange tenderness that left her more breathless than defensive. ''You think about that while I'm gone. You can bet I'll be thinking about you.''

With that, Ben bounded to his feet, grabbed his jeans and shirt and walked off to the lodge without glancing back.

Natalie touched her lips with her fingertips, still reeling from the conflict Ben created in her.

''I'll break you. . . .'' She remembered Ben's words almost as vividly as she recalled his kiss. He wasn't simply after answers, he wanted her—all of her. The persistent question that remained was what would she do if they did make love, if they did lose themselves in each other, even for a brief interval. Could she then pull away from him long enough to devote her time and concentration to her art? Could she function as a charter captain working so close to him each day without becoming distracted by his presence? Natalie had planned this venture so carefully to give herself a chance to prove she could take care of herself and still enjoy her art. Now Ben was undermining Natalie's resolve. He was tempting her with a possibility she had not considered in her cool, methodical program for the spring.

Suddenly Natalie sat upright, staring out over the pale sand. Nothing about Ben made him seem like a man who acted on impulse. Yet he had sought her out here on this isolated stretch of beach and tantalized her with soft caresses and talk of making love.

Perhaps Ben was playing a game of his own, and it was Natalie who didn't know the rules.

Nat closed her eyes tightly at the thought, trying to force it out of her mind. The face that appeared before her, the one that had haunted her dreams, was lined and rugged, but not cruel. Ben was tough and complicated, but surely he couldn't be so devious. If this passionate interlude was part of his own calculated plan to unnerve her, intimidate her and then make love with her, he had almost succeeded. He had undeniable skill in exciting her, and the intensity of the attraction between them was magical and compelling.

Natalie took a deep breath to dispel the depression that had settled over her. If she was being manipulated, then Ben was more ruthless than Natalie could imagine. Gradually the image of Ben's face was replaced by a sharper, more arrogant countenance— the smug face of Angela Sutton. Angela was no inexperienced woman. Every movement she made exuded a studied sexuality. The way Angela placed her arm on Ben with such easy familiarity spoke of an intimacy that required no preliminaries, no soft, seductive overtures. *So what does he want with me...?* The question loomed again in Natalie's mind.

So far, Ben had been very circumspect. He had made no gesture or comment of a personal nature in front of any witness. Around the lodge and the boathouse, everything was strictly business. Publicly, Ben was taking no risks. Natalie picked up her shirt and sketch pad, then stood and lifted up the beach blanket, draping it over her arm. For a moment she stared thoughtfully at the imprint in the sand that their two bodies had made. When they were that close together, everything seemed so natural and so special. But when she had time to think, Natalie couldn't make all the pieces fit. Ben puzzled her as much as she puzzled him.

Natalie was already up to her neck in challenges. "Don't take on more than you can handle," her father had always advised her. She could still hear Ben saying "Don't take any chances," when he began his instructions. Natalie wrinkled her nose, recalling that even in the midst of this tender scene, Ben had lectured her again. His first priority was the business—the boats, the gear, the customers. Natalie kicked at the sand in frustration, sending up a fine powdery white spray into the wind. She had priorities of her own to consider. She had her work on the *Calusa*, her art and her pride.

Hector had a net full of blue crabs ready for steaming when Nat climbed up the steps of the beach house. "We even got a lemon," he said, grinning. Gradually Nat was weaning him off his hot sauce and had introduced him to the delights of parsley-and-lemon butter for dipping seafood.

"This must be some kind of sympathy gesture before you take off for Bimini," Nat teased him.

"I ain't goin' to Bimini with Ben," Hector grunted. "He never takes me out on tournaments when the Suttons are going."

"Why not?" Nat pitched her beach blanket over the railing to dry and grabbed the net with the wriggling crabs.

"I'd rather not talk about it," Hector mumbled. Nat simply shrugged and headed into the kitchen.

Hector came after her, leaning against the counter glumly as she put a pot of water on to boil.

"I guess you might as well know," he finally drawled. "I got picked up for possession once...." He wouldn't look at her. "Marijuana...just a couple of joints," he added. "I'm on probation."

"So?" Nat shrugged. There had been a lot of pot smoking going on at college. Possession wasn't anything particularly unusual. Getting picked up and put on probation was a bit severe. "What does that have to do with your going to Bimini?" Nat asked.

"So...Ben wants to be careful. No telling what might end up on one of these boats during a tournament," Hector observed. "If I was on board, it wouldn't look good."

"There's *dope* at fishing tournaments?" Natalie hated to sound naive.

"Not during the tournament," Hector insisted. "But there is a lot of partying goin' on. I guess there's some buying and selling...."

"And *importing*?" Nat turned to stare at Hector.

"I wouldn't know." He'd tried to duck the question.

"Are you suggesting that Ben allows drugs on his boat?" Natalie began to feel apprehensive. Ben had a strict *public* policy of keeping the lodge clean—no drugs allowed on the premises. If he occasionally smuggled some in, no one would suspect him.

"It ain't Ben," Hector hedged. "The only time I sorta saw something I shouldn't have...it wasn't Ben who was doin' it."

"Okay, then—" Nat bridled at the evasion "—who was it? Who had drugs?"

"If you tell anyone I said it, I'll say you're lyin'," Hector warned her. "I can't afford to get tangled up with any of this stuff."

"Who had the drugs?" Natalie pressured him.

"Daddy Big-Buck's daughter," Hector muttered. "An-gee-la. She had a package of the white stuff—I guess her crowd is into cocaine."

"And Ben knows it?" Natalie didn't think Ben would have jeopardized his business for anyone... not even for Angela.

"I can't say," Hector answered solemnly. "I didn't ask. I didn't see him near the stuff."

"But he does leave you here...." Natalie felt her heart sink. Ben wouldn't take such precautions unless he knew there was a chance drugs might be found if the *Southwind* was searched.

"He gave me the job," Hector reminded her. "He gave me a chance to make good. What his friends do ain't none of my business. Ben is careful not to get me in any trouble... so I'm keepin' my mouth shut. I shouldn't have said nothin' to you," he groaned.

"If Ben is being this careful because he knows what Angela Sutton is doing, he's already in trouble." Nat shook her head sadly. "He's as guilty as she is."

"You ain't gonna tell anyone?" Hector turned dark, worried eyes toward her. "This was just between you and me. I don't want it to get out."

"What is there to tell?" Nat sighed. "That you *think* you saw Angela with some cocaine... and that I *think* it all looks pretty suspicious for Ben to leave you behind? It takes more than *thinking* to accuse anyone of doing something illegal. Besides—" Nat's tone became cynical ''—who would believe respectable and upright Ben Andress would dabble in drugs?'' One reason Buzz Cochran had agreed to set Nat up with the job here was because of Ben's reputation for running a clean operation.

"Maybe it was a one-time thing. . . ." Hector was trying to placate Natalie. "Maybe An-gee-la don't do it anymore."

"And maybe she does," Natalie countered. "Either way, you can be sure that I don't want to get messed up in this either. I have too much going for me right now to get sidetracked by whatever else is going on here."

"And you'll still be my friend?" Hector sounded bereft. "Even if I'm on probation?"

"I'll still be your friend—" Nat walked over and hugged him "—as long as you don't bring any drugs or marijuana around here."

"Hey, I'm clean," Hector insisted. "I learned my lesson. I ain't dumb enough to take any chances. . . ."

"Just don't try smoking my parsley. . . or the oregano," Natalie teased him. Hector broke into a broad grin. They could smile and joke, so things were back to normal. Natalie turned her attention to the huge pot of boiling water, then carefully dropped the crabs one by one into the liquid. While Hector cheerfully set the dishes on the table, Natalie's thoughts shifted to Ben. She had added more pieces to the puzzle, but instead of fitting together into a coherent image, the pieces of Ben Andress kept coming apart, falling away from each other, making him more elusive than before.

Priorities, Nat reprimanded herself, hoping to regain the sense of orderliness that made her feel secure. Yet like the sand shifting beneath her feet when the waves rolled in one after the other, her golden moments with Ben were slowly being eroded by suspicions and doubts and the questions that remained could not be ignored.

"Be careful...." This time the warning came from Hector who handed Nat an oven mitt. "Don't get burned," he cautioned her. Natalie glanced from Hector to the pot of crabs.

"I'll be careful," she replied with a slight smile. Her response was for herself as well as for her dark-eyed Cuban friend.

CHAPTER FOUR

"SOME GRIM NEWS, I'M AFRAID." Mac waited for Nat and Hector on the steps of the lodge on Monday morning. Ben had left the previous afternoon, heading out to Bimini in the *Southwind*, so Mac would be running the outfit for the rest of the week.

"What's wrong?" Nat's first thought was of some mishap with Ben and his boat.

"South of here—" Mac tilted his head "—an abandoned cruiser was picked up by the Coast Guard." Hector moved up closer to Nat and stood beside her waiting to hear the rest of the story. "It was the *Sea Gypsy*," Mac said solemnly.

Nat shrugged in relief. It was a name she did not recognize. "So?" she finally prodded Mac.

"The *Sea Gypsy* was a Key Largo charter boat a little bigger than most of ours," Hector explained. "She was reported missing a few weeks ago—before you got here—along with her captain, a mate and a passenger."

"Oh, no...." Natalie guessed the rest. "She's been recovered—but what about the crew?" She knew enough about hijacking in the Keys to expect the worst.

"Nothing," Mac said evenly. "She'd been scuttled with almost five tons of marijuana aboard. Whoever comandeered her ran her as long as they could, then simply abandoned her when the Coast Guard spotted her. The original crew was probably dumped over the side when the boat was first taken. These guys don't leave witnesses.''

"But they'll ditch a boat if the heat is on," Hector grumbled. "Then they'll be after another one quick to take her place. These guys don't waste no time.'' He shook his head emphatically.

"We'll all have to be more cautious than usual,'' Mac asserted. "We'll double-check anyone we take out or any boat that gets a little too close. I just want you on alert,'' he warned, "or you may find yourselves belly up with the barracuda.''

"But we're already careful." Nat followed Mac into the lodge. "We're armed—we have the gun on board—and we can radio for help.''

"The *Sea Gypsy* had the same stuff as we have,'' Hector noted. "Lot of good it did them. You gotta understand, Nat-a-lee, whenever these guys scuttle a boat, things get real tense around here. You *know* it's just a matter of time until they cover their losses. If it ain't us, it'll be someone else they get.''

"I figured that with Ben gone, we'd better tighten up our defenses,'' Mac said, crossing the dining room with the other two in his wake. "I don't want anything to happen to either of you or to the cruisers,'' Mac stressed. "We'll try to act normal—'' he lowered his voice as Maggie's bright face peered out from the kitchen "—but we'll keep an eye out for each other and an ear out for the Coast Guard, and we'll get through this just fine.'' He managed to conclude with a hopeful smile.

Maggie's cheerful "Good morning," and the rapid arrival of hot biscuits and ham did little to dispel the gloomy atmosphere that engulfed the breakfast table. One by one, Greg, Fuzzy and Herb arrived, heard the news of the *Sea Gypsy* and slumped over their hot coffee, staring thoughtfully into its dark surface.

"You ever shot a gun?" Mac asked Natalie. "I know you can load and unload one, but have you ever shot anything with one?"

She glanced up at him, wide-eyed. "I've shot a rifle at empty cans," she answered self-consciously. "I've never tried a handgun."

"You better let me show you how to pump off a few rounds with the .357 before you leave today," Mac said calmly. "We'll set up something at the beach for target practice." He took a sip of orange juice, then looked over at Nat again. "Speaking of targets, you may be a more likely one than any of us. Some guys would figure a female wouldn't put up much of a fight."

All five men stared at her in silence.

"Maybe I could go with Nat-a-lee on the *Calusa* for a few days," Hector suggested. "I could do the shootin' if we have any company out there." He made a pistol with thumb and index finger.

Mac was already shaking his head. "No way, you Cuban cowboy," Mac kidded him. "You know the rules—if you work together, you don't bunk together. Ben doesn't want anyone getting an overdose of anyone else. You wanna be her first mate, then you let someone else bunk with Nat," he challenged the dark-eyed fellow. "Besides, I'm booked for three shallow-water trips out the back this week and that means you have to take over here.''

"I'll be all right," Nat interrupted. "I don't want any special treatment. I'm the one in charge of the *Calusa* and I'll do my job. Besides, I'd hate to lose a good roommate—" she smiled across at Hector "—or a good crewman." She patted the arm of her bearded shipmate, Greg Owens.

"I won't let nothin' happen to you," Greg muttered quietly. "We don't need no one else buttin' in." The slender, solemn fellow didn't look up as he spoke. "So, maybe I'm gettin' used to her." He defended himself against the amused smiles that turned in his direction.

"Just in case, I'll give Natalie a little target practice after breakfast," Mac concluded cheerfully. "Business as usual," he said, waving them all back to their half-eaten breakfasts.

"It can't hurt to be prepared," Nat nodded. The six of them sat in silence, each engrossed in thought.

With the *Southwind* off in Bimini with Ben, only two charters went out. Fuzzy and Herb took out a couple of New Jersey businessmen on the *Suds Buggy* and Nat and Greg provided a great day's fishing for an Orlando realtor and his client. Every twenty minutes they checked by radio with each other, then with Hector back at the marina. The day passed without incident. Nat made one last call in to Hector at two-thirty, then set her homeward course.

"No trouble?" Hector stood in the late-afternoon sun grinning at Nat as she returned from the day's trip.

"Not a bit," she called back to him. As an extra

precaution, Nat had tucked her long braid up into one of Mac's peaked caps. With her height and clad in a loose shirt, she looked more like one of the guys—particularly from a distance. Except for a brief squall that had swept across the open water about noon, both of the charters had been normal, tranquil trips.

"Any news?" Nat asked uneasily over the throb of the engine as she maneuvered the *Calusa* toward the dock. "Anything from the other charter outfits?" She was hoping no other boats along the Keys had been reported missing and no crews lost.

"Too early to tell," Hector shouted as he caught the bow line Greg pitched in his direction. "Sometimes it takes a couple of days before anyone reports a missing boat."

Nat cut the engine and drifted in to bump her boat against the strips of old tires along the pilings. Her two male passengers nodded to each other in silent admiration of her skill.

"You know how unpredictable fishermen are," Hector said in a normal voice, smiling at the two sun-reddened passengers rising from their seats at the stern of the *Calusa*. "They might just hitch up to one of the smaller keys and keep on fishin'. We'll just take this one day at a time." He tried to sound reassuring. "Besides," he said softly to Nat as she hopped onto the dock beside him, "we're small potatoes."

Nat smiled and chatted with the two fishermen as they stood beside Hector on the dock and watched Greg unpacking their catch. Nat had taken them along the deep waters just past the reef where the bot-

tom dropped to 120 feet. After fifteen minutes cruising, they had hit a school of black grouper and the
two delighted businessmen had pulled in five large
fish each. But the big excitement had occurred an
hour later when a hundred-pound tiger shark hit the
line held by the round-faced realtor. There were forty
minutes of yelling, tugging, fighting and cursing until
the shark was brought alongside for Greg to gaff and
haul aboard. Spread out on the dock, with jaws held
wide open by a length of metal pipe, the shark made
a fine trophy photograph for the real-estate man to
take back to Orlando. It had been a great day for the
fishermen. Hopefully, they would go home pleased
and full of stories for their friends about the fabulous
charters run by Gold Coast Lodge.

Thirty minutes later, Nat maneuvered the *Calusa*
around into the covered boathouse. Greg leaped out
and secured the lines as Hector entered from the
front door of the building.

"We'd better lock her in good." Hector glanced
across at the securely moored *Suds Buggy* in the next
slot. "Looks like Fuzzy used everything but the
clothesline," he chuckled.

"You think a hijacker would take a boat from
here—from inside our boathouse?" Nat asked, her
brow furrowed in concern.

Hector shrugged, then replied in a slightly con-
spiratorial tone, "Depends on whether they've been
casing the joint," he offered in his best cops-and-
robbers jargon. Nat shook her head and managed a
little smile, though she knew he was serious. "I mean
it." Hector stepped closer to Nat to add, "Somebody
coulda come in here anytime—like on a charter or

checking for a charter...anything—and scouted us out, even picked out what kinda boat they're after." He looked from Nat to Greg and back again. Greg, silent and efficient as always, shrugged and began securing the stern lines.

"We'd better lock things up tightly," Nat agreed as she and Hector looked around the boathouse. "Why take any chances?"

Hector nodded vigorously in agreement, then turned to head back to his duties at the main dock. Nat climbed back up to the pilot's seat atop the *Calusa* and locked the ignition. She then opened the gun-cabinet door and removed the .357 Magnum pistol from its secure holder. The weight of the lethal weapon in her hand and the recollection of the fate of the scuttled *Sea Gypsy* made her throat feel dry. Cautiously she peered into the shadows of the dim boathouse, listening for stealthy footsteps as her imagination began working on embellishing the situation.

"Come on, come on," she whispered to herself a warning. "There are no brigands lurking in the corners with cutlasses." Still Nat had the unmistakable feeling the danger was real, and that no one in the Keys was entirely safe.

"You about ready?" Greg called up to her from the dock. Apparently he was feeling a little uneasy himself, since it was unusual for him to hurry anyone along.

"Sure," Nat called back crisply, then came down the ladder and climbed over the side onto the dock. Greg had all the gear neatly stacked and ready to be carried to the storage room. After two trips each, the task was done and their workday finished. "I'll get the lock," Nat offered when Greg turned at the door and reached for the padlock hanging open on the latch.

He mumbled something that sounded like "Okay, good night," and walked off toward the lodge.

Nat snapped the lock closed, gave it a second pull to check it was secure, then, gun in hand, she proceeded up the white shell path toward Beachside One. For the first time, she was actually relieved to be off the cruiser and away from the water.

As she walked along, Nat examined the silver handgun with the dull wooden handgrip. *I wonder if I could do it,* she thought as she rotated her wrist and watched the shiny pistol glimmer in her right hand. *Could I really shoot someone?* That morning Mac had taken her down onto the beach and lined up cans atop a graying, weathered log. She had listened attentively to his directions about how to hold and aim the weapon, then had leveled it at the first can, the gun steady and motionless in her right hand with the left hand bracing the pistol from below. When she squeezed the trigger Nat was momentarily startled by the boom of the explosion as the first shell fired. The considerable kick forced her two extended arms skyward.

"It's a real cannon, ain't it!" Mac laughed at her wide-eyed surprise. "Now this time, be ready and relax your shoulder for the kick. Let it lift your arms—not shake 'em in their sockets. That's it... stiffen your arm muscles a little...now...squeeze the trigger...*now*!"

The second shot was straight and true. The tin can on the left end of the row instantly disappeared.

"Wow," Nat had uttered breathlessly. Mac

laughed, offered another couple of suggestions, then let Nat blast away at the rest of the targets. One after another the cans leaped into the air as the gun boomed. Each can had fallen back into the sand punctured with a penny-sized hole in the front, a massive opening in the back where the bullet had passed through.

Could I do that to a person, Nat asked herself as she walked along the path, her arm still a bit sore from the morning's target shooting. Silently she crunched along the pathway. She hoped there would never be a time when that question would have to be answered.

As she neared Beachside One, Nat deliberately turned her thoughts to the pine-shrouded deer refuge and the quiet, tranquil moments shared there with Roger Embry. He liked painting with her. He made precise, perceptive suggestions about her work. Already Nat could see a difference in her paintings—a new depth of color, a sharper edge in her line drawings. But more than that, Roger offered her quiet approval and unobtrusive companionship. Just as Ben had said—she preferred "safe" relationships.

It was almost 5:00 P.M. when Nat started down the steps of Beachside One on her way to the Refuge.

"You goin' somewhere?" Hector approached clutching a beer can and staring at her change of clothes as Nat lifted her car keys from her bag. She stopped to look down at him. The disappointment in his voice was evident.

"Not necessarily," she said quietly. "What are you going to do?" She watched him shuffle uncomfortably at the foot of the steps.

"Oh, nothin'." He tried to cover his embarrassment.

"Hector—" Nat grinned and came down to face him nose-to-nose "—what did you have in mind?" she inquired, pressing him for an explanation.

"I...I thought maybe...if you aren't too busy, and if you don't mind drivin'—" he struggled to formulate his proposal "—I thought you could go with me to the lodge and ask when Maria gets off work. If you and me take her home, we could meet her uncle." He spoke slowly, as if he'd planned it all carefully.

"Then *we* could ask her uncle if *we* could take Maria out for a date." Nat smiled sympathetically.

"That's the idea." Hector breathed a tormented sigh. "I figure if there are two of us...." His voice trailed off. "Besides, you talk to her. She likes you," he said, recalling all the times Maggie and Maria had invited Nat into the aromatic kitchen that was unofficially off limits to the men.

"And if *we* get the date," Nat continued, including herself in the scheme, "where will *we* take her?"

"For a picnic?" Hector said hopefully. "Maybe take out one of the runabouts and ride over to one of the little islands and fish."

"Whatever happened to the good old days—dinner and a movie?" Nat kidded him.

"She looks at dinners every night," Hector replied. "Maybe she'd like to get outside for a change. Besides, I like to fish," Hector protested. "I like to be out on the beach. If she likes it too, *then* I'll take her to dinner and a movie once I know she likes the things that I like most."

Nat reached out and hugged the dark-eyed Cuban. "You're a smart fellow, Hector," she laughed. "I can't tell you how many times I've had a pleasant dinner and seen a good movie then ended up late in the evening finding out the guy didn't like *anything* I liked—least of all fishing!"

"So we go ask Maria." Hector backed away and grinned.

"We go ask Maria," Nat agreed.

It was almost ten-thirty before Nat and Hector returned from taking Maria home and meeting the Calonge family. Maria had invited Nat and Hector inside and the brief introductions had stretched into a two-hour visit, complete with dark Cuban coffee and a guitar serenade by Louis Calonge, Maria's uncle.

"We have heard from Maria about the lady captain," Iris Calonge, Maria's aunt, had greeted Natalie. "And we also have heard the name of Hector mentioned," she added with a shy smile. Within minutes, Nat and the women had discreetly withdrawn into the kitchen while Louis and Hector settled on the living-room sofa.

"Uncle Louis will probably know his birth date and his social security number before he's through." Maria cast an anxious glance at the two men in the next room. "He is very protective," she sighed.

"I have a couple of brothers and a father who belong to the same club," Natalie sympathized. "I think Hector will handle this just fine," she reassured the girl.

Nat had been right. Soft-spoken and quick to smile, Hector had eased any doubts the Calonge patriarch may have had. When he and Nat finally departed, Hector was grinning from ear to ear, and Nat was wide-eyed from drinking so much coffee. But an agreement had been made. On Sunday, when the restaurant was closed, Hector would be allowed to take Maria on a picnic—with Nat and young Carlos, Maria's nephew, for chaperones.

Long after Hector had trudged off to bed, still grinning, Natalie sat up reading in an attempt to lull herself to sleep. The dark tanned face of Ben Andress kept haunting her, as thoughts of hijackers and drug traffickers and shiny, deadly guns mingled with visions of bright water and leaping fish. Mac had said that there were so many amateurs in the drug business that no one knew whom to trust. "So don't trust anybody," he'd said as he watched her reload and fire the handgun. Now the shiny weapon lay on the top of the chest of drawers across the room, lustrous and ominous in the moonlight. "Surely not Ben," Natalie groaned, pitching aside the book in frustration.

She couldn't picture Ben as a cold-blooded criminal smuggling kilos of cocaine into his respectable marina. But since the Coast Guard knew his boat, and Ben had established a reputation for barring drugs on the compound.... Natalie shook her head, trying to drive out the suspicions. Maybe Hector was mistaken. Maybe Angela Sutton had had something else in that plastic package. Maybe....

Finally Nat bolted out of bed, pulled on her jeans and a jacket and stuffed her bare feet into her sandals. Tomorrow she had to work. That meant tonight she had to sleep. She could not sleep with her mind churning about Ben and his drug entanglements, but if she took a walk, hopefully the salt-tinged breeze from the Atlantic and the steady sweep and rush of the waves would bring tranquility...and finally restful sleep.

Nat could hear Hector's steady breathing as she tiptoed across the living room. He was sound asleep. The ceiling fan turned with a soft hum as it stirred the air. At least one of them would be bright-eyed and rested. Natalie slipped silently out the door, then stood at the foot of the beach house debating which route to take. She considered jogging past the row of beach houses to the thick line of trees where Ben always went at the end of the day. He lived somewhere beyond the trees, withdrawing into a world of his own when he finished his labors at the marina. She reminded herself that would be trespassing before her curiosity overcame her good sense. Instead, she settled for the open space of a more familiar route—back toward the parking lot and the boathouse. Lifting her knees and jogging with an even-paced step, she loped along beside the shell path, determined that either the exertion or the fresh air would make her tired enough to finally fall asleep.

Nat barely reached the near edge of the parking area when a slight movement in the shadows by the boathouse brought her to an abrupt halt. Someone else was out there. Nat stood rigid, listening to her pulse pounding in her temples, as she stared into the darkness for a further sign that she was not alone. Nothing stirred. Natalie hugged her arms about her, fighting off the cold, uneasy sensation that whoever lurked nearby was watching her as intently as she searched the shadows.

"Is someone here?" Nat steadied her voice and called out into the black surroundings. The only reply was the whisper of the wind in the drooping palm fronds and the distant swish of the waves at low tide.

"Mac?" She tried again hoping that he might have come out for a security check of the premises. Still no response. The lodge was totally dark except for one small light above the front entrance that spread its dim glow over the porch, sending eerie shadows twisting over the pale shell parking lot. That patchwork of light became the only source of comfort in sight. Natalie started for it with slow, careful steps. The dull crunch of shells marked each movement she made.

The night air brought a distant scene drifting across the parking area—the faint odor of smoke, marijuana smoke. "If one of you guys is hanging around here taking a few puffs," Nat addressed the darkest end of the boathouse, "I'll make you a deal. I'll just keep moving on toward the lodge and you take off the other way. I won't tell anyone," she promised. "Just let me know if it's one of you...." She waited anxiously for a sign.

From the corner of the boathouse came a thin spiral of smoke as someone expelled a long breath.

"Thank goodness," Nat sighed, relieved that whoever was there was one of the crew. "So...I'm on my way," she started for the lodge steps. Between the steady beat of her own steps, she could hear another pair of footsteps, heavier and more rapid, moving off in the opposite direction back toward the crew's beach houses.

This isn't what I had in mind. Nat collapsed onto the porch and flopped beneath the dim light. "I was after something calming," she groaned. She lay there staring up at the three gray moths circling and bumping into the round white bulb while her staccato heartbeat gradually resumed its normal pace.

Natalie gave the silent smoker several minutes' head start before she went back down the path toward Beachside One. She stayed in the center of the walkway, refusing to peer into any more shadows for fear her imagination would fill them with other specters. Ahead, all the beach houses were dark and still, yielding no clue to the identity of her companion in the dark.

"I'm sure glad it wasn't you...." Natalie paused by Hector's half-open door. His regular, heavy breathing continued as before. Hector had sworn he was off dope for good. He'd had one brush with the law, and he didn't want to risk his future with another arrest. Nat listened a moment longer, then retreated to her own room.

Without bothering to turn on the light, she undressed quickly and slipped back into her bed, nudging aside the book that still lay unread on the pillow. "Sleep...." Natalie closed her eyes and inhaled a long, deep breath, expelling it slowly through pursed lips. "Relax," she commanded herself as she breathed in again and again, filling her lungs with air and willing herself to sleep. At last the tension ebbed and the languid effects of the deep breathing set her adrift with only the soft whirr of the overhead fan whispering in the night.

"THAT MAKES TWO...." Mac's disgruntled reply came over the radio telephone when Natalie called in her message the next morning. She had barely got beyond Newfound Harbor Channel before the *Calusa* broke down. "Fuzzy is already being towed in," Mac explained. "Something fouled his gas lines, so he says."

"That sounds like the same trouble I'm having," Nat replied. "I've checked everything I could, but the fuel pump isn't working right."

"Don't worry," Mac answered. "Just drop anchor and I'll send Hector out to get you right after he brings in the *Suds Buggy*."

Nat placated her two passengers by switching to light tackle and having them cast from the stern. She tried her own hand, casting her favorite bucktail jig and catching a plump gray snapper. She cut it into strips, had Greg bait the fishermen's lines and had them cast again. This time they hooked a couple of hungry barracuda that put up a terrific fight. By the time Hector passed by, towing the *Suds Buggy* and its crew and passengers, one of Nat's fishermen was on his second barracuda and was in no hurry to return to shore.

When the *Calusa* was finally dragged back into the marina, Mac had already been working on the engine of the *Suds Buggy* and greeted her with his bleak appraisal. "Looks like somebody dumped something in the fuel tank." He jerked his thumb toward the first boat. "Salt...sugar...something. I won't be surprised if you show up with the same stuff."

"Sabotage?" Nat whispered.

"Either that or incredible stupidity," Mac replied.

"And I sure hope we don't have anybody that stupid working for us." He narrowed his eyes and peered out over the marina. "If one of those dope runners wanted to snatch a boat, I sure could have thought of some better ways to disable one...."

"We must be dealing with some real jerks." Fuzzy poked his head out the *Suds Buggy*. "Whatever they dumped in the fuel messed up the lines, but it also tore up the engine. You can't run dope without an engine."

"Amateurs," Mac hissed angrily. "Damned amateurs. The Keys are crawling with 'em."

Natalie's wide hazel eyes shifted to the three crewmen who had gathered farther up the dock. She hadn't actually seen the midnight smoker down by the boathouse. It had been too dark. But she had assumed it was one of the crew. She stood staring at the familiar faces wondering if there was a saboteur among them. "Don't trust anyone," Mac had said. Nat didn't realize she might have to take his words so literally.

Mac walked over to the charter passengers who were waiting on the porch of the lodge. He stood speaking with them for several minutes then shook hands with each of them and headed back in Nat's direction. "All they want is a rematch," he announced with a broad smile. "First good news I've had all day," he chuckled. "Your two passengers were quite taken with you, Nat," he noted. "They asked specifically for you on their next trip. That's how we build a clientele." He patted her on the shoulder.

"Yeah... well, how do we fix the boats?" Fuzzy interrupted. "We can't expect our clientele to *swim*."

"What about calling the police?" Nat brought

everything to an abrupt halt. "Don't you think we should call the sheriff?"

"We don't have the time," Mac replied. "By the time they sent someone out to investigate and maybe another guy to take fingerprints, we'd lose a full day. Even if there were fingerprints, they'd need a full set of them to get a match, *if* there is a match on file somewhere." The tone of his voice made it clear that the procedure would be time-consuming and probably futile. "We're losing money as it is," Mac added. "Let's cut our losses by getting these boats back in working condition. We'll just take this as a warning and tighten up our security."

"If these amateurs are as dumb as they must be," Fuzzy asserted, "they'll figure we'll be on our guard from now on, and they'll try somewhere else."

"I hope so." Nat fell into step beside Mac who was heading for the *Calusa*. Before the repairs got under way, Mac would have to see just how badly the engine was damaged. While the crew moved the *Suds Buggy* into the boathouse, Mac and Nat studied the second damaged boat.

"We've got real trouble," Mac groaned at last. There was nothing surprising about his verdict. Nat had stayed by his side, handing him tools and holding wires in place while Mac turned, twisted, and blew through tubes. She could see that the mixture in the fuel had heated up, become sticky and had seized up the engine.

"This is beyond me," Mac said dejectedly. "I can handle the minor repairs, but this baby is really a mess." He stood up, stretching, staring forlornly at the massive engine.

"Let me make a phone call." Nat touched his arm gently then hurried off toward the main desk in the lodge. Smudged and sweaty, she stood by the phone, dialing the number.

"Uncle Buzz—" she controlled the tears that threatened to erupt "—I need *another* favor."

Buzz Cochran arrived forty minutes later. He hugged the slim, long-legged girl who greeted him, then followed her, toolbox in hand, to the boathouse. After eight years working on ships for the navy and fourteen years as a marine mechanic, Cochran was a skilled specialist who happened to dote on his late sister's only daughter.

Cochran muttered repeatedly as he poked and probed. "Whatever was dumped in here—salt, sugar, whatever," he groaned, "it seized up the entire works."

Mac cursed quietly beneath his breath.

"You can't fix it?" Nat gasped.

"Oh, I can fix it," Buzz grunted. "It'll just take about a week and a big layout in cash for parts and labor." His narrowed eyes rested on the next boat. "If the same thing's wrong with that one, then you can double the cost," he stated.

"What if we all worked on it?" Natalie pressed him. "What if all of us pitched in and you supervised? Couldn't we cut the costs that way?"

"You'll cut the labor costs, but the parts don't care how many folks carry them around. It will still run you close to a thousand apiece."

"Plus we'll have to call off all our scheduled charters for the week." Mac shook his head.

"Should we call Ben?" Hector asked.

"And where is Ben?" Buzz Cochran watched his niece's face as he asked.

"Bimini," Mac replied. "With Charles Sutton and some sports equipment dealers in a tournament."

"How long will he be gone?" Buzz asked.

"He may be back late Sunday." Mac already sounded as if he was preparing to face the dark-eyed fury of his friend.

"I'll tell you what—" Cochran slipped a consoling arm around Nat's shoulders "—if we can line up the parts tonight or early tomorrow...and if we drop everything and all pitch in...dawn till dusk," he stressed, "maybe we can get these two in shape by Saturday night."

"But then there's the matter of money," Mac sighed. "I may be able to swing a thousand, maybe fifteen hundred. But then there's the labor. You don't work cheap." He spoke with respect to the mechanic who had a reputation for fine work.

"I'll make you another deal," Buzz continued. "You keep an eye out for my baby here—" he squeezed Nat's shoulders "—and slip me a few decent fish for the next year or so...."

"Ben would shoot me," Mac protested. "From what I hear, you two aren't exactly on good terms." Both men glanced at Nat. Apparently she wasn't the only one on Ben's enemy list after his begrudging agreement to let her work.

"So, who plans to tell Ben that I've been around?" Buzz replied innocently. "And who would mention just how extensive the damage is?"

Hector had stood silently listening while the others

negotiated. Now he broke into a wide grin. "I ain't tellin' anybody," he offered.

"I can get the other guys to keep their mouths shut," Mac surrendered.

"You don't have to worry that I'll talk," Natalie joined in. "I sure wouldn't tell him I had to call in help."

"Then let me get a list of parts," Buzz concluded. "You can start calling around and see what we can find. Maybe we'll have to send one of the guys to Miami if we come up short."

"They'll go," Mac assured him. "Or we'll send Nat."

Buzz Cochran shot him a dubious look. "You've never seen this kid tear down an engine?" he asked incredulously. "She's the best hand I've had around in years."

Mac cast a bewildered look at the tall, golden-haired young woman. "She didn't mention that," he muttered.

"I bet that's not all she didn't mention," Buzz snickered. "Anyhow, she stays. You start rescheduling your charters for the week," he told Mac. "I'll be in with the parts list in a while."

With another long look at Nat, Mac finally retreated toward the boathouse to retrieve the list of charter bookings. Buzz simply winked at Nat then turned noncommittal dark eyes to Hector. "You the roommate?" he demanded.

Hector nodded.

"You two getting along all right? No problems?"

"We got everything worked out," Hector answered. He had the distinct impression that the tall mechanic was weighing his response carefully.

"You agree?" he turned to his niece.

"We're fine," she assured him.

"Good, then let's get to work." Buzz dropped the inquisition and turned his attention back to the boats.

Hector merely rolled his eyes behind the tall man's back and gave Natalie a weak smile. Natalie simply shrugged. Maybe tonight she and Hector would have a long talk and clear up some of the details she had avoided discussing earlier.

"Well?" Buzz said a bit too loudly.

Nat grinned broadly at her uncle, put her hands on her hips and assumed a defiant, feet-apart stance. "Well, let's get to work!"

Buzz stepped forward to plop a big, greasy wrench in her hand. Nat strode purposefully to the *Calusa* to begin pulling down the engine.

CHAPTER FIVE

NATALIE LEANED AGAINST THE RAILING of the water-side balcony of the beach house, sipping her coffee and watching the morning sun turn the eastern sky into bands of gold and beige. She and the men had finished their four-day engine-repairing marathon at three minutes after nine the night before, and traces of dark grease were still visible around the outer rims of Natalie's ragged fingernails. "The hands of an artist," she sighed at their disreputable appearance.

Low stripes of stair-stepped clouds promised that a gusty, slightly overcast Sunday was in the offing. Mac had given everyone the day off to recuperate. Nat and Hector had made other plans. The gentle breezes would keep the temperature bearable and keep the insects from hovering around. It would be a good day for painting. It would be a good day for their picnic, too, Nat noted as she downed the last few drops of coffee and hurried back into the beach house. Ben would be coming back from the tournament in Bimini sometime during the day. When he pulled into the boathouse with whatever cargo or passenger might be aboard, Natalie did not want to be there. She would wait until things settled down a bit and the news of the sabotage and repairs had been relayed before she faced him again. Throughout the days of laboring over the engines, her thoughts had been filled with Ben Andress. She could wait a little longer before she looked into those intense eyes to see if he had been thinking of her.

Hastily Natalie rinsed out her cup, refilled the coffee maker with a fresh supply of water and ground coffee, then penned a note for Hector. He had dragged himself in from work the night before, sipped a cold beer and collapsed, exhausted, into bed. While Nat was eager to get an early start, Hector could enjoy a few more hours of sleep.

"Plug in the coffeepot," the note read. Then it followed with instructions about joining her at the Refuge with the skiff and remembering to bring the lunch that Maggie had packed for the picnic. Nat set the alarm clock for eleven, taped the note to the clock, then slid the clock inside Hector's darkened room. With her canvas carrying case of sketching materials under her arm, Natalie proceeded with her own agenda for the morning.

Roger Embry made a practice of getting up early on Sunday mornings when the other human occupants of the Refuge compound were still asleep. It was an exceptionally tranquil time when all the vehicles were silent and the entire area seemed to be subdued and serene. Natalie had not left the lodge during her four days of almost round-the-clock repairs, so she eagerly hurried to join her friend in his early-morning routine. When she parked alongside Roger's cottage, it was barely six o'clock.

"We'll have our juice by the seaside." Roger handed her an orange then picked up his drawing materials. With soft deliberate steps, they made their way across the dew-damp grass to the water's edge.

At noon, after spending almost six hours side by side in silent concentration, Natalie glanced over at Roger's detailed drawing of a bird's nest, a hollow scooped out in the sand, lined with a few twigs and feathers, upon which a lackadaisical pelican had laid three coarse, white eggs. With less pleasure Roger gazed at Natalie's unfinished sketch of the mother bird who had flown off earlier to forage for food.

"Looks like the mama bird isn't the only one off in the clouds," he muttered over Nat's incomplete drawing.

"I've been a little preoccupied," Natalie conceded. As the morning had progressed, Nat had found her thoughts wandering every time she heard a distant boat motor. Ben was coming home. No matter how she struggled to keep her attention focused on her work, Natalie kept returning to that one refrain. Ben Andress is coming home.

"You can't force it, Natalie," Roger said sympathetically. "Either the inclination and inspiration are there...or they're not. If it doesn't come to you now, it may later."

"Maybe," Natalie agreed. Almost apologetically, she rose from the outspread blanket, recovered her sketch pad from the short, scruffy grass and gathered up her pencils and brushes. The morning had not been a total loss. In the stillness of the quiet Sunday morning, she had felt once again the soothing power of nature to release the tensions she had accumulated in the week. She had breathed the clean air and felt the wind against her skin and with great admiration she had watched Roger draw. It had been a wonderful morning, Nat admitted with a rueful smile.

The sound of an approaching motorboat made her spring to attention. Glancing at her wristwatch, Natalie smiled more broadly. "I bet this is Hector in the skiff," she announced. "Time to close up shop and get this picnic underway."

"Aye, aye, captain." Roger hastily scooped up his pad and supplies and began stuffing them inside his carrying case. He followed Natalie to the dock. Hector appeared around the point, one hand on the motor and the other waving broadly to his waiting passengers.

"What about the others?" Roger asked Nat as he squinted into the noon sun. Roger had been informed of the purpose of the outing—a well-chaperoned date for Hector and Maria—and had been invited along as friend and fellow chaperon.

"We'll pick them up, too," Nat explained. "The Calonges live on Summerland Key. We'll just cut back through the channels to get them. They'll be looking for us about noon—which in the Keys means any time from about eleven till two."

Hector cut the motor off and stared up at Natalie and Roger. Now it was his turn to scrutinize one of Nat's companions. He looked closely at the light-haired artist and at the gold wedding band worn conspicuously on Roger's hand. As if he anticipated Hector's distrust, Roger managed to work into the first few sentences of their conversation his wife's name, the fact that he missed his children, and that he was eager to go on the picnic just to be around a youngster. From that point on, the suspicion dissipated. Roger and Hector were like old friends.

"What happened to the ice chest?" Nat squealed when she saw only the picnic basket in the skiff.

"Your note didn't say anything about the ice chest." He rubbed his chin in distress. "I do remember stepping past some big thing on the kitchen floor. I shoulda thought to bring it," he admitted. "I guess that means I go back?"

"You and Roger can take the boat," Natalie suggested. "The two of you can head back by the lodge. I'll drive to the beach house and pick up the chest. Just swing by the back of the beach house to pick me up."

The *Southwind* was entering the marina when Natalie drove through the parking lot. The sleek white cruiser with its sapphire blue canopy top disappeared behind the boathouse, then the rumble of its engine became muffled within the covered mooring. Natalie bit her lower lip, suppressing the urge to stop her car and run to greet Ben. Natalie pressed her foot slowly on the accelerator. There would be time for her later, after Ben learned about the damage to the boats and the charters that had been canceled or rescheduled.

Natalie parked by Beachside One, hurried inside for the ice chest, then dragged it out onto the back balcony overlooking the water and then out to the shore.

Within minutes, Hector steered the skiff across the inlet. He leaped out and held the boat steady while Natalie and Roger loaded the ice chest onto the floorboards, then once again they were on their way. Hector cut across the channel, rounding the bend on the next key. Natalie glanced back toward the boathouse and breathed a sigh of relief.

"Something wrong?" Roger leaned forward and called out so he could be heard above the motor of the skiff.

"Nothing...nothing at all," Nat assured him. Only now was she beginning to feel the peculiar tension ease from within her. It was almost as if she could breathe more freely now, knowing that Ben had returned safely to the compound. Natalie contemplated the bright peaks of water that slapped against the underside of the bow. She hadn't realized how much Ben's absence had affected her: he had become an essential part of Natalie's world, a world that seemed strangely incomplete when he was away.

"Here's the rest of the group." Hector waved to the cluster of people on the dock at Summerland Key. The Calonges were all lined up waiting for the small boat to maneuver into place. Hector stared at Maria so intently he almost ran the boat into the dock. With an idiotic grin, he leaped out to meet her.

Smiling slightly, Nat watched Hector greet the Calonge family. His head nodded up and down politely, but his eyes returned constantly to Maria. There was a joy in his expression that Natalie understood.

After a flurry of introductions, greetings, and farewells and a few uncertain looks at the sixteen-foot, flat-nosed boat, Maria and her twelve-year-old cousin, Carlos, climbed aboard. Hector followed, still grinning, but he did remember to unhitch the tie rope before trying to push off from the dock.

"Adios." The elder Calonges waved from shore as the boat bounced over the choppy water of the channel.

"It will be calmer on the Gulf side," Hector yelled, trying to reassure Maria and Carlos.

"We're not worried. We can swim," Maria yelled back. The loud putt-putt of the motor and the steady slap of the waves made further conversation impossible. Then the boat skimmed out onto the smoother water beyond the channel, as the warmer greenish water of the Gulf spread out before them.

Hector guided the party of picnickers back into the maze of mangrove islands that fringed the keys, over the shallows where tarpon, grouper and bonefish skirted the labyrinth of islands. He steered through a narrow pass between two overhanging mangroves, then abruptly brought them into an inlet where two other flat runabouts had converged.

He moved on through another close passage into an open stretch of water. Finally he cut around a low-lying group of newly forming keys, each containing only a few mangrove trees and their outstretched, airy roots, then he curved back through a break in a thick wall of mangroves into a horseshoe-shaped lagoon where a sandy crescent of beach spread out to welcome them.

"This is it." He cut off the motor and let the boat glide up onto the soft, pale sand that lined the water's edge. "I can guarantee you privacy here," he promised.

Nat turned to look back at the mouth of the inlet.

The trees almost totally obscured the opening and the lovely beach within its confines. "If anyone wanted to disappear for a while," she remarked, "this would be one place you could do it." The secluded location was separated from the outside world by a tangled wall of tropical vines and twisting trees.

Already Roger had dropped his shoes on the bottom of the boat and was climbing over the side.

Once Roger and Hector pulled the skiff up on more solid sand, the rest of the party disembarked. Maria and Natalie trudged across the beach and picked out a shady spot for the picnic. Carlos stalked the beach in pursuit of the little scurrying hermit crabs, which disappeared into damp holes in the sand whenever someone approached. Roger brought the ice chest. Hector carried the picnic basket, and they all settled down for a long, leisurely luncheon.

Much later in the afternoon, Roger and young Carlos explored the undergrowth of the island and Natalie spread out her paints and sat cross-legged on the beach, blissfully daubing bright colors onto the sketch pad. Roger had told her to try quick, light strokes and fill the scene with color. He was making an effort to break her of her tendency to ponder a scene too long and lose the spontaneity that he liked best in her work. So she painted Carlos beneath the deep green overhanging mangrove; Hector just as he cast his line into the inlet; Maria in red, gold and black wading in the mud searching for hermit crabs.

Nat sketched the inside of the inlet with the skiff beached and empty. This one was for Mac. Then she painted the picnic basket, propped open in the shade, in rich browns and bright oranges. That one was for

Maggie. The last picture broke Nat's rhythm and returned her to her slower, more contemplative form. This was her sketch of the graceful, twisting mangrove at the mouth of the horseshoe. Its long dark roots were almost grotesque with their angles and turns. But there was something elegant about the mangrove, something strong and brave and... moody.

This one was for Ben. Ben had said she was like a mangrove—drifting in, sending out shoots, touching people but remaining independent. Perhaps part of what he said was true. But this particular tree wasn't her metaphor—it was his. Ben had reached out and claimed his surroundings, like this majestic tree, creating life and expanding his boundaries. He had touched her, drawn her close to him, filled her consciousness with memories and sensations that refused to release their hold on her and made her long for his presence. Somehow this tree possessed the same quality that Ben had—a persistence and strength that was almost mystical. If she could capture that quality, it would convey to Ben a message so poignant, no language could compare.

The more Natalie anguished over the twisting lines of the tree, the more dissatisfied she became with the results. All the other sketches had burst forth in flights of color and form, but the drawing of this tree eluded her.

"Stop now," Roger addressed her over her shoulder. "You have part of it." He touched the two outstretched limbs that she had colored in lightly. "If you keep pushing it at this point," he warned, "you'll lose whatever it is that you feel. You'll just end up with a tree."

He was right. Part of Roger's skill as a painter and as a tutor was knowing when the creative intensity was missing. "That tree has been here a long time," Roger consoled her. He clasped her hand and helped her to her feet. "It will wait for you. When you're ready, you'll come back here."

"I'll get it yet," Nat sighed and looked down with some comfort to her other paintings. They all needed to be finished, but the impressions she had to work with—flashes of something immediate and personal—would allow memories of this picnic to last far beyond the limits of this day.

Later, when the sun was low in the sky and dark shadows crept across the lagoon, Hector guided the skiff back through the narrow mouth of the inlet out into the clusters of other small islands. Nat watched his route carefully, memorizing the location of the small key with the secret lagoon in its heart. She would come back to this nameless key and look at the remarkable mangrove that guarded its gate. She would paint the tree that now would haunt her night and day. . . as Ben did.

The trip back seemed to progress more rapidly than the departing boat ride. The weathered dock on Summerland Key loomed ahead as Hector cut through the channel to drop off the first load of passengers.

"She said she had a wonderful time," Hector announced as he climbed back into the skiff after delivering Maria to her family. "And she said she doesn't like going out to dinner—" he grinned smugly at Natalie ''—so she invited me over to eat with her family next Sunday.''

''That's great,'' Roger declared. ''Now all we have to do is find someone for Natalie,'' he joked.

''I'm not looking,'' Natalie cautioned him. ''I have as much as I can handle right now.''

''That's always when it happens,'' Roger professed. ''Precisely when you are not looking, and when it is absolutely *not* convenient, that's when it happens.''

''Then I'd better watch out,'' Nat joked to dismiss the subject. The words echoed in her mind as they bounced across the choppy waters of Newfound Channel. As they moved along at a good clip, Nat looked over the water toward the beach where she and Ben had lain together. Fondly, she remembered the warm sun, the cool green water...and Ben's smooth hand stroking her bare back...and his low, throaty voice speaking her name.

''Nat-a-lee,'' Hector yelled above the sound of the motor. ''Get the bow line, Nat-a-lee.''

She snapped her attention back to the present and bent forward to find the coiled rope in the bow of the skiff. When the boat had glided soundlessly to shore behind Beachside One, Nat and Roger stepped out and began unloading the supplies.

''I'm going to unpack, and then I'll take Roger home,'' Nat called over her shoulder to Hector. ''Or do you think we have enough fish in the refrigerator to invite him to dinner?''

Hector smiled, reached into the boat, and passed her the three good-sized sea trout that he'd caught back at the inlet.

"I gather this is your way of saying he can stay." Natalie accepted the catch.

"Only if you clean them," Hector insisted.

"*I'll* clean them," Roger offered. He took the stringer of fish from her.

"Now we got teamwork." Hector smiled broadly at his new friend. "I'll hose down the boat, you clean the fish and Nat can cook."

"How about dinner in thirty minutes?" Natalie suggested.

"Good deal," Hector agreed. "I'll make sure everything is locked up, then I'll hurry back here." Hector started the motor and chugged off toward the boathouse.

Roger stood at the water's edge with the three fish suspended at arm's length. He seemed uncertain about what to do next.

"Roger. . .have you ever cleaned a sea trout?" Natalie eyed him suspiciously. "Come on, city boy," she teased.

"I've usually been on the eating end of this fish business," he confessed. "Eaten many. . .cleaned none."

"Perhaps you'd like a lesson?" Natalie offered to be the teacher for a change.

"In addition to speeding things up considerably—" Roger linked his arm through hers as she reached his side "—it may guarantee a more respectable-looking result."

"Then I'm at your service." Natalie laughed at the relieved expression on his face. It was only then that Natalie glanced at the piers supporting Beachside One and noticed the tall figure that had been leaning against the building move away. Ben turned and walked off briskly along the shell path toward the lodge.

"Oh. . . darn." Natalie replayed the entire scene in her mind and surmised what Ben must have thought. This certainly wasn't the homecoming reception he had been expecting. He had asked Natalie to think about him. Now it appeared that her attention had been devoted to someone else.

"I assume that's Ben Andress." Roger stared after the man. Natalie nodded. "And I assume he was hoping to find you. . . without an unfamiliar male at your side. . . ."

"At least he won't think that I've been moping around waiting for his return." Natalie tried to make the best of the situation.

"And would he be correct?" Roger gave her a sidelong look. "Is *he* the distraction that has been interfering with your work?"

"Keep walking, Embry." Natalie refused to answer. "We have some fish to cook."

"Whatever you say," he chuckled low in his throat. As they scaled, gutted and filleted the fish, Natalie only half listened to Roger's progress report on his commission at the Refuge. Her thoughts kept returning to the tall man in the sun-bleached captain's hat.

Natalie kept assuring herself that she hadn't moped around waiting for Ben while he was gone. She'd worked on the engine repairs with the skill of an expert. She'd been cheerful throughout the labors, joking with Buzz and Hector and the other men while the greasy work progressed. But she had thought about Ben almost continually. She'd wondered about his days out fishing with Charles Sutton and his evenings in Bimini, when crews and competitors gathered in lounges and on patios to joke and brag about the day's escapades. There would be music and cocktails and soft breezes…and Angela Sutton. Would Ben gaze into Angela's cool blue eyes and listen to her soft laughter? Nat had wondered about the package of white powder that Hector had caught a glimpse of months before. She had thought about a number of things in Ben's absence, but she hadn't moped.

"Let's get these under the broiler." Natalie stacked the sea-trout fillets upon a platter and scraped the remainder of the fish into a paper bag. "You pitch this in the garbage and I'll do the rest."

"Looks like you've got plenty," Roger said, eyeing the stack of fish. "Maybe Captain Andress might like to join us?" he suggested with a sly smile.

"If you don't mind, Roger," Natalie cautioned her friend, "I'd prefer to work this out on my own. Stop worrying. I'll talk to Ben a little later."

"Ben?" Roger smiled at the tone of her voice as she said the name. "My, things are progressing…." He winked, then hurried off in search of a garbage container in which to deposit the fish residue.

Natalie started to climb the stairs up to the beach house kitchen, then paused to look down the empty path where Ben had gone. She had wanted to wait until Ben had tended to business before she spoke with him. She wanted their first moments together to be calm, open and casual. With a shrug, Nat proceeded into the beach house to prepare the dinner.

The fantasy reunion she had planned would just have to wait.

At nine-thirty, Roger slid into the passenger side of Nat's Mustang, well fed and ready to go back to the Refuge. He and Hector had spent most of the meal-time discussing the numerous offshore reefs where sea creatures sought food and safety. Hector had given Roger a hasty course in the types and sizes of fish that frequented the waters, and by the time they were finished eating, the two men were planning some weekend fishing trips of their own.

"I'll be back in a few minutes," Nat called to her housemate who stood on the rear balcony. "Don't forget the dishes," she reminded him. Hector grimaced and then nodded.

"Someone's working late," Roger observed as they approached the boathouse. "Perhaps your Captain Andress is burning off a little pent-up frustration," he added mischievously.

"I doubt that Ben is frustrated about anything," Nat commented dryly. She sat forward in the seat, observing the brightly lighted end of the boathouse where the old cruiser was in dry dock. "He must be working on his favorite project," Nat noted. "He's restoring an old cruiser. . .and he's not *my* Captain Andress," she added, refusing to let Roger get away with his teasing.

"Is he anybody's?" he persisted.

"I'm not sure," Natalie replied thoughtfully as she drove across the parking lot and served out onto the roadway. "Ben keeps his private thoughts pretty much to himself."

"Then that gives you two something in common,"

Roger smiled. "Something besides fishing," he added smugly.

"Roger. . . ." Nat left the warning incomplete. He leaned back in his seat. He obviously sensed that he'd reached the limit. When Nat pulled up before his cottage on the Refuge, Roger made his farewell with a brief wave of gratitude and let her go on her way.

The light inside the boathouse was still glaring brightly as Nat pulled into the parking lot. She hesitated, trying to catch a glimpse of movement near the old cruiser, then she parked by the boathouse entrance. If Ben was in there, she would at least stop and welcome him back from his trip.

The boathouse door was unlocked so Nat let herself in and strolled along the wooden landing toward the end where the cruiser was housed. Two bright lights were focused on the underside of the old boat, but there was no sound or movement to indicate Ben was there.

"Ben?" Natalie stared at the eerie scene—a repair site without a worker—and slowly backed away.

"I don't know how to let you know—"

Natalie gasped and jumped before the voice completed the sentence. She whirled around. Ben had entered from behind her and stood holding a few sheets of sandpaper in one hand and a cup of steaming coffee in the other.

"I was about to say," he began again, "that I didn't know how to let you know that I was here without startling you." Natalie stood with one hand pressed against her chest, gasping. She managed a weak smile and nodded so Ben would know that she understood the dilemma.

"I just went to pick these up—" he held out the sandpaper sheets "—and you must have just slipped in before me."

"I was coming back from taking a friend home." Nat had finally caught her breath enough to speak.

"A friend?" Ben echoed her words. Then he stood looking at her as if he was waiting for further explanation.

"Yes, Hector and I had a friend stay for dinner," Natalie said simply. "How was your trip?" she continued, changing the subject abruptly.

"My trip was fine," Ben replied evenly. "It was the coming home that wasn't so great. I heard about the damage to the boats." He tilted his head toward the *Calusa* and the *Suds Buggy* secure in their moorings.

"That was pretty discouraging," Natalie agreed. "But at least everything is in working order now."

"I gather you were able to find something to occupy your time while Mac and the guys worked on the boats," he said without looking directly at her.

"I served lemonade and cookies," Nat shot back at him sarcastically. Mac had told the fellows to keep quiet about how much work had been done and how much of that work Natalie and Buzz Cochran had performed, but Nat resented the implication that she had sat idly by while everyone else pitched in. "I did dust the sea gulls and knit little booties for the pelicans," she added with a patronizing smirk, "between hauling parts and tools back and forth and holding whatever it was that needed holding. I worked with the men every minute."

"Okay, okay...so you helped," Ben conceded

unconvincingly, then stepped past her on his way back to the old cruiser. He landed his coffee cup with a thud on the dock and leaped down beside the hull to resume sanding the bottom. Natalie stared after him angrily, then followed his route, sitting down on the dock just behind him.

Ben ignored her presence as he scrubbed away on a strip of cracked paint. With infinite patience, he pried the old paint off, then smoothed and sanded the hull. Natalie didn't budge; she simply sat there, studying his movements and feeling her own anger fade with the soft, steady sounds of his labor. She watched his broad shoulder muscles stretch and ripple as the intensity of his action gradually subsided. Finally he stopped altogether and turned to look up at her.

"Your coffee is getting cold," Nat informed him. Without a word, he picked up the cup and drank, keeping his dark eyes locked on hers.

"I don't see why you're so angry with me," she said softly. "If you'd say what you're thinking, you wouldn't have to take out your anger on the bottom of the boat."

"I'm not angry," Ben insisted.

"I thought you were a little brusque." Nat maintained a wide-eyed innocence. "I had hoped that when you returned, we would be on more civil terms. Apparently I was overly optimistic." Ben placed the cup back onto the dock then looked up at her with a tight, noncommittal smile.

"I was overly optimistic myself, it seems," he said pointedly. "I don't like coming home to bad news. I had hoped it would be different." Natalie knew he was not referring to the trouble with the boats. What had angered Ben was the encounter he'd witnessed between her and Roger—arm in arm by Beachside One.

"Oh," she whispered. "That wasn't what you thought...."

With a sudden thrust, Ben vaulted up onto the dock beside her. He sat close to her, waiting for her to continue, while his leg pressed against hers. Nat glanced at the rip on the upper leg of his old jeans, still unrepaired, and felt the warmth of his body against hers.

"Well?" Ben leaned against her shoulder, coaxing Nat out of her sudden silence.

"Well, what?" Natalie replied.

"How about giving me a lesson in telling someone what you're thinking. Start with telling me why you came in here tonight...and why you won't look me in the eye right this minute." Without having to see his face, she knew he was smiling.

"I stopped in to welcome you back," Nat said simply. "I was just trying to be friendly."

"Friendly...." Ben repeated her word.

"I was curious about how you were." Nat felt her color deepen.

"Speaking of curious—" his tone lost its good-natured quality "—I don't suppose you'd like to tell me what you were doing out here by the boathouse the night before the engine breakdown?"

Now Nat turned to look up at him with wide, surprised eyes. "How did you know?"

"So you were out skulking around...."

"I wasn't *skulking*," Nat protested. "I was jogging. I couldn't sleep and I came up this way. I saw someone in the shadows near the end of the boathouse. Whoever it was left, then I went back to the beach house and went to sleep."

"And you didn't bother to mention it to anyone?" He shook his head in dismay. "You didn't see any connection between the person in the shadows and the damage to the boats?"

"I didn't actually *see* anyone," Nat responded in her own defense. "I thought it was one of the guys out for a quick smoke. I was a little frightened, so I promised I wouldn't mention it if the person would just go on back to his bunk. All I saw was a puff of smoke."

"Then what makes you think it was one of the guys out there?" Ben asked.

"It must have been," Nat replied. "Apparently he must have mentioned it to you...otherwise, you wouldn't have known that I was there that night. All I heard was someone running off toward the boathouse, and all he saw was me jogging along the path to the porch of the lodge. After that I went straight back. If anyone was *skulking*, it wasn't me," she insisted. "And when it became apparent that someone had tampered with the boats, there wasn't much point in saying anything simply because I had no real evidence. All I could do was to help out while the repairs were made."

"You should have mentioned it to Mac," Ben stressed.

"But why?" Natalie frowned. "What good would it have done?"

"It could have eased his mind, for one thing," Ben

countered. "I don't know who the guy was out by the boathouse," Ben informed her. "I heard that you'd been wandering around from Mac, not from one of the guys. Mac saw you just as you were leaving the parking lot. He figured that when you suggested bringing in the police, you didn't have anything to hide...but he still was uneasy because you'd never mentioned what you saw."

"You mean what I *didn't* see," Nat corrected him.

"Report *anything* suspicious," Ben replied wearily. "From now on, for security reasons, and to avoid any unnecessary speculation about who is where," he directed, "it would be better if you stayed in the beach house after dark."

"Just me? Or is everybody at the lodge confined to quarters, captain?" Natalie balked at the limitations unless they applied to everyone.

"*Anyone* who doesn't have a good reason to be wandering around should stay in," he asserted, "at least until this hijacking business dies down a bit."

Natalie's jaw tensed as she looked from her clenched hands to Ben's leg still touching hers. "I must have time to visit my friend," she said cautiously. "Sometimes I don't leave there until after dark. Do I need your permission for that?"

"No," Ben growled. "I certainly have no right to interfere with your social life, but at night when you're here, stick close to your beach house." Abruptly he stood and clicked off one floodlight. He took a few steps, then switched off the second one. Apparently he had lost interest in working. The dim light from the office at the opposite end of the boathouse barely illuminated that part of the interior of the long building. Ben offered Natalie a hand and silently hoisted her to her feet. She was being dismissed again.

"Good night," Nat said softly, then moved past him to the distant doorway.

"Wait...wait just a moment," Ben said as he followed her. "I don't want you to feel like you're being treated unfairly." He caught her by the shoulder and turned her to face him. "But there is a lot at stake here. You're here only temporarily, Natalie," he said with surprising gentleness. "What happens to the lodge and the boats really is no great concern of yours. But Mac and Maggie and I have made this our home as well as our business. So maybe we have a right to be very cautious about who comes and goes."

"I guess you do," Nat agreed.

"If something threatens the business, I take it very seriously," he admitted. "We have trouble enough making bank payments, finding good workers and keeping the equipment working, so all it takes is something like sabotage to put us in real trouble. For the time being, I want to keep a close check on everyone and everything."

"I understand."

"I'll do anything I have to do in order to keep this outfit," Ben said quietly. "There are too many others waiting in line at the bank to pick up the payments if we fall through. This place has great possibilities. Even Charles Sutton has tried to buy into the partnership, but this dream is Mac's and mine...and Maggie's too. We don't want outsiders interfering with our plans."

Natalie looked into his dark, solemn eyes. When he said *outsiders*, she wasn't sure if he meant to include her.

"I'm trying to help," Natalie responded. "Please quit trying to push me out. Believe me, I'm on your side. I want your business to do well." She raised her chin stubbornly. "After all, I do have my future to think of, too...and I *have* to do a good job here. I won't let you down, Ben," she concluded in a whisper.

"It would be a lot easier if you'd turned out to be a disappointment." Ben reached out and brushed aside a wisp of hair that had drooped across her temple. "But you keep coming up with more surprises, and each thing I learn about you is more intriguing. You just don't know what you've stumbled into, Natalie. I sure wish you'd come my way some other time."

"I've thought the same thing about you," Natalie replied with a glimmer of a smile. Then that same smile formed on Ben's lips, as if for once they understood each other perfectly. Very gently he clasped her shoulders, pulling her close to him so her pale hair brushed against his cheek. At first they held each other tentatively, reluctant to disrupt the fragile peace they had achieved.

Then the warmth they shared took on a new character—a softly surging wave of heat and pleasure. Natalie pressed her hand against Ben's chest, moving away from the source of the tantalizing warmth. He looked down into her eyes with an apprehensive quality that Natalie couldn't decipher.

"You aren't imagining it, Natalie," Ben whispered. "When I touch you and hold you, something ignites. . . like coals catching fire."

His eyes shifted to her soft, half-parted lips. Ben lowered his mouth to hers, letting his lips barely brush their surface as his breath mingled with Natalie's. The pressure of his lips subtly altered from the tentative softness engulfing her in a warm cocoon to a more passionate, sensuous tension that summoned her to respond.

"Touch me, Natalie." Ben's words rippled over her lips. "Warm my body with your hands. . . ." He pressed her closer to him. Natalie was for a moment indecisive, then she closed her arms around him, sliding her hands beneath his shirt, tracing the broad, corded muscles of his back with her fingertips.

Ben sighed, pressing his taut body against her as his hands slid downward, over the curve of her hips. With a moan of pleasure, he tantalized her lips with the tip of his tongue, then penetrated the velvety softness with an intimacy that held them both suspended. Inside his powerful embrace, Natalie drifted on a current of liquid fire, separated from reason—conscious only of the scent and taste of Ben Andress.

He grasped the back of her shirt, pulling it free from the waistband of her jeans, then he moved his hands beneath the soft fabric, tracing the contours of her bare back with his rough fingers. The gesture was at once exciting and familiar as the memory of the afternoon on the isolated beach mingled with present time. But now there was no golden sun flooding the scene with light; now the dark interior of the boathouse muffled the sound of the world beyond and surrounded them in near darkness.

"Come with me," Ben whispered. "Come into the cruiser, Natalie." The breathtaking urgency in his voice sent a shiver of comprehension through Natalie. He was not about to hold her like this and simply let her walk away. He was a man who obviously knew that she wanted him, that her response to him was instinctive and unrestrained. Nat had always been able to pull away with other men, to halt the lovemaking before it reached the point of total commitment. With Ben there had been no boundaries, no clear barrier to warn either of them that they had gone too far. Somewhere in a time already past, they had moved into a realm where passion was endless.

"I'm not sure—" Natalie gasped for a breath as Ben broke the embrace and bent down to scoop her into his arms "—that I'm ready for this," she concluded softly.

"Then obviously you haven't been paying attention," Ben answered in a throaty voice. "Your body has been talking for you, Natalie—" he kissed her again lightly "—and it's time you listened to it."

Ben brushed the tip of his tongue very lightly across her lips, holding her cradled in his arms. "Listen to your body," he murmured, punctuating his words with soft languid kisses, offering erotic promises.

Unwilling to let the kisses end, Natalie lifted her hand, clutching his dark cloud of hair at the nape and pulling his lips down to hers. All her reservations were washed away like scattered bits of driftwood on the outgoing tide, and the steady thunder of her heart pounded out the rhythm of his name. Inside her head, tangled images of nature overwhelmed her. Waves and tides swept in; sands shifted; twisted mangrove roots took hold then drifted apart, free of connection, free of certainty. The sound of the wind in the leaves of the trees and the rush of the waves drummed out the low and vibrant murmur of her name. "Natalie. . . come with me."

Ben crossed the few paces to the side of the old cruiser, took her hand and stepped into the old boat, nodding toward the dark interior. Without a word, Natalie followed him down into the depths where they had first met.

In the stillness of the master cabin, Ben unfastened her shirt, button by button, without any sign of haste. With rough, gentle hands, he stroked her long smooth arms and trailed his fingertips lightly between her breasts. He proceeded with the unhurried grace Nat had witnessed before as he'd labored over the cruiser or sent a captured fish back to the reef. This time, *she* was the object of his attentions. She was the still, quiet creature he was caressing and offering new life.

Ben knelt before her in the darkness, pressing his lips against her arm, soft skin as he slid the remaining clothes to the floor, letting her step free of them. He stroked her hips and long tanned legs with his rough hands, brushing his lips back and forth across her naked midriff, inhaling the warm scent of her body.

Natalie stood above him, barely breathing, feeling the sweep of his thick dark hair as it rippled below her breasts. His obvious delight in feeling her skin next to his own melted away the apprehensions. His tender caresses were so sensuous and soothing that

Nat moved freely beneath his touch, silently conveying her increasing pleasure. When Ben lifted his lips upward, Nat embraced him, lowering her breast toward his eager mouth. All inhibitions disappeared as the heat and touch of one enveloped and infused the other. With one smooth gliding motion, they clung to each other as they rolled onto the wide cabin bed.

"Natalie," Ben spoke her name with a low, throaty sigh.

"Nat-a-lee!" came the echoing voice of Hector Ortiz from the parking lot outside. "Nat-a-lee!" he yelled. "You around here, Nat-a-lee?"

"It's Hector...." Natalie froze.

"I *know* it's Hector," Ben groaned. "Just stay here and be quiet." He stroked her bare shoulder. "He'll go away."

"But my car is out there." Natalie sat upright. "I have to answer or he'll think something is wrong...."

"Damn," Ben muttered, his voice still breathless with passion. "You and your *friends*," he added without amusement. For a few seconds, he stared at her steadily in the dark room, then he thrust a hand through his thick hair and expelled a long breath. "I'd better go first," he said matter-of-factly. "You'll need a little time to get your clothes back on." He collected her scattered clothing and handed it to her. Only then did Nat realize that Ben was still partially clad. Wearing only his jeans, he climbed up onto the deck, leaving her to dress as he flicked on the floodlights and headed for the boathouse door.

From above, the sudden glare of the work lights

sent shafts of harsh white light into the gangway of the cruiser where Natalie hurriedly stepped into her jeans and pulled on her shirt.

"She's here." Ben's distant voice summoned Hector from his search. "Hector," Ben called louder, "she's in here." Hector circled the threshold of the boathouse just as Natalie became visible above the deck of the old cruiser.

"You okay?" Hector asked with wide-eyed concern. "Man, I was so worried. . . ." He caught his breath.

Natalie's racing pulse had calmed sufficiently that she could force a vague smile to greet her housemate. "I'm fine," she said with just a trace of breathiness. She followed Ben's route, leaping over the side of the boat onto the dock, then crossing the wooden landing to the two men.

"Boy, I was afraid somethin' was wrong." Hector looked from Natalie to Ben, his expression one of bewilderment.

"Natalie stopped by to take a look at the progress on the cruiser." Ben managed to make it sound so casual. "We were below deck. I guess we didn't hear you right away," he added with a slight smile.

"It's okay now." Hector grinned. "I just wanted to know if anything had gone wrong with the car or something." He shifted his feet awkwardly. "Say. . . you finished lookin' at the boat?"

"I guess I am," Natalie answered quietly. Hector was obviously ready to escort her safely back to the beach house. "See you tomorrow, Ben," she said, looking up into his dark liquid eyes.

"Sure, good night, you two." Ben stepped back

and let Hector start for the door a step ahead of Natalie. "Sweet dreams...." He lowered his voice, barely breathing the words as Nat moved beside him. There was no sound of distress or disappointment in his voice, only a warm, calm quality that conveyed his assurance that there would be time again for them.

Hector talked nonstop all the way to Natalie's car, oblivious to her preoccupation with the tall form silhouetted in the boathouse door. "Man...I was really worried," Hector repeated. "You said you wouldn't be long...and I got the dishes done and cleaned up the place. I kept watching the clock and waiting for you to get back...and you didn't come." He paused only long enough to catch his breath. "So I came lookin' for you, and here your car was sitting out empty and the lights were out in the boat-house...well, almost out," he stammered in embarrassment.

At least in the darkness, Hector couldn't see how her cheeks were flushed.

"I didn't interrupt something I shouldn't have... did I?" He lowered his voice and turned to look at her anxiously. "I just wanted to make sure nothin' had happened to you." He grimaced as if he'd overstepped the bounds of their friendship.

"I'm glad you came looking for me." Natalie flashed him a quick smile. "Nothing happened. I got a little carried away...and forgot it was so late." That much was the truth.

"Okay, then," Hector sighed. "Let's go home."

Natalie switched on the ignition and backed around so she was facing the shell road that led to the beach house. The floodlights inside the boathouse still glared, making large patches of light across the parking lot beside her. For Natalie the day was over. Apparently Ben had decided to work late after all.

She recalled his words as she followed the moonlit path toward Beachside One. ''Sweet dreams,'' she echoed as she brushed the back of her fingers across her lips where the taste of Ben Andress still lingered.

CHAPTER SIX

ROGER EMBRY WALKED OVER TO NATALIE and stood peering over her shoulder at the exquisite lines and curves that were soon to become a picture of the aged mangrove. He glanced from her canvas to the twisted tree that guarded the mouth of the inlet, and he smiled. They had spent the entire afternoon off Big Pine Key, sketching in near silence and it was clear that the time had been well spent. "You've got it," Roger said at last.

Ben had been nowhere in sight when Natalie had brought in her morning charter. Still filled with memories of their intimacy on the old cruiser, Natalie had rushed off to the Refuge to try to capture her unspoken feelings in a painting that would have an eloquence of its own. Now as evening approached and long shadows cloaked the lagoon, Natalie contemplated the tree she had drawn.

"It isn't like anything else you've done before," Roger observed. "This one looks like something out of a dream." He glanced back at the distant tree she was using as her model, as if to verify that such a magnificent tree existed.

"Well, I've been dreaming about it, that's for sure," Natalie replied. "It's been on my mind for days."

"What else has been on your mind?" Roger asked quietly. "You've been working without a pause for hours—almost as if you were possessed. I admire determination," he noted, "but there's something more to this than simply the desire to paint a tree."

"I can't explain it, Roger," Natalie answered without looking over at him. "I just know I have to finish this painting."

"You'll have to finish it some other time." He tilted his head to the increasingly dark sky. "We've got to get back before they send a search team out after us. The fellows at the Refuge like to have all their boats accounted for by nightfall."

Reluctantly Natalie packed up her canvas and drawing equipment and loaded everything back into the Refuge skiff that they had beached on the sandy crescent of the lagoon shore.

"Don't worry," Roger comforted her. "You've captured the spirit of the thing. When you come back to complete the work, you'll find that it all comes back to you—all the feeling and mystery—because it's already there. You'll feel like you've never even been away from it."

The boathouse was locked securely and totally darkened inside when Natalie drove back into the compound. She parked her car by Beachside One and climbed the stairs, expecting to find Hector waiting for her to cook dinner. Instead she found a note.

"Gone out with the guys. Be back late. Hector."

The rest of the evening seemed to move in slow motion. Nat fixed herself a sandwich and a salad, put on some music and sat on the rear balcony looking out over the water as she dined alone. Long after she had cleared away the dishes and slid into bed, she lay awake listening for a knock at the door, hoping that Ben would stop by to see her. It was almost midnight before the shuffle of footsteps and the click of the lock indicated that Hector and "the guys" had returned.

"You didn't have to wait up for me." Hector stumbled slightly to the right as he spoke. "We were out havin' a few beers." He grinned sheepishly.

"I wasn't waiting up." Nat crossed the room and draped Hector's arm over her shoulder. "But as long as I'm here, let me steer you into your room," she offered.

Hector's "few" beers had sufficiently affected his coordination, so that it took three attempts to get him through his bedroom door, but once he was inside, he immediately curled up on his bed ready to sleep.

"I hope the other guys aren't any worse off than you are." Nat tugged the covers up over him.

"Fuzzy hardly drank anything," Hector replied with a sleepy smile. "It was Greg and I who kinda overdid it."

"How about the others?" Nat asked casually, trying to find out if Ben had been out with them.

"There was just us," Hector yawned. "Greg and Fuzzy and me." Without another word, Hector rolled over and promptly fell asleep. Nat stood next to him in her robe, staring down at the steady rise and fall of the covers as he breathed. Ben was not with the men. He hadn't stopped in to see her at the beach house even though Nat had been careful to leave several lights on so he'd know she was home.

Then where was he? Slowly she left Hector's room, pulling the door half closed, then she walked through the beach house, turning out the lights one by one.

The next day passed just as strangely. While Natalie brought in the *Calusa* from her charter, Ben was already driving out of the lodge compound in his battered Jeep. Nat spent three hours with Roger at the nameless key, putting the finishing details on her mangrove painting. Late that night, long after everyone else had turned in, Natalie heard the muffled sound of Ben's Jeep as it passed by the row of beach houses and disappeared into the wooded area beyond. Natalie stared up at the stars for almost an hour after that, growing sleepier all the time. Finally some light clouds moved in from the west and winked out the stars one after the other. When the final star of the Big Dipper disappeared, Natalie's eyelids fluttered closed and at last she fell asleep.

By the third morning, a slightly overcast Wednesday, Natalie resolved to make herself less available. If Ben was trying to avoid her, for whatever reason, she would make it easier on him. She showed up for breakfast before Ben and the other men arrived, grabbed a couple of sausage-filled biscuits and a thermos of coffee and went out to the *Calusa* to eat her breakfast in tranquility and to recheck all the gear that would be carried along that day.

At 6:30 A.M., she crossed the open area between the lodge and the boathouse, glancing up at the few slowly moving clouds, calculating wind speed and direction as she planned the day's fishing trip. Her two passengers were returning for their half-fare consolation trip after the engine breakdown the week before.

Nat would take them east off the reef and let them fish for the big ones that lived deep in the cool water along the craggy cliffs of varicolored coral.

In the boathouse, behind the counterlike structure that served as an office, storage facility and loading area, there was another early riser. Mac was already on duty, twisting dials and making faces at the radio as the Coast Guard service gave the day's weather forecast. Mac looked up to smile and give her a signal with thumb and forefinger to indicate an encouraging forecast.

The *Calusa* sat almost motionless in place number one at the wide dock. The sea was so calm today that her boat wasn't even tugging at its lines. "Hot, hot, hot," Nat mumbled as she anticipated the weather she would encounter on the water today.

She stepped aboard the *Calusa*, placed the thermos of coffee beside the refrigerated fish-storage box, then glanced over the lower deck. Still munching on the last of the thick sausage-stuffed biscuits Maggie had given her, Nat climbed up to the captain's seat and tapped all the gauges on the control panel. She inserted the key and turned over the *Calusa*'s powerful diesel engine. The throaty, musical throb of the engine confirmed the information she read on the dials. The *Calusa* was in top shape. Still, Nat was taking no chances. Down in the cabin on the lower level of the boat she secured the bright red toolbox just inside the cabin door. In addition to the usual emergency repair equipment all charter boats carried, Natalie made a few inclusions of her own since the threat of sabotage still loomed over the Keys.

Just as Nat throttled back the engine to idle and

started down the ladder to the lower deck, Greg saun-
tered into the boathouse, lugging a large bucket full
of fresh bait. On this charter he wasn't taking any
chances, either. If the artificial lures and spoons
didn't attract the fish today, his supply of shrimp,
squid and cut bait would perk up some appetites.
When he looked at the boat and saw Nat nod a greeting, Greg's usually inscrutable countenance, silent
and impassive behind his bushy beard, remained un-
changed though he did grunt "Good morning."

Nat leaned over the side of the boat and watched
him deposit the bait into the built-in wells at the
stern. "Let's really give these two guys a big day."
She'd said what they both had been thinking. "They
were pretty tolerant after the last disaster. Today
maybe we can get them a fish worth something."

Greg simply replied with his customary shrug and
proceeded to check the tackle as he always did. With
slow, methodical steps, he passed from one storage
locker to the next, returning to the boat with an additional gaffing hook and a larger landing net than
usual. If Nat was going after a trophy fish, he was
prepared.

Within the next few minutes, the boathouse was
echoing with men's voices as the crews of the *Southwind* and the *Suds Buggy* arrived. Natalie backed the
Calusa out of its mooring, ready to move it around to
the outside dock where her passengers would meet
her. Before she pulled out of the enclosure, she
glanced over toward the *Southwind* where Hector
was moving the tackle at a slightly slower pace than
usual. He caught her eye long enough to clutch his
head and gesture about his excesses with the guys.

Above him, at the controls of the *Southwind*, Ben stared at her intently. When Nat smiled and nodded, he returned the gesture, keeping his dark eyes locked onto her until the *Calusa* passed.

Nat took her two cheerful passengers out beyond the reef, almost ten miles out, where the clear Gulf Stream waters sparkled in the morning sun. She checked the depth sounder, watching the round green screen carefully as the electronic impulses registered the gradual increase in depth as the sea floor angled away from the shallows. Suddenly the wavering white line on the screen headed sharply downward, indicating that the depth had just dropped from 150 to 400 feet. This was the spot.

Nat reached for the throttle and controls and shifted into reverse to get a better angle for trolling. The engine raced momentarily, but the boat didn't alter its position. Nat rolled her eyes and tried shifting gears again.

"Looks like we've got trouble again," she groaned.

"What is it this time?" one fellow looked up from his fishing rod to ask.

"I think we've thrown a propeller," Nat grumbled. "How about you guys trying for a few little tuna while I check it out below. Then we'll go after some tarpon."

"Below?" The more slender passenger frowned. "You mean you're going over the side?" Abe Bodner pointed from Nat to the water. He was a man of about sixty who was obviously uneasy about this young lady swimming around in the open ocean.

"Just for a few minutes." Nat smiled reassuringly

as she ducked into the cabin and retrieved a snorkel and face mask. "I won't let you guys down again," she insisted as she adjusted the strap on the mask then held it up to the sunlight to check that it was clean and in good condition.

Abe Bodner looked at his fishing companion and shrugged. "Well, she seems to know what to do. I sure as heck don't." He grinned.

Nat quickly stripped off her shirt, jeans and deck shoes and stood in her one-piece swimsuit, making a final adjustment to the mask. She slipped it over her eyes and nose, pressed it tight with the palm of her hand and hopped over the side into the cool water. She blew out a sharp breath to clear the snorkel of water, then glided back toward the *Calusa*, her intent gaze playing along the keel and stern. Sure enough, the propeller was totally gone—nut, keeper ring, washer and prop—had all dropped into the Atlantic, leaving the bare shaft.

Nat surfaced and pushed the mask onto her head. She peered up to see Greg flanked by the two passengers staring down at her. "It's the prop," she announced, then took a deep breath, repositioned the mask and snorkel and plunged under once more. This time she made a close inspection of the shaft itself. There was no way all the pieces could have worked themselves loose. The keeper ring had metal tabs that locked over the nut and held it in place. Nat could see the freshly scraped metal where something had scratched the dull surface of the steel shaft. Someone had been working on it. Someone had to have cut the washer tabs and loosened the nut, so it had finally worked loose under the stress and motion of the water. Nat's earlier shift into reverse was the last kick it needed.

"I think I can handle it." Nat clung to the side of the boat while she caught her breath. "Boy Scouts and charter captains always come prepared," she joked to the men on board. Greg clasped her wrist and yanked her into the boat.

In minutes, Nat had retrieved the necessary parts from the storage cabinet in the cabin. "Uncle Buzz, thank you." Nat whispered as she lined up the equipment. Buzz Cochran had listened intently to his niece while she'd recounted the difficulties she'd faced with Ben.

He was even more concerned that someone had tried to sabotage her boat. The *Calusa* was the only single-engine boat in Andress's charter outfit. "If somebody is out to lame you," Buzz had brooded, "they'll go after something that'll let you get out, then cripple you." So he had set out a series of options that could disable a craft, and he'd made sure Nat had the materials to fix any of them.

Nat came back on deck with her arms loaded with the equipment. Without prompting, Greg stepped over and aided her. He cut several two-foot lengths of tough fishing line, made large loops in them and tied them to the two wrenches at Nat's feet. Nat stuffed the spare washer, keeper ring and nut into the top of her swimsuit, hung the wrenches around her neck and picked up the spare propeller. It was a dingy, scarred instrument that Buzz had supplied, but it would be good enough for this trip and perhaps even for years to come. And it had been free. Clutching it in one hand, Nat eased over the side, her mask already in place. She let the weight of the prop and tools pull her down until she was level with the shaft, and she began a slow, rhythmical frog kick to maintain her position. Methodically, she put each piece in place, then tightened the nut by hand. Rising to the surface for a brief rest and a couple of deep breaths, Nat smiled up at her impassive mate and returned to finish the task.

Occasionally a sizable barracuda would swim by and circle slowly around, gawking at her with curious iridescent eyes. "Keep coming, baby." Nat glanced at a thirty-pounder, knowing that as long as a 'cuda was nearby, there were no sharks in the vicinity. Nat tightened the nut with the wrench and surfaced for another breath. She took her last dive, hanging onto the drive shaft with one hand as she tapped the keeper tabs over the nut. *Almost done,* she thought to herself.

Suddenly a smaller, more aggressive barracuda cut near her. *Too near,* she thought. Then she realized what it was after. The slender thread of gold around her neck had caught its attention and the long, thin fish was circling for another lunge.

Nat clasped one hand over her throat to cover the shiny target and jerked backward as the 'cuda made another pass. She hadn't noticed the rudder right behind her. It slammed into the side of her face mask, knocking it askew and sending a silent cry of pain bubbling to the surface. Stunned by the blow and momentarily blinded by the rush of salt water into the mask, Nat thrust out her hand to grasp something solid until she could reestablish her equilibrium. Suddenly there was a searing stab of pain up her right arm. She had jammed her arm straight out at the motionless brass propeller. One of the blades had scraped off a long swatch of skin from her wrist to her elbow. Peering through the stinging salt water that filled the mask, Nat watched the thin cloud of pinkish blood slowly spread underneath the keel. Very soon there would be fish swimming around her that were larger and much less friendly than the barracuda. Blood in the water means sharks. She had no time to waste.

Still gritting her teeth from the pain in her right temple, Nat used a firm steady kicking motion to back out from under the boat and to rise to the surface.

"Oh, my Lord!" Mr. Bodner gasped when he saw her pained expression and the tinge of red in the water around her. Greg instantly sprang forward and reached low over the side to pull her aboard. Instinctively he scanned the blue gray surface of the ocean for any ominous triangular fin, but the dreaded sharks had not appeared this time. "Oh, my Lord," Bodner gasped again when he leaned down to see Nat at closer range, "What have you done to your face?" Looking further down he added, "And to your arm?"

"Just took off the surface skin." Greg quickly evaluated the crimson wound on her arm, then studied her temple closely. "This looks like quite a bump."

Nat looked from Greg to Abe Bodner and rose from her seat on the railing. "I'm okay. I'll get some antiseptic for the scrape and put some ice on this." She winced as she gently probed the knot on her right temple. "You fellows go on back and get us some tuna for bait. The boat is fine now—all fixed—and I owe you for the last trip."

Abe Bodner gave her one more distressed look and returned to the stern with his fishing partner. Greg followed her a couple of steps toward the cabin, saw she was moving steadily and returned to his duties.

Nat stepped into the cabin to tug on her shirt and jeans over her wet swimsuit. Then she washed the scrape with soap and water and patted it dry. Greg was right. It was just a surface scrape. She sprayed on the antiseptic then turned her attention to her throbbing head. What she saw in the mirror was grim. The rudder had left a deep reddish purple line across her temple, down to the base of her cheek-bone.

"No doubt about it," Nat lamented. "It's going to be one fine shiner."

Nat had been back at the wheel for a half hour when Mac radioed for the second time. He just wanted to make sure everything was going all right on the *Calusa*. The first time he called had been before the boat had reached the reef or lost the propeller. This time when he radioed from the boat-house, Nat truthfully told him she was trolling east of the reef and her passengers were having a great time hauling in mackerel and marlin. Nat didn't mention trouble or propellers or keeper rings since she now had everything under control. She had managed to make the repairs without asking for help or taking anyone back at the lodge away from his job.

By Mac's third call, Abe Bodner had hooked a beautiful blue marlin and was screaming and fighting to bring it in. The creature pitched and flew into the air while Nat remained at the helm, cautiously watching the fish and coaching Bodner on his technique. All the while, she kept a towel full of crushed ice pressed against her bruised temple. The scrape on her arm was no problem. Now, after three hours, there was only a grim dull reddish stripe remaining.

Nat kept the charter out an extra hour to compensate for the lost time and the interrupted journey the week before. When she finally maneuvered the *Calusa* into Newfound Harbor, her right eye was swollen half closed, but her two passengers each had a blue marlin that would weigh in at over 250 pounds.

Mac was waiting on the dock along with Hector and Ben. All the other charters had already come in and were stowed in the boathouse.

Nat angled her boat in cautiously, letting the left side bump against the dock. She held her head tilted to the side so she could break the news of her mishap to them gradually.

"You're sure you didn't have any trouble, Nat? You sound a little—" Mac stopped cold when he saw the two fine marlin. "Whooo-whee!" he exclaimed. "No wonder you took your time!" He grinned broadly.

"You all right, Nat-a-lee?" Hector narrowed his eyes suspiciously because Nat hadn't come out of the shadows of the canvas-topped pilot house atop the *Calusa*.

Ben stared at her curiously. Nat busied herself at the console, ostensibly putting away some folded charts and empty glasses.

"You shoulda seen what this gal did." Bodner stepped out and began praising Nat's skills. "This darn boat threw a propeller. Just pitched it off ten miles out." He waved his hands as he spoke.

Nat could see a trace of a frown on Ben's face. One thing he didn't need was more trouble.

"But it didn't phase her," Bodner beamed. "She just hopped right in and fixed it—slick as can be."

Ben's expression stiffened.

"Yes, sirree," Bodner continued, as he looked over his shoulder at Nat as she climbed down the ladder from the pilot house. "She had us on our way again in no time," the enthusiastic angler declared.

"There was only one little problem." Nat spoke up at last as she reached the dock side of the boat, then turned to face the men. "I tried to get out of the way of a 'cuda and I bumped into the rudder." She tilted her head so they could see her right temple.

A series of gasps erupted. "It's just a bruise," she insisted as Hector burst into a stream of Spanish obscenities and leaped aboard for a closer inspection. Mac just stood where he was, openmouthed. Just behind him, Ben turned a peculiar shade of gray.

"It's all right." Nat flinched as Hector pulled her out into the full light of the low afternoon sun.

"And your *arm*—what about your arm?" Hector groaned as he bent to look closely at her scraped forearm. He clutched her wrist and held up the scrape for Ben and Mac to see.

"The prop got me. It's nothing—really," Nat said wearily.

"Better tell Maggie," Mac finally said. "She'll want to take a good look at it. She's gonna be madder than...." The rest was lost as he hastily left the dock area and took off across the parking lot for the lodge.

"Let's just get things unloaded so these gentlemen can take their prizes home." Nat took command of the confused scene. "I'm really quite all right. I've been out there most of the day like this. A few more minutes won't kill me."

Abruptly Hector, Ben and Greg shifted into fast motion. The marlin were lifted up by the hoist, the gear was unloaded, and the well emptied of mackerel and grouper. While they worked, Nat eased back into the fighting chair, reluctant to get too near the men. Her wound looked worse close up. She knew that for a fact.

When she saw Maggie, white-faced and wide-eyed, coming down the lodge steps two at a time, Nat felt a sudden rush of tears about to break. With three long-legged strides, Nat passed Greg and leaped out of the boat, dashing across the dock to meet Maggie and assure the woman that she was feeling better than she looked.

As Nat spoke, Maggie inspected first the eye, then the scraped arm. "You just come in and let me put something on these." Maggie pouted in an attempt to keep back her own tears. "This is really awful," she muttered in one breath, then promptly consoled Nat with "It isn't so bad," in the next.

"I hoped we could take care of this with a little less spectacle," Nat said, as Maggie insisted on helping her up the steps of the lodge.

"You must come around the back and give me a chance to fuss over you." Maggie whisked her through the kitchen and into the pleasant living room beyond. This was the inner sanctum, the private section along the back of the lodge where Mac and Maggie made their home.

Maria came in right after them, carrying a fresh ice pack. "Works better than steak," Maggie had insisted on the way through the kitchen, "and it smells a lot nicer."

Maggie dabbed on peroxide. She poked and prodded and muttered, but finally she went back to the ice pack, convinced that the scrape was clean and the puffy eye really wasn't as bad as it looked.

"I need a couple of aspirin." Nat winced slightly as she touched her fingertips to her tender temple once again. "And I think I'd like to go to my room and rest," she finally announced.

"I'll take you," Ben said from the hall doorway at the other end of the room. Apparently he had come in somewhere in the midst of Maggie's first aid. Nat couldn't read the dark, solemn expression on his face, so she hastily looked away. She was a sorry sight—and she knew it. She didn't want to look into Ben's eyes for further confirmation.

"I don't want to stir up any more trouble than necessary," Nat replied wearily. "I'll just wander up the path by myself if you don't mind." She wasn't being obstinate. She simply wanted to put a little distance between herself and everyone else.

"I'll walk along with you," Ben persisted. "You don't have to talk to anyone—not even me," he smiled weakly. "I'd just like to be sure you make it all right."

"Have it your way," Nat sighed. Without help

from anyone, she rose from the chair and started from the room.

"I'll send you some supper," Maggie proposed. "You tell Hector to come get it in a few minutes. *I'm* cookin' for you two tonight."

Nat nodded and kept walking.

"You eat before you go to bed," Maggie insisted. "Promise?"

Again Nat nodded as she left the living room.

Ben stayed beside her all the way to Beachside One. He didn't touch her or speak; he just matched his pace to hers and kept his eyes locked on her profile. Everyone else had taken a turn staring at the puffed, purplish eye. Ben was perceptive enough to stay on her "good" side, to avoid making an uncomfortable situation seem worse.

Hector came loping along the path behind them, anxious to see how successful Maggie's treatment had been. He caught up with them just as they reached the steps of the beach house.

"Before you guys start offering to tuck me into bed—" Nat turned on them with firmness "—just pretend it was Fuzzy or Greg, or even one of you who had been bumped. You'd expect them to manage on their own. Believe me, I can manage on my own, too." Her voice caught suddenly. "I would just prefer that you wouldn't hang around watching me." She turned away quickly so they couldn't see the two big tears inching their way down her cheeks. She had handled everything fine so long as they had been fishing, but now she was back on shore she couldn't tolerate looking grotesque.

"Maggie said she's cooking for you two tonight," Ben told Hector. "She wants you to pick it up."

Nat couldn't see, but she guessed that behind her Ben was motioning Hector off to the lodge.

"Sure." Hector started away. "I'll bring it down— soon," he concluded feebly as he left them alone.

Ben rested his hand on Natalie's shoulder. "I sure am sorry," he whispered. "I didn't expect you to go under to repair it."

"You would've done it if it had been your charter," Nat replied evenly.

"Sure, but—"

"I don't need any special concessions. I wanted you to see that I take my job seriously—and that I'm good enough to deserve to keep it. The rest of this was just bad luck," she added, with her bruised right temple and puffy eye turned away from him. "In a few days I'll be as good as new."

Ben smiled sadly and shook his head slowly. "You are quite a remarkable lady."

Natalie sniffed but said nothing.

"If you need anything," Ben stressed, "let me know." His hand slowly stroked her arm. "You get some rest."

Natalie stepped up the stairway into Beachside One and closed the door behind her, without looking back. She knew he was still standing there, but she didn't want to see the somber look in his eyes. And she didn't want him to see her crying. She was just one of the boys now—and boys don't cry.

NATALIE AWOKE AT DAWN the next morning, took one long, sorrowful look at her bruised face reflected in the hazy mirror and hurriedly dressed. The dark purple shiner was no longer swollen, but the deep reddish purple color was a chilling sight. The previous night Ben had sent Hector back with the message that Natalie was not to report to work the following day, but rather than stay locked up like an invalid, Natalie wanted to get out of there—away from the worried, caring eyes of her friends at the lodge.

"What happened to you?" Roger gasped when he pulled open his cottage door and found her standing there.

"You should see the other guy...." Nat tried to make a joke of her damage. "Actually, I was given the day off," she said, "the *whole* day, for service beyond the call of duty." Roger's blue eyes narrowed as he leaned closer to examine the bruise. Then he caught a glimpse of the scab along her forearm.

"What exactly did you battle with?" he asked with marked distress.

"I got under the boat to fix a propeller. Then I bumped my face and scraped my arm." She proceeded past him into the kitchen where she had left some of her painting gear. "It was nothing spectacular," she insisted. "Just an accident."

"You could have sliced your hands...." Roger wasn't reprimanding her. He was just stating a grim possibility.

"But I *didn't*," Nat stressed. "So how about spending the day with your technicolor student. If you can stand to look at me, I sure would like to do something productive."

"Let's take a lunch out to one of the sand keys," Roger suggested. "You, me and a few pelicans and driftwood. The sun doesn't look too bright today.

I'll pack the umbrella and a couple of straw hats and we can pretend that we're stranded.''

"I'd like that.'' Natalie began assembling the items she planned to take along. "I don't want to go anywhere public where some unsuspecting soul might stumble upon me. I'm tired of being examined and coddled. I could use a few hours of feeling inconspicuous.''

"I must admit—'' Roger tried not to stare at her "—you did give me quite a start when I first saw you.''

"I reacted the same way," Nat sighed. "And it is *my* face. But when I translated it all into gold, purple and a dash of alizarin crimson,'' she said, smiling, "naturally I thought of painting with you.''

"Naturally.'' Roger began rummaging through his refrigerator for picnic fare. "You and your eye for color,'' he chuckled.

The two of them staked out separate portions of the flat sand key that poked above the waves like the back of a partially submerged beige whale. Except for the striped beach umbrella that Roger erected on his end of the sandbar, the strip of land was almost barren.

Natalie collected several large, sun-bleached shells, rough and chipped from age and time, and placed them on the pale sand. Using pinks and beige and the palest ivory, she began to brush them into a new existence on her canvas, where tides and the hot sun would no longer wear away their beauty. Most of the day, Roger had labored intently over his own projects, but now he ventured down to Natalie's end of the sandbar and crouched beside her, regarding her work intently. "Those pastels almost fade into the canvas." His tone implied praise. "You've done a great deal with very little color. I don't suppose you'd be interested in giving that one to a certain blond-haired friend?"

"I'm afraid this one's already spoken for," Nat said quietly. She had wanted something for the wall of the beach house—something tranquil and pretty to make the place more comfortable and personal. "This one's for me," she said, smiling. "I've got something else planned for you, Roger. Something special. When it's ready you can have it."

"While we're on the subject of paintings—" he scratched a few lines in the sand while he spoke "—have you made any plans for the mangrove masterpiece?" When Nat failed to reply immediately, he looked up at her curiously.

"You did it for Ben Andress," he guessed. "I should have known. You were getting your inspiration from somewhere or someone." He smiled at her solemn, silent face. "Well, well," he chuckled. "Someone finally got under your skin."

"Let's just say that I find Ben very intriguing," Natalie hedged. "I've never met anyone quite like him. Not that it's going to be the romance of the century," she hastily added. "He isn't exactly consistent. He keeps me off balance. I never quite know what he thinks or why he is doing some of the things he does. There are a lot of things I *don't* know about him."

"That should make the two of you even," Roger replied. "There's a lot he doesn't know about you either. I'm sure he wonders where you go when you disappear from the lodge and spend hours here. He certainly must be impressed with the way you handle the charters, yet you surely aren't the run-of-the-mill seafarer.'' He sat back on the sand and looked at Nat uneasily. "Andress isn't a fool," he added pointedly. "It must have caught his attention by now that some of this sabotage business seems to coincide rather conspicuously with your arrival here."

"But nothing that has happened is my fault," Nat protested.

"I'm not suggesting it is," Roger stressed. "I'm just pointing out what may be Andress's perspective. If your relationship is becoming more than a business one—" he watched the color of Nat's cheeks deepen "—then perhaps it would be wise for both of you to clear the air a bit. Maybe you should tell him what you're doing here and why it's all so important to you."

"I can't do that yet." Natalie shook her head emphatically. "I want to keep the job *only* because I'm good at it," she explained. "I don't want anyone over at the lodge to make special concessions for me because of anything personal. *I* have to know that regardless of anything else, I can handle the charter job. In ten days, my trial month will be over and Ben has to decide if I stay on. As soon as he makes that decision, I'll tell him all the rest."

"If you last ten days," Roger said. "At the rate you're going, you may not make it." Natalie frowned and methodically began rinsing out her brushes in the seawater. Curling spirals of pinks and ivory mingled into the soft sweep of the waves.

"I suppose you heard there was a hijacking yesterday," Roger disclosed. Natalie stiffened and turned to stare at him. After her accident with the propeller of the *Calusa*, no one had disturbed her with any kind of news.

"No, I hadn't heard."

"Private boat—forty-two-foot Bertram—brand-new," he informed her. "Apparently the owner took it out on its maiden voyage just off Key West. He was found floating in a life jacket...with a bullet in his head."

Natalie's mouth dropped open, but not a word came out.

"Now you see why I'm concerned for your safety." Roger's blue eyes narrowed anxiously. "When you first told me about driving a boat, I thought it sounded relatively harmless. Now there are accidents and a murder. I don't like the thought of someone sending all this talent—" he waved toward her painting of the shells "—into the stomach of a shark."

At last Natalie took a breath. "That poor man...."

"You could be the next one," Roger persisted. "Someone seems to be out to get you...or at least the boat you're driving."

"Not now...." Natalie stood and looked out over the water. "This will be on all the news broadcasts and in the papers," she said dully. "They usually lie low for a while after something big like this hits the news. The Coast Guard and the police will really be on alert. But it's sure a shame...." Her voice trailed off.

"Maybe whoever *they* are won't be so accommo-dating," Roger noted. "They may have their own ideas about when to strike. And who's to say if the ones who did this in Key West are even remotely connected to whoever had been causing you trouble here. Didn't you say that some of these so-called amateurs are likely to show up anywhere? Maybe they don't know they're supposed to let things cool off for a while. I don't care what any of them are thinking,'' Roger fumed. "I don't want anything to happen to you.''

"I'll be very careful,'' Natalie promised. "I'll concentrate on every detail, and I won't take any risks. But you can forget about trying to get me to quit. I've come this far and I'm closing in on the end of the month. The hijackers will be wise to steer clear of me. I'll send out word that it simply isn't convenient for any further interference from them.'' Natalie tried to dispel his worry with her joke.

"And what message will you send to Ben Andress?'' he asked coolly. "What if he has a few questions that need answering?''

"They'll have to wait,'' Nat said firmly. "It just isn't the right time to go into all that...not yet.'' She stopped and contemplated the slightly amused expression on Roger's face.

"Inconvenient,'' he chuckled. "That's precisely how it was with Sue and me. Wrong time...wrong place...wrong finances,'' he laughed. "Inconvenient and unexpected. My dear, I have a feeling you're in more danger than simply from those seafaring hijackers. There may be a touch of the pirate in Andress.''

Nat turned solemn as she remembered what Ben had told her during their first confrontation in his office. He had gazed at her and said that she would bring out the pirate in a man. They were talking about the security of the boats and the crew members. . . but the prize she had almost given willingly to Ben Andress was something far more personal.

"Maybe I should meet this fellow," Roger offered. "I could have a nice man-to-man talk with him to see if his intentions are honorable. . . ."

"You'll do nothing of the sort," Nat gasped. "I've had two brothers and a father who interrogated every date I had in high school. . . and even a few while I was at college. I'm a big girl. . . and I don't need anyone running interference for me. Whatever Ben's intentions may be are my business. Right now, you and I had better agree that you will *not* do any detective work on my behalf. Roger. . . ." She stood with her hands planted on her hips, waiting for him to agree.

"This guy has really got through to you." He sounded delighted. "I've never seen you so. . . volatile. This is absolutely wonderful. No wonder your work has taken on a sudden tension and drama. You've fallen in love with what's-his-name. . . ."

"His name is Ben Andress," Nat stormed. "And I'm. . . ."

"Don't go any further." Roger stopped chuckling long enough to silence her. "Don't say anything that may not be true." He grinned smugly.

"Then I won't say anything at all," Nat answered. "And don't you say anything either. . . certainly not to Ben."

"Ben. . . ." He repeated the name quietly. "It has a certain charm," he teased.

"Roger...." Nat threatened him with a fistful of brushes.

"I shall remain silent," he promised. "I won't interfere in your inconvenient and unexpected relationship," he smirked. "But I'll join forces with Hector and dismember the brute if he hurts you, Natalie." His smile had faded abruptly, and there was no mistaking the serious tone in his voice. "Some of these beach types are said to be a little undependable when it comes to longterm ties. Romances may last a night...or a weekend...or a season," he warned her.

"*I'm* one of those beach types," she reminded him. "And I'll watch out for myself," Nat replied softly. "I didn't come here looking for romance. I'll stick to work."

"That's what I said the spring I went to New Orleans and ran into an antique dealer named Susan Fleury...."

"Roger, you have a terrible habit of undermining my nice, logical plans with your tales of true love."

"Just preparing you for the worst...or the best...depending on how you look at it," he defended himself.

"Well, I just wish you'd be consistent," she muttered.

"The only people who are consistent," he philosophized, "are those who refuse to be flexible."

"Then be a little less flexible," she said, grinning. "What we need here is a little iron will—unyielding to temptation and undaunted by adversity."

"What we need is to go in and steam a few pounds of shrimp and ask Jack Wilson to have dinner with us.'' Roger cast a concerned look at the dark clouds moving in from the Gulf of Mexico.

"I'm not interested in him, either," Nat cautioned her tutor. Roger had repeatedly tried to arrange for Nat and the Refuge manager, Jack, to spend some time together.

"Once he sees you in your current condition, I doubt if you'll have to fight him off. He may not be as enthusiastic as he was after your first meeting. You certainly don't look like the lovely young artist I introduced to him."

Nat lifted her slender fingers and lightly touched the bruised area surrounding her right eye. "I'd forgotten about this," she said softly. She had managed to spend the entire day so intent on her work that she'd become oblivious to the massive bruise. Only now did the realization revive the old feelings of self-consciousness that had driven her from the Gold Coast Lodge.

"I guess you have no intentions of matchmaking," she said. It wouldn't be too successful with her in that condition.

"None. This is a strictly friendship dinner," Roger insisted. "The poor guy spends all his time with deer and raccoons and diligent conservationists. He might enjoy an evening with some artsy types."

"Then let's go," Nat agreed. Cautiously she packed up all her art paraphernalia, depositing the seashell canvas in the center of the flat skiff, well away from the spray of the waves. Roger sat in the bow of the boat. Nat stayed in the stern so she could operate the outboard motor. Carefully she maneuvered around the pale sandbar off toward less isolated keys where small clumps of sprawling mangroves stretched their roots from solid land out into the spongy bottom of the shallow water. Gradually the falling leaves and debris would collect around the outermost roots, slowly building a new outcropping of land that would connect to the former. Then the roots and seed pods would drop farther out into the water, extending the islands by slight degrees until a new key was formed.

In silence, Nat and Roger wound their way through the scattering of green-shrouded islands. Occasionally they passed a grotesque skeleton of a dead tree—one of the many that had not survived the ravages of wind and water—still clinging to a half-eroded sandbar. There was something timeless and eternal about these trees, as if they embodied life's cycle of growth and decay, birth and death. The gnarled and sprawling mangroves filled her with awe, with serenity... but mostly with love.

CHAPTER SEVEN

NAT COULD TELL SOMETHING WAS WRONG the moment she walked into the lodge the next morning. All the men were seated at the breakfast table as usual, with the exception of Ben, but there was none of the customary grumbling and teasing that accompanied most meals. Maggie came around with the pot of steaming coffee, quickly refilling the cups, then she nodded toward the kitchen, indicating that Nat should follow her.

"It's her again," Maggie muttered as she hastily cracked two fresh eggs and plopped them on the griddle. "Here at the crack of dawn."

"Who?" Nat asked.

"Angela," Maggie replied with an indignant sniff. "You'd think she had enough men trackin' after her without having to keep after our Ben."

"Angela Sutton...." Nat recalled the dark-haired woman with the icy blue eyes.

"You just stay in here and eat in peace," Maggie insisted. "I wouldn't want to give her the opportunity to make something out of your shiner."

"Why on earth would she bother with me?" Nat accepted the plate of bacon and eggs from Maggie.

"She just might." Maggie avoided looking directly into Nat's eyes. "She's got a mean streak, that one."

"Is she going out on a charter today?" Nat inquired. "I'm supposed to take out the *Calusa*. It will be a little difficult to avoid her if she's on one of the charter boats."

"You've managed to avoid the rest of us for the past couple of days," Maggie replied testily. "You can certainly avoid her. Besides, she only came to see Ben. I doubt if she'll be hanging around the boathouse."

"Are you angry with me?" Nat asked quietly between bites.

"I've been a bit concerned about you," Maggie answered. "We all have. You certainly have made yourself scarce."

"I didn't have to work yesterday," Nat explained. "And I didn't want everyone feeling sorry for me. So I went off for the day."

"And a good part of the night," Maggie commented.

"I had dinner with a friend—in fact, two friends. I'm sorry if you were worried. Hector knew where I was."

"I wasn't the only one who was concerned." A slight smile tilted one corner of Maggie's mouth. Natalie arched her eyebrow in interest but kept on eating her breakfast.

"Aren't you going to ask me?" Maggie teased.

"All right," Natalie answered the smiling woman. "Who was concerned—besides you?"

"Ben. He's been finding all sorts of reasons to wander in here...not that I mind," Maggie chuckled. "Ben is very dear to me. But he wasn't comin' around to see me. I think he was hopin' to find you...or at least find out how you were doing." She lowered her voice. "He's really been upset about what happened to you."

"He's probably afraid I'll sue him," Nat said wearily. "You can assure him I have no intention of doing that."

"I don't think that was on his mind at all," Maggie admonished her young friend. "There's something more to it than that. I don't suppose you have any clues to his *personal* interest in this." A peculiar mischievous glint in Maggie's eyes made Nat once again focus her attention on her plate.

"Not the faintest," she murmured.

"Well, just in case there was some reason," Maggie continued, "I thought I should mention that a couple of summers ago, when Miss Fancy-pants was simply *Angie*, she and Ben had a little romance."

"I don't think you should be telling me this," Nat protested.

"You just be quiet and finish your breakfast," Maggie persisted. "Anyhow...when the summer ended, Angie simply took off for France on a tour with several of her friends...without so much as a fare-you-well. She was gone for over a month. When she came back, she had some foreign student in tow." Maggie clasped her plump hands in front of her. "Ben didn't say much, but I know it hurt him."

Natalie had stopped eating and stared, transfixed by the tale.

"The next spring, she was back again," Maggie reported. "Just smiling and being *so* cute." Her voice had a bitter edge. "I don't know what she told Ben, but he must have believed it. She started to invite him up to her father's place in Miami, to introduce him around her father's big fishing buddies,'' she muttered, ''so he could pick up a few lucrative charters. Apparently he didn't make enough money fast enough for her tastes,'' Maggie observed. ''By summer, she had joined the yachting set and her face was on the society pages every weekend...each time with a different fellow.''

''That's too bad,'' Nat whispered. She was beginning to understand why Ben had been so antagonistic about her expensive-looking sports car. Maybe he thought she was another Angela, drifting in for the season, slumming with the working class.

''And now she's back again....'' Maggie's eyes drifted to the kitchen door. ''I kinda hoped it wouldn't work this time.'' She turned a meaningful gaze toward Natalie.

''I see.'' Natalie lowered her eyes.

''I just wish Ben would see,'' Maggie declared. ''That woman is as transparent as they come. She just wants to snag him again—play him along for one reason or another. Then it will be the same story all over.''

''Maybe she's just here on business,'' Nat said grimly.

''At five-thirty in the morning?'' Maggie hissed. ''She didn't have to drive all the way down here just to schedule a charter,'' Maggie insisted. ''She knows how to use the telephone. If all she wanted was a charter, she could have called.'' Maggie's round face darkened with concern. ''No, sir, she's up to something. I sure wish I knew what it was.''

''I'm sure Ben will be able to handle whatever she

wants.'' Natalie tried to ease the older woman's distress. Natalie's own uncertainty was increasing as she stared into her coffee cup.

"I guess so," Maggie said without confidence. "But you just remember to stay out of her way. If she picks up on anything goin' on between you and Ben...she'll give you more trouble than you know." Suddenly Maggie glanced up at Nat's shiner. "Well, maybe not that kind of trouble," she amended, "but trouble nevertheless."

"I'll go straight to the boat," Nat promised. "She won't even notice me."

"So you say." Maggie retrieved the empty plate and shooed her on her way. Natalie pulled her white sun visor low over her forehead and made a hasty exit through the opposite end of the kitchen, heading into the hallway that led through the living quarters end of the lodge, avoiding the dining room. With long, rapid strides, she cut across the parking lot. Mac had already brought the boat around to the open dock, so Nat leaped onto the rear deck of the *Calusa* and looked over the equipment.

"Almost ready?" she asked Greg, who was dumping bait into the well.

"Yeah, but no sign of the two guys we're taking out," he replied. Natalie turned to scan the distant shell road for some sign of an incoming car. Then another figure crossed her line of vision—the dark-haired, petite form of Angela Sutton. Nat stepped up into the cockpit then bent down out of sight, diligently concentrating on the wiring of the depth finder.

"Didn't I see your lady captain come this way?"

Angela's clear voice called to Greg. Greg simply glanced at Nat and grunted something indistinct.

"Miss Bishop, are you aboard?" Angela inquired.

"I'm getting ready for a charter." Natalie stood, keeping her right side turned away from the other woman. "Did you want something, Miss Sutton?" she replied with the same formality Angela had used.

"I'd rather not have to discuss this from such a distance." Angela climbed aboard. "It has something to do with a social event...." She had reached the cockpit and now stared at Natalie's blackened eye. "My goodness, you do like to roughhouse with the boys," she breathed with exaggerated amazement.

"You wanted to speak to me?" Natalie replied without any visible show of emotion.

"Well, it is hardly appropriate now." Angela smiled a tight polite smile. "We're planning a cocktail party to kick off a conservationist tournament...." Her icy blue eyes were riveted on Natalie's bruise. "I had thought it might be amusing to have you there...perhaps stir up a few fellows who might bring you some additional business. I like to give Ben a little publicity whenever I can...." She batted her eyelashes at Greg who had paused in the midst of his preparations and stood watching the two women.

"Ben said there had been a couple of problems with the boats lately—expensive problems. I'm trying to stimulate business," Angela breathed.

"I'm sure Ben appreciates your help," Nat replied evenly.

"I certainly doubt if you'd make the right kind of

contacts if you showed up with that,'' Angela said, wrinkling her nose. "I'll just *tell* them about you,'' she asserted. "I'm sure Ben will charm the people all by himself.''

With another tight smile at Natalie and a flutter in Greg's direction, Angela stepped off the *Calusa* and onto the dock. A pale cloud of dust far up the shell road signaled the approach of Nat's passengers.

"Let's get out of here,'' Nat said between clenched teeth. Across the parking lot, Angela had already reached the steps of the lodge. "Stimulate business. . . .'' Nat brooded over the possible implications of that statement. She had an uneasy feeling that the business Angela meant might involve drugs as well as fish. "The right kind of contacts,'' Nat found herself repeating over and over in her head. If Angela Sutton was as tricky and conniving as Maggie said, she could be leading Ben into her circle of fast-living friends— many of whom would pay well for a delivery of cocaine.

"Oh, Ben,'' Natalie whispered as she stared toward the windows of the lodge. *Don't get involved,* she silently begged.

Two straw-hatted men emerged from the parked car and came briskly across the parking lot. "Sorry to keep you waiting,'' the heavier of the two called out. "We hope a few minutes one way or the other isn't too disastrous.''

"No problem.'' Natalie waved them aboard. The fishing trip would be unaffected by the delay, but the few minutes—those spent with Angela—were enough to ruin Nat's entire day. Perhaps even more disastrous than that, they might mean trouble for Ben.

Nat turned on the ignition and let the rumble of the engine fill the still air. *Nine days to go,* she noted. Nine days until the month trial period ended. Then she would find out where she stood—with Gold Coast Lodge and with Ben Andress. Then she'd make a point of determining Angela Sutton's role in Ben's life.

WHEN NAT BROUGHT HER BOAT IN after her charter, the *Southwind* was already secured in the boathouse and neither Hector nor Ben was anywhere in sight.

"What's the matter with you?" Natalie climbed up the two lower steps of Beachside One and found Hector forlornly staring into an open beer can.

"I've been volunteered," Hector replied dejectedly. "Ben is taking me to Miami next week—all week," he lamented. "I was gonna have a real date with Maria."

Natalie's sigh of disappointment was as much for herself as it was for her Cuban friend. "That's a real shame," she said with genuine regret. Apparently Angela got even more than she'd come after. She'd have both Ben and Hector on her home territory.

"I'm supposed to have Sunday dinner with Maria's family tomorrow," Hector groaned. "I was gonna ask her Uncle Louis if I could take her to a movie, maybe Tuesday. Now it's all messed up."

"How were you planning to get to the movie?" Natalie thought she knew what was coming next.

"I was gonna ask you if you and Roger wanted to go along with us," he replied sheepishly. "Really, I was gonna ask you tonight," he offered. "But it doesn't make any difference now."

"It sure doesn't," Nat agreed. Ben had obviously decided to accompany Angela, for whatever reason. "You're going to be gone the entire week?" Natalie eased the conversation back to the trip.

"Ben says it's some conservation thing," Hector reported. "Mr. Sutton wanted Ben to get in on it. Apparently it pays good," Hector conceded, "and Ben could use some money to make up for the days we lost fixing the engines."

Nat nodded in acknowledgment, wondering whether it was Angela or her father who was coming to Ben's financial rescue.

"There's some sort of party at the start of it." Hector filled in the details. "Then we go out five days straight after sharks—not to kill them, just to drag them alongside long enough to tag them. It's some sort of scientist's project." Hector jerked his shoulders indifferently. "Something about tracking them."

"And Charles Sutton has hired the *two* of you?" Natalie sounded vaguely relieved. It was possible that this would be strictly business—sports fishing business—after all.

"I don't think there will be any trouble." Hector tried to sound confident. "Ben wouldn't get me into anything that...that looks like trouble. Angela probably just wants to get her picture in the paper with Ben. Some magazine is supposed to be covering the story, too. There'll be lots of social stuff," he muttered, "between meetings."

"Social stuff?" Natalie was disturbed to hear there might be a number of gatherings where contacts and deals could be made.

"They're having food and drinks and stuff between the meetings and the tagging. Some scientist guys will be talkin' about sharks and things. Ben said I didn't have to go to any of that. I just work the boat on the trips out. When we're docked, I stay on board and keep an eye on the boat."

"While he goes to meetings and dinners and makes new acquaintances," she said bitterly.

"Yeah, Ben and Mr. Sutton and An-gee-la," Hector acknowledged. "They get to rub shoulders with the fancy people who are putting on this shark hunt."

"I sure hope Ben knows what he's doing," Natalie sighed and stalked up the stairway into Beachside One. She slammed the door and sat down on the army cot. Apparently Angela had done it again. Whatever she had that had drawn Ben back to her time after time—whether it was romance or the lure of money—was still working. And there was nothing Natalie could do about it. At least not this week.

She leaned back across the small cot while two forlorn tears trickled from the corners of her eyes. Ben had said he would do *anything* to keep his business—and now Nat wondered just how much "anything" might include. Her mind turned back to the night Ben had swooped her into his arms and invited her into the dark seclusion of his old cruiser.

"If we had made love," she brooded, "would things be any different now? Would Angela have lost her hold on Ben?" But there was no way of knowing what would have happened after that night. If they had made love to each other, if they had spent the night holding each other in the wide bed in the cabin where they had first set eyes on each other, it might still have turned out this way.

Natalie sat bolt upright at the thought. Angela had a long head start with Ben. Regardless of what Nat might mean to him, Angela could still walk back into Ben's life and lure him away. "And then where would I be?" Nat murmured. "Moping around feeling miserable," she sniffed. "Just like now—only worse."

Resolutely she changed into a brightly flowered sundress and touched a few daubs of makeup over her unsightly shiner. "Come on, Hector," she called to her housemate. "Put on a clean shirt. We're not going to sit here and feel sorry for ourselves," she declared. "We're going to pick up Roger and maybe even Jack Wilson." She hurried him along. "Then we're going to find a nice pizza parlor, and we're going to stuff ourselves."

Hector moved with uncharacteristic speed. The prospect of good food had that effect on him. Arm in arm, they pranced to the little car parked between two shade trees. "Do you have a license?" Nat hesitated as she got out her car keys. Hector looked at the red Mustang hungrily, but he shook his head no.

"I don't have a car, and I don't have a license either," he confessed.

"Then we'll have to work on that," Nat proposed. "You could use some transportation—especially if you plan to go out on any dates." She winked with her unbruised left eye. "In our idle moments—" she forced a smile "—I'll teach you to drive, and I'll help you study for the driving test. I'll even lend you my car to take the examination in.'' She slid behind the wheel and reached over to unlock his door.

"You want to start tomorrow?" Hector eyed her cautiously. "Like at dinner time?"

Natalie sighed and turned to glare at him. "Do you mean that you *don't* have a ride to Maria's house?"

"I was gonna ask you," Hector moaned. "Really, Nat-a-lee," he grinned at her like a child caught misbehaving.

"Knock off the phony charm." Nat switched on the ignition. "I've had enough phony charm to last me a lifetime." She could still see Angela Sutton's cold blue eyes and her tight little nicey-nice smile as she pretended to be so thoughtful by drawing Ben into her circle of affluent friends.

Natalie's car moved abruptly from the grassy area onto the shell parking lot. The tires spun, sending a cloud of sand and dust into the air. Nat's frustration had increased the pressure on the gas pedal.

"I sure hope *this* isn't my first lesson." Hector clutched the armrest and stiffened his legs to brace himself.

"No, but it sure might be one for me," Nat observed. When it came to thoughts of Ben, she had to face the fact that his actions were beyond her control. Proceeding at a much more reasonable speed, she pulled across the parking lot onto the shell road that led to the highway. On the last turn, she swerved aside to let the approaching disreputable-looking Jeep have the right of way on the narrow road. Just before it passed her on its way to the lodge, Nat glanced into the dark, curious eyes of its driver—Ben Andress.

"Talk about poor timing," Natalie sighed. Roger had said he'd met Sue at the wrong time, in the wrong place and with the wrong finances. *But at least he wasn't too late,* she noted silently. With Ben, Nat hadn't been quite that lucky.

"DRINK YOUR JUICE, take your vitamins, and keep putting hot and cold compresses on that eye," Maggie Butler prodded Natalie. "It isn't over yet," she insisted as she poured Natalie's glass full of juice for the third time. No one was pleased that Hector and Ben had gone off to Miami with the Suttons, but Maggie wouldn't let her distress show. "Ben said it was a business trip," Maggie insisted. "He said he'd be sitting in on some seminars about sharks and their tracking procedures. Just maybe, it isn't as bad as it seems."

"Right," Nat replied without enthusiasm. Ben and Hector had been gone for most of the week, and Maria had been just as depressed as Natalie.

"At least when he gets back, you'll be as pretty as ever," Maggie continued hopefully. "All this vitamin C and vitamin E and compresses...." She bent forward to peer at the injury. "It's really clearing up," she smiled.

"I wish I could say the same for the weather," Natalie responded. Mac had called off the charters for the day and rescheduled an outing he was guiding into the shallow Gulf side because of the shroud of low gray clouds that had settled over the central Keys. The steady drizzle had begun well before dawn and showed no signs of lessening as the morning progressed.

"If it's any consolation, it's raining in Miami, too," Maggie noted. "Ben and Hector are probably sound asleep on the *Southwind*, enjoying a day off like the rest of us." Even she frowned at the unconvincing ring to that story.

The sound of heavy footsteps echoed through the empty dining room as some refugee from the storm made his way toward the kitchen. "You seen Natalie?" he called out. Mac stopped when he caught a glimpse of the honey-haired captain.

"My goodness, what's wrong?" Maggie stared at her husband. Mac's worried face peered out from under his slouchy hat.

"I sure hope it isn't bad news—" he beckoned to Natalie "—but some gal is on the phone—person-to-person and long distance for you." Natalie leaped to her feet and started out the door after him.

"Wait for me," Maggie insisted and trailed along after the two of them. "Oh, dear," she muttered over and over as she hurried along.

"Hello. Yes, this is Natalie Bishop...." Nat's heart thundered as she waited to hear the voice on the other end.

"Janie?" Her voice rose to a squeak of anxiety. Mac and Maggie stood beside her, staring at her expression for any indication of the content of the message.

"Oh...no," Nat groaned. "When?" Two more oh, nos followed, then there was a long silence. Finally Nat glanced from Mac's anxious face to Maggie's. The two of them were obviously in torment over the unknown plight of their friend. "Let me call you back." Natalie finally calmed the speaker on the other end. "In a few minutes," she assured the caller.

As she hung up the receiver, Nat raised one palm to reassure her two companions. "It's bad news for me...but it isn't the usual type of bad news," she said calmly. "Let's all go and have a nice soothing cup of coffee, and I'll tell you the details." Mac and Maggie breathed a joint sigh of relief and headed back to the kitchen.

"The bad news," Nat began glumly, "is that my father has finished his shrimping trip a little early. He's letting my brothers bring the trawlers back... and he's flying to Atlanta."

Mac, Maggie and now Maria stared at her in bewildered silence. None of them knew anything about the father, brothers, or the trawlers that Natalie mentioned. Nat looked up at their blank faces.

"Maybe I'd better back up a little more," she reconsidered. "I'm supposed to be in college in Atlanta, while my father and my two brothers are out shrimping. I finished school a quarter early so I could come here to get some experience with a charter outfit before I tell my family that I'm not going to teach art after I graduate in June. I need to do something physical, something near the water—" she struggled to communicate her dilemma "—because something inside me needs it. If I can make a living running charters and paint in my off time, when the inspiration is there...."

The light was beginning to go on in Maggie's gray eyes. "You mean your father is on his way to visit you up there...at the college," Maggie said, "and here you are with us?" Now Mac began nodding in comprehension.

"I didn't want my father to know about this charter idea until I was sure I could do it well enough to support myself," Natalie admitted. "I've been working on my paintings in my off-duty hours. They're the best things I've ever done. I've even worked on some for you." She glanced from one bemused face to the next.

"Maria knows that I paint...." Natalie wasn't sure if she needed a witness. Dark-eyed Maria nodded solemnly to corroborate her statement.

"I've been working with an artist over at Big Pine Key," Natalie sighed. "I didn't want anyone to figure out what I was doing. I wanted everyone to think that I was giving my full effort to the job here...which I have been doing." She looked from Maggie to Mac and saw that they were not about to dispute that fact.

"It isn't as irresponsible as it sounds," Natalie insisted. "I really thought I could work out all the rough spots and show myself—and my dad...and Ben—that I could handle the job with no special considerations." Nat gazed up apprehensively. "If I had made it a few more days," she stressed, "just long enough to convince Ben he should keep me through the summer, I would have told you everything."

"You sure had plenty to tell." Maggie shook her head and chuckled.

"When is your father getting into Atlanta?" Mac asked abruptly. "Maybe we could get you those extra days you wanted." His weathered face crinkled into a smile.

"He'll get there the day after tomorrow...Saturday afternoon," Natalie replied. "I've got charters scheduled every day," she added glumly.

"You could fly up after work," Maggie suggested. "When you finish visiting with your father, you could catch a later flight back." Natalie was already shaking her head. It simply wouldn't work.

"My father bought me that little car I drive. If I didn't show up in it, he'd worry that something had happened to it. Besides," she continued, "he likes me to drive him around up there. He hates all that traffic."

"Then you take a little longer. . .and you drive up there," Maggie suggested.

"My dad will be staying till Sunday. I usually drive over to the hotel and have breakfast with him. . .so he can see that I'm eating well." She smiled. "Then I take him to the airport. He won't leave until almost noon. Even if I hurried, I'd have to miss two days of charters, then I'd have the long drive back." She raised her large, sad eyes to Maggie's. "It wouldn't be fair to the passengers or to the charter business," Nat noted. "Ben would have more than enough reason to have me replaced."

"Now don't let's get ahead of ourselves," Mac soothed.

"It was worth a try," Natalie smiled bravely. "But it's time to call it quits. I'll just cable my dad and tell him to alter his plans. I'll tell him that I'll be waiting at home in Key West."

"Now if I take over your charters for Saturday and Sunday," Mac proposed, "and if we found some way to pacify Ben. . . ."

"Mac. . . ." Maggie gave him a gentle nudge.

"Now, Maggie," he continued, "Greg will do the hard work." He turned his bright eyes back to Natalie. "You took a real long shot getting into something like this," he acknowledged. "So it must be pretty darn important to you. If this is what you want to do, there's no sense caving in this close to the end of your month. You get your things packed," he ordered. "And you get a lot of rest today... we both will." He looked at Maggie. "After your charter in the morning, you take off for Atlanta. The fellows and Maggie and I will hold things together until you get back."

"What about Ben?" Natalie frowned.

"If this rotten weather holds, we may have to postpone a few charters here—" he smiled slyly "—and Ben may get hung up in Miami. If he doesn't get in till Sunday, he'll never have to know a thing," he added hopefully. "One way or another," Mac assured her, "we'll work it out."

"I'll take care of Ben," Maggie promised.

"When the time comes, we'll just do whatever we think is best." Mac refused to surrender. "If it comes down to it, we'll tell him the truth." He narrowed his eyes at Natalie. "You keep in mind that you're a darn good captain. Even Ben knows that. You come back here safely, and we'll face him together. You've come this far—" Mac hugged her "—we'll stick with you the rest of the way."

"You don't know how much this means to me," Natalie said, trying to sniff back the tears that threatened to overflow.

"I'm beginning to learn," Maggie said softly. "Now finish your juice and take a couple more vitamins. Put another compress on that bruise while you take your nap."

Dutifully Natalie downed the remaining juice in her glass. She left the trio at the table and walked once more out into the lodge foyer. She stopped by the telephone and dialed a direct call to Atlanta.

"Please get my bed ready," she told Janie Hitchcock. "I'll be driving up tomorrow...and I won't get into Atlanta till early Saturday morning—very early. I'll just flop into bed and sleep a few hours." She listened for a moment while Janie replied.

"Be sure to tell all the girls that I'll be there. Tell them *not* to act surprised if they see me strolling around," Natalie added. As far as her father was concerned, everything was to appear normal.

Taking a deep breath, Natalie strode out into the drizzle and hurried along to the beach house. "Take this one day at a time," she mumbled, trying to keep calm. "And don't quit yet."

CHAPTER EIGHT

"NATALIE. . . ." Janie Hitchcock gently nudged the sleeping form. "It's almost noon." Janie stood and waited while Natalie stretched and moaned. Almost apologetically Janie spoke again. "Natalie, you said to wake you at noon."

"I'm moving," Natalie replied without rolling over. She wriggled one bare foot back and forth to indicate that she was in fact moving. "Let me have a couple of minutes to pry open my poor eyes," Natalie pleaded. "Has my dad called yet?"

Janie plopped down on the adjacent bed and smiled sympathetically at Natalie. "No call yet," she reported. "How are you feeling?"

"Like I drove all night," Natalie groaned.

"That's appropriate," Janie chuckled. Natalie had left the Keys at two o'clock Friday afternoon and had driven straight through to Atlanta along the interstate. At seven that morning, as commuter traffic was beginning to crowd the eight-lane highways of Atlanta, Natalie had reached her destination.

"Maybe you could get a few more hours of sleep before your father comes." Janie looked at the weary face of her friend.

"He'll expect to see me sparkling clean and smiling," Nat countered. "I can still smell the salt water in my hair,'' she remarked, brushing back a few loose strands. ''And the Braves are playing at the stadium tonight.'' She had heard that on an all-night radio station during the long drive. ''You know how my dad loves a baseball game.'' Natalie finally cracked both eyes open. ''I'll have to go to pick up some tickets.''

''Oooooh, my!'' Janie leaned forward and inspected the remnants of Natalie's shiner. ''I love the touches of lavender around your eye.'' She made a clicking sound with her tongue and shook her head reproachfully. ''You said the work was hard,'' she commented, ''but you didn't say they beat you.''

''It was an accident.'' Natalie tugged herself into a sitting position. ''Do you think we can cover it up with makeup?'' She tilted her chin up so Janie would have an unobstructed view of the damage.

''How about an eye patch?'' Janie wrinkled her nose. ''It would fit in nicely with your nautical occupation.'' She reached over to touch the discolored tissue lightly. ''It's not going to be easy to make you look normal,'' she asserted. ''In the first place, you don't usually wear makeup. Your dad is used to seeing *your* paint on a canvas.'' She grinned at her own cleverness.

''What's the *second* place?'' Natalie prodded her roommate to get on with the diagnosis.

''In the second place,'' Janie said gravely, ''the makeup it would take to cover this may make you look like a painted floozie. I don't want to be an accomplice to such corruption,'' she proclaimed with feigned innocence.

''A painted floozie?'' Natalie gasped melodramatically. In their years of rooming together, Janie's flamboyance had done wonders to erode Natalie's own cautious reserve. Janie was a theater major who never really left the stage. She created one wherever she happened to be, filling every conversation with broad, dramatic gestures and off-the-wall comments. Fortunately for Natalie, some of Janie's ebullience had been contagious.

"I've really missed you," Natalie burst out in a giggle, as Janie flounced across the room in a pantomime of a floozie.

"Did you miss me enough to change your mind and run off to New York with me after we graduate?" Janie teased.

"Not that much," Natalie replied honestly. "I had just forgotten how long it was since I had a good laugh. You always manage to cheer me up." Now Janie's eyebrows arched in sincere curiosity.

"Is something wrong down there that you need some cheering up?" she asked, picking up on Natalie's comment. "You mean everything is not pleasant in paradise?"

"It's been a little bit more difficult than I'd expected," Natalie sighed. It wasn't just the physical strain but the emotional conflicts that had weighed upon her.

"You can always change your mind," Janie persisted. She had never endorsed Natalie's adventure. It was only because they were good friends that she had allowed herself to become the middleman in Natalie's mailing system.

"It may already be over," Nat said solemnly. "When I get back to the Keys, I have to face a very uncompromising gentleman. It's up to him whether I get to finish the season or get sacked on the spot.''

"No wonder you're depressed." Janie moved over and sat beside her. "Come on. You get cleaned up and I'll take you out to lunch. I'll even go to the ticket office with you and pick up tickets for the ball game. See how nice I am?" she joked. Nat had to smile again. If there was anything Janie Hitchcock hated, it was sports events. "All that fuss over a little ball. . . ."

"You're a true friend," Nat replied.

"One who could use a few original N. Bishops to adorn the walls of my New York penthouse." Janie waved her long fingers along an imaginary wall. "When I'm the toast of Broadway," she added.

"If you want paintings, you'll get paintings," Nat agreed. "You've done so much for me."

"Of course I have," Janie asserted, grinning. "So you go shower and I'll try my own brand of artwork on your lovely face." She herded Natalie off toward the bathroom. "It would have to be the right side," Janie muttered. Nat gave her a quizzical look.

"When you drive your father around town," Janie noted, "that's the side facing him." Now it was Natalie's turn to grimace in distress. "Never mind, never mind," Janie rallied. "We'll do something with your hair. Droop it over one side," she suggested. "You know, the sultry-wench look." She tossed her own dark hair dramatically.

"I guess sultry wench is an improvement on painted floozie," Natalie giggled again.

"I shall get my curling iron hot and meet you in the boudoir." Janie flounced off with a flutter of her long eyelashes.

Natalie stood beneath the steaming spray, with billows of foamy shampoo rolling down her back. The long thick braid that she had worn while she worked on the charters was easy and natural, she mused, but the thought of letting her streaked hair flow, of dressing up in something soft and feminine appealed to her. *Papa Bishop would like it.* Natalie smiled under the coursing water of the shower. He'd like to sit in the stadium, watching the Braves play ball and to have a tall, lovely lady at his side. It had been a long time since she'd felt like a lady. Maybe it would be just the thing to lift her spirits, and, at least for a while, she could forget about Ben Andress.

Just before Natalie and Janie left the sorority house, they stopped to post a note by the bulletin board. "If my father calls, please tell him I'm out getting tickets to the ball game tonight. Have him leave his number, and I'll call him as soon as I get in." It was signed Natalie Bishop.

"He usually has some business to attend to," Natalie explained to Janie. "Either he'll get some gadget for the boats, or he'll check with the Fisheries Bureau about shrimping conditions off the coast." She crossed the grassy strip that separated the old sorority house from the parking area on the adjacent lot. "We'll catch up with each other sometime this afternoon."

"Just keep draping that hair over your eye, and he won't notice anything alarming." Janie smiled with satisfaction at how well she had camouflaged Nat's bruised temple. "He may think you look a little tired," Janie sighed, "but he'll assume it's from laboring over your studies. At least he'll be close to the truth with that," she conceded.

"I'm afraid 'close to the truth' is all he's been getting for a while now," Natalie frowned. "I'm sorry it all has to work out like this," she admitted, "but my father is *so* hardheaded."

"You don't have to tell me," Janie countered. "I've lived with his daughter for two years. Hardheadedness is a Bishop family trait."

"It certainly is," Natalie acknowledged. "But up until now, my father and I have managed to be hardheaded about different things. I've always complied with his wishes...and avoided an open confrontation. When I finally face him with this one, I'd like to be able to make a reasonable, convincing case for myself."

"With a little more luck, you'll do just that." Janie tried to sound confident. "Just three and a half weeks till graduation," she calculated. "Your dad will be so proud that a Bishop graduated from college, he'll probably go along with anything you choose to do."

"I'm counting on that," Natalie said grimly as they reached her car. "When I finally tell him what I've been up to, I intend to remind him that I tried it his way first."

"So what are we worried about?" Janie tried to lighten the somber tone of their conversation. "A little dinner, a ball game, breakfast in the morning, a trip to the airport...." She ticked off Natalie's schedule. "What could possibly go wrong?"

ATLANTA STADIUM's loudspeaker system broadcast a loud organ fanfare into the cool evening air as the baseball players took their places on the field waiting for the game to begin. The huge circular concrete stadium with its upper tiers of bright red seats and lower tiers of two shades of blue opened above the playing area to the graying evening sky. It was still light enough for the game to get under way without the giant clusters of overhead floodlights that would eventually fill the arena with a harsh, almost surrealistic light. For now, the light was subdued and the outside sounds of downtown Atlanta were muffled in the immense enclosure.

Natalie settled back into her seat, sighing in relief, as Bill Bishop's attention became riveted on the action taking place on the grassy playing field below. It was early in the season, so almost the entire red upper section and large portions of the blue seats were unoccupied, but it made no difference to Bill Bishop. He leaned forward, hands clasped between his knees, staring intently at the infield. All he wanted was to see a ball game.

Natalie had chosen the seat on her father's right side, so even if the wind should blow her hair back from her face, the slight discoloration along her temple would be on the side farthest away from him. Finally able to relax, Natalie followed the first few innings, occasionally shifting her attention to the scattered sports fans who filled the lower sections of the stadium.

Gradually the color was fading from the circle of sky above the field, and section by section the stadium lights went on. Now the Braves' crisp white uniforms with red-and-blue trim appeared more dazzling against the bright green infield. Natalie found herself smiling in spite of her weariness.

"How about some popcorn?" her father leaned over and suggested. "I'll pay, you go get it."

"I suppose you could put up with a nice cool beer to go with it?" Natalie draped a long, tanned arm across his shoulders.

"I sure could," Bishop grinned. He peeled several bills from his wallet without even lifting his eyes from the base runner.

"Back in a few minutes." Natalie patted his arm, but Bishop was inching forward in his seat, intent on the next pitch. Smiling to herself, Natalie climbed the stairs to the landing and headed through an exit ramp toward a refreshment booth. Moments later, armed with two overflowing boxes of buttered popcorn and one paper cup full of beer, she stepped back into the open stadium and stopped in mid-step. Her father was no longer bent forward observing the game. He was leaning back in his seat conversing cheerfully with the dark-haired man sitting one row behind him. Bill Bishop stood and shook the man's hand and invited him to move down a row so they could enjoy the game together. None of the exchange would have been particularly surprising, if the dark-haired man hadn't happened to be Ben Andress.

Natalie stood motionless for several minutes, clutching the still-warm popcorn and squeezing the paper cup until the foam on the beer began to trickle over the sides. Finally bracing herself for the encounter, Natalie descended the narrow stairs until she reached the two men.

"You'll never guess where this young fella is from." Bishop grinned as he relieved Natalie of her containers. Without waiting for a reply, her father went on enthusiastically, "He's from the Keys. He just happened to be up here for the weekend and we started talking." He was obviously pleased with his discovery. "He even knows your Uncle Buzz," Bishop continued, oblivious to the look of amazement on her daughter's face.

"Come on, sit down, Natalie," he insisted. "Oh, this is my daughter, Natalie," Mr. Bishop said, introducing them. "Andress. Ben Andress." He tilted his head to the man on his left.

"I think I may have seen you somewhere before," Ben said with a slight smile. "Either you or someone who bears a striking resemblance to you. Nice to meet you, Natalie," he said politely, then settled back, just like her father, his eyes fixed on the action on the ball field. Natalie managed to mumble a response and sink into the seat next to her father. Stunned and rigid, Natalie stared straight ahead, afraid to glance over at either of the two men.

"You say you run a charter outfit?" Bill Bishop spoke with interest. He passed one container of popcorn back to Nat.

"On Little Torch Key," Ben replied easily. "That's how I got to know your—" he hesitated as a batter swung at the ball and missed "—brother-in-law." Ben cast a sidelong glance at Nat, smiled and continued. "Yes, Buzz Cochran has taught me a lot about repairing and restoring boats."

Natalie anxiously stuffed some buttered popcorn into her mouth.

"He's quite a guy," Mr. Bishop agreed. "He used to take Natalie off to the shop with him when the boys and I were out shrimping. He'd let her crawl right in and haul things apart. He'd have made her his partner if I'd have let him.'' He took a sip of beer, then chuckled. ''Worst thing is, Natalie would have gone along with him. Thicker than thieves, those two,'' he asserted.

''And are you still interested in boats, Miss Bishop?'' Ben leaned farther forward so he could glance past Bishop and watch Natalie's profile.

Natalie licked her lips apprehensively, then ventured a look in Ben's direction. The pleasant tone of his voice did not match the chilling intensity of his eyes.

''I'll always love boats,'' Natalie replied softly.

''And are you and Buzz going into business together?'' he persisted.

''No, sirree,'' Bill Bishop said. ''Nothing like that for Natalie. She's done with the smell of diesel fuel and fish. She's an artist,'' he pronounced proudly. ''She paints and draws beautifully. She's going to teach art,'' he boasted. ''She's in college up here. Graduates in June,'' he noted. ''She's the first Bishop to get a college education.''

''An artist,'' Ben said quietly. ''I'm sure you're very proud of her.'' He addressed his comment to Mr. Bishop whose eyes had never left the ball field.

''Proud of myself as well,'' Mr. Bishop chuckled. ''If she'd had her way, she'd have stayed in the Keys like her brothers—I couldn't pay them to go away to college. But there was Nat, right beside them, trying to work a man's job, and when she wasn't working she'd be out fishing or poking around underwater after all kinds of critters. No, the Keys can be rough on a woman. If she'd stayed, she would've ended up

weatherbeaten and tough like the rest of us Conchs."
He turned to grin at Ben. "I didn't want that for my
daughter," he declared firmly. "I want her to be a
lady—a fine, gentle lady—who can paint so pretty it
makes your heart break." He rested his rough hand
on Natalie's arm. "She wouldn't admit it, but she
turned out even better than I dreamed."

"I'm sure she did," Ben responded solemnly.
Natalie closed her eyes briefly and took a deep
breath. The calm, polite conversation was keeping
her nerves on edge. It was like the placid, still period
before a tropical storm. Natalie simply wished the
deluge would begin. At least then she would know
what Ben was doing here.

In the fifth inning, the Atlanta Braves had a comfortable nine-to-two lead over the Chicago Cubs, so
Bill Bishop decided to stretch his legs. "Anything I
can get you two?" he asked his companions. "Coke,
a beer. . .a hot dog?" He glanced from one to the
other.

"Nothing for me," Ben replied politely.

"Natalie?" Bill Bishop looked down at his daughter.

"Nothing for me either, daddy," Nat responded,
sounding more like a little girl than she intended.

"Let me know if I miss anything important." Mr.
Bishop patted Ben's shoulder. He stepped past Natalie and climbed the aisle stairway, leaving Natalie and
Ben together, with just one empty seat separating
them.

"Well. . . ." Ben spoke first.

"Well, what?" Natalie refused to look at him.

"Are you enjoying the game?" Ben asked quietly. Natalie wasn't sure what game he was discussing.

"What are you doing here?" She turned to face him. "I thought you were in Miami." She had to bite her lip to avoid adding "with Angela."

"I came back early. You were gone. I took out your charter this morning, then my curiosity got the better of me and I flew up to see for myself what kind of double life you were leading." There was still no warmth in those dark eyes.

"I thought Mac was—"

"Covering for you," Ben interrupted. "He sometimes takes on more than he can handle." He watched her closely. "Maybe you'd never noticed, but Mac doesn't take the deep-sea charters out— except on rare occasions."

"This was a rare occasion," Nat replied evenly. "I didn't know that my father was going to drop in for a visit."

"Did you know that Mac has a heart condition?" Ben shot back. "Didn't anyone ever explain why Mac runs the business end and the shallow-water trips?" He stopped and stared at Nat's shocked expression. Ben took a slow breath and calmed himself. "No one told you," he noted flatly.

Natalie shook her head from side to side. "Mac insisted that he could take care of my charters. I wouldn't have asked him," Natalie said softly. "My mother had a heart condition. . . ." Her voice was barely audible. Her long slender fingers moved to the gold chain at her neck, the one her mother had given her for Christmas the year she died. "I wouldn't have asked. . . ." Nat's voice trailed off.

"And Maggie didn't put up any argument?" Ben quizzed.

"She told me not to give up," Natalie answered. Suddenly her eyes widened. "He is all right, isn't he?" she gasped. "Mac didn't have an attack—"

Ben was already shaking his head as he moved into the seat next to her. Now his arm stretched along the back of her seat, and his hand brushed her shoulder. "He's fine," Ben assured her. "It just wasn't a very smart thing for him to take on."

"I'm sorry." Nat couldn't think of anything else to say.

Ben let the silence linger for a moment, then glanced over at her. "How's the eye?" He reached out and touched her hair gently. The intimacy of the gesture sent a ripple of pleasure through her.

"Better." Natalie turned her head slightly so he could see that the traces of purple were almost entirely gone.

"I had a little trouble spotting you in the stands," he commented. "I kept searching for the *other* Natalie—long legs and swaying braid." The coldness had left his eyes. "But once I saw. . . still *another* you—" he stopped when Nat raised her gaze to him "—I began to realize how much I didn't know about you." He stared at her as a lopsided smile tilted one corner of his mouth. "I think you and I had better have a long talk," he said, finally breaking the next silence.

"I think so," Nat whispered.

"Let's just call a truce for tonight," he suggested. "Maggie said you were driving back tomorrow. Let me drive with you. We'll talk then."

Natalie nodded in agreement. By now Bill Bishop

had completed his tour of the facilities and returned, bearing a cardboard tray heaped with hot dogs and iced soft drinks. Ben eased back over into his own chair, then stood to help the older man with his load.

"I know you two said you weren't hungry," Mr. Bishop commented, "but the stuff smelled so good. I figured if I came back with just one, I'd have to fight you off." He handed out the food and drinks as he explained. "By the way did I miss anything?" he asked Ben.

Ben looked hastily toward the huge computer-controlled scoreboard. He had not been paying any attention to the action on the field while Mr. Bishop was gone.

"Nothing much happened," Ben reported vaguely. Fortunately, no one had scored in the interim. "And thanks for the hot dogs," he added, to change the subject abruptly. "They look great."

Mr. Bishop settled back down between the twosome. With a hot dog in one hand and a cold drink in the other, each was again attentive to the final innings' action on the field.

When the game was nearly over, Bill Bishop had related the family saga from the early settlers in the Bahamas through their migration to Key West, up to the building of the two-trawler shrimp business that the men in the Bishop family ran. "I've been checking on shrimping in the Gulf." Bishop spoke easily with Ben. "Too many boats in the area," he said, frowning. "I think the boys and I will try the Georgia coast next week. I want to be near enough to the Keys for all of us to make it up for Natalie's graduation."

"When is that?" Ben made it sound like casual conversation.

"Ninth of June." He named the date with pride. "Even Buzz said he'd drag his old bones up here to see our girl," Mr. Bishop grinned.

"I'm sure it will be a proud day for all of you." Ben leaned back and glanced over at Natalie. "No one should miss it," he said with a smile.

"Say, would you like to stop off for a drink or a cup of coffee?" Bishop suggested as the game reached the top of the final inning with the Braves ahead by three runs. "Natalie has her car. If you're driving, you could follow us to the hotel."

"I had intended to get a taxi back," Ben began.

"No such thing," Mr. Bishop insisted. "Natalie can drop you off after we have a quiet drink together. I can't tell you how much I enjoyed having you to talk with tonight. Natalie only comes along to humor me." He winked. "At least you keep up with the action."

"I certainly enjoyed spending the time with you," Ben replied, returning the compliment. "How about letting me take the two of you out for a drink?" he offered. "It's only fair, since you bought the food here."

"You are a real gentleman." Mr. Bishop slapped Ben on the shoulder. "That's what I want for Natalie. Some nice, rich, well-mannered fella who will hire a maid and let Nat spend all her time painting." He leaned closer to Ben. "I know too much about the life of the working man to want her to end up with the likes of me. I made sure she became a lady," Bill Bishop insisted, "and I plan to keep her a lady."

The stadium emptied rapidly as spectators strolled into the parking area and went off into the night. Natalie walked a few steps ahead, her arm linked with her father's. Only when she unlocked the car door and pulled the seat down for Ben to enter did she notice the solemn, remote expression on his face. But Bill Bishop hurried her along, insisting that they go to his hotel.

"There's a nice place on the top floor with a view of the whole city," Mr. Bishop remarked. "It's quiet...and I won't have to squeeze back into this midget-sized car another time." He grumbled as he slid his thick frame into the passenger seat. "Not that I should gripe—" he turned halfway back to face Ben "—it was me who made her get this little thing. She kept insisting her old Cutlass would make it a few thousand more miles, but I wanted her to have a car with a lot of pizzazz. I won that round."

By now Natalie was in the driver's seat and had started the engine. As she swung around to back out of the parking place, her hair swirled over one shoulder and stayed there. Ben glanced at the dark streak along her temple that the hair had concealed then looked anxiously at Bill Bishop. "Now what do you suppose that is?" he asked, hastily directing Mr. Bishop's attention to a square-shaped object on the top of an adjacent van. Mr. Bishop promptly leaned forward to get a better view of the attachment.

While Bill Bishop's attention was directed out the front, Ben reached forward and lifted the softly curled hair back into place. Natalie gave him a grateful smile. She had forgotten all about the "sultry-wench" swoop that Janie Hitchcock had labored over so carefully.

"Air conditioner," Mr. Bishop said aloud. He had finally figured out what the object on the van roof was. "One of those self-contained units," he added.

"How about that?" Ben nodded with interest. Mr. Bishop had once again turned so he could occasionally glance into the back seat as they made their way out of the parking lot and out into the night traffic.

An hour later, in the lounge atop the Peachtree plaza, Bill Bishop said good-night. "I'm getting old," he declared. "I'm going to leave you younger folks to enjoy the view." He leaned over and kissed Natalie's cheek. "You get this fellow to his hotel and go on to the sorority house," he reminded her unnecessarily. "Come over in the morning and have brunch with me, then—"

"Then I can take you to the airport," Natalie finished, smiling.

"That's the worst thing about these college girls," Mr. Bishop joked. "They think they know it all." He reached out and shook Ben's hand. "Now you drop in any time you're in Key West," he insisted. "And if I come up your way, I'll do the same. Real nice meeting you, Ben," he said warmly, then he made a slow retreat toward the elevator.

Natalie stared at the slim glass in front of her. Ben sat across from her, watching her, but not speaking. Finally he managed a weak smile. "Alone at last." He'd tried to make it come out like a joke, but somehow the humor dissipated when Natalie raised her eyes to his.

"An artist?" Ben tried again. "Another piece of

the Natalie Bishop puzzle.'' He reached across the table and trailed a single rough finger over the back of her slender hand. "You're an artist...and you climbed under the boat and with your bare hands...."

"You're going to lecture me again," Natalie reprimanded him gently. "I'm really too tired to be scolded."

"Maybe that's just as well." Ben pulled back his hand and again assumed a remoteness that made Natalie uncomfortable. Bleary-eyed and exhausted, they both seemed out of place in these surroundings, with groups of people laughing and talking nearby. High above Atlanta's network of bright lights, they sat in silence. Finally Ben touched her hand lightly.

"Let's get out of here," Ben suggested. "If we're going to make that drive back to the Keys tomorrow, maybe we'd both better turn in," he added. "It might be simpler if I catch a taxi to your sorority house and meet you after you drop your father at the airport. What time do you want me to show up?"

Natalie had expected their exchange to be a little less businesslike, but she knew they both needed a good night's rest.

"Twelve-thirty," she answered simply. Then she narrowed her eyes and looked at him curiously. "How did you know about the sorority house?" she asked him. "And how did you know we'd be at the ball game?"

"I pried the address out of Maggie," he answered quietly. "Then once I got to the city, I called the sorority house and asked for you. One of the girls there read some kind of note about picking up tickets to the game. She thought I was your father,'' he said dully.

"She was close. You're my father's *friend*,'' Nat noted. "The two of you really hit it off well.'' She was genuinely pleased.

"A friend doesn't keep the truth from you,'' Ben said critically. "I should have told him the whole story. I really like your dad. I don't like the way you play games with the people who care about you—and I don't like playing your game with him.''

"This is no game,'' Natalie bristled. "And I don't like deceiving him either. But he'd worry if he knew what I was doing. He has my whole life all planned out for me. He wants me to teach in a nice school and use whatever time I have left over to dabble in paintings of my own. I want to make my own plans. I want to work on a boat in the Keys. I'm only trying to convince him that I'm quite capable of taking care of myself—my way—without dad or my brothers playing bodyguard.''

"I see.''

"You don't see,'' Natalie shot back. "And you couldn't tell my dad the whole story if you tried. You only know part of the story yourself. There's more involved than your charter business.'' Here she was, face to face with Ben, and all they could do was argue.

"Let's go,'' she said softly. "I don't want to fight with you—and I'm too tired to tell you everything now.''

"Fine.'' Ben promptly stood and came to help her slide out of her chair. "We'll talk tomorrow.'' He pressed one hand on the curve of her waist as he guided her through the lounge and out to the elevator. This was one of the few times he'd touched her without generating some sensuous response.

Natalie at the wheel with Ben sitting stonily in the passenger seat, they drove the remainder of the trip to his hotel in silence. Only when the car came to a halt at the entrance did Ben finally speak.

"Twelve-thirty?" Natalie nodded in acknowledgment. "I'll see you then," he said, hesitating as if he was waiting for her to turn to face him.

"Okay." She kept her eyes straight ahead. "See you then."

Still Ben made no move to open his door.

"Natalie, turn off the ignition for a moment." He touched her shoulder.

Nat reached down and clicked the key to the off position.

"Well?" Natalie looked over at him.

Ben expelled a long breath. "What am I supposed to do about you?" His dark eyes were masked in the shadows.

"I don't know," she barely whispered. Again, he lifted his hand and gently touched her hair. Softly, he trailed one fingertip down her temple, as if he wished his touch could erase the dark traces of the bruise. Natalie closed her eyes and leaned against his palm, letting his warm hand caress her cheek.

"I came here planning to fire you," he said with a peculiar hoarseness that made Natalie's skin tingle with anticipation. "All I wanted was a few answers, face to face. Now that I've found you, I don't know what to do next. I was hoping for a simple solution."

He bent toward her. "Even with all the trouble

you're causing me, I'd settle for having the problem last a little longer."

Very softly, he kissed her. Natalie lifted her hand to Ben's face, then slid it behind his neck so she could prolong the pressure of his kiss just a few seconds more. When he began to withdraw she held him to her, parting her lips as a gentle invitation.

"Natalie...." He murmured her name again and again as he brushed his lips over hers. "You don't know what you do to me.... Park this thing, come with me to my room, spend the night with me. There's no one to intrude. We could hold each other and close out the world."

Natalie looked into Ben's eyes...smoldering with desire. It would be so easy to go with him, so easy to be carried by the current of their passion. But there was still too much unsettled between them. Eventually they would have to come back to the real world, where boats are sabotaged and drug deals are made, and people get caught up in currents of another kind.

"I can't...not now, not here," she whispered against his throat.

When he clasped her wrist and lightly lifted her hand so he could move away, there was an unexpected trace of sadness in his expression. For a fleeting moment, Natalie felt he was about to speak—to reveal something very important about himself, something he desperately wanted her to know. But then his eyes became darker and more distant. He placed her hand on her lap and cleared his throat.

"See you tomorrow," he said abruptly. Then he opened his door and disappeared into the hotel.

Natalie sat for several seconds staring after him with the soft trace of his kiss still on her lips. Perhaps she knew only too well what she did to him...if the electric effect of his presence on her was a similar response.

"Tomorrow," she whispered as she started the car and drove off. The characteristic remoteness had returned to his eyes just before he hurried away. They kept doing that...moving closer, then retreating into some situation more secure.

"Tomorrow," she repeated as she drove, trying to decipher the unspoken message in Ben's eyes. They would have the long trip back to the Keys...just the two of them. Maybe then she would find out what made him leave her so solemnly.

CHAPTER NINE

When Natalie returned from the Atlanta airport thirty minutes later than she had intended, the old two-story brick sorority house with its gabled windows and trailing ivy looked placid and serene. One of the young women was sitting on the porch swing with her boyfriend, but Ben was nowhere in sight. Natalie parked her car by the side entrance so she could hastily load the few belongings she needed. As she crossed the broad, columned porch that fronted the sorority house, Nat glanced through the long windows of the living room. Ben was there all right, standing, coffee cup in hand, surrounded by six smiling young women who apparently were cooperative enough to keep him company until Natalie returned.

Natalie let herself into the large foyer then stood in the hallway momentarily, curious to observe the exchange between Ben and the college girls. In his open-collared shirt and dark sports jacket, he towered over his companions. He appeared as at ease with them as he was with the fishermen back at the lodge. *What else would you expect,* Natalie mused as she listened to his low laughter. She tried to suppress a vague displeasure at the thought that even here, he was comfortable.

Before she could move from her vantage point in the dim hallway, Ben turned slightly, glancing above the heads of his companions to greet her with a silent half-smile.

"I'll be just a few minutes. . . ." Natalie tried to recover from the distress of being caught eavesdropping. Six other heads turned in her direction. Ben nodded and placed his coffee cup on an end table.

"Anytime," he said agreeably. A chorus of disappointed "Oooohs" emanated from his numerous hostesses. Only Janie Hitchcock came to help Natalie assemble her belongings.

"You didn't mention that your captain was so gorgeous." Janie trudged up the stairway behind Natalie, complaining good-naturedly. "If I had known you were stranded in that desolate place with the likes of him, I wouldn't have been a bit sorry for you. I kept picturing some grizzled old seaman." Janie rambled on with her usual enthusiasm. "Did you get a look at those wonderful large muscles moving under that shirt?" she sighed. "I'd get stranded with him. . . anywhere," she declared.

Natalie proceeded in silence, methodically lifting a few items of clothing from the closet and stacking up several books she had left behind. Janie dutifully placed the items in Nat's suitcase, occasionally glancing up to examine Natalie's expressionless countenance.

"If your father knew that you were living in close contact with such an attractive man, he wouldn't approve," Janie said slyly. "I can see how quite a romance could blossom under those circumstances," she smiled. "Warm, tropical nights. . .the slow pounding of the surf...just the two of you...."

"My father wouldn't approve of *any* of this," Natalie corrected her roommate. "And there are *eight* of us—Maggie and Mac, Fuzzy, Herb, Greg, Hector.... It's a little less exotic with *eight*," she stressed.

"Surely you two must be alone some of the time," Janie protested. "I saw how his eyes lit up when you came in. I'd think someone so obviously forceful...and interested would find a way to get you alone...." Again her voice took on the lilting dreamlike quality that was beginning to irritate Natalie. "Or perhaps you could arrange it yourself...."

"Time to get on the road." Nat snapped the suitcase closed and started for the door. Janie took another close look at the deep color on her roommate's cheeks, then she smiled smugly.

"Ready?" Ben came to the foot of the steps to take Natalie's suitcase from her hand. The group of girls keeping him amused had dwindled to two, but they still stood nearby, staring up at him. "So long, ladies," he said, nodding to them. "It was nice to meet you." With a polite smile, he stepped to the front door, holding it open for Natalie.

"Are *you* ready?" she muttered as she passed him. At last the irritation she felt surfaced. Ben simply grinned and followed her out onto the porch while Janie giggled and came along with him.

"Now the two of you have a safe trip." Janie handed two large art books to Ben as he packed the rear of the car. "And don't worry about a thing on this end," she insisted. "I'll keep sending on all your mail...." She kept grinning as her silent roommate handed the car keys to Ben. "Nice to meet you, Ben," Janie called across the roof of the car. "Perhaps I'll see you at graduation," she added mischievously.

"It was nice to meet you, too, Janie." Ben ducked into the driver's seat and looked at Natalie cautiously. He did not respond to the comment about her graduation.

"Bye, now." Janie waved and stepped back to let the car door on Natalie's side swing closed. Natalie looked up to say farewell, only to see Janie roll her eyes dramatically and mouth the words, "He's so gorgeous...." This time Natalie couldn't suppress her own smile.

"I know," she whispered back to Janie. "I've noticed."

"Well, then—" Janie patted Natalie's arm "—good luck." This time she was obviously not referring just to the trip back to the Keys. "See you in June," she called out as the little red car backed out of the driveway.

"I gather your father caught his flight back all right?" Ben asked as he maneuvered the car through Atlanta's Sunday traffic.

"There was a twenty-minute delay," Natalie replied. "I assume you didn't mind waiting." The words were out before she realized how bitter they sounded.

"I didn't mind." Ben smiled slightly.

"You were quite a hit with the girls," Nat observed dryly.

"They were very friendly," Ben replied non-committally. "I think they were just curious." He glanced over at her. "They all knew you were working on a boat somewhere in the Keys. They wanted a close look at whomever it was you were working for."

"You're far too modest," Nat replied sarcastically.

"Then they're far too easily impressed," Ben responded. "Maybe they should take a good look at the business before they form any conclusions. If they have any illusions of a huge fleet of cruisers and people lolling around in yachting clothes, they're sadly mistaken. It's a far cry from the bedraggled outfit I run."

"The Gold Coast Lodge is not a bedraggled outfit," Nat protested.

"Well, it surely isn't glamorous," Ben asserted. "On paper it sounds great...but the bank owns more of the equipment than I do. We're barely squeaking by with the payments each month. I just don't think your sorority friends considered that."

"I don't think it was your *business* that fascinated them," Natalie said quietly.

"Anyone a little out of the ordinary can be amusing—in small doses. I've seen that reaction before," Ben remarked with a solemn tone. "It doesn't last long. They'll be more permanently impressed by an engineer or an architect—maybe a business executive," he suggested, "someone a little more conventional—and affluent." Natalie looked over at him curiously. Perhaps he was thinking of something other than his effect on the girls in the sorority.

Perhaps Angela Sutton had again enjoyed his company during the shark expedition, then discarded him once the fascination wore off.

"Speaking of amusing," Natalie said, venturing into dangerous territory, "how was your sharking adventure with the Suttons in Miami?" Now it was Ben who turned to her with a curious look.

"It was fine. They closed down early because of the bad weather, but it went better than anyone had expected." He kept his eyes on the traffic ahead.

"You must have had a lot of free time on your hands. . . because of the rain." Natalie pressed on.

Ben shifted his eyes from the highway traffic to her attentive expression. "I didn't have *any* free time," he said quietly. "There were all kinds of seminars and discussions going on. Hector stayed on the boat, but I went to everything that was available."

"What were they about?" Nat asked, feeling increasingly hopeful Ben had not been drawn into anything involving drugs.

"Everything you could think of," he smiled. "Feeding patterns of sharks. . . mating habits. . . migration routes. They had some incredible films," he continued. "One film about the great white shark was spectacular. A great white the size of a school bus was literally ferrying around a marine biologist who had been studying them for years. It was huge and awesome, yet it treated her so gently." His tone captivated his audience of one.

"They did point out a curious phenomenon that has everyone interested in sharks upset." Ben glanced to see if she was still listening. "There has been an unaccountable increase in the number of shark attacks on bathers already this year, both on the California coast and down our way. No one seems to have an explanation," he informed her. "It could be that something has fouled up their usual feeding places and routines, or it could be some kind of cycle they are going through. Some of this tracking information could shed light on the cause of these attacks. Sharks usually stick to fish."

"Studies like that take time," Nat remarked. "Isn't there anything that can be done to protect swimmers in the meantime?"

"There's some talk of running offshore nets along the Florida and California coasts to blockade the swimming areas," Ben replied. "But that can do incredible damage to the migratory patterns of fish, not to mention destroying an enormous number of sea turtles, rays and dolphins that get tangled in the nets and die." His grim face reflected his concern. "As a fisherman, I'd hate to see what it would do to our catch," he commented. "The nets could upset whatever natural balance there is. There's nothing *natural* about those nets. Besides, the sharks and sea creatures belong there—the sea is their home, not ours. Sticking a net in just to fence them off so humans can swim seems rather unfair."

"Not to mention deadly," Nat added quietly.

"These conservation folks have me convinced that the only way to solve this mess is to learn more about the sharks and other sea life," he stated with conviction. "There are *more* sharks this year," he stressed, "as well as more shark attacks. This tracking business could give some reason for the increase in both."

"What exactly were you doing to the sharks you caught?" Nat asked him after a brief silence. She knew they were doing some kind of tagging, but at the time she had been more concerned about Angela Sutton—a predator of a different species. So far Angela's name had not even entered the discussion. Perhaps Ben had resisted whatever enticements she offered.

"We hooked a lot of lemons—they were the easiest to catch." Ben referred to the smaller, greenish yellow sharks that frequented the waters between the Florida coast and Bimini. "They've really multiplied in the past two years. I did learn one curious thing," he noted. "If you ever catch a shark and you don't want it fighting you, simply roll it over on its back." He paused and smiled at Natalie's bewildered expression.

"If you turn it over, it will go limp," he informed her. "You can tag it and get the hook out without any struggle. Then you let it go."

"I'll remember that," Nat chuckled. "I'm sure it will be a handy piece of information. . . the next time I'm out clutching at sharks."

"I just wanted to share my wealth of information with you," he grinned.

"I appreciate that," Nat replied graciously.

"You might keep an eye out for one of our specimens," he added, apparently confident that she would be out on the water just as before. "The dorsal fins tagged in international orange are simply for tracking by sight," he explained. "The yellow tags have radio tracking devices. They can be monitored from the various sites set up along the coasts."

"If I see one of your friends, I'll be sure to mention it," Natalie promised. "I'll roll him on his back and have a nice long chat." Ben smiled appreciatively at her humor.

After that they settled down in comfortable silence, listening to a tape of classical music that Ben slipped into the player in the dashboard. The miles of Georgia countryside slipped by as they headed for the Florida state line and began the long route down the Florida peninsula and across the stretch of the Keys. Nat leaned her head back against the seat, planning to relax for only a few minutes. However, the steady hum of the tires on the interstate highway, the soft music and the warm sun shining in from the west soon lulled her to sleep. When she finally awoke, the sky was nearly dark and the Florida line was over a hundred miles behind them.

"Hungry?" Ben asked when he saw that she was awake. "I need to stop and fill the gas tank. Maybe we should get some dinner as well."

"Let's just pick up some hamburgers and keep driving," Nat suggested. "It's going to be dawn before we get to the lodge as it is. I feel bad enough about all the time you've missed because of me."

"Then I'll get the gas, and you run in and get the food," he suggested, as he swung off the interstate toward a cluster of service stations and restaurants. He pulled up to a self-service gas pump, stepped out and stretched. "Get a cup of coffee for me, please," he groaned. "I could use a little caffeine to jar my system."

"I'll get you some." Nat strode off in the direction of a fast-food shop. "And one for me," she muttered under her breath. *The least I could do is to stay awake to talk to him,* she reprimanded herself. She was slowly realizing how exhausted she must have been after driving to Atlanta herself. *If I'd tried driving back alone today, I might have fallen asleep at the wheel....* The sobering thought made her terribly grateful for Ben's presence. *If it wasn't for him....* She left the thought unfinished. If it wasn't for Ben, a number of things would have been different. The drive back to the Keys was simply one of the changes he was making in her life. There were numerous others that she couldn't even put into words.

"Your turn to talk." Ben braced the cup of coffee between his legs and took a huge bite out of his hamburger. Natalie unwrapped her hamburger and squeezed some mustard onto the bun.

"What do you want to hear about?" she asked apprehensively. She knew that they had agreed to talk the night before, but she wasn't quite ready for a deeply personal discussion over hamburgers.

"Tell me about painting," he said between bites. "What's the difference between what you want to do with your painting and what your father wants?"

"You sure know how to pick your questions," Nat sighed. She had grappled with that one for years. "Let me see where to start." She rewrapped her hamburger and put it back into the sack. "Maybe our differences began when I was still in high school," she said aloud. "Back when I painted or sketched just for fun...." She stared out at the nearly empty highway ahead. The huge roadside billboards and the miles of grassy grazing lands and occasional orchards were disappearing into the night. It was going to be a long, dull drive...and it was her turn to keep the conversation going and keep Ben alert. The story of her career in art was hardly a thrilling topic, but if that's what he wanted to hear about, then that's what he'd get.

"I started sketching when I was just a kid." She'd backtracked even farther than she intended. "When my dad took me out on his shrimping trips and we went miles and miles out. I used to look for sea gulls and pelicans or an occasional boat," she reminisced, "then I'd pass the time by drawing them in a big sketch pad. Sometimes I'd make up a story and write the words under the pictures. I'd have names for the birds, and they would all have great adventures." She smiled fondly. "I still have a whole stack of those books at home."

"From those trips?"

"I save everything," Nat admitted. "I'm a regular pack rat. My mother used to save the normal things—photographs, diplomas, awards—and I kept bits of driftwood, shells, birds' feathers...and anything else I ever picked up. The attic of our house is full of—" her voice softened abruptly "—memories."

"I suppose the walls are hung with your paintings, too," Ben remarked, easing her out of her sudden silence.

"Not really. I've done a few for our house," Nat replied. "Usually I do something that seems right for someone I know, then I give it to that person. I've never really wanted to put a price on anything I painted," she noted. "I've always looked on my talent as a gift...something that I simply have. I pre-

fer to paint only when I feel something special...
and then I pass my gift on to someone else...." Her
voice trailed off.

"Your father seems to think you'd make a good
teacher," Ben noted. "Maybe that would be another
way to pass on your gift."

"My father is more interested in my eating regular-
ly than in passing on my talents in art." Nat smiled
slightly. "He knows that very few people make a decent living as artists, but teaching is steady work with
a regular paycheck. He's concerned with security
more than with aesthetics."

"He has a valid point," Ben observed.

"Of course he has," Natalie agreed. "I'd like to be
financially secure, too. But I also want to be free to
paint when the desire is there, not just when school is
out for the day or the weekend. I've tried painting on
a schedule. One summer I agreed to do some quick
watercolors for a shop in Key West to sell to tourists.
They expected a certain number every Monday morning. I found under that kind of routine all my work
began to look pretty much the same. The paintings
lost their uniqueness. I don't ever want to mass-
produce my work to support myself," she said with
conviction. "I'm concerned that I'd lose even more
of my special feeling for things if I spent all week
teaching. Sharing with the students takes so much enthusiasm and patience...there isn't a whole lot left
over for my own work."

Ben kept looking straight ahead as car after car
zipped past them on the interstate. He kept the
accelerator steady, with the speedometer reading
precisely two miles over the legal limit. He ig-

nored the temptation to speed as flagrantly as the others.

"I *need* to be outdoors a lot—for inspiration," Nat stressed. "If I can make a living doing some *other* kind of work—something that I enjoy and find stimulating...."

"Like running a charter...." Ben was already nodding his head in comprehension.

"Right. Then I can paint what I want—when I want—without feeling compelled to produce something just so I can pay the rent," she explained.

"There must be less strenuous ways to make a living." Ben looked at her fleetingly. "Charter work is tough. And working for someone else doesn't pay that much. Getting your own boat and your own business is even tougher."

"I've been around Uncle Buzz's business enough to know what to expect," Nat replied confidently. "If I show him that I can do the job and if I come out of here with a solid recommendation from you, Uncle Buzz will be on my side when I talk to my dad about becoming an independent operator."

"But what about a boat?" he asked.

"My mother left me some money when she died, and I can sell the car. If that isn't enough, I'll work part-time with Buzz to cover the costs." She spoke with a quiet assurance that indicated she had given the financing considerable thought.

"Then there's the maintenance," Ben added.

"And insurance...and tackle." Nat smiled knowingly. "Believe me, I've really looked into this. I've learned a lot simply from watching your operation."

"Ours isn't a particularly impressive example,"

Ben acknowledged. "At least, not yet it isn't. Mac and I started this business on a shoestring. He took his army retirement and stuck it in the lodge. I put my savings in the land and the boats. Just lately when we're beginning to show a profit," Ben said glumly, "something breaks down or something goes wrong."

"Like the trouble with the boats," Nat remarked. Ben still had no idea of the extent of the damage to the two engines or the actual cost of the labor she and Buzz had supplied free.

"Like that," Ben nodded. "I'll tell you something that I haven't mentioned to a soul, not even to Mac," Ben said from the darkness. "For the past couple of months, I've had some company interested in buying us out—land, boats, lodge...everything. One of their men has called back several times, raising the price. I keep hoping we can keep our finances straight until the fall season begins. If we have any more big expenses or a string of bad weather or too many charters we have to cancel because a boat is laid up...." He took a deep breath. "Mac and I may have to bail out and let this company take the place. Financially we'd come out all right, but we'd lose the location. Maybe we could start over somewhere else in the Keys," he said softly, "if worse comes to worst—but it certainly wouldn't be the same."

"That's why you were so upset when I showed up." Nat realized that his distress was financial as well as personal.

"I told you that I couldn't afford to fool with you," he conceded. "Money was part of it. The rest—well, let's just say I don't like to have someone play games with me. Buzz should have told me you were a female.''

''But then you wouldn't have let me work for you,'' Nat objected.

''That's right,'' Ben replied. ''Think of the problems I would have saved myself—the problems we could have saved each other.''

Natalie tried to examine the expression on Ben's face. Just as she hoped they were beginning to resolve their difficulties, he had come out with that grim statement. In the glare of the headlight beams from a passing car, she could see his rugged profile, stern and pensive as they continued on in uneasy silence.

''If you'd like to take a break, I'll drive for a while,'' Nat said.

Ben nodded. ''I'll pull off at the next exit.'' He sounded tired. ''Maybe you'd like something to drink—Coke, coffee?''

''I'll take the coffee,'' Natalie replied. Driving at night was always more tiring than during the day. At least in the daylight she could enjoy the scenery, but the night view from the interstate was simply long, flat, dark areas punctuated by occasional exits and signs. After a few miles, the surroundings all began to look monotonously like what she'd already passed by and those she knew still lay ahead.

Ben slept for the next few hours of the trip. He stretched his long legs out, slid down in the passenger seat so his head was resting on the back and closed his eyes and slept while Natalie drove. Occasionally she would take her eyes off the road long enough to glance at him. But the serenity in his face while he slept was so unlike the troubled expression she had seen so often lately that she would feel an inexplicable twinge of regret for having come into his life. Perhaps her working for Gold Coast Lodge had caused him some extra problems. But she had helped repair the damaged engines free of charge and she had proved to be a good fishing guide and charter captain. *Maybe it's a fair bargain,* she consoled herself. Yet there was definitely more to the tension between them than either of them bargained for. There were moments when they looked into each other's eyes, and neither one of them could speak or look away. There were those rare moments when they touched and kissed...when time stood still. She could hear Ben's words echo in her ears, "Touch me, Natalie." They had talked on this trip about a hundred things, but deep inside, Nat knew they had not spoken of the one thing they both sensed—the intimate bond that left them breathless.

"Maybe later," Natalie muttered as she glanced at the glow off to the east. Beyond the Atlantic horizon, the sun was beginning its climb. The dark sky turned from black to gray, then gradually grew brighter as she took the expressway around Miami in the direction of the lower tip of the Florida peninsula.

"Let's stop somewhere and watch the sunrise," Ben said without moving. Nat suddenly realized he might not have been asleep as long as she'd believed. "Pull off into the park when you hit Key Largo," he suggested. "We'll get out and jump around and get our blood stirring while we watch the day begin."

The park overlooking the ocean was abandoned that early in the morning. Nat pulled up beside a clump of straggly pine trees, slipped off her shoes and leaped out of the car onto the sandy beach. With long, rapid strides, she strode to the water, stopping knee-deep in the chilly surf.

"If this doesn't wake us up, nothing will." Natalie clasped her arms around herself as the cool waves licked her legs.

"I'm sure it will," Ben replied from the shore. He had stopped several feet behind her to roll up his pant legs. Then he waded in next to her and stared across the water at the spreading slash of light that was the edge of the rising sun.

The entire surface of the ocean, as far as they could see, was peaked in brilliant light, shimmering with the movement of the currents. The still-cold water would eventually grow warmer as the sun climbed through the sky, but for now, Natalie felt as if she was poised on the brink of something wonderful, suspended in the moment, as the chill at her feet was countered by the heat from the sun sliding up out of the Atlantic.

She stood with her eyes half closed, savoring the sensations, listening to the whisper of the waves, the soft sounds of homecoming. When she turned to look beside her, Ben was gone.

"Surely it isn't too cold for you?" she teased as she waded back closer to shore. He was waiting there, ankle deep in the gentle surf, watching her. "I thought you were tougher than that," she grinned.

"I'm not as tough as you think." His voice was soft and low. "I'm not as tough as I'd like to be." Something in the way he looked at her made her stop in mid-step.

"If I were stronger," Ben continued, "I could

look at you and simply enjoy the vision...without wanting to hold you.''

''I love it when you hold me.'' Natalie's impish grin faded. Ben opened his arms. Natalie stepped willingly into his embrace. His lips brushed hers in soft, barely perceptible movement that left her smiling lips parted, awaiting the tender invasion of his tongue. Silhouetted by the dawn of a new day, they clung to each other, buffeted by the incoming waves, their bare feet half buried in the sand.

Natalie could feel the hammering of Ben's heart, her own pulse echoing his as she pressed against him, eager to feel the way his lean, hard body fitted into the curves of her own. A new dream stirred within her, one that encompassed all the things she loved: the wind and sea, the Keys, a kaleidoscope of colors...and Ben Andress.

''You're not going to believe this.'' Ben grasped her shoulders and gently moved her away from him. Glancing behind her over the wide parking area, he heaved a deep uneven breath. ''But we aren't alone—even here.'' He nodded toward an old station wagon that rattled to the beach with fishing poles protruding from the rear window. Two early-morning fishermen had come to try their luck.

''Maybe I should get the message.'' Ben turned his attention to retrieving his socks and shoes from the beach.

''And what message is that?'' Natalie steadied herself long enough to ask.

''Something about the wrong time,'' he said enigmatically, rolling down his pant legs and starting back to the car.

Half skipping, Natalie hurried along after him.

At the parked car, they brushed the sand from their feet, slid their shoes on, then sat—without speaking—looking at the bright sun that had finally cleared the rim of the horizon.

"You *do* know that my month is up tomorrow," Nat reminded him before he turned the key.

"And?"

"And I'd like to get this settled. You haven't actually said whether or not you're satisfied with my work. I'd like to know whether you intend to let me keep working at the lodge. Am I staying on through the season?" She simply had to have an official decision.

"I wish I had an easy answer for you," Ben replied thoughtfully. "If you continue working, we can still run charters on the *Calusa* and try to keep our heads above water financially. But it looks like you may be too tempting a target for somebody. First it's damage to the fuel lines, then it's the propeller dropping off and you getting hurt. I really don't want to risk someone taking another try at you."

"I'm not frightened, and I'm not helpless," Nat argued. "Surely whoever has been tampering with the boats has figured that out already. I can take care of myself as well as any of the others. I won't let anything go wrong."

"You didn't *let* the other incidents occur," Ben said solemnly. "They just happened—and they happened to you. What I'd like to do is put you in a nice safe place for a month or so until a lot of things here are settled. Then I'd be in a position to keep a closer eye on you."

"I have no intention of hiding away for a month or whatever." Natalie bristled in indignation. "I've got too much to do. You don't have to feel so darned responsible for me. I don't know what these things are that you have to settle before you can give me your attention. They're your problems, not mine. But we have an agreement—a business agreement—that I want settled."

"Don't tell me you're going to threaten me with your attorney again," Ben groaned. "You can't sue me for trying to protect you."

"I don't want to sue you for anything," Nat declared. "I want to keep on working on the *Calusa*. That's all. You must admit that I've done pretty well with my end of the bargain. I've worked hard. I've been doing a good job." She wasn't going to let him ignore her skill on the charters.

"Except for being somewhat accident-prone," he said evenly.

"Accidents and sabotage are not the same thing," she countered. "I've done my job in spite of *both*. I'm not going to be intimidated...not by some idiot who tampers with my boat and not by you."

"*Your* boat?" Ben paused.

"You know what I mean," Natalie replied crossly. "It's *your* business and *your* boat...but it's *my* job. And I intend to keep it."

Ben hung his head forward, running his hand through his thick hair. "If you stay," he finally said with a trace of resignation, "you'll have to be extremely cautious about everything and everyone. I can't get any more enmeshed in your life than I already am. And you'll be better off if you keep out of the marina area and the boathouse whenever you're off duty." His eyes met hers meaningfully. There would be no more intimate encounters in the old cruiser.

"It's not that I don't want to make love to you, Natalie," he said softly. "You know what happens when I touch you...and when you touch me. We slip into another world," he said simply. "What I'm involved with in the *real* world is going to take all my time for a while. Having you close to me causes more trouble than you realize."

"Just what is it that you're so involved with?" Natalie demanded. "And what does it have to do with you and me?"

"I don't want it to have *anything* to do with you." Ben's voice had a melancholy quality. "I want you to lay low for a while. Just keep to yourself. I don't want anything to happen to you, and I don't want you poking your nose into anything that doesn't concern you."

Natalie sat staring at her hands as Ben spoke. All the old suspicions about Ben and Angela Sutton and the drug connections that may have been made during the Miami shark hunt began to surface again. If Ben was planning something illegal, she could see how a passionate romance could interfere with his clandestine activities. "It's a little late for anyone to decide what concerns me." Natalie cleared her throat to relieve the tension. "*You* concern me," she said softly. "I won't complicate your life any more than I have already...." She hesitated. "But I won't leave my job...and I won't pretend that I don't care for you...because I do."

Ben sat rigid, refusing to look at her. For a long time, he stared out over the water. "I used to be a lifeguard at the swimming pool on the army posts wherever we happened to be at the time," he began. "All the girls at the pool would fall in love with the lifeguards—" he drew in a breath "—until the summer ended. I'm a little older. . . more experienced in some ways, I'm sure. . . and certainly willing. There's no arguing about the attraction we both feel," he said slowly and thoughtfully. "Wanting someone isn't the same as loving someone." He lowered his eyes and looked at the rugged hands clasped atop the steering wheel. "When the season is over, and you've proved yourself. . . and your father accepts your plans, you'll find that the attraction will have worn off. I'll just be someone you once worked for. Up to now we've simply been accessible to each other. Working together made a romance convenient."

"Believe me," Natalie said, "I don't find anything about this convenient. Being accessible has nothing to do with what I feel for you. Is that how you felt about me all along?" She frowned. "Is that why you only show affection when there's no one else around? You find me *convenient* when Angela Sutton isn't draping herself all over you?"

"She does have a tendency to do that," Ben remarked, "particularly in public. But Angela Sutton has nothing to do with what's going on between you and me. I don't want anything that happens to be for the wrong reasons. And *convenience* isn't the right reason. Other women can move in and out of relationships without any particular concern, but not you. . . and *not* with me," he insisted. "Until we've both taken some time to think this over, I want you to keep your distance, and I'll keep mine. This has already turned into something more than either of us is in a position to handle."

"I'm not going to promise anything," Natalie quietly replied.

"Then I'll do both of us a favor," he declared. "I'll see that we're both too busy to cross paths with each other."

"You don't have to go to any great lengths to avoid me," Natalie sighed. "I'm not going to throw myself at you. I won't intrude on your personal affairs more than I have to. But I don't want you to pass this off as some schoolgirl crush...or a casual fling," she stated firmly. "You're the last thing I was looking for when I came back to the Keys. I came here to pick up a little experience with the *charters*, nothing more," she said sharply.

Ben's firm jawline softened slightly.

"So you just go on with your pressing business—" she refused to back down now "—and I'll be as inconspicuous as possible." She glanced sidelong at him to see if his profile seemed less severe.

"Sure you will," he muttered as he turned the ignition key. Only then did a little smile cross his lips.

"So we have a deal," Nat said evenly, "for the rest of the season."

"As long as there's no more trouble." Ben qualified the tenuous agreement.

Nat pursed her lips in resignation. It wasn't the deal she had hoped for—but it was the only one to which Ben would agree.

"No trouble." Nat accepted his condition.

Ben maneuvered the car back onto the highway and accelerated smoothly. As the scruffy, low-lying keys skimmed past the windows and the distant, wider, pine-shrouded Lower Keys loomed ahead, Natalie felt that familiar tingle of pleasure that welcomed her whenever she was nearing home. Only this time, the anticipation began a little earlier, and the "home" she yearned for was the Gold Coast Lodge.

CHAPTER TEN

A RELIEVED MAC BUTLER greeted the two travelers when they pulled up by the boathouse. The *Suds Buggy* had already gone out on an early sports-fishing charter and Mac had telephone numbers of two other parties who had called about charters.

"Call them back," Ben directed Mac. "Tell them we'll be ready in an hour if they're still interested." A few minutes later Mac returned. Both replies were positive. The *Southwind* and the *Calusa* were going out.

Nat hurried down to her beach house to shower and change clothes. She had managed to get a little sleep during the all-night trip from Atlanta and the knowledge that she was staying on at the lodge had her adrenaline flowing. The trial period was over; she'd earned the right to stay.

It was a great day for fishing, and the *Calusa* found the big ones. After delivering her satisfied passengers back at the dock, Natalie had helped wash down the boat, then had grabbed a two-hour nap. Still she could feel the effects of the long drive as she walked back to the boathouse in the late afternoon.

"If we're going to celebrate tonight, you'd better come along and help me round up our dinner," Mac insisted as he looked up from refueling the *Calusa*.

"We *are* going to celebrate, aren't we?" Mac looked at her closely. He had spread the word that she would be on the job through the rest of the season, and Maggie had put the champagne on ice. Mac's big grin wavered as he waited for Nat to respond.

"Of course we're going to celebrate." Nat summoned a smile. Mac and Maggie had been so relieved when they saw Ben and Natalie drive in that morning that Nat didn't have the heart to pass up the seafood dinner they had promised. "And I'll be glad to help you catch a few fish for dinner," Nat added.

"Fish?" Mac replied indignantly. "You think we'd have plain old *fish* for this?"

"Then where are we going?" Nat climbed in the boat.

"Just drive." Mac cast off, then climbed into the cockpit and sat down next to her. "You'll see," he promised. With an accommodating nod, Natalie switched on the ignition and steered out into Newfound Harbor toward the Atlantic.

"Head for the old wreck just before the drop-off to sixty feet." Mac settled back to enjoy the ride. Natalie accelerated, letting the *Calusa* skim over the water more rapidly than usual. She had not had the *Calusa* out except to run charters, and the chance to open her up and let her run was too much fun to pass up. Grinning like a child with a new toy, she raced across the water, swerving occasionally to follow the channel and delighting in the immediate response of the boat to her touch.

"Mine are the green buoys with an orange star on the top," Mac announced as they approached the location he had designated. Then a comprehending grin spread across Natalie's face. Just beyond the shoal where an old freighter had gone down, the uneven bottom changed depths erratically, varying from eighteen feet to thirty, then dropping off to sixty.

"Lobster!" Nat squealed with delight. "We're having lobster. I love it."

Clustered between the shoal and the drop-off were twenty buoys of different shapes and colors, all bobbing about, each marking the location of a lobster trap.

"When I say celebrate, I'm not kidding," Mac chuckled. "Let's just hope those spiny little critters got the message and showed up for the party." Natalie cut the motor and coasted to the buoys, spotting three of them with the green color and orange star that Mac claimed as his own insignia. She anchored upstream so the current would pull the *Calusa* up beside them, then she scrambled down to the lower deck to help Mac tug the large cages aboard.

"Welcome, welcome," Mac greeted the first load, as they eased the cage onto the side of the boat. The two-foot cube-shaped cage was built of cypress slats then a concrete weight was connected to the bottom to hold the cage on the ocean floor. Mac had pulled on a thick pair of gloves and started lifting the scurrying Florida lobsters into the bait well. "Let's hope the other traps did as well." He placed the empty cage against the far side of the boat. "I haven't tried this in a while, so I was a little unsure about how big a haul we'd get." Eagerly he grasped the buoy rope of the next trap and began pulling it to the surface.

They had twenty-one lobsters when all three traps were aboard. The clawless, spiny creatures skittered over one another in the bait well, peering up with protruding beadlike eyes. "A little lemon butter, and we'll be in heaven." Mac poured a bucket of water over the lobsters and slammed down the lid to keep them alive and shaded. "Now *that's* what you have with champagne," he declared.

BY 7:30 THAT NIGHT, the large open fire that Hector and Mac had built behind Beachside One had subsided into a thick layer of dull, reddish coals. Mac propped a metal grill above the hot surface, then one by one plopped the lobsters onto the grill. "Just like my dad," Nat noted as Mac pressed another metal grid over the layer of sizzling lobsters. Bill Bishop considered it a waste of good lobster to throw it in a pot of water and let it cook. "Do it like a native," he insisted, then he'd broil them out in the open sea air.

By 8:00 P.M., they were all inside, seated around the small living room, using anything they could find for tables. Mac and Maggie shared the small kitchen table while Hector, Maria, Greg and Fuzzy sat cross-legged on the floor, balancing their platters on their laps. Roger and Natalie sat across from each other at the upturned crate that was now a coffee table.

"Is Andress being antisocial?" Roger had asked after Nat introduced him to the few folks he had not already met. "I'd rather hoped I'd get to meet your mysterious employer."

"He's working on his boat," Nat said quietly.

"Apparently he hopes to get it finished as soon as possible."

"And he couldn't spare a few hours?"

"He's avoiding any complications," Nat whispered. "That means *me*," she stressed.

"Ah...." Roger smiled. "You must have had quite an interesting time in Atlanta...."

"Not interesting enough, it seems." Nat turned her attention back to the hot lobsters before her. Mac had been the one who had invited everyone to the party, but it was Maggie who had told Nat about the absentees. Herb was visiting a girl friend over on Summerland Key and Ben would be working on the old cruiser. "But this night is for you, honey." Maggie had refused to let her irritation with Ben spoil the celebration. "I'll get to the bottom of this some other time."

"Let's have a little music." Hector struggled to his feet. "How about it, Nat-a-lee?" He bounced back and forth. "A little boogie music for the party?"

"Sounds like a good idea," Nat agreed as she licked the lemon butter from her fingertips.

"And a little more champagne." Mac circled the room refilling each glass. "To Natalie." He held his glass aloft.

"To Natalie," came the chorus from her friends. The soft rock music that Hector had selected set a soothing, steady rhythm for the remainder of the feast. When the last lobster had been devoured and the celebrants were well fed and mellow, Nat quietly slipped off into her bedroom and returned with a stack of paintings.

"Now I have something for each of you." She

placed the stack in the center of the room. One by one, she passed out the works she had completed. "For you." She handed Maggie the painting of the picnic basket amid the trees that she had begun two weeks earlier. For Mac, she had completed the picture of the skiff afloat in the secret inlet.

"Ah, so you've found my island." He held it up for everyone to admire.

"I think you might like this." She gave Hector the painting of Maria, wading in the shallow water of the mangrove-rimmed inlet. "And for you...." She gave Maria the one of Hector, casting into the water, his pants rolled above his knees, his dark hair tousled by the wind. "Now if you want to exchange with each other," Nat suggested, "you certainly are free to trade."

"Not me." Hector clutched his picture of Maria. "This one stays with me," he insisted. Maria lowered her dark-lashed eyes and held her painting of Hector closer.

"One for you...." She handed Roger one she had been working on while he was preoccupied with his own work. It showed him in a straw hat and blue jeans, his bare back reddened from the sun, staring intently at a curious sea gull, which was in turn staring at him. There was nothing but the two figures in the painting, yet the intimacy of that moment brought an immediate smile.

"Fuzzy...." She handed the grumpy captain of the *Suds Buggy* a pale sketch of his battered peaked cap sitting atop one of the dock pilings. Fuzzy stared at it for a moment, then he climbed to his feet and kissed her cheek. "Ain't big on pictures," he muttered, "but I like this."

For Greg she had a brown-and-gray painting of the back steps of Beachside Two, showing only the railing above the stairs and Greg's long legs propped upon it. He accepted it with a slight nod, but Nat was accustomed to his remoteness. A nod from Greg was almost an entire conversation.

"What about that one?" Mac clasped his boat painting under his arm and stared down at the largest painting of them all. It was the mangrove one Nat had made for Ben.

"I'll have to deliver that some other time," she said softly. Then, resuming her cheerful demeanor, she propped her hands on her hips. "Well?" She grinned from one to the other. "If you're all satisfied, they're yours."

"I'm satisfied." Hector began the chorus. "Me, too." The comments flew from one delighted recipient to the next.

"Then let's clean up this room and give Natalie a chance to get some sleep." Maggie stood and hustled everyone into action. "We've got her for the next couple of months, so we can all get back to normal." Everyone pitched in, clearing away glasses, bottles and stacks of well-cleaned lobster shells. In minutes, everything was packed up. The extra plates and glasses would go back to the restaurant with Mac and Maggie. Greg and Fuzzy carted out the garbage.

"I've offered to give Hector a ride to Maria's house," Roger informed Natalie. "We'll drop her off, then I'll bring him back. I think you've had enough driving to last you a while." He hugged her.

By now, everyone had moved out onto the shell path that ran from the parking lot, past the four beach houses, then on through the trees to Ben's quarters. Amid a flurry of thank-yous and good-nights the assembly scattered.

"I love my painting." Roger kissed Natalie on the cheek. "I just wish I could see Andress's face when you give him the mangrove." He looked at her intently. "Maybe it would be better if you made that a private presentation. I have a feeling Mr. Andress will be amazed by your talent."

"We'll see," Nat said warily. "He hasn't found anything I do particularly amazing," she noted dryly.

"Then the man is a fool," he said with a terse smile. "Either that or he's crazy about you and he just doesn't want to admit it."

"Good night, Roger...." Natalie nudged him toward the waiting vehicle. The dull green Refuge truck was parked next to her little Mustang. Hector and Maria had already squeezed into the front seat and were ready to go. "See you tomorrow," he called as he climbed in next to them. Nat stood there watching the pickup bounce across the grassy space to the parking lot. Once it had disappeared along the narrow roadway that led to the highway, Nat saw Ben's tall figure heading toward her through the darkness.

"If you'll wait a moment, I have something for you." She stood in the center of the pathway, waiting for him.

"I'm pretty dirty." He held his hands out to show her he was indeed covered with sweat and grime.

"And I'm tired," he added. "Can't it wait till tomorrow?" In the dim light from the beach house, she could see the deep shadows of weariness in his face.

"Sure, it can wait," she managed to reply. She wanted to reach out and brush aside the sweat-dampened hair that pressed against his forehead. The temptation to massage the tight muscles of his neck with her cool hands was almost irresistible. But Ben had warned her not to touch him. . . not to complicate his life any more than she already had.

"I'll see you tomorrow." She stepped back to let him pass freely.

"Are you going to see *him* tomorrow, too?" Ben asked in a low voice.

"Who?"

"The guy in the truck. . . the guy from the wildlife Refuge." He turned his gaze in the direction Roger had gone. "Another one of your friends?"

"The same friend you saw in the skiff that night, the same one who stayed for dinner with Hector and me, the same one I drove home afterward. He's my friend—and my *tutor*," she stressed. "I see him as often as I can. . . and we paint together."

Ben slowly turned back to face her. "That's where you've been going all along?" He sounded relieved.

"Hector could have told you that," Natalie answered.

"I didn't ask Hector," he replied.

"You could have asked me," Nat said calmly.

"I told you once before. . . whenever you were ready, you could tell me everything." His expression was unreadable. "I assumed he was just another one of your secrets."

Natalie stood there, trying to piece together what Ben must have been thinking. All along he'd suspected she had been racing off for romantic interludes with Roger while Ben was just an infrequent though passionate convenience.

"Roger Embry is an artist from Atlanta with a commission to do some illustrations for the wildlife Refuge," she explained. "He's also a happily married man with two children," she added, with a slight smile, "just in case you were wondering."

"It's not my place to wonder," Ben stated evenly. He stepped past her and steadily made his way beside the beach houses to the cluster of trees beyond.

I'll give you something to wonder about.... Nat turned and stamped up the stairs. She stormed into the living room and retrieved the awesome mangrove painting she had struggled to perfect. With the painting braced beneath her arm, she strode along the shell path in the direction Ben had gone.

When she cut through the near-black shroud of trees that separated the lodge compound from Ben's private place, Natalie stepped into a moonlit clearing and confronted a house that took her breath away. Poised against the dark sky, like a specter from a time long past, was a structure of magical proportions. Natalie had glimpsed only a portion of the rear of the building from the waterside, but all that had been clearly discernible was a long porch flanked by thick foliage. She had assumed it was some type of deck, but she had not approached closely enough for a more exact inspection.

Now, from the land side, the home of Ben Andress looked like something from the Key West settlement of a hundred years ago. The old, two-story Bahama-style house with weathered clapboard sides and metal shingled peaked roof had a wide veranda encompassing three sides of the house—on both the upper and lower floors. Natalie moved toward it, spellbound, trying to skirt the thick palmetto plants and low shrubbery that obscured the path.

From inside the shuttered windows, the bright glow of electric lights sent swatches of ivory zigzagging onto the porch floor and out into the night. Set high on stone piers to protect it from high water, the old building stood prim and elegant, like a dowager aunt, somehow stranded in the moonlight, entranced by the heady aroma of the night-blooming cereus on the evening air.

Something to wonder about.... Natalie remembered why she had come. Still clasping the mangrove painting, she sought the front steps and climbed onto the covered porch. On closer inspection, she could see that the house was in serious need of repair and restoration. Some of the spindles on the porch railings needed replacing. The shutters were scarred with peeling paint, but the structure itself was solid. There were houses like this one farther down the Keys in the heart of her hometown—old houses from the past that had been ignored for years but now were preserved and maintained with loving care. Many were more elegant than this one, many far larger, but each had a timeless quality that evoked the gracious ambience that had been Old Key West.

Ben had knocked her off balance again. Somewhere in the back of her mind, Nat had expected to see another beach house like the four set together back on the lodge compound. Even a mobile home wouldn't have seemed unusual. There were hundreds of them in the Keys. But this lovely old house, so in need of care, yet rugged enough to have lasted through years of tropical rain and hot sun, had caught her totally off guard.

Something to wonder about. She smiled to herself. Ben wasn't the only one who was getting a surprise. Resolutely, Natalie headed for the door and knocked with firm, even taps. When there was no immediate response she waited a minute, then knocked again, even louder.

"I thought we had an agreement." Ben stood there wearing only his oil- and grease-stained jeans. Silhouetted by the light from inside the house, his body seemed as if it were rimmed in gold. His arms were propped against the doorframe. In the moonlight, the dark mat of his chest hair glistened, its density diminishing nearer to his narrow waist. Natalie had apparently intercepted him on his way to the shower.

"I finished this *before* our agreement," Natalie forced herself to say, determined to keep her eyes locked onto his. "If you had been able to attend our little party tonight," she said pointedly, "I would have given it to you then." She turned the painting toward him and held it out. "I did this for you."

Ben stared at it intently, then stepped back so the light from inside the house could illuminate its surface. "I've wondered what your paintings would look like," he said almost in a whisper. For a moment, he simply stood looking at it with a peculiar half-smile on his face.

Then he stepped back abruptly, gesturing for Natalie to enter. "I can't touch it with these hands." He pushed the door shut behind her. "Come in and make yourself comfortable. I'll clean up and be back in a couple of minutes." He left her standing in the hallway while he climbed the stairs to the second floor.

Natalie stood for a moment, looking up at the high-ceilinged hall with two large fans suspended motionless above her. Then with undisguised curiosity, she moved from room to room, switching on the overhead lights for a better view of the dim interior. The old house was so like the ones in the restored section of Key West, with a long central hall and a stairway leading upward, high-ceilinged rooms to keep the hot air from becoming trapped inside, one room spilling into another with every area opening in one way or another onto the wide verandas that offered a view of the harbor. There were only two long rooms on the lower floor—a living room along the left side of the hall and a kitchen-dining room on the right side. Upstairs, where the sound of a shower signaled Ben's presence, Natalie presumed there would be two or even three bedrooms.

The house, like the boat Ben was restoring, showed the results of careful labor. The brickwork in the fireplaces had been redone. A new tile hearth had been installed. Wall paneling was shiny and new. In the kitchen, all the plumbing and appliances were modern. "So he's working on you, too," Nat said aloud in the immaculate kitchen. She could imagine how lovely the old place would be after he had returned it to its original beauty. Upstairs, the water stopped running. Nat scampered into the living room, settling into a huge wicker chair at the far end so it would appear that she had been calmly waiting there all along. *He doesn't like anyone to invade his privacy,* she reminded herself.

"Sorry to take so long." Ben reached the bottom of the stairs and turned into the living room. His freshly shampooed hair had been hastily combed into place, and a pair of khaki shorts replaced the jeans. The still-damp chest hairs were visible in the deep V of his knit shirt. "Now that I'm clean, let me have a close look at your painting."

"*Your* painting," Natalie stressed as she handed it to him. Ben held it at arm's length, examining it closely as he moved nearer to the light.

"You're very good," he said softly, without lifting his eyes from the twisting form of the tree. "Your father said you were good, and he was right. I can't accept this, of course," he added as he came close to her again. "But I can tell you how beautiful it is."

Nat kept her hands clasped in her lap. Even when Ben held out the painting to return it to her, she would not unlock her fingers. "It isn't polite to refuse a gift," Natalie said in disappointment. "If you're the gentleman my father thinks you are, you'll accept it. . . as a present from a friend."

Ben lowered the painting, holding it by his side. "If I were the gentleman your father thinks I am, I wouldn't have done a number of things that I've done," he countered. "And I wouldn't have invited you in. You're not going to pretend that I'm your *friend*—or that you're mine." He glared at her. "Mr. Embry is your *friend*, Hector is your *friend*, Maggie is your *friend*." He recited the list coolly. "Mac is your friend." He stared down at the painting once more. "It would be a gross understatement to pass off this painting simply as a gift from a friend."

"Call it whatever you like." She held up her palms in surrender. "It's for you." Nat stood to leave. "I don't know why it's just yours, but it is. It was yours even before I began to paint it," she said quietly. "I wish you'd keep it." She took one step, then hesitated. "There are no strings attached," she added.

"You're far more generous than I would be if the roles were reversed," Ben commented. "But then, I'm not in a position to put strings on anyone." He lifted the painting carefully. Then his eyes scanned the long room. "How about over the fireplace?" He crossed the room and held the picture above the mantel. "I haven't finished decorating in here...as you probably have noticed. Perhaps this will make the old place seem more like someone actually lives here." He propped the painting up, then backed away from it to gauge the effect.

"It looks nice there," Nat attested. "Even if it is my own work that I'm admiring. It's such a marvelous tree," she smiled.

"Thank you." Ben cleared his throat self-consciously. "I've never had a real piece of art before...." He shifted his gaze from the painting to her serene face.

"You have this house," Nat responded. "It's a gorgeous old thing...a real work of art in its own right."

"It was here when I bought the land," Ben explained. "It was left over from the old days when the railroad ran the length of the Keys. Apparently someone settled here and eventually abandoned the place. The lodge and the boathouse were some kind of storage sheds." His dark eyes glistened with deserved pride. "Mac and I brought this outfit a long way," he noted. "Now all we have to do is keep the charters running until we can get the marina extension built up."

"The marina extension?" Nat looked at him curiously.

"We're going to build in the whole inlet with facilities for mooring boats. We can rent the space out, expand our tackle business, put in a grocery store and refueling station. . . ." He moved his hands from place to place around the imaginary replica of the lodge and dock area. Natalie found herself hypnotically watching his rough hands as they shaped his vision, constructing so vivid an invisible model of the fishing camp that she could visualize it.

"This inlet would be the ideal place for it," she remarked. "It has the perfect natural setting." She was caught up in the scheme. "You could do it." She stared at the space between them where only the vision existed. "It's a wonderful place, a wonderful idea."

Ben had stopped, his hands in midair, watching the rapture on her face. "I've never really had a place that felt like home," he said as he lowered his arms to his side. "My father was a military man—we moved a lot. When I joined the army, I moved, too. But this feels right, as if I've always belonged here, as if I could make it into something." Slowly he dropped his gaze. The magic faded. The earlier remoteness inched between them like a chilly wind from the north, and they fell silent.

"I'd better be getting back," Natalie said. She had made the delivery; there was no longer any excuse to stay.

"We have a busy week," Ben acknowledged, starting to the door slightly ahead of her. "We're booked full. Word must be getting around."

"I'll spread the word myself, once I've convinced my father to go along with my career change," she volunteered.

"*If* we're still in business," he said ominously, as he opened the door to let her out.

"You'll be in business," she said with conviction. "Your luck is changing for the better." She smiled slightly. "You said yourself, word is getting around. We've got plenty of bookings."

"And there's a tropical depression in the Caribbean," Ben informed her. "If it builds into a full-fledged hurricane, we might be in real trouble." Natalie's brow furrowed into a frown. She'd seen it happen year after year in Key West: the anxious fishermen keeping one ear on the radio and both eyes on the horizon, watching and waiting to see how far the storm would progress and how ferocious it would be.

"This place has survived storms before," she said, looking up at the old house, "and it will survive them again. So will the rest of the lodge. This new storm may just dwindle away," she added hopefully.

"Then there's always the next one," Ben commented, "and the one after that. That's part of the gamble, though.'' He stepped out into the yard and looked up at the tall palm trees silhouetted against the velvety sky. Nothing stirred. It was like that when a storm was building somewhere far away. It might be three or four days before the wind picked up and started gusting. But when it did, it meant trouble.

"You'll make it...." Natalie followed his gaze into the clear sky. "Just like that mangrove, you'll hang in there...you and Mac...and you'll make it.''

Ben turned toward her. She couldn't see his face clearly for the shadows. The moon was at his back, making his rugged face an indistinct mask of deep planes and angles. Her own hair, moon-bleached and pale, created a soft ivory halo effect, with loose tendrils spiraling down her cheekbones. Ben lifted his hands and softly framed her face with his palms. For a moment, Natalie held her breath, waiting for him to kiss her.

Instead, hc spoke.

"Natalie...starting with you is the easy part. Being able to stop is almost impossible. Go home, Natalie,'' he rasped.

Nat could smell the muskiness of his body, just inches away from her own. She had promised not to throw herself at him, but she could not move away from him.

"Please...for both our sakes...go home.'' He dropped his hands and quietly turned away.

Long after Ben had disappeared into his exceptional house, Natalie stood there, wishing he had relented and had held her once more. At least he now had the painting, she consoled herself as she made her way back along the shell path. As long as Ben had it in his home, he had something of her with him. Perhaps he would realize that the painting was merely a beginning—incomplete without its creator—and then he would come for her.

CHAPTER ELEVEN

By MIDWEEK, it was clear that the storm coming was a fierce tropical one, but no hurricane. Along the Lower Keys, the reported sightings of waterspouts mounted as heavy, erratic bursts of air sucked wind and water into spirals that skirted across the water, threatening swimmers and boaters alike.

Ben summoned them all together on Wednesday morning. "When you get in today, we'll start tying everything down. We'll just close up for a couple of days and not risk having to make last-minute preparations if this storm changes its mind." Often a tropical depression turned to a storm, seemed to subside, then lingered out in the Caribbean long enough to lull weather-watchers into complacency. Then with chameleonlike speed, the storm would feed on the warm tropic air and the swirling winds that were drawn to its center, and it would emerge as a full-blown hurricane with winds well over the seventy-four mile-per-hour velocity that moved it out of the "storm" capacity.

The *Southwind* was already unloaded and moored in the marina when Natalie brought in her charter on the *Calusa*. She and Greg unloaded the gear as usual, washed her down and moved her into the boathouse to secure her. Mac was nowhere in sight, but he had brought in stacks of discarded car tires to use for additional buffers, just in case the rough water jostled the boats against the pilings.

"I'm going to pick up some supplies for Maggie," Ben said, striding into the boathouse with two coils of additional rope for tying down the cruisers. "Extra ice, batteries in case the electricity goes out. Anything either of you can think of?" Maggie had already decided that all the workers would move into the lodge for the night, and her food and water supply would take care of everyone.

"I need to gas up my car just in case we have to evacuate," Nat explained.

"Go do that now," Ben said calmly. "I want everyone here before dark. The traffic is already picking up on the highway. I don't want anyone far from home when the rains hit." Natalie promptly dropped the tire she was holding and hurried off to the beach house to get her keys. "Natalie," Ben yelled after her. "When you get back, hang around the radio in my office until you hear from Fuzzy. Keep an ear out for anything that may affect us here." Natalie waved an acknowledgment, then jogged on down to Beachside One where her car was parked.

Ben had been right about the increase in traffic on the Overseas Highway. Instead of taking Natalie five minutes to get gas and return, it took twenty-five, even when the station attendant recognized her and let her slip in while a truck with a camper attachment maneuvered closer to the pumps. When she returned to the boathouse, she was all alone. The *Calusa* sat just as she left it, with the tires still waiting to be strung between the boat and the dock pilings. Nat hesitated before deciding that the radio duty came first. When Ben came back, probably with Greg accompanying him, they could all get the *Calusa* secured.

Natalie clicked on the radio receiver, adjusting the knobs so the static faded, and she could eavesdrop on the exchanges over the system. Several calls concerned the increasingly rough waters and high tides. One fellow was calling his son to meet him at another fishing camp on the north side of Little Torch Key. Fuzzy called in his location; he was off Sugarloaf Key and was on his way in. Natalie sat in Ben's armchair monitoring the calls, smiling occasionally when some of the comments distinguished the old seamen from the novices. "Poker game tonight?" the unperturbed old-timers asked, to summon their pals for a friendly game. "Load up plenty of beer," another ordered.

"Seems to be a skiff in trouble out Big Spanish Channel." This call was to Ben. "One of your men is out of gas," the caller said. "Older fellow. Maybe you better send someone to tow him in."

A flurry of garbled sounds interrupted the transmission. Anxiously, Nat adjusted the receiver. When there was no further message, she hastily requested one. "Could you give me the location of the skiff?" she asked. Mac was the only one who took the skiff in that direction. With a storm coming and Mac stalled in the channel, he'd be anxious to get in and help secure the lodge. "With his bad heart," Natalie muttered, her own pulse pounding loudly as she waited for a reply.

"Spanish Channel...Cutoe Banks," came the

broken message. Nat was already nodding. It was not far from Mac's favorite little island, but it was about seven miles from the lodge.

"Relay the message that help is on the way," Nat said into the transmitter. There was no acknowledgment. Hastily she scribbled a note and taped it to the radio. "Mac having boat trouble. Gone to get him. Back soon. Natalie."

She had the *Calusa* skimming along Pine Channel in minutes, staying in the deeper water as she headed out toward Harbor Channel instead of cutting through the shallows into Big Spanish Channel. This way would bring her in behind the stalled boat, but she would also avoid the sea grass and sandbars that could give her own boat serious trouble. Maneuvering around the varying-sized clumps of mangroves, she swung into open water. There was no sign of Mac or any skiff around Cutoe Banks.

Skirting the shallows, Natalie cut across the banks and circled Big Spanish Key. The only other boat out was idling between two half-formed mangrove islands. The two men aboard spotted Natalie. . .and she knew it was a setup. Their boat was the new Bertram that had been stolen from Key West. She had seen the picture in the newspaper. . .right alongside the photograph of its owner, the one found dead in the lifejacket.

"Hijackers. . . ." Natalie gritted her teeth and slammed the *Calusa* into high gear. "Not me. . . ." She cut back around Big Spanish Key and aimed for the Cutoe Banks. Then the first gunshot cracked. Loud, brittle, unmistakable, it made her snap her head around in disbelief. "They're shooting. . .

they're really shooting at me," she moaned. "Move, *Calusa*!" she wailed as the next shots rang out. She cut closer to the mangrove clumps that twisted and turned and linked long fingerlike roots. The *Calusa* was a smaller boat than the stolen Bertram. It could navigate in shallower water, but Nat knew she could not outrun the bigger craft. She could try playing hide-and-seek amid the mangroves, but all it would take was a bad turn to end up face to face with the gunmen.

"If you want me, you'll have to find me," Nat hissed through clenched teeth as she dodged around a string of mangroves and aimed for the familiar mazes off Big Pine Key. "Hide-and-seek...big time." She watched the bottom grow dangerously shallow as she held her breath, hoping her propeller would manage to clear the soft sand. Farther away, the Bertram was cutting her off, staying in the deeper channel, but blocking her way into the safety of the populated keys.

With a final surge of power, Nat aimed the *Calusa* for the narrow opening into Mac's secret inlet, grinding its bottom on the extended roots of the twisted tree that guarded its mouth. The boat leaped into the enclosed waters just as Nat switched off the ignition. Still moving forward from the momentum of the approach, it slid up to the soggy sand and silently nudged its hull against the shore.

Natalie snapped open the holder on the console and lifted out the .357 Magnum. She rolled up her pant legs and hastily lowered herself over the side of the boat. With her bare feet sinking into the soft, gooey sand, she waded in to shore, holding the hand-

gun up out of the water and pulling the heavy tie line
with the other hand. She knotted the rope securely
around the base of the nearest mangrove tree, then
retreated into the bushes, waiting for any sign of her
pursuers.

Crouched under the drooping branches, Natalie
braced the heavy gun between her knees, holding it
with two hands just as Mac had taught her. She could
hear the engine of the Bertram as it circled closer.
Then it stopped abruptly. Natalie sat rigidly, aware
that the driver and the gunman had finally realized
her boat was no longer running.

After a moment, the Bertram started up again, this
time passing near the opposite side of her little island
where the undergrowth was the thickest. Natalie
sprawled on her stomach and wriggled under the
trees, inching her way toward the sound of the Bertram engine. Then there was silence as the hijackers
shut off the engine and tried to pinpoint her location.
One of them bent over the console. The new-model
boat undoubtedly had the latest electronic equipment. Natalie peered out at the drifting cruiser,
guessing that the man in the cockpit was scanning the
radio signals, trying to locate her by her own transmission if she called for help.

She could see the second man more clearly. He was
a short, thin man, strangely dressed for a boat
outing—in a suit and tie. He was obviously the one in
charge of this attack. He scanned the dull waters and
muttered instructions to the boat operator. They let
their boat drift for several minutes more, then the
engine rumbled and they began weaving between the
islands, looking for her again. Once the sound had

faded into the distance, Natalie crawled out from under the bushes and crouched on the sand.

Already the sky was dark and rumbling as the approaching storm spread its irregular gusts and thick clouds ahead of it. The heavy air was thick with the scent of pine and dead fish as the weighty clouds compressed the air and made it throb with anticipation. Natalie hurried back onto the *Calusa*, retrieving another rope, then yanking out a heavy canvas cover to snap closed over the rear of the cockpit. From the cabin, she grabbed a box of matches and several flares, a flashlight, some insect repellant and a container of meat tenderizer that she carried to subdue the bug bites. Her legs were already spotted and itchy from insect bites, and even with the insect repellant, the bites would only get worse as nightfall approached.

Nat hitched the second tie rope to the rear of the cruiser and pulled it to a scruffy Australian pine that had somehow found a foothold amid the mangroves. Now the cruiser was tied loosely at both ends. If the storm came, it could ride out the rough weather without reeling around and scraping against the nearby roots. Natalie retreated once again into the bushes, armed with the .357, the matches and flashlight and the tenderizer. If the men came back and happened to spot the boat through the circle of trees, Nat wasn't going to be anywhere near it.

The boat did return one more time, again avoiding the narrow, shallow stretch near the mouth of the inlet and passing on to the densely covered side. Nat waited in the bushes, clasping the heavy gun and bracing her weary arms upon her knees. "Just forget

it, boys,'' she pleaded as their boat moved along
slowly. Perspiration trickled down onto her lips as
she took silent, shallow breaths and waited for them
to leave. She could remember the ragged hole the
gunshots had made in the tin cans the morning Mac
had given her shooting lessons. If these men knew
where she was, Nat might have to turn that gun on
one of them.

"Go away. . . ." She pressed her lips together and
waited. Then the wind gusted and a new sound swept
across the labyrinth of small islands. It was the soft
rush of the rain as it blew over the water and whispered in the leaves of the trees. Now the departing
boat accelerated, cutting through Big Spanish Channel back toward the main line of the Keys.

"Thank goodness," Nat sighed. She sprawled out
on the ground in relief. Gradually the trickles of rain
leaked down onto her outstretched form, so she
moved farther under the thick-leaved mangroves for
shelter. She broke off several branches and made a
blanket of them on the ground at the base of one
thick trunk for storing the gun and the other supplies. Then she opened the meat tenderizer and began
sprinkling it onto the collection of red insect bites.
The tenderizer immediately dulled the itching. At last
Nat leaned back against the trunk and listened to the
rain as the sky grew steadily darker, finally engulfing
her small island in darkness.

The steady downpour had lasted almost two hours
when Natalie finally decided to go back into the boat
to search for food and something to wrap up in to
sleep through the night. It was still too risky to call in
her location. If the hijackers were within radio range,

they might still reach her before anyone else could. Resolving to wait through the night, she made a stealthy foraging trip into the dark interior of the *Calusa*.

By the time she had carried one load of scrap canvas under the cover of the trees and returned to the boat for the boxes of crackers and lukewarm soft drinks left over from a charter, she was soaked to the skin and shivering. The only item of clothing in the boat was a dull greenish work shirt, grease-stained and ragged, that had been stored with the tools. "At least it's dry," Nat sniffed, stuffing it into a plastic bag. "And it matches the leaves," she noted as she tucked it under her arm and once more jumped over the side of the boat.

She had barely situated herself in her primitive but otherwise snug enclosure when she heard the steady put-put of a smaller boat winding closer and closer. Every few moments, the swish of the rain or the rumble of the thunder would drown out the sound, but when the storm noises subsided, the relentless put-put of an engine would be heard approaching.

Nat grabbed the .357 Magnum and tugged the collar of the work shirt up over her streaked hair for camouflage, then inched back under her canvas canopy. Through the trees, she could see the glare of a hand-held searchlight slashing through the thick tangle of trees. The small boat passed the mouth of the inlet, proceeded on a short distance, then turned and came back. Now the light settled on the huge mangrove that stood like a sentinel at the narrow passage into the heart of her sanctuary.

The skiff motor cut off, then the sound of paddling accompanied its cautious movement up to the roots of the massive old tree. The boat stopped there while the bright light was aimed into the interior, pinpointing the cruiser in its straight beam. Natalie bit her lower lip and willed herself to remain motionless as the bright light zigzagged back and forth across the beach, then skimmed the trees that rimmed it. Nat held the gun low so it wouldn't catch the light and reflect it, giving away her position. *Don't come near me,* her inner voice wailed as the driver used the oar to propel the skiff into the water where the cruiser was moored. Natalie pulled back the hammer into the cocked position and leveled the gun at the shadow holding the light.

The bright light skimmed the outline of the *Calusa* as the skiff pulled alongside. It lingered on the waterline below the neatly lettered name. Nat knew there had to have been some damage to the propeller and rudder when the cruiser had slammed over the entangled roots at the mouth of the inlet. Maybe the intruder would reach the same conclusion and abandon the cruiser as a lost cause.

"Natalie?"

The gun quivered and almost fell from her hands at the sound of her own name.

"Natalie!" The call was more urgent, and the voice was unmistakable. Ben had come for her.

"I'm here." Natalie choked back her tears as she crawled out into the pouring rain. "Here!" The blinding light swung sideways and flashed straight into her eyes. Holding up one hand to deflect the strong light, Natalie loped across the sand. Ben was onto the shore in a matter of seconds, lunging through the soggy beach toward her.

"Put that down," he yelled when the light glinted off the gun in her hand. "It's cocked! You'll blow off a foot—" he snatched it from her grasp "—or my head!" Proficiently he stuck his finger in front of the hammer to block its firing and pulled the trigger to release it, then he eased his finger out and lowered the hammer into place. With a quick motion, he stuffed the weapon deep into the pocket of the raincoat he wore. "Now," he said, as he opened his arms and hugged her. With the rain pouring down around them and the thunder grumbling above, he held her close.

"What the hell are you doing out here?" he finally said, although he didn't release her. "And why didn't you call in?" he demanded. "Is your radio out?"

"The radio is all right, but I think I lost another propeller," she added dutifully.

"Then why didn't you call in?" He moved her back a bit and peered at her through the rivulets of rain streaming down his face.

"They set me up for a hijacking...some men—" the story came out in a torrent "—they shot at me...." She found the words choking her as the sudden onrush of tears poured forth.

"It's okay, it's okay...." He held her against him and stroked her hair. Her shoulders quaked as the terror she had subdued turned into broken sobs of relief.

"Come on." He tugged open the raincoat and

pulled her against his side. "Let's get out of this flood." He led her out to the cruiser, then boosted her aboard, stroking her and calming her while she gasped, trying to squeeze out the details of her escape.

"I thought Mac was in trouble...someone called in...." She shuddered as he switched on the light and began rummaging around the boat for something dry to wrap around her.

"Mac is fine," Ben soothed her. "He was up at my place loading up storage jugs for extra water. When he came back to take over for you at the radio, you were gone...and so was the boat."

"I left a note," Natalie sniffed.

"We didn't find any note." Ben stripped off the wet raincoat and draped that over her while he continued his quest for dry clothing.

"It was taped to the radio."

"It doesn't matter." Ben gave up the search and pulled off his own T-shirt and handed it to her. "We didn't find any note," he said quietly. "But I found you...." He turned to the radio transmitter. "Now you get changed while I let everyone know you're all right."

"If you use the radio, they'll be able to find us...." Nat bolted out of the seat to stop him. "They were *shooting*," she stressed. "They'll come back."

Ben put his hand on her shoulders and eased her back into the seat. "If I don't call in, a lot of folks will be worried sick...about *both* of us," he replied evenly. "I'll make it very clear that I'm here with you...and we're both well armed." He held her still until her muscles relaxed.

"You brought a gun?" Natalie looked up at him.

"I brought a spotlight and a sack of flares," he confided, "but I'm not about to announce that to anyone."

"Aren't you worried that they'll come anyway?"

"From the looks of the *Calusa*, that boat isn't in any condition to do anyone much good. If they were after a boat to run dope, they'll pass this one up for sure." He switched on the radio and called in to the office receiver. "She's safe," he announced rapidly to ease the anxiety of the folks at the other end. "The boat is a mess...rudder and prop are smashed but she's secured for the night. We have a sizable arsenal aboard," he asserted for all who were tuned in. "Send out a boat and tow rope in the morning, and call the Coast Guard and tell them we've located her."

Nat unbuttoned the soggy work shirt and pulled Ben's T-shirt over her head while he was busy with the radio call. "And call Embry," he added.

Nat glanced up in surprise. "Is that how you knew to look for me here?" she whispered. Ben didn't respond. "Come early," he said, signing off.

"Then how did you know I was here?" Nat inquired.

"I didn't know," Ben said as he turned to check that she was dressed. "We tried every place we could think of while it was still light. When I called on Embry, he mentioned the painting...and this island... and that it made a good hiding place. I didn't know if you were in trouble or whether you were just stupid going out like this...but it was a matter of sitting around worrying. . . or taking a chance and running out here.''

"They really shot at me," she said quietly. "It was the new Bertram that was taken from the Keys, the one whose owner. . . .''

"Was murdered," Ben finished. "Well that's the end of our deal," he said evenly. "You're fired. I'm not letting you take any more chances. I was afraid they'd think a woman was an easy target.''

"I won't be so gullible the next time. . . .''

"There won't be a next time," Ben declared flatly. "The boat will be out of commission for a while. It will be a long time till I can afford to fix it. You're out of a boat, Natalie," he stressed, "and out of a job. I won't let you risk your safety again.''

"I'll fix the boat myself," Natalie countered angrily. "I'll pay for the parts with my own money. . . and you can forget about this firing business. I kept them from getting your boat," she stormed. "And if they try it again, I'll stop them the next time.''

"Now take it easy," Ben soothed. Her entire body trembled from both the cold and the stress she had suffered. "Let's just settle down and ride out the storm." He stroked her hair as he sat down beside her. "I'm glad you're all right." He brushed away the tears that streaked her cheeks. "Why don't you go below and crawl into the bunk? I'll keep watch up here, just in case we have any visitors.''

"I'll get seasick," Nat replied. The driving wind and rain was making the *Calusa* bob about like a cork, jerking against the tie ropes like a rodeo mustang. Nat could handle the motion as long as she was upright, but there was no way she could sleep with all that bucking and pitching. On top of that, she still had the uneasy feeling that the two men might return. If they did, she didn't want to be on the boat.

"I see what you mean." Ben grabbed his raincoat as it slid onto the floor. "Do you want to try camping out under the trees again?" He pulled the weather-proof coat over her shoulders.

"I made a dry spot," Nat said, brightening. "I'd feel better out there."

"Then let's go." Ben snapped open the canvas covering that had kept the wind from blowing into the cockpit while they called the lodge. "I'll get the mattress off the bunk so you won't have to sleep on the ground." Natalie waited with the flap held open while he went into the cabin and emerged with the rolled mattress. "Stick it under the coat and I'll piggyback you to shore," he directed, then switched off the light in the boat. Nat expelled a long breath when the darkness again filled the inlet.

"They aren't coming back," Ben insisted. "They aren't that stupid." He was already drenched again as he leaped over the side and reached up for her.

"I hope you're right." Nat braced herself and slid onto his back, still clutching the foam rubber bunk mattress under one arm.

"You've got the gun?" Ben asked abruptly. Natalie could feel the weight in the coat pocket. She didn't have to check.

"I've got it," she confirmed. A sudden flash of lightning followed by a snap of thunder filled the inlet with an eerie light as Ben carried her onto shore. Hugging his neck with one arm, she held on tight, relieved that she had him close to her, and she would not have to wait through the night alone.

They won't be back, she repeated inwardly, hoping desperately Ben was right. *They aren't that stupid,* she insisted.

From the piece of canvas Natalie had found and the large rubberized raincoat of Ben's, they expanded the makeshift canopy into a dry haven large enough for the two of them. In his last tour of the *Calusa*, Ben had located two towels, one that he rolled into a pillow, the other Natalie spread over her as she nestled on the mattress. Ben sat upright, leaning against the trunk of a tree, with a switched-off flashlight in one hand and the gun in the other, while Natalie lay beside him, her hand resting on his upper leg.

Detail by detail, she told him all she could remember about the encounter with the two men in the Bertram, until Ben finally urged her to close her eyes and rest.

"I'll be right here," he promised, putting aside the flashlight so he could cup his hand over hers, reassuring her with the pressure. "You'll have to go through all this tomorrow. The sheriff and the Coast Guard will want to know everything. This time we're calling in the law." His calm voice convinced her he was right. "Tonight, you rest, tomorrow, you talk." Then only the soft rush of the rain and the occasional rumble of thunder filled the dark inlet. With her hand still clasped in his, Natalie lay there with her eyes pressed closed, but sleep would not come.

"I can't seem to turn off my mind." Nat finally gave up trying and pulled herself into a sitting position. "I've got a case of the jitters."

"Come here...lean on me," Ben said evenly. He placed the weapon carefully beside him, then raised his hand, catching her wrist and gently pulling her forward across his outstretched legs. When he had her cradled in his arms, her head resting on his shoulder, he chuckled suddenly. "We really do have to work on our logistics," he asserted. "We can't keep meeting in such uncomfortable places."

"I'm comfortable," Natalie said against his warm, bare chest. Her breath sent a ripple across his dark chest hairs and filled her senses with his delicious scent. When she raised her eyes to his, her entire universe seemed contained in those dark, liquid eyes.

Ben brushed her lips with his, pulling her closer until the contact of her breasts through the thin fabric of the T-shirt separating their bodies sent a shudder of pleasure through him.

"You feel so good," he moaned as he pressed her soft body against his hard, muscular chest. "Natalie...." He moved back and looked down at her hungrily, his eyes, heavy lidded with desire, searching her face for some confirmation.

Natalie parted her lips in a smile, drawing in his hot, moist breath as the tip of his tongue answered her invitation, penetrating deeply, exploring the soft interior with unrestrained sensuality. Barely severing the intimacy of their kiss, Ben slid the thin shirt off, caressing the curves of her breasts, until nothing obstructed the gentle meeting of their bare torsos. His irregular breath fanned across her neck as his dark head dropped to the hollow of her throat.

Ben pressed her back down on the mattress, moving above her as his warm lips traced slow sensuous spirals from the curve of her throat up to her waiting mouth. His soft, moist kisses inched lower in a downward progression between the rise of her breasts. Natalie raked her fingers through his dark hair, arching her back responsively, seeking the contact of his mouth. There were no reluctant whispers haunting her, no reservations, no response other than the soft, repeated sighs that told him *yes*.

Deftly, he slid her jeans from her slim hips. His hands moved languidly over her body, touching and caressing her. Slowly, very slowly, she was seduced by the warm pressure of his hands stroking the soft roundness of her shoulders and breasts.

As he explored the cool silkiness of her skin, he made a low purring sound as if he was luxuriating in the sensation.

"Ben..." Natalie gasped as his fingers boldly discovered her soft hidden recesses. There were no words for the feelings his touch aroused. She could only cling to him and breathe his name.

He caught her whisperings with his lips. She was conscious only of the overwhelming heat in his touch and the exquisite tension of his body as he pressed against the softness of her thighs.

Gently, she drew him closer, removing his jeans. Naked and entwined they lay together feeling the awesome power of their passion. All doubts fled, leaving her in this mist-shrouded inlet, wanting to feel this man move within her and enfold her within his embrace. She had dreamed of this moment. She had often yearned for a moment when passion would overwhelm her and bring her to ecstasy. But the lover she had dreamed of had been faceless and vague.

Now that lover had strength and tenderness and a consuming desire for her. His dark-eyed face was etched into her soul and her phantom lover had a name.

"Ben. . ." she begged him to belong to her.

Ben touched her body with the same unhurried pace that had excited and tantalized Natalie when they had embraced within the darkened cruiser. With deliberate tender movements he stroked her smooth midriff then moved downward, languidly caressing and exploring her body.

For a few seconds Natalie lay in his arms almost motionless as she savored the intensity of the contact. Nat could feel the tremor of his broad back muscles as Ben lifted himself above her, watching her, restraining his own desires until her arousal under his smooth, probing touch told him that her body was ready and eager for his. Then their flesh molded together—their bodies moved together with a time-less instinctive rhythm like the slow insistent sweep and flow of the waves. This time their private world transformed the leafy shelter into a languid sea of sensations as their sighs and soft caresses grew more urgent. The lovers, enveloped in each other's arms, willingly surrendered to the currents of passion, oblivious to the dull rumble of thunder and the steady rush of the tropical storm.

Much later, still side by side on the narrow mat-tress, covered by towels and outspread garments, Natalie finally fell asleep. Cradled against Ben's warm body, she no longer felt haunted by the terror of the chase.

Shortly before dawn, the rain subsided, leaving

only a dull gray drizzle that muffled the early-morning sounds of the sea gulls. When the pale sun-light began to filter through the upper branches of the trees that encircled the inlet, Natalie stirred, roll-ing onto her side so she could face Ben. He was already awake, lying there watching her.

"I'm not sure what the proper etiquette is," Nat said with a slight hesitation. "Do we say 'hello' or 'it was wonderful'?"

Ben smiled at her then pulled her close, lightly kiss-ing her eyelids, the top of her nose, then her lips. His answer was unspoken but eloquent—nothing needed to be said. Gradually the pressure of his morning kisses became more prolonged, instantly bringing back the sensations that had filled their night.

Ben suddenly became still and silent, bracing himself on one elbow while he glanced out into the mist.

"Ben. . . ." Natalie stroked his bare back, urging him to come to her. He raised one finger to silence her. A boat was coming. Its heavy engines droned steadily as it wound through the labyrinth of man-grove islands.

"It might be Mac," Nat breathed, "or Fuzzy."

"Or the guys in the Bertram," Ben said softly. He grabbed the T-shirt from the beach and shook the sand out of it. While Natalie tugged it over her head, Ben unrolled the knotted jeans and panties and passed them to her one at a time, then hastily yanked on his own clothes. "You pull on that raincoat and get back farther in the trees." He picked up the gun.

"I'll stay with you," Natalie insisted.

The low rumble of the boat engine moved closer.

"And do what?" Ben frowned.

"And help. I could light flares and shoot them at the men," she offered as she reached for the matches.

"I'd prefer that you were out of sight," Ben said firmly. "No sense *two* of us taking chances. Now get back in the bushes." He waited for her to move.

"I'll go this way," Nat informed him, starting out the curve of the inlet. "If it isn't Mac or our guys, I'll fire the flares from this side. You can do the rest."

Ben began to argue, then he saw the firm set of her jaw. "Fine," he muttered. "Have it your way. Just try to keep out of sight."

When Natalie was in position on the far side of the inlet, she waved and ducked down behind some scrub palmettos. The approaching boat came to a slow idle, then the engine was cut. After a few seconds, the blue-and-white bow of the *Southwind* eased into the mouth of the inlet.

"Nat-a-lee!" Hector bellowed. "It's me and Mac," he yelled clearly. "Don't you guys shooooot me."

Ben stepped from behind a tall tree, the gun at his side. "Come on in," he called back. "Watch out for the roots."

Across the inlet Natalie was standing and waving with both arms. "Hector, you've never looked so good!" She dropped the flares at her feet then waded into the cool water to the *Southwind*.

The boat couldn't make it into the shallow inlet without suffering some damage, so it anchored outside the mouth while Ben and Hector untied the *Calusa* and moved it into position to force it back over the roots. They swam along beside it. Natalie tied the tow rope to the skiff and pulled it out toward Mac. Once he had it secured to the *Southwind*, he started the engines and tugged it through the mouth of the inlet while Ben and Hector stood on the roots, easing her past.

"I'll bring the skiff." Ben climbed in beside Natalie. "We'll follow you in." Mac pitched two heavy sweatshirts to them, then waved and started for the channel. Hector rode in the crippled *Calusa*, occasionally glancing back to watch the skiff bobbing along in its wake.

"You can call your dad when you get fed and cleaned up." Ben leaned forward as he spoke so Nat could hear him above the sound of the motor. "If he's not in, we call Buzz Cochran."

"I'm not going home." Nat leveled her narrowed eyes at him. "I'm going to fix the boat."

"No, you aren't," Ben countered.

"Yes, I am," Nat replied obstinately. "And when it's fixed, I'm coming back to work."

"You were fired, remember?" Ben shot back.

"I remember that we had an agreement...."

"Which we aren't too successful at keeping." His eyes sparkled with a strange light.

"I mean the *business* agreement," Nat stressed. Other thoughts were making the color rise in her cheeks. In spite of the intensity of her determination, she felt the urge to laugh with joy. "I am *not* giving up my job," she declared.

"You *don't have* a job." Ben considered the subject closed.

Natalie sat for a moment, then she tried again. "If

it's the money that's bothering you, I'll lend it to the business. You can put it on the books and pay me back next fall, after the business picks up.''

''I don't want your money,'' he said sternly.

''You borrow from the bank.'' Nat tried to sound reasonable. ''I'm responsible for the damage to the boat. I'll provide the labor—''

''No deal,'' Ben interrupted.

''You need the boat in the water and operating—''

''No deal,'' Ben repeated.

''You let Angela Sutton do her part in boosting your business,'' Nat blurted out in frustration. ''Why can't I help?'' she demanded. Ben glared at her and shook his head.

''*Mr.* Sutton helps my business,'' he said precisely, biting off his words angrily.

''Then what exactly is it that Angela does with her friends and contacts? Never mind,'' Nat silenced him before he could reply. ''I don't want to know what she does. That was a little bitchy of me to say.''

''I couldn't agree more,'' Ben answered dryly.

''Unless you throw me off your land—kicking and screaming,'' she warned him, ''I'm going to stay.'' Ben slowed the motor to a dull throb and let the two boats move farther ahead. ''I have my work with you and my studies with Roger...and I promised to teach Hector how to drive a car.''

''Does that cover everything?'' Ben shook his head and suppressed a chuckle.

''Almost.'' Natalie refused to be patronized.

''How about taking a few days off? Just keep out of sight while the police and the Coast Guard check into this episode. When we see what they turn up, then we'll figure out what to do next.'' Ben seemed willing to appease her.

''I want to help repair the boat.'' Nat stood her ground.

''Maybe,'' Ben hedged. ''We'll check out the damage and see how much it will cost. If I can scrape up the cash, you can work on it,'' he conceded, ''but for a few days you stay off the water—spend the charter time with Embry. Keep out of sight until we see if there's more to this than we realize.''

''Like what?'' Nat demanded.

Ben closed his eyes momentarily as his jawline tensed in frustration. ''Let me do some checking, then I'll tell you.'' He adjusted the throttle, and the skiff took off rapidly after the larger boats.

''In other words,'' Nat yelled over the roar of the motor, ''trust you.''

Ben turned to look into her questioning eyes. ''Yes,'' he mouthed silently. She slowly nodded, then looked out over the water back toward the nameless key where they had loved and slept and loved again.

When they rounded the tip of Little Torch Key, Ben cut over the wake of the two cruisers and skimmed ahead of them, angling into the Gold Coast Lodge ahead of the others. Already a small reception committee was forming on the dock. Maggie and Maria each had aprons flapping in the breeze. There was a uniformed officer from the sheriff's department, another fellow Natalie didn't recognize and a slender black-haired female.

Angela Sutton. The name leaped into Natalie's mind almost instantly. Clad in the palest pink sundress, with its full shirt fluttering about her legs, Angela waited side by side with an unidentified man.

"Wonderful," Nat muttered dully as she glanced down at the oversize sweatshirt she'd been given. She started to smooth out the numerous strands of hair that had escaped from her braid during the night, then she stopped herself. Ben had told Nat she looked lovely—with words and looks and caresses. There was no reason for her to improve her appearance just to impress anyone on shore. When the skiff glided up to the dock, Natalie stood tall and straight in the bow. She felt she was ready for anything.

CHAPTER TWELVE

"Bringing in the lost lamb?"

Natalie heard Angela Sutton's comment as Ben helped her out of the skiff. Angela was speaking to Ben, not to her, so Nat kept moving toward Maggie whose large arms opened to receive her.

"Let's get something warm in your stomach." Maggie promptly ushered Nat off toward the lodge. "You can tell us all about this mess while you eat. I sure am glad to see you back safe, honey." She kept one arm around Nat as they made their way across the parking lot.

Maria scurried along with them, casting uneasy glances back at the quartet of men who remained at dockside with Angela. "The sheriff wants to talk with you," Maria told Nat, "but he said it could wait until you get some nourishment."

"I wish you-know-who and that guy with her were that considerate," Maggie muttered.

"What are they doing here?" Natalie looked over her shoulder at the twosome. The man in white slacks and a blazer looked as out of place as Angela did, wearing her filmy pink dress in the midst of the charter outfit.

"I haven't the faintest," Maggie huffed. "She called here twice last night—long distance—with a lot of loud music and laughter in the background. From the looks of it, the party lasted all night. She showed up an hour ago with that man in tow. Even with all this going on, they hung around waiting for Ben." Maggie led the procession into the snug kitchen. "Everyone here was in an uproar waiting for the boats to bring you back. The police were gabbing over the radio and makin' phone calls back and forth. . .and *she* wants everything to come to a halt so she can talk with Ben." Maggie tugged open the refrigerator door and harrumphed irritably.

"I sure wish she'd leave him alone," Natalie commented softly as she lowered herself into a chair. There was no trace of jealousy in the remark. Nat was simply voicing her concern over Angela's persistence. Whatever brought Angela and her companion there was not merely a social call—it was something far more ominous.

"I wish she'd leave us *all* alone," Maggie concurred as she poured some hot chocolate into a mug and slid it in front of Natalie. Even though the sun was climbing slowly in the sky, chasing away the low streaks of clouds that still lingered in the wake of the storm, the damp air had been cool enough to make Natalie shiver. Now, the warm liquid sent a comforting sensation throughout her tired body.

Maggie stacked sourdough pancakes on a heated plate and poured herself a cup of coffee. Until now, all she wanted was to warm and comfort her young friend. But the waiting had been difficult, and the time had come to hear the details of Nat's ordeal. Maggie sat across from Natalie and listened eagerly, while Maria leaned against the kitchen door, intent on the conversation, but able to keep a lookout for customers or any incoming visitors.

About midway through Natalie's account, Maria fluttered her fingers and hissed so the twosome would look her way. "The man from the sheriff's department is coming. What should I do?"

"Bring him in here." Maggie waved Maria out to intercept the officer. "I'll get a cup of coffee for him." She paused with one hand on her hip, waiting for Maria to leave. "Go on," Maggie chuckled. "We won't let you miss a single detail," she promised the pretty young woman. "She'll probably have to start all over again, anyhow." Maggie wriggled her finger and sent Maria scurrying out the door. "Go...."

On the next recounting of the events, Sergeant Weekley, a square-jawed, broad-shouldered investigator, sat across from Natalie, diligently taking down the specifics she related. Already he had pages of indecipherable scribbling, which he separated from her section by two thick pencil lines and her name in large letters.

Slowly and patiently, Weekley asked Nat questions, eliciting bits of information about the boat and its two occupants that she hadn't realized she'd even noticed. Occasionally he would suggest that Natalie simply close her eyes and think a moment, to reenact the encounter in her mind. It was like painting without a brush—reconstructing a memory.

"Your friend Hector says you're quite an artist." Weekley seemed determined to call upon all her abilities. "How difficult would it be for you to sketch anything you saw?"

"I'm not good at faces," Natalie replied. She had

seen enough television shows in which the police artist did a striking portrait of a suspect to know that
her skills were no match for that type of challenge.
"I'd have better luck with the boat."

"Just try to give a general idea of this guy's
build." Weekley pulled out a sheet of lined paper and
slid it toward her. "Maybe just the outline of his
face. It might help you recall some crucial information if you fiddle around with the pencil while we
keep talking." He passed his pencil to Natalie.

"I'll try." She took the pencil and stared at the
dull blue lines on the page. Finally she sketched an
oval for the head, and the page was no longer so
empty or threatening. The first stroke was always the
hardest, but once it was done, the creative juices
began to flow. Every few moments, Nat would use
the investigator's technique—closing her eyes and
concentrating. One image would overlap another,
until she finally had provided a reasonably accurate
drawing of the hijackers and the boat they had used.

Maggie sat in respectful silence, watching the
sketches evolve from dull grayish pencil lines into the
angular, evil creatures who had terrorized her young
friend.

"I only saw one face clearly," Natalie said, passing the paper back to Sergeant Weekley. "The one
who drove the boat had a hat on—and sunglasses,
the mirrored kind—and he stayed in the cockpit."

"Sunglasses...." Weekley inspected the profile of
the driver that Nat had drawn. His eyes shifted to the
more detailed sketch. "This other one...the guy
who did the shooting...." His voice trailed off
thoughtfully as he stared at the rough portrait. Nat

had the feeling that Weekley recognized the man, but the officer only nodded at her work and grinned at her. "This is excellent, Natalie," he thanked her. "You'll make a deadly witness when we get these two."

He placed the sketches carefully between the pages of his notebook and flipped it closed. Whatever he saw in the drawing of that face would remain unspoken. "Let me run what I've got through the computer and do a little checking," Weekley said, calmly concluding the interview. "I'll get back to you as soon as I hear anything." He inclined his head toward Maggie Butler. "Thank you, ma'am, for your hospitality." Then he downed the last of his coffee and quietly left the room.

Several minutes later, Natalie stepped out onto the porch of the lodge. Across the parking lot, the blond-haired investigator, Weekley, was engrossed in conversation with Hector and Ben. The men looked up at her, then continued talking as she started across the parking area toward the shell path.

"We heard you eluded an entire gang of hijackers." Angela Sutton's voice came from behind Natalie. Nat turned to find Angela and her friend heading in her direction.

"Not a *gang*," Natalie replied politely, "just two men."

"Maybe it was just a prank," Angela suggested, "to chase you through the swamps...."

"There aren't any *swamps* around here," Natalie bridled, "and—"

"Natalie," Ben called abruptly, "can you come here for a minute?" He sounded insistent. Half relieved to have an excuse for leaving Angela, Nat took long strides to the three men standing by the tackle-shop door. When she reached Ben's side, she glanced over her shoulder. Angela and her companion were following at a much slower pace.

"Don't say anything in front of them," Ben whispered to her as he moved her between himself and Sergeant Weekley. Natalie sighed in exasperation. She had no intention of running through the story again—especially not for Angela.

"Ben, I really hate to rush you," Angela smiled, "but we do need a few minutes alone with you. Andrew and I have to be getting back to Miami."

"In ten minutes. . .in my office," he replied evenly. "Just let me get Natalie settled in her quarters. She's had a long night," he said solemnly.

"I'm sure she can manage on her own, Ben—" Angela's smile became rigid "—and we are rather pressed for time."

Weekley shrugged and tapped Ben on the shoulder. "I've got a couple of calls I need to make. We can talk in the lodge in a half hour." Ben nodded without taking his eyes from Angela.

"Fine," Ben remarked softly. "I wouldn't want to inconvenience you and Andrew."

Weekley departed for the lodge, leaving Hector shifting his eyes uncertainly from Nat and Ben to Angela and the blazer-clad man at her side.

Everything about Hector's look told Natalie something was very wrong with this meeting.

"Why don't you two go on to the beach house." Ben nodded for Hector and Natalie to leave. "I'll take care of this, then I'll check on you in a few minutes.''

Natalie looked at Ben curiously. Something in his manner seemed to indicate that at this moment Angela and her private meeting with Ben and the fellow named Andrew took priority, and Nat and Hector were simply in the way. Without a word, Nat walked off along the shell path, with Hector hurrying to catch up. The last comment she heard was Angela's...something about making this worth Ben's time.

''You mad at Ben?'' Hector kept his voice low as they walked along. ''Look, this Andrew guy could be business—*fishing* business,'' he stressed. ''Ben wouldn't do anything stupid.''

Natalie shook her head angrily. ''That Andrew doesn't look like a fisherman to me,'' she sniffed. ''His fingernails are longer than Angela's.''

''Ooooh, you *are* mad.'' Hector kept in step with her.

''I don't like to be sent off simply because it's convenient for those two,'' she stated. ''And I don't intend to sit in my room like a good little girl and wait for Ben to 'check' on me.''

''What are you going to do?'' Hector asked apprehensively.

Natalie stopped short as she spotted her red Mustang parked in the shade. ''I think I'll take a drive,'' she decided. ''Let's get cleaned up and play hooky for the day.''

''Gee, I don't know. . . .''

''I'll give you your first driving lesson,'' she tempted him.

"You feel like giving me a driving lesson *now*?" Hector blinked.

"If that woman is still here when we're leaving," Natalie said with a tight smirk, "I'll give you parking lessons—*on* Miss Sweetness-and-Light herself. Just imagine gray tire tracks across pale pink...."

Hector burst out laughing. "Oooh, Nat-a-lee," he hooted. "You are one mean ladeee," he cackled. Nat found herself laughing, too, as the outrageous idea broke the tension in her chest. What Nat was feeling was frustration, not anger. Even as she and Hector climbed the steps of the beach house, Ben was in his office discussing something profitable—and possibly illegal—and there was nothing she could do about it.

Natalie showered and shampooed and scrubbed until all the sand and grit from the long night on the nameless key were gone. As she looked at herself in the bathroom mirror, standing naked and glistening with droplets of water, she could see no outward signs of the intimate encounter she had shared with Ben. All the changes were intangible ones. Nat had followed the yearnings of her body and her soul—she had made love with Ben Andress. There had been no sense of surrender, only the joy of sharing sensations—of touching and being touched.

She brushed her long hair until it was almost dry, then pulled on shorts and the frilliest blouse she could find—a white muslin strapless top that made her dark tan seem like burnished gold. Even Hector changed shirts and pulled on a pair of jeans that still retained their original shape.

"Where are we *really* goin'?" Hector asked as she grabbed the car keys and started for the door.

"Away from here," she said with a frown. Then she shrugged and smiled slightly. There was truly nowhere else she wanted to be. "Let's go see Roger... and visit the deer," she said evenly. "Only you'll have to tell him *The Adventures of Natalie*...if he asks...which he will."

"How about if I drive?" Hector grinned slyly.

"Not if the investigator is still here." Natalie summoned him to follow her. "I've had enough cops-and-robbers for today, my friend."

"Sergeant Weekley's all right," Hector assured her. "He's been around here long enough to know I'm not up to anything bad."

Nat looked up curiously. "I've never seen him around here."

"He comes by every couple of weeks," Hector explained. "To see Ben and me—he's the one who picked me up on the possession charge."

"You sure don't hold a grudge," Nat marveled.

"It wasn't his fault, it was mine." Hector shrugged. "He was decent enough to go to court and recommend probation, then he helped me get the job here with Ben."

"He knows Ben that well?" Nat was bewildered. She kept seeing the image of Weekley, Ben, Angela and the mysterious Andrew all standing together.

"No one knows Ben *well*," Hector grinned. "But Weekley did know Ben before I showed up."

Natalie shook her head to clear away the image of Angela and Andrew. It would be just like Angela to parade one of her drug-related friends into Gold Coast Lodge right under the nose of the law. Natalie tried not to think about what they might be talking about in Ben's office.

The car from the sheriff's department was still parked by the boathouse, although Sergeant Weekley was nowhere in sight. Ben stood beside the door, shaking hands with Andrew while Angela smiled approvingly. She looked up when a red Mustang with Natalie at the wheel and Hector at her side zipped across the parking lot and turned toward the highway.

"My, my, she recovered quickly," Angela offered as she scrutinized the golden-haired female with bronze shoulders."

"Drop it, Angela," Ben rumbled. "Give her a little space."

"Let's give her a lot of space, Ben," Angela retorted as she sent a dubious sidelong glance to him. Just then Sergeant Weekley emerged from the lodge and called to Ben.

"Gotta go—big meeting with the chief. I'll catch you later, Ben." They exchanged acknowledging waves as Weekley climbed into his car and left.

Angela heaved an exaggerated sigh. "Now I suppose we can get on with it," she commented. Andrew smiled broadly at Ben. "How fortunate that we need a favor from you at precisely the same time *another* of your boats is damaged," Angela said with a pout. "Poor Ben—so many expenses."

"Right, how fortunate," Ben replied unenthusiastically. When he looked up toward the shell road, the last wisps of dust from Natalie's rapid departure were settling.

WHEN HECTOR AND NAT RETURNED to the lodge late in the afternoon, Nat pulled over at the entrance and let Hector take the driver's seat.

"As long as we're on private property, we're free to practice the tricky parts," she teased, "like starting and stopping." Hector gave her a disgruntled look and clasped the gearshift knob.

On the third try, Hector succeeded. He even managed to get into second gear as they cut across the grassy area to the row of beach houses and the clump of trees where Natalie usually parked.

"Not bad for a beginner...." Hector resumed his usual grin. "Maybe if I practice and get real good I'll be ready to try parking on Ań-gee-la." They were both chuckling when the crunch of footsteps on the shell path intruded upon their private joke.

"Natalie." At the sound of her name, Nat turned abruptly and glanced from Ben to Sergeant Weekley to the man who accompanied them. "Here we go again," she muttered softly.

"This is Joe Caputo," Weekley said to introduce his plainclothes companion. "He's working for DEA on drug traffic from Columbia." Sergeant Weekley caught the bewildered look on Nat's face and interpreted the initials. "Drug Enforcement Administration," he informed her. Natalie extended her arm and shook the man's hand.

"We think we have a lead on your man." The raspy-voiced Caputo sounded more formidable than he looked. He was small and balding, and his appearance reminded her more of an optometrist than a crusader against drug traffickers. "We're just not sure whether you'll be safe out here while we're tracing him.''

''You're kidding.'' Natalie felt her smile waver at the tone the conversation was taking on.

''He's not,'' Ben said. ''Greg has disappeared.''

''You mean someone has kidnapped Greg?'' Nat gasped.

''No, his beach house is cleaned out. It looks like he packed up and took off,'' Weekley cut in with his calm, reassuring manner. ''Ben tells us that these guys sometimes come around and work for a few months, then they move on. Maybe that's it. Then again,'' he added, shrugging, ''there may be more to it.''

Caputo nodded.

Weekley cleared his throat and went on. ''It's possible that some of the things that have been going on around here are a lot more interrelated than they appeared. From your perspective, whatever happens you read hijacking into it. That made sense to us—up to a point. Hijackers usually hit and run. They wouldn't take so many risks and cause so much damage to boats at one outfit.''

''Like the two engines somebody screwed up,'' Hector offered excitedly. ''Boy, they were both seized up tight and steamin' hot.''

''Two?'' Weekley shot Ben a surprised look. ''I thought only one engine was fouled.''

Already Nat could feel the color drain from her face. They had agreed to tell Ben only one engine was severely damaged. Supposedly the other engine only had the fuel lines replaced.

Hector's mouth dropped open as he realized what he had done.

"There were two." Nat figured there was no reason to cover up the extent of the repairs now. "Something was put in the fuel of both boats. We rebuilt two engines. . . but we only told Ben about one of them," she confessed.

"That makes it even more suspicious," Weekley said. "A hijacker doesn't damage the engine of a boat he wants," Weekley stressed. "One boat or two, it wasn't the boats he was after."

"What then?" Nat asked.

"That's what we're working on," the smaller investigator, Caputo, commented. "They apparently came after you a second time."

"You mean when I threw the propeller," Nat nodded. There was no doubt someone had tampered with the *Calusa* that time. Caputo and Weekley exchanged silent looks and went on.

"Then there was this chase yesterday," Caputo declared. "We're not sure if the setup was intended for you in particular or for anyone who answered the call. Who knew you were on the radio at the time?"

"Ben. . .and I guess Greg," Nat said quietly. "No one else was around. By the time I got gas in the car and came back, Ben and Greg had gone for supplies." Again the two officers looked at each other, and Nat had the uncomfortable feeling that they knew a great deal more than they let on.

"And the note you left behind when you went to answer the distress call—" Caputo was mentioninng a bit of information he had to have picked up from Ben or Sergeant Weekley "—simply vanished. Perhaps you were supposed to vanish, too, Miss Bishop," the officer concluded.

"Maybe," Weekley observed. "It looks as if someone was working from the inside, someone who knew when you were the most vulnerable."

"Not Greg," Nat protested. "He's my mate...." Her voice trailed off uncertainly. "When we threw the prop, he didn't try anything then," she argued.

"There were witnesses," Weekley shrugged.

"Maybe he was hoping to let the sharks do it for him," Ben suggested grimly.

"Or he could have been sizing you up for later," Weekley noted. "Look, we don't have all the pieces, either. We simply think Ben has been having more than just a run of bad luck. Until we find out what's happened to Greg, we're gonna keep a closer eye on this place." He glanced over at the row of four beach houses on pilings. "You're wide open here," he commented flatly.

"I think it would be a good time to call it quits, Natalie—go on home." Ben's somber tone matched that of the two investigators.

"I'll go to Roger's cottage," Nat bargained. "It's on the restricted part of the Refuge. No one other than the Refuge staff is allowed in that area. Hector is the only one who's been there with me."

"I suppose that would do," Caputo agreed.

"What about her car?" Weekley tilted his head toward the red Mustang. "Pretty noticeable...."

"I'll take her over there in my Jeep," Ben offered. "We'll put her car in the shed by my place."

"As long as her vehicle is off the road for a few days and Miss Bishop stays out of sight," Caputo stressed, "we may iron all this out without endangering anyone." He seemed satisfied.

"Then I suggest you make the arrangements, Natalie." Sergeant Weekley hurried her along. "If Ben is going to take you over there and get you settled, you'd better do it now. Once it gets dark, I don't want anyone unaccounted for."

"Come on, Hector." Nat headed for the beach house. "You moved me in, you can move me out again... *temporarily*," she added loudly for the benefit of Ben Andress.

JACK WILSON, the Refuge manager, met the Jeep at the entrance to the restricted area and stayed on guard at the gate while Ben drove his rattling vehicle right up to Roger's door. Ben unloaded Natalie's suitcase and followed her inside.

"I'm giving you the bedroom." Roger ushered them right through the house to the small room at the rear. "I'll take the sofa, of course." His ears turned reddish under Ben's stern gaze. "You must be the renowned Captain Andress," Roger continued nonstop. "I've heard a great deal about you."

"Roger," Nat said as she turned to give the artist a curious look, "what's the matter with you?"

"I'm nervous." Roger's color deepened. "All this business about guns and hijackings has got to me. I'm not really the heroic type—and here you are, and I don't know if you'll be safe here or not. And they've put another guard on for the night," he rambled on. "This one has a gun. Nat, I can't believe anyone would try to harm you. Perhaps I'm overreacting," he apologized.

"This is just a precaution." Nat walked over and

hugged him. "You really are a pillar of stability," she teased.

He expelled a long breath. "Perhaps we could all use a cup of tea," Roger rallied. "Captain Andress?"

"Just *Ben*," he said, reaching out a hand. A relieved Roger shook it.

"Ben," Roger said, "would you like some tea?"

"I need to get back to the Lodge," Ben insisted. "I'm pleased to meet you, and I appreciate your hospitality—" he seemed comfortable with the artist "—but we want things to look as normal as possible."

"Normal—certainly." Roger understood immediately. "Then you just go about your regular routine. I'll just brew some tea for Natalie and myself." He led them from the bedroom door back through the living room. With a sly look at Natalie, he made his parting comment. "Maybe you could give Ben a quick tour of the dock...while I get the kettle to boil."

Natalie smiled at Roger's convenient disappearance and turned to look up at Ben. He was smiling, too.

"Come on." She took his hand and led him out the side door of the cabin, down to the water where the runabout was tied. "Sometimes we take the boat out to one of those islands." She shaded her eyes, blocking out the low sun, as she looked out across the channel. Far out, over the clumps of mangrove islands, a dark cormorant spread its long wings and sailed on the wind. Then the great bird swooped behind one cluster of tangled trees and disappeared.

They stood hand in hand, watching in silence as the setting sun spread its golden carpet of shimmering light for them.

"I love it here," she said in a voice soft with awe. Ben slid his hand from hers and raised his arm to embrace her shoulders, pulling her against his side.

"It's beautiful...and peaceful, for now." Ben stroked her shoulder gently. "I'm just not sure you wouldn't be safer at your father's house."

"I'll be fine here," Nat insisted. "Besides, I'll be able to get some work done. You don't find many frigate birds building their nests in downtown Key West."

"I just don't want anything to happen to you," he said with difficulty.

"I'll keep that in mind," Natalie said softly. "I just hope you're careful not to jeopardize anything either," she added pointedly.

"Now what's that supposed to mean?" Ben looked down at her.

"It means that I hope you can wait out this investigation and keep things going at the lodge—without making any mistakes."

"What kind of mistakes?"

"Mistakes with Angela Sutton and her friend." Natalie watched as Ben's eyes narrowed slightly, then he turned his gaze to the far line of clouds out over the islands.

"I'm not making any mistakes," he said quietly.

"Then what's going on between you and them?" Nat couldn't stop the question she had held back so long.

"I can't tell you," Ben replied evenly. "I might be

able to talk about it in a couple of days, but not now.''

"Here we are with investigators all over the place, and she shows up with her buddy, trying to manipulate you and drag honest, upright Ben Andress into their little business.''

Again his eyes narrowed, but this time he did not respond.

"Don't you know that Angela Sutton has ice in her veins?'' Nat spoke with real anger in her voice. "She's like a barracuda—taking bites out of people whenever it pleases her. Once she gets what she's after, I doubt that she'll care who gets chewed up in the process. Please, Ben...don't let her get you involved with drugs.''

"What a pair we make.'' Ben turned his solemn eyes to meet hers. "I'm worried about you...and you're worried about me. Believe me, Natalie, I have no intention of jeopardizing anything important,'' he insisted, "but I can't talk to you about any of this yet. I have to make a run on the *Southwind*, and I'll be gone for a couple of days.''

Natalie turned away from him abruptly as tears began to well up in her eyes. Still, he did not touch her.

"If you care for me...if you care about us... you'll keep your mouth closed and your suspicions to yourself. If anything leaks out about me or Angela or Andrew...I want to be sure that it could *not* have come from you. Just trust me,'' he requested. "Two days, no more. Believe me, everything will be all right.''

"All right? How can anything between us be all

right now?'' Natalie sobbed as tears streaked her face. ''If you go on some errand for Angela, you're risking everything—your business, your freedom... maybe even your life.'' Nat knew only too well how high the casualty rate was among people in the drug trade. ''But it isn't whether or not you get caught.'' She turned to face him, brushing the tears aside with her fingertips. ''What matters is that *I* know you have no scruples. You'd actually deal in drugs...and expect me to overlook it. Well, I can't do that.''

''I'm not asking you to overlook anything,'' Ben answered. ''I'm asking you to give me two days of silence—two days of suspended judgment. It took a long time to set things up. There's nothing I can tell you about it until it's over.'' The tremor in his voice made her look away.

''There's nothing to wait for,'' Nat stormed. ''Anything we had between us is over. You underestimated me, Ben. You think just because I care for you, I'll look the other way...I'll get over this. Eventually the tears will go away, but I'll know the truth about you.'' It frustrated her that just when she wanted to appear so formidable the tears wouldn't cooperate. Tears simply kept coming. ''And I'll never be able to trust you again.''

''Natalie....'' He reached toward her.

''Don't you touch me.'' She gritted her teeth. ''You have to hurry back to your schemes. So go!'' she demanded, raising her voice.

Ben glared at her, the muscles in his neck tensing. After several seconds he spoke. ''I'll call you in a couple of days.'' He backed away slowly.

"Don't bother," Nat shot back. "I've heard enough to last me for a long time."

"Stay safe," he said firmly.

"Go away," Nat sniffed and turned her back to him. She could tell he remained there for a few seconds, then his steps across the dock signaled his departure. "Ben," she lamented in a whisper. "How could you be so dumb?"

When the engine of his Jeep switched on, she stiffened, but she did not turn away from the water. Natalie felt as if something important and good had disappeared from her life. Slowly she raised her chin and dried her tears as the last gleam of light from the white gold sun slid beneath the horizon.

CHAPTER THIRTEEN

"SINCE IT LOOKS LIKE YOU HAVE MORE TIME on your hands than we expected—" Roger smiled across the breakfast table at his guest "—I might as well spring this on you now."

Natalie looked up from stirring her coffee.

"I hope this isn't more bad news," she said forlornly. She had barely slept, worrying about Ben and his illicit business with Angela.

"Yes and no." Roger stood and retrieved a manila folder from the counter. "A fellow I know approached me about doing the illustrations for a children's book—about the Keys," he stressed. "It really isn't something I can get excited about," he confessed. "I'm more interested in getting through here and going back to Atlanta. *This* would keep me here." He passed the folder to Natalie.

"So?" She eyed him curiously.

"So I showed him a few of *your* things," Roger replied smugly. "He picked up right away on the touches of humor—the goofy expression on your sea gull, the spraddle-legged deer you did. He really liked what he saw. He said *maybe*—" he emphasized the word "—if you would do a couple of preliminary drawings, he could offer you the commission instead of harassing me."

Natalie flipped open the folder and began reading the neatly typed pages of the manuscript. It was called *A Child's Guide to the Florida Keys* and was divided into sections about the birds, tropical plants, sea creatures, boats and landmarks that children might see and identify if they had a picture book to follow. A slight smile tilted one corner of Nat's mouth as she read the brief but amusing commentary. With the right artwork it would be the kind of book she would love to give her nephews and nieces...*even a child of my own....* The thought drifted through her mind.

"What about it?" Roger leaned forward anxiously. "I'd rather hoped it would appeal to you."

"It appeals to me," Nat said softly. She remembered all the sketch pads full of drawings she had done as a child—with fat pelicans and soaring frigate birds. Now that her talents were developed, she could do what her father had dreamed: "capture whatever your eyes see and your spirit feels." She could capture these things and pass on her visions to children.

"I had a feeling this project was for you," Roger sighed in relief. "I'm sure once my friend Jerry Potter sees your first few paintings, you'll get the commission. I won't even need to use my influence and powers of persuasion," he chuckled.

"You don't mind losing the money?" Nat asked him.

"You need it more than I do," he responded. "From the look of things at the lodge, unless you do this, you may be an unemployed college graduate."

Natalie stared down at the pages. He had a point. Regardless of what the drug investigators turned up, there was no need for her to remain at the Gold Coast Lodge. Roger had known this last night. After a dinner eaten in near silence, Roger had come around to her side of the kitchen table to clasp her hand and say, "When this all settles down, get out of here, Natalie. Go back home to Key West. You should put some distance between Ben and you so you can take a long look at where your life is heading. There's too much pressure on you here for you to make any important decisions."

Nat hadn't told him about her suspicions—nothing about Angela and her friend Andrew. Roger was speaking as a friend who knew only that something was troubling her.

Natalie looked up from the manuscript. "Are you sure you aren't offering this simply because you feel responsible for me in some way?"

"You must be kidding," Roger grinned. "A fool I am *not*. Sooner or later you'll make it on your own. I just wanted to help make it *sooner*. I'll get your eternal gratitude—*and* you might find some commissions for me down the line that aren't right for you," he smiled. "And besides, it's right for you, your style. Jerry Potter will be indebted to me for finding him such a wonderful illustrator. So you see, I can't lose."

"Then I'll see what I can come up with." Natalie returned the warm smile and tucked the folder under her arm as she sipped the last of her coffee. "Where are we working today?" She was eager to begin.

"Let's stick close to the Refuge," Roger suggested cautiously. "At least until we hear from the investigators that it's safe to wander around."

"I really would like to do some bird-watching," Nat proposed. "I could use an egret, maybe a couple of gulls, a great white heron...." She named some birds from those mentioned in the manuscript.

"I'm working on a deer," Roger said. "Wilson has one over at his place with real personality," he laughed. "I'll finish working on it while it's still recuperating."

"Recuperating from what?"

"Jack removed a splinter from its foot," Roger explained. "As long as the deer's foot is still too tender to use, it doesn't seem to mind posing while I draw."

"Then you go finish your work—" Nat deposited her coffee cup in the sink "—and I'll sit on the dock and pitch out a few bread crumbs. Maybe one of our feathered residents won't mind posing for me." The two of them packed away the remnants of their breakfast and collected their painting paraphernalia, each aiming for a different location to spread out supplies and begin work.

Natalie found herself working with an intensity she hadn't felt in a long while. Perhaps it was the excitement of the commission she could win, but at the edge of her consciousness was Ben. All day long, Natalie worked hard, almost furiously, to keep the image of his tanned face and solemn eyes from her mind.

It was almost three in the afternoon when Roger came to sit beside Natalie on the dock.

"How's it going?" he asked, as he looked at the pages of discarded sketches.

"Promising," Nat responded. "I know where I *should* be sitting. There must be a nesting place for

egrets on the other side of Howe Key." She pointed
to the low, tree-shrouded key to the west. "I watched
them come and go all day. Hardly any came this direction." She dropped her sketching pencil atop the
scattered pads. "I could take the runabout—"

"Hey, you'd better check with the guys from the
sheriff's department who told you to stay out of
sight. Jack said no one called today, so why don't we
go in and call them?" he suggested. "If they say you
can go out in the boat, then you can go."

"It's just right over *there*." Natalie pointed at the
island. "This is almost like having to get a note from
your parents," she muttered. But she knew Roger
was simply looking out for her safety. "Come on—"
she hopped to her feet "—let's call the lodge first.
Maybe they have some news."

By the time Nat and Roger cut across to the cabin,
the tan-and-gold car from the sheriff's department
with Sergeant Weekley at the wheel was already pulling into the restricted area. With him was Joe Caputo
from the Drug Enforcement Administration.

"How about looking at a few of *our* pictures for a
change," Weekley greeted the two artists. "See if any
of these faces look familiar to you," he called to Nat.
The four of them proceeded into the living room of
the cabin where Weekley spread a stack of photographs on the table.

Natalie bent over the photos, inspecting each one,
then sliding it to the side and examining the next. In
the midst of the assortment was the thin man who
had pursued her in the boat.

"That's the one with the gun." Nat rested an index
finger on the photograph. Weekley never said a

word. He seemed to have anticipated her identification of that face.

"You're sure?" Caputo urged her to take another look.

"I'm sure," Nat replied. "Who is he?"

"I'd rather not get into that just yet." Caputo slid the pictures into a stack and tapped them on one end until they made a neat pile. "Let's just say we may have a tiger by the tail. We've been trying to get this guy—and make the charges stick—for a couple of years. He's been involved in drug deals from Turkey to Colombia, but we've never been able to prove it. If he's the one who was after you, we're not dealing with any small-time trafficker—and we're not talking about amateurs. This fellow has finally made a bad mistake," Caputo declared. "Attempted murder and leaving a live witness are bad enough, but the boat he was in links him with the murder of the Bertram owner."

"This guy has never been the kingpin in any operation," Weekley added. "He's always the errand boy for someone higher up, but whenever a raid was made, we could never nail him red-handed. It looks like you may have uncovered something a lot bigger than any of us expected, Natalie."

"I suppose I should be thrilled." Natalie stared somberly. "But I guess this means I have to keep on hiding out here, doesn't it?"

"You're darn right. This guy is big trouble," Caputo asserted. "You keep a low profile until we pick him up. Now that we have your positive identification, we'll transmit his photo to the police, the Coast Guard and the FBI. Our own investigators are already on his trail for a few other reasons. Sooner or later, he'll slip up.''

"And what am I supposed to do in the meantime?" Nat shook her head in distress. "I can't stay here forever."

"Just give us a couple of days to see what turns up," Weekley said, trying to appease her. "Your mate, Greg Owens, hasn't shown up anywhere yet. We have a flyer out on him—just for questioning," he noted. "For now, you stay away from the lodge—totally," he cautioned her. "Ben is gone for a while, and Mac is managing the charters without any trouble."

"She'll be fine here," Roger said. "Nat has a lot of new work to do, and time is precisely what she needs."

"Time. . . and a little cooperation from the birds," Nat added. "Do you guys think it would be all right if I took the runabout just across to Howe Key to do some painting? Some egrets are nesting there."

Caputo and Weekley looked at each other and shrugged. "Just *there*?" Weekley could see the top of Howe Key from where he stood. It was only a hundred yards farther up the channel. He nodded at Caputo.

"Your friend Mac Butler said you can handle this," Caputo said as he lifted the familiar .357 Magnum from his pocket. "He asked me to give it to you. I'll make you a deal—" he smiled sympathetically "—if you want to go over there and paint, you take this with you. Check in and out with the Refuge manager or Embry here and come straight back when you're done."

"Okay," Nat promptly agreed. She felt she had been given her freedom again. The Refuge she had looked upon as a lovely, inspiring haven had begun to feel like a temporary prison. Now, the boundaries extended out to the next key. She felt as if the restrictions had vanished. She was eager to paint again.

"Can I go *now*?" Nat asked as she picked up her paints and sketch pad. "There's still plenty of light left today and all the birds are coming in from their foraging."

"You can go," Weekley grinned at her. "Just carry the gun and keep it handy."

Natalie took the handgun from Caputo and placed it inside the canvas bag that accommodated an assortment of pencils and brushes.

"I'll be back at six-thirty," Nat promised, glancing at her watch so she could judge the alloted time.

The three men watched as she strode out the door and down the path to the dock. Her deep gold braid swung from side to side as her step accelerated. She could already see in her mind's eye the nest of the egrets...the colors she wanted to capture in her painting. She made herself concentrate on these details—on anything other than what might be going on at the lodge...or what Ben was doing away on the *Southwind* at this time. She must paint...work... stay busy—and not brood.

The motor's steady put-put made her smile as she maneuvered the small boat across the narrow strip of water and around the curve of Howe Key.

The thick canopy of rubber trees, buttonwood, and mangroves on Howe Key provided a secure nesting place as well as a plentiful supply of food for the snowy egrets that claimed it.

From time to time during the two and a half hours Nat worked on the island, the sound of a distant boat weaving its way among the islands caused her to sit motionless as the ominous recollection of the thin man with the gun surfaced to trouble her. Once, just beyond the dense undergrowth of the island she shared with the egrets and deer, a larger boat passed nearby. It had a powerful inboard like the stolen Bertram. It skimmed past the island on the opposite side, apparently on its way to some other destination. Yet it sent a shudder through Nat, and she moved the canvas bag closer to her so she could feel the reassuring outline of the handgun.

At precisely six-thirty, Natalie pulled the runabout up to the dock at the Refuge. Roger stepped out of the cottage long enough to check that she had, in fact, arrived. He waved and stepped back inside. Nat reached the side door before she heard the sound of familiar voices and knew they had visitors.

"We just had to come to see you." Maggie hugged her. "I brought you two some fried flounder and hush puppies." Maggie winked. Nat could already smell the heavenly aroma from the kitchen. That was something else from the lodge she'd missed—the enticing scents in Maggie's kitchen.

Mac just stood there waiting his turn. When Maggie finished her barrage of words, he edged over to her and got his hug.

"How's the boat?" Nat asked him as she plopped her painting gear beside the sofa. She knew he'd have the *Calusa* out of the water and have the repairs appraised.

"Not too bad. We'll get a new rudder, a new prop. . . maybe patch up the paint a bit."

"When are you going to start fixing it?" Nat asked him anxiously.

"Ben said we should have some extra cash in a few days. He's working an overnight charter that pays well," Mac replied. "We'll get on it right after that. It ain't doin' us much good up on hoists."

"I told Ben that I'd help fix her," Nat said with resignation. Her offer hadn't been enough to stop him from making this trip with Angela.

"Ben thinks you've helped too much already— especially since he found out it was *two* engines you fixed. He figures he owes you for the work you did rebuilding them." Mac avoided her eyes. "He still doesn't know Buzz Cochran worked on them, too." Mac had always felt uncomfortable keeping the truth about the damage from Ben.

"Ben Andress doesn't owe me a thing," Nat said angrily.

"You'll have to settle that with him when he gets back," Mac commented.

"Where did he go?" Nat asked before she could stop herself.

"Don't really know. He and Hector took off this morning. Said they'd be back sometime tomorrow."

"*Hector* is with him?" Nat gasped. The thought that Hector was being dragged into this business made her feel even more desolate.

"Poor Hector," Maggie chuckled. "Maria's uncle, Louis Calonge, came by to drop her off and saw the sheriff department's car at the lodge and started asking questions. Well, he found out that Hector is on probation. Now Maria says she can't see him anymore since her family doesn't approve. Hector's gone all hangdog. And Ben doesn't look much better. You never saw two sorrier expressions when they left. In fact Ben looked about as glum as you do.'' Maggie took Natalie's hand and stared into her eyes. ''I don't know what's gone wrong between you two, but you just wait for the dust to settle before you make any decisions. Ben isn't perfect,'' Maggie stressed. ''Some men take a little longer than others to sort things out.''

''I've sorted it out for myself already,'' Nat replied. ''There isn't anything left between us.''

''I'm not so sure,'' Maggie said softly. ''Anyway—'' she squeezed Nat's hand ''—you look as though some of my good cooking will help your spirits, so get to it before it goes to waste.''

''The food!'' Roger was suddenly enthusiastic. ''We can even have wine with dinner—even *you* don't mind cheap Californian.''

''I think we'd better slip out and let you enjoy the dinner yourselves,'' Maggie replied. ''We left Maria running the lodge and Fuzzy watching the boats.''

Mac stepped over to give Natalie a hug. ''Maybe when Ben gets back tomorrow, he and I should have a little talk,'' he proposed. ''Maybe a nudge in the right direction. . . .''

Maggie poked him in the ribs. ''You stick to your own concerns. This may not be the right time to push anybody. Natalie, you go on and eat your dinner. I'll call you tomorrow to tell you any news.'' For a moment Maggie's smile wavered. "You be careful, honey," she said softly just before she stepped out the door.

Mac turned to echo Maggie's concern, but for him the words wouldn't come. He simply nodded and gave his thumbs-up signal that had been the first friendly gesture to mark Nat's commitment to the lodge. With his mouth held tight to conceal his misgivings, Mac nodded again and followed Maggie to the car.

"Food...eat...now." Roger broke Natalie's solemn vigil as the green car wound its way along the Refuge roadway.

Slowly she turned and followed him into the kitchen.

LATE IN THE EVENING, Natalie sprawled across the bed, flipping slowly through the manuscript pages of the children's book, trying to select the entry she would illustrate next. She had never liked selling her works, but doing illustrations meant only that she'd give up the original. She would always have the picture as it appeared in the book. Being paid to paint for the enjoyment of children made the prospect even more satisfying. The book was to have twenty-eight entries, all distinctive, wondrous things that would amuse and inform any child. And it could be only the beginning of innumerable picture books, which could include stories from her childhood, memories shared by relatives, tales of shipwrecks and pirates, legends of Indians and settlers that had made her imagination soar and her gangly limbs shiver with excitement when she was a child in Key West.

Nat wanted to talk. Talk about the projects. She cracked open the bedroom door and peered out. Roger was asleep on the sofa. She had wanted to tell someone, to let the ideas spill out. But there was no one to tell.

If things were different, if she didn't have to stay locked up like this, she could find someone who would listen and share her enthusiasm. No matter how she tried to suppress the thought, Natalie knew that someone was Ben. She could almost see herself on the dock while he labored over his old cruiser, sanding and scraping, turning his dream into a reality while she talked to him of dreams of her own. Or they could line up two chairs on the veranda of his old Conch house and rock back and forth and talk.

"I belong there, too," Natalie whispered as she realized how easily she had put herself in that scene—in his house. "I belong with him. . . belong *to* him," she breathed. Even beyond the soul-shaking intensity of their lovemaking, she had no doubt that she had found a part of herself that she had never anticipated, an intensity of feeling that had charged her life and her art with a new energy. With Ben in her life, all the images of Natalie Bishop—all the pieces of the puzzle—seemed to emerge into a new design, one more complete than ever before.

Maybe that was what Maggie sensed before either Natalie or Ben had realized it themselves. They belonged together—like creatures of nature, drawn to a new locale, learning to live compatibly. They belonged together—at the lodge and on these islands. Mac and Maggie Butler had taken Natalie to their hearts as if she was one of their own, and they had encouraged her and supported her—keeping her with them—for Ben. Now they urged her to wait a little longer, to give him time.

Outside the leaves rustled again, only this time there was something about the sound that made Nat freeze. The sharp crack of a twig was followed by another...then another...as some creature moved step by step through the woods. "A live witness...." Natalie recalled the words of the investigators. "We may have a tiger by the tail...not amateurs."

The outside noises receded as if the unseen prowler was moving down to the water.

"It's just another deer...or a raccoon...." Natalie tried to chase from her mind the image of the thin man in the suit...with the gleaming weapon pointed at her. Surely she was safe here on a government Refuge...among the creatures protected from predators.

Out in the channel, the engine of a large boat thudded along steadily. There were often fishermen out at night, spearing flounder or angling for the crafty fish that came close to shore to feed under cover of darkness.

Nat crept to the window and peered down through the trees and shrubs between the cottage and the clearing by the dock. Just a flicker of the running lights on a large boat was visible through the foliage. Then a bright searchlight swept the waterfront, hesitating on the dock and on the runabout, then sweeping back again.

"Probably the Coast Guard cruiser." Natalie felt her heart hammering in her breast as the boat continued on its way. From this distance, it was impossible to tell.

She dropped down and crept across the floor on her hands and knees, locating in the darkness the canvas bag that contained the handgun. This time she lifted out the weapon and placed it on the floor under the bed, within easy reach. Then she slid back into bed and lay motionless, hoping that no sounds or shadows would torment her further.

Once the sky took on the bluish hue of morning and the routine noises of the Refuge vehicles and residents assured her that another workday had commenced, Natalie closed her eyes, free at last from the perils and promises that had haunted her long night.

CHAPTER FOURTEEN

IT WAS ELEVEN-THIRTY when Natalie finally awoke to the scent of spiced tea and the sound of rattling dishes in the kitchen. Outside the bright sun was high in the sky and the still, oppressive heat of a windless day had settled over the Refuge. Natalie swung her feet to the floor and struggled to open her bleary eyes. The restless night was finally over and the few hours' sleep she did get had made her rested but certainly not alert.

"Thanks for letting me sleep in." She stood by the kitchen door as she tried to suppress a yawn. "You didn't happen to hear anything peculiar around here last night, did you?" She wandered over to the table and collapsed into a straight-backed chair.

"I'm a city boy," Roger chuckled. "Put me out here in the wilderness and *all* I hear are peculiar sounds. Why?" He looked at her anxiously. "Do you think we had a prowler?"

"Maybe I just had a bad case of nerves...." Natalie glanced to the window. "I thought I heard something or someone in the bushes...then I saw the light from a boat skimming the dock area."

"Could be one of the Refuge staff—" Roger tried to make a rational explanation "—or a Coast Guard patrol. I'll see Jack Wilson after lunch and have him check with the other workers. Sometimes they go out at nights when the deer are less skittish. Then again, it could have been a deer you heard.''

''I did come up with some new ideas.'' Nat perked up as she began relating her ideas for children's books. ''There are so many great stories about the Keys,'' she noted. ''Stories about pirates, wrecks, Indians...and sharks.'' The list went on and on. ''If this Mr. Potter likes my work—''

''Which he will,'' Roger cut in.

''Anyway,'' Nat went on, ''maybe I could get him interested in some other books—mostly pictures but with good information in them.''

''It seems as if my instincts were right,'' Roger said smugly. ''I did get the right person matched with the right project and the right publisher.''

''I think you did,'' Nat agreed.

''Let me see if I can speed up a face-to-face get-together between you two,'' Roger said. ''I'll get in touch with Potter. He's vacationing in the Caribbean. I'll give him a call in St. Thomas. I expect him to show up here sometime in the next week or so. We'll let him browse through whatever you've finished and see if he's ready to make you an offer.''

''I was so excited last night,'' Nat breathed. ''I kept thinking about the books.''

''I thought you were thinking about prowlers,'' Roger teased.

''I was thinking about lots of things,'' Nat responded. Part of her night had been spent brooding about Ben's dealings.

''Well, think about piling up a few more paintings for Jerry Potter. If you're interested in the publishing business, you might as well overwhelm him with your talent. Eat some lunch and go find a few birds.''

''What are you going to be doing?'' Nat asked while Roger started laying out mustard, mayonnaise, sliced tomatoes, ham and dill pickles for sandwiches.

''I'm going to find Jack and call the sheriff to discuss the prowler precautions,'' he said calmly. ''Then I have a hot date with a mama raccoon and her youngsters. I'd tell you how many offspring she has, but they never hold still long enough to be counted.'' Very methodically he dealt out slices of bread and began putting together his lunch creation.

''I'll be over on Howe Key again,'' Nat said as she followed his lead and began stacking ingredients on her bread. ''And I'll be back by six-thirty,'' she added before he reminded her.

Roger looked over at her and smiled. In the past weeks of working together they had shared more than talents and techniques. They had become comfortable companions. Sometimes they could almost anticipate each other's next move, passing a brush or a tube of color—whatever was needed—a split second before it was requested.

''Maybe we could disguise ourselves and go out to dinner tonight,'' he smiled. He suspected that any outing beyond the confines of the Refuge would appeal to her as a respite from the pressures of waiting out the investigation. ''No one would notice us in Jack's pickup truck.'' He lowered his eyes momentarily. ''If it's dark, maybe we could even swing by the lodge and see how things are going over there.''

Ben and Hector were due back sometime during the afternoon. Going to the lodge in some sort of disguise, against the orders of the investigators, would be foolhardy and irresponsible, and precisely what Natalie wanted to do. It was as if Roger had read her mind. She missed them all—Hector, Maggie and Mac, Maria, Fuzzy—but most of all she wanted to see Ben. Whatever she would see in his eyes would make her next move clearer. She was tired of grappling with suspicions and fears. All she wanted was the truth.

"I'd like that," Nat said softly.

"Then you get back here early," Roger went on, describing his scheme. "You might like to change clothes or wear a hat." His big blue eyes glistened sympathetically.

Nat started to protest, then smiled. "I'll be back from Howe Key about five. Then we'll see about going out." She threw her supplies together after their meal and started for the runabout, her mind racing with the idea of actually sneaking out to visit the lodge after dark.

Natalie spotted the broad-winged cormorant before she even had the runabout untied. It soared above the buttonwood and pine trees of Howe Key, then settled down in the treetops. The large, nearly black, clumsy-looking bird always seemed to be poised at an awkward angle. When it flew, it kept its head upright and its squat legs tucked under so it seemed to be flying upward. Actually, it would be flying straight, which made the sight even more curious. But in the water, the bird was masterful. Its streamlined body was tapered back so the powerful legs, like the propeller on a boat, could drive it swiftly along.

The adult cormorant, which breathes only through its mouth because its nostrils grow closed as it matures, can dive beneath the water in pursuit of small prey and stay under for thirty seconds. When they were children, Natalie and her brothers used to watch the gawky big birds disappear under the surface and try to pick the second they would surface. "Now," each one would guess.

"Now...." Natalie steered around Howe Key in search of a new spot to beach the small boat. As she passed along near to shore, the squawk of restless birds and the indignant shriek of others filled the sky above her with angry or frightened creatures. "It's just me," Nat called up to them. "Remember me... the one who sat watching you all day yesterday?" Apparently they didn't remember, since the cries of birds and the rustle of wings continued as she inched along the outer rim of the island. "Settle down...." She stared skyward at the pandemonium above her. She turned the boat between two airborne mangrove roots and steered it onto a sandy strip of open beach. "Come on back, you guys," she whispered amid the clamor of the birds.

Natalie had the boat secured and most of her belongings spread out on her huge striped beach blanket before she went back to the boat for her thermos. Then she sat cross-legged on the blanket, sipping her lemonade, waiting for the creatures on Howe Key to adjust to her presence once more.

"Oh, come on now," Natalie said, wrinkling her nose as another commotion in the dense interior of the island sent the skittish birds into the sky. She sat very still, listening as she had in the night to the movement of something in the bushes. As she slid her hand inconspicuously into her canvas bag, she realized what she had forgotten. Still tucked underneath her bed as protection from the terrors of the night, the silver-barreled .357 Magnum had been overlooked in her hasty departure.

Nat stood up, clutching the canvas bag and staring at the boat, trying to decide whether to make the return trip to get the weapon. Above the island, the birds sent up another chorus of squawking.

"Shut up and let me think!" Nat growled impatiently.

"Take all the time you want, honey. . . ."

The voice from behind her made her squeal and spin around. Natalie stood face to face with the man in the silver sunglasses. It was too late to worry about her handgun. Looking down the barrel of a gigantic weapon with a long, gray silencer attached to it, she froze.

"It's about time you showed up." The man grimaced as he examined her from behind his mirrored mask. "I damn near got eaten alive by the bugs," he grunted.

Gradually the birds returned to their perches in the treetops, staring down cautiously at the two intruders in the clearing. Natalie realized now that it had not been simply the approach of her boat or her arrival on the island that had been responsible for the hysterics of the birds. It had also been the passage of "Sunglasses" through the undergrowth as he stalked a prey of his own.

"Are you going to shoot me?" Natalie finally got her mouth to function.

"Not unless you try something stupid. . . like making any loud noise and trying to attract anyone's attention while we take a little trip."

"Trip?" Natalie could feel a clammy feeling beginning to creep down her spine. "Where are we going?" she squeaked.

"We're goin' fishing." Sunglasses chuckled at his version of humor. "Get your stuff back into the boat and let's get out of here." He waved the long shaft of the weapon at her. Wordlessly, Natalie complied, picking up her thermos, sketch pad, the striped blanket and her drawing equipment.

"Just throw it all in the boat and take off that way." He pointed the gun toward the west end of the key, in the opposite direction from the Refuge. "Keep looking up at the trees like you did before," he directed. "In case anyone's around, act like you're enjoying yourself."

Natalie sat at the stern of the runabout, operating the outboard motor, while Sunglasses sprawled between the center and bow seats, trying to appear less conspicuous than he would be if he sat level with Natalie.

Slowly Nat steered out around the twisting mangrove roots where her haughty friend from the day before, the soft-plumed, elegant egret, watched their departure with one unblinking yellow eye.

"You know where Content Keys are. . . Content Channel?" Sunglasses clasped the gun low between his knees and pointed directly at Natalie's chest as he spoke. She nodded and kept the boat at a steady pace. As long as that gun was aimed in her direction, she intended to cooperate.

"Head out that way," Sunglasses indicated, waving the gun. "And give this thing some more gas. Let's get moving."

MAGGIE BUTLER stood back in the shadows beside the lodge front door watching the square-built visitor who had pulled into the parking lot. The man sat in his car for several minutes as if he was deciding whether he should stay or leave. At last, he stepped from the car and looked over the area, carefully scrutinizing each building and every vehicle nearby. He was obviously not one of their regular customers, so Maggie kept a cautious eye on him.

Mac was across the parking lot in the boathouse working on the books. As soon as the stranger stepped into the boathouse, Maggie could take a closer look at the man's car while Mac took over the surveillance business.

Notepad in hand, Maggie hurried out to scribble down the license number once the boathouse door closed behind the stranger. She wasn't taking any chances. If this was one of the "bad guys" looking for Natalie, Maggie was going to have a record of his visit. She'd have Steve Weekley trace the license number before the car left the lodge compound.

"Steve," she found herself whispering into the telephone, even though there was no one nearby. "This is Maggie Butler. We've got someone snooping around. Here's his number."

Weekley took down the make and model of the car and the Florida tag number and promised to call right back. "It doesn't cost us a thing to be this careful. Keep up the good work. I'll run this through motor vehicles' division and see what shows.''

Maggie was still waiting by the telephone when Mac and the stranger—looking almost like carbon copies of each other except that the visitor was taller—came across the parking lot. Just as they came through the front door, the phone rang. Trying to appear nonchalant, Maggie let it ring twice, then picked it up. "Gold Coast Lodge," she said in a cheerful voice.

The thickset, gray-haired man waited with Mac while Maggie carried on a brief conversation with Steve Weekley. He glanced over Maggie's shoulder at the two bright acrylic paintings exhibited prominently behind the reception desk. Then a sly smile tilted one corner of his mouth.

"Oh, my goodness," Maggie said twice before she stared at the visitor. Without saying goodbye, she dropped the phone back onto its cradle.

"Maggie—" Mac stroked his stubble and shrugged "—I don't know how to tell you this. . . ." He tried to make the introduction as painless as possible.

"I know," Maggie said, nodding and stretching out a hand in greeting. "You're William Bishop, Natalie's father."

Bill Bishop shook her hand then jerked his thumb toward the two paintings. "I can see my tip-off was right. She's here." He leaned forward a bit to get a closer view of the two colorful scenes. "From the looks of it, she's been here a while. . . ." He didn't sound particularly pleased.

"Maybe you could come in and join us for a cup of coffee," Maggie suggested, "and we'll try to get this

all explained.'' She shot Mac an uncertain look behind Bishop's back.

"It's better that you hear this sittin' down.'' Mac
took over. "Come on in, Mr. Bishop.'' He led the
way into the deserted restaurant.

"I'd be a lot more comfortable if you called me
Bill,'' Mr. Bishop confessed. "When that fella called
me and said Natalie was here, I was sure he had to be
wrong.'' Now it was Mac's turn to roll his eyes
anxiously.

"Natalie has been perfectly all right here with us,''
Maggie insisted. "Well, almost....'' She hesitated before she made too many reassurances. "Just
take a seat—'' Maggie waved the two men toward a
table "—and I'll get the coffee.''

JACK WILSON parked the Refuge pickup truck in
front of his cottage and unloaded two boxes of government forms that had to be filled out over the next
months. He already had a backlog of reports waiting
on his desk, and he muttered as he balanced the new
forms on one knee and struggled with the door.

"Want an extra hand?'' Roger loped across the
grassy area between the two cottages.

"I didn't think you were anywhere around.'' Jack
stepped back and let Roger open the door. "I didn't
see the boat down by the dock.''

"Natalie is out on Howe Key in it,'' Roger replied,
somewhat surprised that Jack had forgotten.

"I thought you were with her.'' Jack moved into
the room and placed the boxes on his desk.

"I was over at the nursery painting Rosie the Raccoon,'' Roger grinned.

"Then who was that with her?" Jack lowered his voice and cast an apprehensive look at his blond companion. "One of the staff saw Nat in the run-about with someone that looked like you in the front of the boat. They were heading out around Howe Key looking up at the trees at something."

"She went alone." Roger's eyes widened in distress. "You don't think someone could have gone after her there?"

Almost in unison, the two men reached for the telephone. Jack began dialing rapidly while Roger paced back and forth. "Sergeant Weekley, please." Jack got through to the sheriff's department. "This may be nothing to get hysterical about," he began, "but Nat Bishop took off along Howe Key in a run-about with some blond dude—and we can't figure out who he is or how he got to her." There was a brief pause while Weekley responded.

"One of the workers was just checking things out with his binoculars," Jack explained. "He saw the guy and thought it was Roger Embry. *I* thought it was Roger." Again there was a quick exchange.

"Maybe twenty minutes. Maybe half an hour ago," Jack guessed. "Heading west. We thought they were just moving up the key to a different location. They didn't seem to be in any hurry." He nodded while Weekley gave his instructions.

"Okay," Jack agreed. "We'll get all our men on it. We'll start our boats from here." He paused again. "Sure, we've got weapons," he said evenly. "Right, see you out there." He clicked the receiver down. "We're going out looking for her." Jack turned to the pale-faced Roger who still paced the floor.

"Call the lodge. Roger jumped past the Refuge manager and snatched the telephone off its cradle. Hastily he dialed the number Natalie had given him. "Maggie," he gasped into the phone. "I think one of those people may have kidnapped Natalie," he said rapidly, as the intake of air on the other end ended in wail. "They went west off Howe Key." He gave the directions he had heard from Jack. "The police already know. Just ask anyone you can reach to get over this way to look for her." He listened to Maggie's anxious questions. "They've got about a half-hour lead on us," he answered. "Be sure to tell them to bring weapons—and *hurry*," he added, panic apparent in his voice.

SUNGLASSES DIRECTED NATALIE straight to the thickest string of mangrove islands that were beginning to close the gaps between the larger, sandy keys along the outer rim of the shallows. Standing like soldiers on the front line, these outer islands faced the Gulf of Mexico and received the first onslaught from wind and rain. Because some trees clung more desperately to the sandy bottom than others, large stretches of water bore only bleak, half-submerged sandbars and grotesque skeletons of defeated trees and failed colonies between the thick, tightly knit clumps of mangroves that survived.

Natalie waited until Sunglasses looked away, then she dropped two more pencils into the water behind the boat. She had managed to slip in most of her pencils and brushes along the way, hoping that some of them would float to attract the attention of a Refuge warden or a fisherman coasting the area. If and when the folks at the Refuge realized that she was missing, perhaps they would come looking for her and run across someone who had seen the drifting brushes and pencils. It wasn't much of a trail, she realized, but it was the only thing she could think to do.

"That way," Sunglasses said sharply. Nat followed his gun barrel, which was aimed toward the irregular coastline of the largest of the Content Keys. Anchored in the inlet was the white Bertram. Waiting by its stern was the thin man in the business suit. This time he had taken off his jacket, but the shirt-and-tie outfit still made him look out of place on the sleek vessel. As she pulled alongside the larger boat, Sunglasses caught the tow rope thrown from above. Natalie looked from the deckhand who had thrown it, to the dark form at the wheel. When the bearded operator glanced her way, she knew where her shipmate, Greg Owens, had gone so suddenly.

"Oh, Greg." The disappointment in her voice caused Greg's eyes to narrow, then look away.

"Leave her in there." "The Suit" now gave directions. Sunglasses climbed aboard and let the runabout drift out behind the larger craft. He let out enough rope to keep the runabout from swamping once the Bertram's twin engines were running.

"Move away from the motor." The Suit waved his own ominous handgun at Natalie. Obediently she slid into the center seat of the runabout. The dull roar of the Bertram engines broke the silence as the deckhand secured the anchor. Then Greg shifted into gear and steered to the northwest. Natalie sat watching helplessly as the tow rope tightened and three expressionless faces looked back at her from the stern of the

Bertram. They had painted a name on the back of the boat, some of the trim had been removed and the numbers painted on the craft for identification looked authentic, but it was clearly the same boat that she had seen before. It was a top-of-the-line cruiser whose proud owner was dead.

One forlorn tree trunk protruded out of the water ahead. Greg slowed the engines and coasted up beside it.

"This is where you get out, honey." The Suit spoke over the rush of the water. Natalie stared at him.

"I said *get out*." The Suit raised his voice. "Climb over the side and get in the water."

Nat crawled to the side of the runabout and swung her feet over the edge. Facing outward, she pushed off and dropped into the Gulf. The water where she went in was well over her head, but she kicked across to an old stump and touched a submerged sandbar with her toes.

Sunglasses and the deckhand were already reeling in the runabout as Greg pulled the Bertram about fifty feet ahead and let the engine idle again. Once the runabout was alongside the Bertram, the deckhand took a gaff hook and slammed it into the bow of the little boat. After several mighty swings, he had battered a hole in the hull. The three men stood staring while the runabout filled with water and sank.

Natalie clung to the twisted trunk, dreading what was coming next. If they left her there alive, she was a strong enough swimmer that she could make it over to the smaller islands. . . and on to even larger ones until she waved down a passing boat. When the faces of the three men turned back toward her, Nat knew they were not finished with her yet. Momentarily she closed her eyes and whispered an anxious prayer. The specter of the murdered Bertram owner loomed in her imagination—the form of a man, harnessed in a life jacket, with a bullet hole through his head.

The Bertram pulled ahead, then turned and circled back toward her, keeping away from the shallow submerged strip on which she stood. Like one of those gigantic, pale sharks that used to circle and appraise the shrimping trawlers out in deep water, the sleek white craft passed around her forlorn outpost. But these predators were not going to lose interest and swim away like the big sharks did. These human killers circled closer.

On the next trip around, Sunglasses and the deckhand hoisted a couple of metal buckets onto the side of the big boat and began scattering the contents into the water. In that instant, Natalie knew they were not going to shoot her. Instead, they were dumping cut fish, blood and offal into the water. They were "chumming" the sharks...luring them to Natalie with the scent and sight of blood.

With the circle of blood and refuse enclosing her, Natalie inched higher onto the barnacle-encrusted tree trunk. The higher she climbed, the more it listed to the side, dropping her back into the water. When Nat tried to switch her weight to the opposite side of the stump, the sharp edges of the barnacles scraped her legs, letting her own blood mingle with the enticing supply already surrounding her.

Her mind raced over all the things she knew about sharks. Already this year there had been an unprecedented number of shark attacks along the Florida coast...several of them in waist-deep water. She knew the warning signs—the rapid twitching swimming motions, the arched back and the lowering its pectoral fins...all tense, vibrating movements that were intended as a warning. But those were aspects of behavior that were visible *under* the water...and in water clear enough to see into. Already the water around her was cloudy with sand and blood stirred together by the circling motion of the boat and the currents moving over her sandbar.

One final time the Bertram came past. This time the deckhand pitched lumps of bloody meat closer to her. Once the sharks picked up the scent, they would close in for the meat...then, in the frenzy of feeding, they would discover her...and come in for the kill.

Now the Bertram and its grim-faced crew moved off in the direction they had come, back along the outlying mangrove islands. The last view Natalie had of them before they swerved amid the trees was the bright reflection of the sun glinting off the mirrored sunglasses, and the dull gleam of binoculars focused back on her.

Once the Bertram was out of sight, Natalie braced one foot on the submerged base of the tree trunk and clasped two of the three broken limbs that protruded above the water. Leaning back and shifting her weight from side to side, she broke its hold on the spongy sandbar and dislodged it. Now at least, if sharks came, she had something to thrust between herself and the hungry creatures. As long as she could remain upright and not get swept off her narrow rise of sand, she might be able to withstand the onslaught.

Apprehensively, she glanced out over the water, scanning its bright surface for any sign of a disturbance. Sharks generally stayed out of the shallows until nightfall when they snaked their way amid islands and sandbars in search of food. Sleek, gray and silent, they would cut through the channels from the Gulf to the Atlantic, avoiding all contact with humans. Only when they were uncharacteristically active or hungry did the huge missile-shaped creatures skirt the shoreline in the daylight.

This time the feeding impulses of the shark had not been left to nature. This time they had been given a pink-tinged invitation, with promises of rich rewards if they would only follow the trail to Natalie's sandbar.

"Turn them over and they go limp...." Natalie remembered what Ben had told her after his shark-tagging expedition. "Orange tags for sight tracking, yellow ones for radio monitoring. Keep an eye out for any of the species we tagged," Ben had asked.

"Sure," Natalie groaned as she shifted her eyes, constantly checking and rechecking the surface. If the only ones who came near were the little greenish yellow lemon sharks, she could turn them back... maybe. But if the dark, large-headed great white— the size of a boat—answered the summons...or the torpedo-shaped tiger shark with its blunt snout came along, there would be no way to avoid the notched teeth that could tear her and her mangrove-stump shield to pieces.

The flash of gray that pierced the water just past

the drop-off several hundred yards out removed all doubt about who was coming to dinner. Natalie kept her eyes locked on the surface, trying to make herself believe that what she saw was a dolphin's fin. If there were dolphin in the area, there would be no sharks nearby. She could then drop her tree shield and start swimming to land. But the pattern of movement was not that of a dolphin. There was no rolling motion as it surfaced and breathed then plunged back into the water. This dark fin cut through the water smoothly. There was none of the carefree, playful leaping of the dolphin.

Shark. No doubt about it. Shark.

Cutting back and forth, its zigzag pattern bringing it closer each time, the dark-finned creature sliced through the sun-dazzled water. About eight feet long, it skimmed below the surface, only once exposing itself long enough for Nat to see the sharp-pointed elongated upper tail fin.

"Tiger shark," Natalie whispered as she wedged her legs between the limbs of the blackened tree stump and aimed one jagged limb at the approaching shark.

CHAPTER FIFTEEN

MAC BUTLER stood by the radio monitoring the calls and passing information on to the *Suds Buggy* and Ben's incoming *Southwind*. Both boats had responded immediately to Mac's message and had brought in their passengers, pausing only long enough to pick up extra fuel before heading to the Gulf in search of Natalie and the little Refuge runabout. Ben had gained one other passenger in the brief stop—Bill Bishop.

Mr. Bishop stood on the upper level of the *Southwind*, his legs planted apart to steady him as he scanned the shores along Pine Channel just in case the boat had backtracked to the Refuge. With Ben's binoculars propped against his nose, he took the right side, while Hector, standing below on the deck, scanned the northwestern shoreline of the Torch Keys to their left. Once they reached the pass between Howe Key and Big Pine where Natalie had last been seen, they separated, the *Southwind* swinging northeast toward Big Spanish Channel, while Fuzzy and Herb who had been following in the *Suds Buggy* proceeded up the back side of Howe Key, out toward the Content Keys.

The Refuge cruiser with Roger and Jack Wilson aboard had already circled Howe Key. Jack called

out through the loudspeaker as they scrutinized every
indentation that may have harbored the runabout.
They had already radioed the grim report to other
boats coming to join the search. No Natalie Bishop,
no runabout, and no blond companion on Howe
Key.

The Coast Guard had dispatched two cruisers,
each staffed with well-trained, well-armed crews.
One had Sergeant Weekley aboard; the other was
carrying Phil Caputo and an agent from the FBI.
Natalie Bishop had been snatched while she was on a
government Refuge. In addition to the other charges
that would face her captors, the crime on the Refuge
had drawn federal agents into the search.

The alarm was hastily transmitted to every boat
within radio range. Professional charter operators
and private boat owners had taken to the water, fanning out amid the mangrove islands and large keys,
scouring the water for a runabout containing a blond
male and a tawny-haired girl with a long braid.

Ben guided the *Southwind* into the shallow water
at the mouth of the nameless island where she had
hidden the *Calusa*. The still waters within the
horseshoe-shaped inlet were undisturbed. Hector
leaned out and held onto the aged mangrove at the
mouth, keeping the *Southwind* from drifting past.

"Nat-a-lee," he bellowed into the heart of the
island, but there was no reply. With a forlorn shrug,
Hector looked up at Ben.

"I'll head out past the Harbor Key banks." Ben
thrust the boat into gear. "We'll work our way back
bit by bit." He kept a cautious eye on the irregular
bottom as they swerved between a sandbar and the

sunken roots that stretched out from an overgrown strip of land.

Amid the increasing clamor of startled birds and search boats, another sound overhead snapped Bill Bishop's head out from under the cockpit canopy. Coming from the southwest, soaring over the sprawling islands, a stark white Coast Guard helicopter joined the search mission, its brilliant orange stripes aflame against the sky.

NATALIE STOOD HER GROUND on the sandbar, keeping her legs still amid the pronged branches of the partially submerged tree trunk. The sleek gray tiger shark made a pass within six feet of her, but its interest had been in the lump of reddish meat that it snatched away in one gulp. So far, the creature was absorbed in picking up the scattered "chum" that settled to the bottom. Its movement became increasingly frantic as a second shark began its attack. Now the water around the sandbar began to cloud as the motion of the two sharks, each intent on snatching up the meat before the other devoured it, stirred up the soft particles of dirt and sand on the bottom. It was the frenzied head- and tail-shaking that signaled disaster was imminent. No longer simply feeding, the two creatures were racing erratically after anything that caught their attention.

Natalie's feet, buried beneath the silt deposits, began to shift slowly beneath the weight of the tree stump. As they sank deeper into the sand, the level of the water inched from mid-chest level up to her throat. If she remained motionless, the sharks would not be attracted to her. They were striking at everything in their path that moved in the churning water. Their eyesight was poor, particularly in the muddied water, but their keen senses of sound and smell could draw them with uncanny precision to the least movement.

When the distant chop-chop sound of the helicopter became loud enough to drown out the thunder of her heart, Nat felt as if the cavalry had come to the rescue. Still clutching the tree stump, she looked up in anticipation as the white copter made a pass above her and continued on its way. Then it banked and made a smooth, arcing turn and approached from the opposite direction, cutting lower over the water. Like a bloody mouth grimacing at her plight, the stripes on the aircraft scowled overhead.

On its third pass, the copter hovered out from her position as an armed guardsman aimed his rifle at the water. He shifted position, shaking his head, unable to get a clear shot at either of the sharks. Beneath the pulsing roar of the copter she couldn't hear the seaborne rescuers skimming over the water toward her. The *Southwind* was nearly upon her before she deciphered the message being relayed over the copter's loudspeaker. Coming up behind her, Ben cut the motor of the *Southwind* so the action of the propellers wouldn't add to the frenzy already in the water around her. The force of the boat sent waves of salty water over Natalie's head, nearly knocking her off the narrow sandbar. Just as she dropped the tree stump and struggled to keep her head above the choppy waves, Hector and Bill Bishop each thrust a hand under her arms and yanked her up onto the side of the *Southwind*.

From the copter came the loud report of a rifle shot followed by several more as the spray from the bullets hitting the water leaped into the air. Bill and Hector tugged Nat's legs into the boat while the guardsmen kept the sharks at bay.

While Ben swung the boat out past the sandbar, the hulking, weathered old tree trunk listed to the side and slowly slipped beneath the surface.

"Hector!" Ben yelled for his mate to take over at the controls, but Hector wasn't budging. Holding Natalie's hand and weeping openly, the young Cuban wasn't about to leave his friend's side. Amid the tangle of welcoming arms and bodies as Bill Bishop clung to his daughter, Hector managed to keep a firm grip on her hand.

"How is she?" Ben shouted down at them. Natalie looked up at the urgent plea in his eyes that searched her face.

"I'm all right," she choked, "and you've got some explaining to do, Ben Andress!"

His worried expression transformed into a wide, relieved grin. "I guess that means you're all right," he beamed at her. He shook a triumphant fist in the air. Then he shifted around in the pilot's chair, turning on the engines of the *Southwind* and steering in the direction of the far islands and the deeper channel beyond.

"It's the Bertram," Ben yelled over the whine of the engine. He hit the gas with a force that sent the threesome below sprawling across the lower deck. "Grab a gun," he bellowed at them as he set out after the large cruiser easing out from between the islands to the southeast.

Penned in by the rescue boats that converged on the area, Natalie's captors had tried to stay hidden. But with the copter overhead and the Coast Guard cutters alerted and closing in, they were making a run for it.

"The Bertram." Ben had the message on the radio, summoning anyone who was listening to move in and cut off the escape. "Off my bow to the southeast," he informed the Coast Guard copter team.

Bill Bishop remained on the lower deck with Natalie, but Hector climbed up beside Ben. Clutching the canopy support with one hand and a long-barreled .45 in the other, Hector peered ahead at the white boat cutting across the open water.

The Coast Guard helicopter took off out over the Gulf, then curved back well ahead of the stolen Bertram. To avoid a head-on confrontation, the Bertram swerved back toward land. By now two other large sports-fishing boats appeared from amid the outlying islands and blocked that route. Now the Bertram was forced back toward the *Southwind*.

Hector started bobbing up and down, shouting in Spanish, ready to blast away at the men in the Bertram.

"Greg is driving that thing," Natalie called up to him. Hector's enthusiasm ebbed as he looked from Nat to the approaching cruiser. When it cut across their path, again aiming out into the Gulf, he seemed relieved.

Now Ben steered the *Southwind* after them, staying within the wide path of their wake, but not moving in close enough to exchange gunfire. The copter zigzagged above the Bertram, ordering the boat to halt and surrender. When The Suit fired at them, the guardsmen returned a few rounds, shooting close enough to make it clear that after this first series of warning shots, more deadly ones would follow.

The futility of escape became indisputable as the two armed Coast Guard cutters, closing in on the area, converged on the Bertram. Seeing his boat was boxed in on all sides by fishing craft and Coast Guard cutters, with the copter hovering above, Greg Owens slowed the Bertram to a halt. Ordered to drop their weapons on the deck, the four men awaited the boarding party from the cutter while the copter loomed above like an ominous bird of prey.

From one Coast Guard vessel, Steve Weekley boarded with the armed guardsmen then finally signaled for Ben to bring the *Southwind* closer to the stolen Bertram. Bill Bishop and Natalie had climbed up into the pilot's area beside Ben and Hector so they had a better vantage point for making the identification. This time it was Ben's rough hand that held on to Natalie's while she studied the faces of the men and confirmed they were the ones who had tried to kill her.

Once that formality was concluded, Inspector Caputo radioed from the other cutter with permission for Ben to send his boat and passengers back to the lodge. "You come with us, Andress," Caputo asserted. "We've got to do everything by the book."

Natalie looked from the radio to Ben. His face was serene. "You aren't going in with us?" she asked softly.

"Everything will be all right, Natalie," he promised. "My explanations will have to wait."

The radio came to life again with Caputo's voice. "Have one of your people take her in. Have her checked out by a doctor for exposure or whatever. We'll get her full statement later," he declared.

"Later," Ben repeated softly as he raised Natalie's fingers to his lips and pressed a kiss upon them. Then reluctantly he released her again to her father, who had not left her side. Ben leaped across onto the deck of the Coast Guard craft while Bill Bishop whisked his daughter down below into the cabin where at last she could rest.

With the *Suds Buggy* leading the procession and eight other cruisers of varied shapes and sizes bobbing along like a mother duck and her string of ducklings, the *Southwind* with Hector at the helm made a triumphant return to the Gold Coast Lodge.

Natalie stayed below deck with her father while Hector steered the craft in, calling out reassurances and greetings to the assortment of boats and crewmen who had not heard the outcome over their radios. Some who were obviously aware of the results of the search paused along the route to show their good will. Others stood out, eager for a glimpse of the damsel in distress and the handsome captain who came to her rescue.

In the cabin, Natalie sat quietly as her father dabbed peroxide on the scratches that covered her long legs and graceful arms. She kept seeing Ben's wide, serene eyes, kept hearing his assurance that everything could be explained.

"I suppose we'll get this all ironed out somehow," Bill Bishop mumbled. There were some explanations he needed to hear.

"I'm still going to graduate," Natalie blurted out. "I finished all my course work. I didn't miss a thing. . . ."

Mr. Bishop looked at her reproachfully. "I'll say you didn't miss a thing," he muttered.

"I'm sorry, daddy." Nat reached out and hugged his neck. "I really didn't want you to find out this way."

He shook his head and chuckled. "I'm sure you didn't." He sat back and looked at her solemnly. "You're a real corker, Nat," he muttered. "And I thought the boys were the only ones who got into breakneck predicaments. You've got us all beat with this one." There was a trace of admiration beneath his rough humor.

"I'll get everything all straightened out when we get back to the lodge," she promised.

"Lodge, my foot," Bishop sniffed. "You're coming home with me, young lady. Until these folks get all this hijacking and drug business settled, you're going to stay away from that place."

"Oh, no, I'm not." Nat braced herself for a battle.

"You are," Bishop said with an inflexible set to his shoulders. "If they want to see you, they can come down to Key West. Look at you—" he reached across and rolled her arm over gently "—you're all banged up. You're exhausted. Some hoodlums tried to kill you. This is ridiculous. . . ." He blinked back the tears. "You're coming home. If I have to drag you. . . ." His chin trembled. "I can't let anyone do this to you. I want you home where your family can take care of you."

"Okay." Natalie finally surrendered and hugged

him again. "I'll come home." With a weary sigh, she leaned her head on his shoulder as the *Southwind* moved steadily into Newfound Harbor.

Bill Bishop ran interference for Natalie from the first step she made on dry ground. "Forget the car," he insisted when Hector offered to get it from Ben's storage shed. "I'll send somebody up here for it and for the rest of her stuff later on." Bishop tried to make the move home as swift and smooth as possible. "If there's anything she needs, we'll call you."

Maggie hurried along the shell path with Natalie while Bill Bishop followed them in his car. Only Hector, left behind on the *Southwind* at the dock, hadn't been delegated some responsibility in the move. He had been intercepted by several of the local newsmen anxious for full details about the kidnapping and the rescue.

"Give us the story," they were yelling as two television videotape crews elbowed their way to dockside, jostling the four newspaper reporters in the process. "Come on, Hector," a TV commentator called, "we got part of it over the radio—how about answering a few questions?"

"Just a minute!" he called over the hubbub. There was a moment of quiet. Hector cleared his voice. "Until I get an okay from the investigators, I got nothin' to say."

The dockside exploded with complaints and shouted questions. Hector stood firm, his arms crossed over his chest.

At Beachside One, Bill Bishop and Mac Butler were hastily loading some of Natalie's clothes. Mac had sent Maggie to the lodge to phone the Bishops' family doctor in Key West to have him standing by to check Nat when they arrived at home. Maggie hurried back to help with the packing of a few personal items for Natalie.

"We had to tell your father," Maggie apologized in the few moments she had alone with Nat. "Someone called and told him you were here. When he saw your paintings and when Mac sensed how concerned he was. . . ."

"I understand," Natalie said as she patted Maggie's arm. "I never wanted anyone to lie, and I certainly didn't want anyone upset."

"You'll never guess who was behind all this." Maggie spilled out the details between handing items to the men to load. "I mean the man who hired the Cantero fellow." She could tell by the bewildered look on Natalie's face that she was not making herself clear. "The man you drew the sketch of is called Cantero," she explained. "They think the one who hired him was Sutton—Charles Sutton. Angela's father."

"Why. . . why did Sutton want to do this to me?" Nat shook her head in confusion. She was tired, bruised and dirty.

"Maggie, I really don't think we can take any long explanations right now," Mr. Bishop interrupted. "Let's just get her out of here."

"Sure," Maggie said sympathetically. "You'll have lots of time for the details later." She took a pair of jeans out of Natalie's hands and folded them into the suitcase. "Looks like most of your clothes are accounted for." Maggie cast a quick look around the room. "What about the things you took over to Roger's?"

"Forget them." Nat could barely move. Her head ached. Her arms ached. Even her speech sounded slurred.

Maggie had to struggle to keep back the tears. Natalie looked so pathetic. Even in the dry clothes she had tugged on, she looked totally drained.

"You go home, honey." Maggie hugged her. "You go home and rest. I'm gonna miss you." Maggie had the words out before she could stop herself.

"I'm coming back." Natalie turned to face her friend. "You can tell that to *everyone*," she stressed. "You folks haven't seen the last of me." Her voice wavered under the strain. "You tell Ben for sure," she barely whispered. "Tell him I'll be back."

"I'll tell him." Maggie gave Nat a quick squeeze. Then she walked with her down the stairs. "See you. . . ." Maggie peered through the car window.

When Bill Bishop pulled away, driving along the shell path and onto the parking lot, Maggie let her brave facade vanish. While Mac tried to comfort her, Maggie cried.

The newsmen had all assembled in the restaurant section of the lodge, so the dock area was abandoned when Mr. Bishop drove near.

"Wait just a minute." Natalie stopped her father just as they reached the boathouse. "I just want to take a quick look." She was out the door of the car before he could stop her. In several long strides, she was through the door of the boathouse, staring at the *Calusa*, which hung above the water, still scarred on the hull from her collision with the mangrove roots.

"Poor baby," Natalie whispered as she reached out to touch the boat she had come to love. "I'm so sorry." She began to weep as she inspected the bent shaft and the deep scrapes on the underside of the craft. "We're both in pretty sad shape."

"Natalie," her father came up behind her. "Let's take care of *you*," he stressed. He came up beside her and slid his arm around her waist.

"I really love it here," Natalie sniffed through her tears. "I love this boat, these people," she said softly.

"Come on," Bishop urged. Nat reached out once more and touched the stern of the *Calusa* in a gesture of sympathy. Then she looked farther down at the beautiful cruiser, glistening beneath the first of many coats of varnish. "She's going to be lovely, isn't she?" Nat asked her father.

"Sure." His abrupt reply showed that his concern was elsewhere. "Now come along." He took her out to the car.

Natalie leaned back against the seat wearily. "I need to talk to Ben," she mumbled. "Ben...."

"We're not going to Siberia." Mr. Bishop let his impatience surface. "We're less than thirty miles away. We've got roads and we've got telephones. Andress can find you if he needs to," he concluded with an edge to his voice.

"I hope so," Natalie whispered as the exhaustion overwhelmed her.

CHAPTER SIXTEEN

"THE ONE YOU CALL THE SUIT is Bernard Cantero."
Steve Weekley sat across the room from Natalie as he
spoke. All three law enforcement agencies that
assisted in the case had agreed to hold off taking
Natalie's statement until she had a full night's rest.
Even though the matter was no longer under Weekley's jurisdiction, he had come with the other men,
simply because he had worked most closely with
Natalie.

"Cantero is a middleman trying to make it as a
big-time hood," Phil Caputo, the Drug Enforcement
agent stated succinctly. "The brains and money
behind the scheme was Charles Sutton. Sutton wasn't
interested in you or the boats. He wanted the land
that Andress had financed through the bank. When
Ben turned down his first offer, Sutton and his partners in this deal started a squeeze play. They figured
if they caused enough trouble—expensive trouble—
then Ben and Mac would sell out."

Nat remembered Ben had told her once that Sutton
had wanted to buy the lodge. He had also mentioned
another offer for the operation from a man represent-
ing an unnamed company that was offering plenty of
money—enough so he could start over somewhere
else. Charles Sutton was a part of that company.

"Why didn't Sutton and his partners just go out and buy some other land?" Nat asked. "There's always some undeveloped land on the market in the Keys."

"Let me show you something." Webb Hodge, the FBI man spread out a large-scale map of the long string of Florida's Keys. Hodge took out a compass and placed one end on Key West. He drew an arc across the Keys just past Newfound Harbor where the lodge was located. Then he moved the compass farther up the Keys to Long Key. The arc he drew this time came from the opposite direction and touched the first arc. In the center of the two, the only dry land that was habitable was on Little Torch Key. The only protected location that opened to the Atlantic was the site of the Gold Coast Lodge.

"So?" Bill Bishop bent over his daughter's shoulder to look at the map.

"The lodge happens to fall in a weak area as far as our radar coverage goes," Phil Caputo explained. "In these gray areas," he asserted as he peered down at the map, "it's possible to sneak in a small plane or a sizable cargo ship without our being able to pinpoint the location. If their schedule was irregular, and if they played with the weather on their side, waiting for cloudy or stormy conditions—" he leaned back and shrugged "—they could run us in circles. They could bring in a *lot* of dope to this location," he concluded with his finger tapping Newfound Harbor.

"So that's it," Nat whispered.

"That's only part of it. The lodge would also be a great cover for bringing in stuff from offshore boats under the pretext of fishing charters." Webb Hodge added another angle to the scheme. "That's how Greg Owens planned to make his bundle. He knows enough about fishing and these waters to keep up a reputable business. He was to run the charter operation—he's already licensed." Hodge obviously had done considerable checking on her former mate. "He could run regular charters along with several other legal operators. Then every once in a while he could make dummy runs. He could make contact with the mother ships, load up and bring it in."

"With the right men unloading in the boathouse," Caputo noted, "no one would detect anything unusual."

Nat shook her head. "I don't see why they took the trouble to take me out and leave me for the sharks," she puzzled. "If these men smuggle drugs and steal boats and murder crews, why didn't they just shoot me?"

"They couldn't afford the heat," Sergeant Weekley said simply. "Another shooting would be too obvious. It would shift the attention from the theft in Key West up to your area. If you just crashed into a submerged root and were killed by sharks—" Weekley leaned forward intently "—we would have no witness and no link to them, to the Bertram, to this area—and no case against Cantero and his partners."

"How did they know where I was each time?" Nat asked with a slight frown.

"It seems there were *two* insiders. Greg Owens was part of the team and so was Angela Sutton. She set Ben up with jobs away from the lodge so the boats could be sabotaged," Weekley explained. "Generally she showed up afterward to check on the extent of the damage and decide where to strike next."

"So it wasn't *me* in particular they were after, was it?" Nat asked. She was determined to reassure her father.

"You just stumbled into the midst of things," Steve Weekley agreed. "Owens had been planted at the lodge for a few months. He'd worked there long enough to avoid suspicion. When you showed up they figured they had the perfect scapegoat. When the trouble started, it would look like you were either the target or the cause."

"I thought Greg liked me." Nat realized how naive that sounded. She remembered how many times he had worked beside her, and that he had dragged her in the boat after her repair of the propeller.

"He liked you enough to set you up the day before the storm," Weekley told her grimly. "He admitted that he called Cantero that afternoon. They planned to blast the boat, then let you 'disappear' in the storm." Weekley watched Natalie's wide, sad eyes. "He swiped the note you'd left behind. Without the note, no one would know where you'd gone. It would look like you were just a careless boater caught in the storm."

"It seems you fellows have got it all," Natalie said softly. She dared not to ask about the last remaining person in the tangled schemes of the Gold Coast Lodge—Ben Andress. Since he had boarded the Coast Guard cutter and sailed away, Nat had not heard a word from him or about him. Ben had assured her everything would be explained.

"Yeah, we've tied up all the loose ends." Caputo slapped his palm on the map. "Six months of hard, hard work. And now we can put them all away and bust up this drug ring, thanks to you and Andress."

When Natalie looked up, Caputo and Weekley were grinning broadly. "He couldn't tell you," Weekley said as he put his hand on Nat's shoulder. "Ben has been working with the DEA for months—playing along with Angela, tracking down her connections, filling in names and dates and places in our investigation. He wanted to keep the Keys clean, keep dope out of the sports-fishing operations. That Andrew fellow was the last link in a long line of deals. Ben had to hang in with them right up through the last buy."

"Ben pulled it off and no one got hurt," Caputo said. "These guys play hardball, but we got them all—in one clean sweep."

"There is some other good news connected with this," Weekley added, passing her a folded paper. "There was a reward out for the recovery of the Bertram. Two big companies—Bertram and Hatteras—jointly put up $25,000 in an effort to discourage hijackings."

Natalie took the letter, but she didn't unfold it. All she could think about was the poor man whose body had been recovered after the Bertram was taken from him. "I don't think I want any part of this." Nat passed the letter back to the blond-haired officer. "I didn't do anything to deserve a reward. And I don't want to get money this way." Nat was anxious for the officers to wrap up this session so she could call Ben and tell him everything *was* all right.

"Technically," Hodge began, "the reward all belongs to Andress anyway. He was the first civilian to spot the Bertram and help recover it."

"Then why did you mention it to me?" Nat was embarrassed. She had presumed the recovery money was for her.

"Andress wants to split it with you," Hodge smiled.

"I'll stick with what I said before," Natalie replied. "I just can't take that kind of money—not when somebody was killed." She lowered her eyes self-consciously.

Hodge shrugged.

"Where is Ben?" Bill Bishop asked after a brief silence.

Steve Weekley spoke up. "He and Hector are in Miami with some federal attorneys—depositions and the like. They'll be back sometime tonight. I'm sure Ben will get in touch with you," he concluded, looking at Natalie.

"Meanwhile," Hodge chimed in, "we'll get your statement typed up for you to sign." He folded up the microphone and recorder he'd used during the interview. "Other than that, and a few court appearances over the next few months, you can go about life as normal," he assured Natalie and her father.

"It will be quite a trial," Weekley chuckled. "Charles Sutton, big-time sporting-goods dealer, his banker friend who held the note on the lodge and a Key Largo grocer who was going to provide the big trucks to haul the dope up to the mainland from the Keys. They had it all figured out."

"So after it's all over," Bill Bishop thought aloud,

"there's no further danger to Natalie—nobody left to come after her again?"

"Like I said, we made a clean sweep. With all the TV and press coverage of the Lady Captain of Gold Coast Lodge, no other smugglers would come within fifty miles of the place," Weekley smiled.

"Hector Ortiz and Ben Andress are local heroes," Caputo commented as he rolled up the map. "They're getting a lot of coverage for their efforts to keep the fishing sport clean and for their cooperation with the investigating agencies, not to mention snatching you from the jaws of a shark."

"Hector was working on the investigation, too?" Natalie looked from one officer to another. "He never let on to me."

"We got Hector in on it at the last minute," Caputo said. "Ben needed someone he could trust when he was tracking Miss Sutton's Miami connections, someone who wouldn't arouse any suspicion. Hector was the logical choice."

"It should get him a pardon and a clean record," Weekley noted. "He was *more* interested in having us give him a good character reference with the Calogne family." Nat had to smile knowing that Hector's success as an undercover crime fighter would please Maria and her protective family.

"What's going to happen to Angela Sutton?" Nat forced herself to ask. The two officers exchanged uncomfortable looks.

"She was picked up along with the others," Caputo informed her. "When Ben and the Miami agents were working this as a drug-trafficking case, she was only suspected of being a buyer. Now that we've got her and her father tied into this end of the scheme, she'll be facing conspiracy charges...and a lot of years to spend polishing her nails.''

Nat's eyes widened at the thought that Angela could serve a prison term, especially since Ben's testimony would put her there.

"When I said we made a clean sweep, I meant we got them *all*," Caputo stressed, "particularly Angela Sutton. And don't you start feeling sorry for her," he added, "she passed the word to feed you to the sharks, and I bet she didn't lose any sleep over it.''

Bill Bishop put his arm around Natalie's shoulders. "I think we've worn her out, gentlemen." He glanced at her pale face. "It's finally sinking in that she was mixed up with some very ruthless individuals. It's a bit rough having to deal with the fact that someone was actually going to get killed—and that someone was Natalie.''

"Then I guess we've put you through enough for today," Weekley remarked, taking the cue.

"Yes." Phil Caputo and Webb Hodge stood in unison. "We'll keep in touch," Hodge added as he started for the door. "There's a heck of a lot of paperwork, but it will all be worth it. We'll just try not to let it pile up.''

Once the three investigators had departed, Bill Bishop took a long look at his daughter. "I don't suppose that dejected look is for that Angela and her cohorts," he guessed. "There's something going on inside your head that we haven't got to yet." He held her hand in his. "Let's hear about you and Ben Andress.''

Natalie had told her father all about the painting

sessions with Roger, the mail exchange she had set up in Atlanta with Janie, the bank account where she'd deposited all the college money he had sent her, and the work she had done at Ben's charter outfit. She had not told him how much she cared for the handsome captain who had saved her life.

"I'm not ready to talk about him yet," she said in a whisper.

"It's serious?" A small smile formed on Bill Bishop's face.

Natalie nodded ever so slightly, her eyes lowered.

"And is this serious business two-sided?"

"I'm not sure," Nat replied softly.

"Well, someone certainly wanted to see that you got out of the way when all the trouble was brewing," he remarked. "Whoever called here and tipped me off that you were at the lodge wanted to get you out of danger."

"Ben?" Nat asked. "But he knew I was at the Refuge."

"It wasn't Ben but I'll bet it was somebody he put up to it," Mr. Bishop asserted. "Ben knew that if I showed up, the Butlers would tell your own *father* where to find you. It seems there were a lot of good folks looking out for you."

Nat nodded in agreement, though his use of the past tense bothered her.

"When I got the call, I phoned Atlanta and finally got a girl at the sorority house to admit you were down here, then I drove to Little Torch Key and right into a tornado."

"I'm so sorry it was such a mess." Nat shook her head.

"That's all done." He rubbed his hands. "What are you going to do about Ben?"

"The question is what does *he* plan to do about me," Natalie replied. "So far, he hasn't even called. There are a number of misunderstandings that we need to straighten out," she confessed, "starting with which side of the law he was working on...."

"All that seems to be cleared up already," Mr. Bishop observed. "There's more to it than that, Natalie. Why do I keep getting the feeling that you've got a bad case of the fidgets...like you want to get back there?"

"Maybe because that's how I feel," she conceded. "I really want to finish out the season on the *Calusa*. She needs to be fixed, and I want to be the one to work on her. I'm just not sure Ben will let me. Thanks to the reward money he can afford to hire someone else to work on her. I just wish he'd call to talk and give me a chance."

"You do mean with the *boat repairs*?" Mr. Bishop grinned.

"*Any* chance...." Natalie smiled back with a mischievous glint in her eyes. "I miss...everything and everyone back at the lodge."

"Then we wait and see if that *missing* feeling works both ways." her father hugged her.

"We wait," Natalie agreed reluctantly. Slowly she climbed the stairs to the bedroom she had known since childhood. The pale yellow walls and the fluttering curtains were friendly reminders of a time long past. What she longed for was the sound of waves along the shore of Newfound Harbor and the sight of a sun-bleached fishing cap and the dark eyes of Ben

Andress. She no longer belonged in the Key West home that she had loved.

WHEN THE DOORBELL RANG the next afternoon, Natalie almost leaped into Roger Embry's arms. She had spent the entire morning waiting for the phone to ring—for Ben to call. The sound of the doorbell had brought her running.

"You don't have to pretend to be quite so pleased," Roger teased her. The obvious look of disappointment on her face didn't dampen his high spirits. "I may not be precisely the one you were hoping to find standing here," he grinned, "but if you'll let me in, I have some very good news that may put a smile back on your pretty face."

"I'm so sorry." Natalie caught him by the arm and welcomed him inside. "I'm not very good at pretending," she admitted, "but with or without good news, I *am* glad to see you."

"Just to be safe, I'll start with the news." Roger opened a neatly typed letter as they settled down on the sofa. "Jerry Potter came through today—in more ways than one. He's making you an immediate offer on the Keys book and when you finish that, he wants to talk about some others of a similar kind."

Nat accepted the letter and read it slowly. When she looked up, she was smiling.

"In other words, my friend, you're *in*. Congratulations." Roger patted her arm. "I thought perhaps a nice dinner—on me, naturally—would be a good way to celebrate."

Natalie nodded and accepted with a soft, "Thank you."

"Potter said he'd have a contract in the mail to you this week," Roger added with a tap on the edge of the letter. "We'll celebrate *again* after you sign it."

"Roger," Nat began, trying to thank him for bringing this project into her life.

"Shhh," he hushed her. "Just say yes to dinner. I've got the Refuge truck. You pick the place."

Nat hadn't been out of the house all day. "You've got yourself a deal."

LATER THAT EVENING, Natalie and Roger sat on the pier in Key West watching as the orange sky shifted to crimson and clouds became deep purple. The finale was a triumph of grays and rose. Both the sky and the water were bathed in glorious color. Gradually, even the pinks faded, and only the purplish grays remained. Natalie and Roger sat in reverential silence drinking in the magnificent show nature had provided.

There was something about the remarkable beauty and serenity of the spectacle that made one want to share it. Natalie felt a sudden wave of melancholy. She had watched the sun rise with Ben at her side, once on their unnamed key and once before that on the trip back from Atlanta. But to watch the sun *set*, to watch a day end together would make the cycle complete, with each sunset beginning a new night they could share, followed by yet another dawn.

"Makes you wish you had someone to hug," Roger said, guessing her thoughts.

"It sure does." Nat's chin trembled. "Why doesn't he hurry up and call?" she lamented.

Roger didn't even try to provide an answer. Silently he wrapped a friendly, comforting arm around her shoulders as they walked along the pier toward the darkening expanse of Key West.

"Come on in for a cup of coffee," Nat insisted when they returned to her house. "My father makes a mean cup of Cuban coffee, guaranteed to stand your spoon on end—and keep you awake on the drive back."

"I could use it. My energy level went down with the sun." He followed her up onto the porch that ran across the front of the wood-frame house. As soon as their footsteps against the wooden surface broke the silence of the night, Bill Bishop clicked on the porch light and opened the door.

"You missed him...or he missed you," Mr. Bishop remarked. He had obviously been eager for Natalie's return. "Ben...he was here."

A soft no escaped from Natalie's lips.

"I had no idea where you'd gone to eat," Mr. Bishop apologized. "He waited about half an hour, then said he had to go. He had some work he needed to finish, and there didn't seem to be any point to try to keep him here."

"No sense in interrupting his busy schedule." Nat tried to veil her disappointment with the flippant remark.

"He *did* say he'd call you tomorrow—for sure," her father assured her. "It seems that he's had a work crew in at the lodge that he had to supervise and there were more loose ends with the Miami drug testimony. Then he had a couple of interviews with some TV sports reporters and a writer for one of the fishing magazines. He hasn't had time for anything personal," Mr. Bishop stressed. "Some things just shouldn't be said in a hurry."

"Poor Ben," Natalie muttered sarcastically. "Trying to find a few moments for me in the midst of all that attention."

"Natalie," Roger cautioned her, "give the guy a break. He did come down here to see you."

"He also invited us to the lodge Friday night," Mr. Bishop added to appease her. "They're having some kind of party. Ben said Maggie had something special planned."

Natalie looked from her father to Roger. The two of them seemed to think it was perfectly reasonable for her to wait a little longer to see Ben. Something other than reason told her she had waited long enough. Hastily she glanced down at her watch. It was only nine-thirty.

"Suddenly I feel that I have a desperate need for my car," Natalie smiled. "Since it happens to have been left behind at the lodge—" her smile took on a suspicious smugness "—I'll have to prevail upon Roger to drop me off there on his way home tonight."

"Tonight?" the two men said in unison.

"But it's late," Mr. Bishop protested.

"I'll say it's late," Natalie agreed. "And before it gets any later, I think I'll change into something appropriate for retrieving one's vehicle." She started for the stairway. "You two have a nice cup of coffee while I make myself irresistible."

"At this point, I don't think it would do any good to argue." Mr. Bishop led Roger into the kitchen.

"I've seen that determined jaw many times before—often in the mirror. Stubbornness is an unfortunate family trait," he chuckled.

"Let's just say that the lady has a mind of her own," Roger said diplomatically. "And she definitely has it set on a quiet drive up the Keys."

As soon as Roger slowed the truck for the turn-off, the changes under way at the Gold Coast Lodge were conspicuous. In the glare of the headlights was a new sign situated prominently by the entrance of the shell drive. Natalie sat beside Roger with her hands clasped across her lap, trying to conceal her anxiety. She had worn her ivory eyelet dress with its deep embroidered ruffle around a strapless bodice, but in spite of her cool and serene appearance, her palms were moist and her heartbeat uneven as they drove along the familiar curving road.

Natalie bit her lower lip and brushed aside a strand of golden hair that fluttered in the wind. It had been two days since she had seen Ben—two days since he'd held her hand and told her everything would be all right. Then he had boarded the Coast Guard vessel and sailed away. Nothing had felt right since then.

"Well, look at that." Roger pointed at the boathouse. Nat's little red Mustang sat polished and ready under a light as if it were waiting for her. The sight of the car parked there brought on another rush of memories. It had been in precisely that spot the night Ben had invited her into the shadowy cabin of his old cruiser.

Roger pulled to a stop near the red car. There was no one around. The lodge building and beach houses were dark. The only lighted building was the boat-house; bright spotlights at the far end of the structure illuminated Ben's cruiser. Beside the boathouse Nat could see a flat barge with pile-driving rigging. The string of newly driven pilings, listing at varied angles while they settled, revealed that an extension to the marina was in progress.

"Looks like Ben hasn't wasted any time spending the reward money," Nat said softly.

"Nat," Roger reproached her, "those hoodlums who were after this place *cost* Ben and Mac a great deal of money. Ben can't do anything to bring back the man those creeps killed, but he can go on from here. He can use a reward that he damned well earned to build his future."

Natalie kept her eyes riveted to the awkward poles that one day soon would be linked in a network of new walkways and moorings.

"Sometimes when one dream dies it gives life to another dream," Roger said softly. "Life goes on."

"It's not the money," Nat finally realized. "It's the changes. Everything is changing. Everything is going along fine—without me."

"That sounds a bit self-centered. You almost get killed helping this guy keep his business solvent, and when it looks like he's doing well you don't like it."

"Maybe I like to feel useful," Nat replied.

"I think you want to feel *indispensable*," Roger chuckled.

From inside the boathouse came the soft, clear sound of a man whistling a sea chantey. It was Ben working late on his cruiser.

Without hesitation Roger nodded at Nat. "Give 'em hell, Nat," he chuckled.

With a slight smile, Nat opened the door and stepped onto the crushed shells of the parking area. Slowly Roger backed the truck in a large arc, then eased away into the night, leaving Nat standing in the soft light from the single fixture in the boathouse.

Natalie waited outside the boathouse door until Roger drove off, then she let herself into the long high-roofed building. Inside, the still air was tinged with the odor of fresh paint. The old cruiser, now gleaming in the light, was still in dry dock, but it appeared to be finished at last. Then Nat caught a glimpse of Ben standing barefoot between the propellers at the rear of the boat, his dark head bent in concentration as he balanced a can of paint in one hand and made light brush strokes on the stern.

When Natalie began to cross the wooden ramp to the cruiser, the steady click of her heels on the planks echoed through the boathouse. Ben stopped and looked up at her and smiled as if seeing her there was nothing unexpected or unusual. He let her walk the entire distance around to the side of the cruiser without shifting his gaze from her or uttering a word of greeting.

"Stand back a bit so you won't get messed up," he said, waving her over a few feet. "Being a landlubber must agree with you," he commented. "You look lovely." Something in the silken darkness of his eyes—the inquisitive, almost anxious way they searched her face—kept her from responding. For the past hour, she had been planning this encounter. She had wanted to look so cool and elegant that she'd take his breath away. Ben was the one who was supposed to be overwhelmed when he set eyes on her. Now, as Natalie looked at the broad bare shoulders and the wide smile that had become so familiar to her, she was the one who was overwhelmed.

"I've missed you," Ben said quietly.

"If you missed me so much, you sure have a funny way of showing it," Nat finally said. "You didn't even call...."

"I didn't want to talk to you on the telephone," Ben replied. "I prefer to see you face to face."

"And you would have if you'd stayed in Key West a little longer this evening," she said as he returned to his intricate painting.

"I had some work to finish." Ben kept his hand steady as he made light strokes with the paintbrush.

"And you couldn't spare a little more time just to see me?"

"I wasn't in a hurry," he said softly. "I was willing to wait for a time when we could talk."

"How about *now*?" Nat braced her hand on her hips impatiently. For a moment Ben seemed to ignore her as he dipped the paintbrush into the dark paint and added a few more strokes to the area he was painting so carefully.

"Now is fine...." He stopped abruptly. Then he deposited his paint can and brush on the dock and began wiping his hands on his stained jeans. "You can step around and take a look at this now if you like." He stepped back to survey his own handiwork. Across the stern of the cruiser, in large black letters outlined in gold, Ben had painted the new name of the vessel.

Nat-a-lee. Spelled out boldly, just like Hector pronounced. Nat-a-lee.

"Oh, Ben," Natalie whispered as she stood above him on the landing. He hoisted himself up beside her, then stood with his soiled hands held out while she slid her arms around his neck.

"This was supposed to be a surprise for a little later on," he said without touching her. "I had hoped to be a bit *cleaner*, just in case you got carried away with gratitude," he teased.

"I'm thrilled." Nat looked again at the boat. "I've never had anything named after me."

"There's a little more to it than that," Ben cautioned her. "She's not just named for you—she's yours."

"Mine. . . ?" Natalie gasped.

"Wait till you hear the strings attached to this gift." Ben took her hand and led her to the side. "I remember how generous you were when you gave me the mangrove painting," he recalled, "but I don't have your philanthropic qualities. I drive a much tougher bargain." He helped Natalie over the side so they stood on the polished decks of the *Nat-a-lee*.

"I do love you," he said, looking down at her. "I just want you to think this over very carefully."

"I accept," Natalie grinned at him.

"Don't you want to hear the terms first?" When Natalie shook her head no, Ben took her hand and laughed, pulling her into his embrace regardless of the paint and grease stains and the musky scent of his body. With characteristic gentleness, he stroked her bare shoulders as he kissed her. Then with a languid, gentle pressure, he tasted once again the warmth of her lips. When Natalie slid her hands over the naked expanse of his back, she uttered a soft murmur of pleasure. She had come home again—at last.

"Come with me, Natalie...." Ben released her only long enough to extinguish the work light and return to her side. "Come with me...." He took her hand and started toward the gangway leading to the cabins below.

"Now?" Natalie hesitated.

"One of the conditions for giving you this boat—" Ben led her through the darkness "—was that you would trust me. Another is that you'll marry me and love me forever...." He kept moving even though Natalie's step faltered momentarily.

At the bottom of the stairway, he paused to let her step down next to him. "And if you agree to that—" he slid his fingers through the golden hair that draped over her shoulders "—I'll think up a few more conditions to go along with the old house." Natalie turned her face up to him so he could punctuate his statements with the soft, sensual pressure of his lips on hers.

"There are walls that need wallpapering—" he kissed her "—and windows that need repairing...." He buried his face in her soft tawny cloud of hair.

"I accept...." Natalie held him closer, savoring his warm breath against her skin.

"Do you still want to talk?" he asked in a voice low and thick with passion.

"I love you, Ben...."

"I guess that about covers everything," he chuckled.

"Not quite." Natalie leaned back slightly so she

could look up at him. Even in the darkness she could see his half-smile. "I seem to remember some unfinished business farther down the gangway...."

"I remember...." Ben took her hand and started toward the master cabin. "I also remember when I first saw you down here—two months ago—all dressed in ivory and gold. You looked like you already owned her." He stopped by the cabin door with his face now, just as then, masked in shadows. "I heard you talking to her and I saw you touching her. I envied the way you could show how much you cared." He drew her close against him. Softly he trailed his fingers over her bare shoulders, then slowly moved them downward, brushing the pale ruffle over her breasts.

"You started in on everyone," Ben recalled, "winning them over with your spirit...your skill...your hard work...your willingness to learn...and your humor." His voice was almost hypnotic. "You claimed a part of all of them...and I was afraid to let you claim part of me because there was no way that someone like you...and someone like me...." His voice trailed off as Natalie's hands touched his belt buckle and slowly began unfastening it.

"If we're going to get it right this time," he said as he stroked her long hair hanging free and smelling like the sea, "let's start back at the beginning." He brushed his lips against her temple, inhaling the scent of her.

"Welcome aboard, gold-and-ivory lady. My name is Ben Andress...and I love you."

HARLEQUIN CLASSIC LIBRARY

Great old romance classics from our early publishing lists.

FREE BONUS BOOK

On the following page is a coupon with which you may order any or all of these titles. If you order all nine, you will receive a FREE book — *Doctor Bill*, a heartwarming classic romance by Lucy Agnes Hancock.

The thirteenth set of nine novels in the
HARLEQUIN CLASSIC LIBRARY